# Parallel

Lauren Miller is an entertainment lawyer and television writer in Los Angeles, where she lives with her husband and daughter.

www.laurenmillerwrites.com
@LMillerWrites

Lauren Miller

# Parallel

SCHOLASTIC

First published in the UK in 2013 by Scholastic Children's Books
An imprint of Scholastic Ltd
Euston House, 24 Eversholt Street, London, NW1 1DB, UK
Registered office: Westfield Road, Southam, Warwickshire, CV47 0RA
SCHOLASTIC and associated logos are trademarks and/
or registered trademarks of Scholastic Inc.

First published in the USA by HarperCollins in 2013

Text © Lauren Miller, 2013

The right of Lauren Miller to be identified as the
author of this work has been asserted by her.

ISBN 978 1407 13512 0

Printed and bound by CPI Group (UK) Ltd, Croydon, CR0 4YY

Papers used by Scholastic Children's Books are made
from wood grown in sustainable forests.

1 3 5 7 9 10 8 6 4 2

www.scholastic.co.uk/zone

For Lil Mil

*Life can only be understood backwards;*
*but it must be lived forwards.*
—Søren Kierkegaard

# SEPTEMBER

# 1
# (here)

## TUESDAY, 8 SEPTEMBER, 2009
## (THE DAY BEFORE MY EIGHTEENTH BIRTHDAY)

I hesitate, then point my gun at him and pull the trigger. There is a moment of sweet, precious silence. Then:

"Cut!"

I sigh, lowering the gun. Everyone springs into action. Again.

I close my eyes, silently reminding myself that I'm loving every minute of this. Then apologize to myself for the lie.

"Abby?"

Our director, Alain Bourneau, a man with the ego of Narcissus and the temper of Zeus, is standing so close I can feel his minty breath on my face. I force a smile and open my eyes. His reconstructed nose is millimetres from mine.

"Everything OK?"

"Oh, yeah," I say, bobbing my head enthusiastically. "Everything's great. Just going over the scene in my mind." I tap my left temple for emphasis. "The mental picture helps

1

me focus my energy." The only mental picture I have in my head right now is the bacon cheeseburger I plan to order from room service tonight (extra pickles, mustard, no ketchup). But if Alain thinks I'm giving him less than a hundred per cent, he'll send me to craft services for a "Power Pick-Me-Up", a brownish-green concoction that tastes like chalk and makes my pee smell like cayenne pepper.

Alain gives my shoulder a squeeze. "Atta girl. Now, let's do it exactly the same way again. Only hotter."

Right. Of course. We're talking about a scene that involves my shooting an overweight man in the head while he stands in his kitchen making a bologna sandwich. I can see how that could be *hotter*.

My life has officially become unrecognizable.

When I was in kindergarten, my mom decided that I was a child prodigy. The fact that she couldn't readily identify my prodigious talent did nothing to diminish her certainty that I had one. Four months and twenty-two developmental assessment tests later, she was no closer to pinpointing my supposed genius, but she'd learned something about her daughter that made her exceedingly proud: it appeared that I, Abigail Hannah Barnes, possessed a "strong sense of self".

I have no idea how a five-year-old can demonstrate the strength of her self-concept with a number two pencil and a Scantron sheet, but I apparently did, twenty-two times over.

Until a year ago, I would've agreed with that assessment. I *did* know who I was. What I liked (writing and running), what I was good at (English and history), what I wanted to become (a journalist). So I stuck to the things that came easily to me

2

and steered clear of everything else (in particular, anything that might require hand-eye coordination or the use of a scalpel). This proved a very effective strategy for success. By the time senior year rolled around, I was the editor-in-chief of my high school newspaper, the captain of the cross-country team, and on pace to graduate in the top five per cent of my class. My plan – part of *the* Plan, the one that has informed every scholastic decision I've made since seventh grade, the year I decided I wanted to be a journalist – was to apply early admission to the journalism school at Northwestern, then coast through spring semester.

The centrepiece of this strategy was my autumn course load: a perfectly crafted combination of AP classes and total fluff electives with legit-sounding names. Everything was proceeding according to plan until:

"Abby, Ms DeWitt wants to see you. There's some sort of issue with your schedule."

The first day of senior year. I was sitting in form, debating birthday dinner options while I waited for the parking lottery to start.

"An issue?"

"That's all I know." Mrs Gorin, my form teacher, was waving a little slip of pink paper. "Could you just take care of it, please?"

"What about the parking—"

"You can meet us in the auditorium." She gave the pink slip an impatient shake. I grabbed my bag and headed for the door, praying that this "issue" wouldn't take longer than five minutes. If I wasn't in the auditorium when they drew my name, they'd give my parking space to someone else, and I'd spend senior year in the no-man's-land of the annex car park.

Four and a half minutes later, I was sitting in the guidance counsellor's office, staring at a very short list of options. Apparently, Mr Simmons, the man who created and taught the excessively easy History of Music, had suddenly decided to cancel his class, forcing me to pick another option for fifth period. I know this might not sound like a big deal, but if you'd spent as much time as I had constructing the Perfect Schedule, and if you'd convinced yourself that your future success absolutely *depended* on your taking six very particular courses, then the disruption would feel catastrophic.

"The great news is, you have two wonderful courses to choose from," Ms DeWitt chirped. "Drama Methods and Principles of Astronomy." She smiled, looking at me over the rim of her turquoise glasses. The air suddenly felt very thin.

"No!" She got this startled look on her face when I said it. I hadn't meant to shout, but the woman had just yanked the rug out from under me. Plus, her fuchsia trousersuit was giving me a headache. I cleared my throat and tried again. "There has to be another option."

"I'm afraid not," she replied pleasantly. Then, in a girlish whisper, as if we were talking about something far less important than my entire academic future: "I'd go with drama if I were you."

I should mention something about my high school: it's what they call an arts and sciences magnet, which means that in addition to its regular public school curriculum, Brookside High offers two specialized tracks: one for aspiring actors and performers and the other for overachieving young Einsteins lured by the promise of university-level coursework. I made the mistake sophomore year of assuming that "university-level" meant suitable for the average university freshman, only to learn eight weeks into the harmless-sounding Botany Basics that our final exam would be the same one our teacher had given the previous year. To honour students at Georgia Tech.

So, while courses with names like "Drama Methods" and "Principles of Astronomy" would've undoubtedly been cake classes at a regular school, when you go to an arts and sciences magnet and happen to be neither arts nor sciences inclined, these innocuously titled gems are gruelling, time-intensive GPA busters. Oh, and did I mention the mandatory grading curve?

It was a choice between bad and worse.

"Drama," I said finally. And that was that.

In fifth period that afternoon, our teacher informed us that she'd selected Tom Stoppard's *Arcadia* as our class production. I'd read the play the year before in AP English and loved it (mostly because my essay, "People Fancying People: Determinism in *Arcadia*", won the eleventh grade writing prize), so when it came time for auditions, I tried out for the role of Thomasina Coverly, the precocious teenage lead. Not because I actually *wanted* the lead (or any other part, for that matter – I was lobbying to be stage manager, safely behind the scenes), but because Thomasina's lines were the easiest to memorize, and since the same girl had won the starring role in every school play since kindergarten, I figured at worst I'd wind up as her understudy. Plus, trying out for the lead role had the side benefit of irritating that girl, the self-appointed queen bee of the drama crowd and my nemesis since kindergarten, the insufferable Ilana Cassidy, who assumed she'd audition unopposed.

But two days later, there it was: my name at the top of the cast list. I'd got the part.

This coup caused quite the uproar among the drama kids, all of whom expected Ilana to get the lead. My cast mates were convinced that I, the inexperienced interloper, would ruin "their" show, and I wasn't sure they were wrong. But Ms Ziffren's casting decisions weren't up for discussion, and my grade depended on my participation.

The show opened to a packed auditorium. Seated in the front row was a prominent casting director who'd flown in to see her nephew play Septimus Hodge. This kind of thing happens all the time in magnet school land, so it was easy to ignore (especially since the entirety of my mental energy that night was focused on the very real possibility that I would forget my lines and single-handedly wreck the show).

But then I got a call from that same casting director, inviting me to audition for *Everyday Assassins*, a big-budget action movie that was set to start shooting in Los Angeles in May. According to the casting director, they were looking for a dark-haired, light-eyed teenage newcomer to play the lead actor's silent accomplice, and with my chestnut waves and grey-blue eyes, I was a perfect match. Would I be interested in flying out to Los Angeles to audition for the role? Figuring the experience would be great material for my Northwestern application, I convinced my parents to let me try out.

The whole thing happened so fast. Alain offered me the role on the spot. He and the producers knew about my university plans and assured me that production would wrap by late July, leaving me plenty of time to get to Northwestern before classes started in September. Stunned and more than a little flattered, I took the part.

Life just kind of sped up from there. By February, I was flying from Atlanta to LA for fittings, table reads (super exciting when you have no lines) and weapons training. I missed spring break. I missed prom. Production was scheduled to start the third week of May, so while the rest of my class was enjoying all the end-of-high-school festivities, I was holed up in a hotel room, poring over revised drafts of the increasingly convoluted script (there was a new one every day), intensely aware of the fact that I had NO CLUE what I was doing. One semester of Drama Methods does not an actor make.

At this point, I still thought the film would wrap before autumn semester, so I focused on making the best of it. So what if I didn't get to walk with my class at graduation? I was sharing Vitaminwater with *Cosmo*'s Sexiest Guy Alive. There are worse ways to spend a summer. The thought never crossed my mind that I'd have to postpone university, or do anything other than what I'd always planned to do. But then production got pushed to June . . . then July . . . then August . . . at which point we were politely informed by our producers that we'd be filming through October. Thanks to a very well-drafted talent contract, I was stuck there for the duration. And just like that, my meticulously constructed Plan – (a) four years writing for an award-winning university daily, (b) a fabulous summer internship, (c) a degree from the best journalism programme in the country and, ultimately, (d) a job at a major national newspaper, all before my twenty-second birthday – died a very quick death.

It's hard not to blame Mr Simmons. If he hadn't cancelled

7

History of Music last September, everything would've gone the way it was supposed to, and yesterday would've been my first day of classes at Northwestern. Instead I'm here, trapped on a studio back lot in Hollywood, wearing a jumpsuit so tight my butt has gone numb.

Yes, I know it's the kind of thing people dream about, the kind of thing Ilana Cassidy would've given both nipples for: the chance to be in a big-budget movie with an A-list actor and an award-winning director, and to have it all just fall into place without even trying. Stuff like this *never* happens to me. I've had to work for the things I've accomplished – every grade, every award, every victory on the track. Which was part of the problem, I guess. When this came so easily, I couldn't pass it up.

But I never wanted an acting career or anything close to one, so this dream I'm living isn't *my* dream. Which is why, in these moments – when I'm tired and hot and hungry, and we're on the thirty-ninth take of a scene that, if it makes it into the movie at all, will amount to a whopping six seconds of screen time – it's harder to ignore that little voice in my head reminding me that "once in a lifetime" isn't always enough.

When we finally wrap for the day, I head back to my room. The producers put everyone up at the Culver, this completely cool, old Hollywood hotel that was once owned by John Wayne. Everyone from Greta Garbo to Ronald Reagan has stayed here. Somehow, the fact that the studio is paying for me to live here feels like a bigger deal than the fact that they're putting me in their movie.

The sun is low in the sky as I cross the street to the hotel. The smog in LA makes for some pretty funky sky colours, but this evening's palette is especially unskylike. The horizon is streaked with fiery reds and oranges, swirled with shimmering shades of bronze and gold. But that's not the unusual part. Amid the unusually bright colours, there are darker patches – places where the colours are so deep that they nearly disappear into black. It's almost as if night has already fallen in these spots, while it's still daylight everywhere else. Despite the balmy weather, I shiver.

As I'm walking through the Culver's black-and-white-tiled lobby, my mobile phone rings. Every night at eight, like clockwork.

"Hi, Mom." I pass the lifts and enter the stairwell, picking up the pace as I hit the stairs. The three flights from the lobby to my floor constitute the entirety of my cardiovascular exercise, so I try to make it count. I used to run six miles a day (always outside, even in December); now I'm lucky if I walk six streets. Alain doesn't want his female assassins to get too thin, so our trainers have been told to lay off the cardio. Not running has been brutal for me.

"Hey, honey! How's it going? Having fun?"

"Yep!" I enthuse, trying to sound upbeat. The only thing worse than admitting to yourself that you made a colossal mistake is admitting to your parents that you did. Especially when the thing you're regretting doing is something they were lukewarm about from the beginning. It wasn't the acting thing that made mine wary, but the fact that the movie I'd been cast in lacked a coherent plot.

"Learning a lot?" Mom asks. Her standard question.

"Oh, yeah. Definitely." *Today's lesson: how to pick a Lycra wedgie with the corner of a kitchen stool.* "How are things with you guys?"

"Well, we miss you, of course," Mom replies. "But otherwise, things are fine. Your dad starts trial on Monday, so he's been working like crazy." In my seventeen-almost-eighteen years of life, only five of my dad's cases have ever made it to trial, which is sad, because being in the courtroom is pretty much the only thing he likes about the practice of law. Dad was a painter when he met my mom. In fact, art was what brought them together. They were standing side by side in front of Dali's *The Persistence of Memory* at a surrealist exhibition at MoMA, when he looked over at my mom and said (in what my mom insists was a non-cheesy fashion), "The trouble with Dali is that it's hard to look at his work without thinking that you could live a whole life and not feel anything as deeply as he felt everything." They were married less than a year later, the day after my mom graduated from Barnard. After struggling as a painter for a few more years, my dad finally gave in and applied to law school, mostly because my grandparents said they'd pay for it. The plan was to practise for a couple of years to save some money. Twenty years later, he's the head of the litigation department at a big Atlanta law firm, working sixty-plus hours a week. And most of the time, he's bored senseless.

"How are things at the museum?" I ask. "Did the Picasso exhibit open?" My mom is the head curator at the High Museum, a job she absolutely adores. Last autumn, a Seurat exhibit she put together made a big splash in the art world, and other, bigger museums started courting her, but Mom told them she had no interest in leaving the collection she'd spent the last ten years trying to build. Instead, she used her new reputation to bring a string of really stellar exhibits to Atlanta.

"Not until tomorrow," she replies. I can hear her smile. "Speaking of things happening tomorrow. . ."

"I meant to tell you," I say quickly, knowing where this is going. "Some of my cast mates are taking me out to dinner tomorrow night. Some trendy place in Hollywood." Not true, but I know how much my mom hates the idea of my being alone on my eighteenth birthday with no one to celebrate with. I also know she can't afford to be away from the museum right now.

"That's great, honey." She sounds relieved. "I wish your dad and I were going to be there, too. Eighteen! Good grief, I feel old."

The line beeps as I'm unlocking my door. "Hey, Mom, that's Caitlin. We've been playing phone tag all week, so I should probably. . ."

"Oh, of course, honey. Say hi to her for me."

We hang up, and I switch over to my best friend.

"Thank God. I thought I was going to have to leave hate voicemail to get you to call me back."

"Sorry. I've been on set all day. What's up? Everything OK?"

"Better than OK," Caitlin replies. "The geek in me can barely contain herself." My best friend is, for sure, a raging geek – at least when it comes to science. Her inner nerd just happens to live in a supermodel's body. She gets her looks from her mom, an ex-model turned handbag designer. Her brain, on the other hand, she gets from her dad, a structural engineer and quite possibly the geekiest man I've ever met. Although she didn't inherit the geek gene (it was overpowered by her mom's fashion gene) Caitlin did get his left-brained love of the excessively detailed and mind-numbingly complicated. In high school, she spent her weekends working in an astrophysics lab at Georgia Tech (the chair of the department is an old friend of her dad's), helping grad students with their research and doing some of her own. Our classmates at Brookside weren't sure what to make of her. I'm guessing she blends in a little better with the Ivy League crowd. Not that Caitlin cares about blending in. She never has. At Brookside, she and I sort of floated on the periphery of the popular crowd. The social hierarchy was a little warped because of the magnet school thing – athletes generally dominated the scene, but if you were a science track or drama kid with above-average looks and decent social skills, you had mainstream cachet. So the "cool" crowd was a fairly eclectic mix of kids from each track. Caitlin and I were part of that crowd, but since we hung out with the golf team instead of football players and sometimes skipped parties to do homework, we weren't social royalty.

"The best part is, Yale doesn't have course requirements," Caitlin is saying, "so I can basically take whatever I want. Today I shopped Statistical Thermodynamics and Intro to Relativistic Astrophysics, both of which were awesome. I'd love to take them both, but they overlap by fifteen minutes. Plus, IRA has a prereq . . . which I could probably get them to waive . . . but I dunno. I think I'm leaning towards Thermo."

Only Caitlin would be this excited about classes with names like "Statistical Thermodynamics" and "Relativistic Astrophysics". I mean, seriously. What do those words even mean?

"Although it's not like I have to make a decision today," she adds, finally pausing for a breath. "I have till the end of the week to decide."

"Didn't classes start last week?"

"Yeah, but we get two weeks to finalize our schedules," Caitlin explains. "They call it shopping period. You can visit any class you want, and your schedule isn't final until it's over. Did I mention how much I love this place?" As if there were any doubt; Caitlin has wanted to go to Yale since primary school.

"Life should have a shopping period," I muse. "It'd keep people from getting stuck with life-altering decisions they didn't really want to make."

"Ab—"

"How are things with Tyler?" I ask, steering the conversation towards happier ground. Three weeks ago, our best guy friend stood up on a chair at a packed party and proclaimed his love for Caitlin, call-and-answer-style (I'm not exactly clear on the mechanics, but apparently, there were some cheerleaders at the party who assisted with the effort). With my being gone for the summer, Caitlin and Tyler had spent nearly every day together. She had to have known how Tyler felt about her, but Caitlin says she was too busy pretending things hadn't changed to see how much they had. To be fair, I don't think Caitlin was quite as shocked by the big announcement as Ilana was. I'm not sure which shocked her more – that I stole her part or that Caitlin stole her boyfriend.

After waiting four days to go on their first date (Caitlin wanted there to be a "respectable gap" between the end of Tyler's relationship with Ilana and the beginning of his relationship

13

with her, plus, although she'd never tell Tyler this, she was totally weirded out by the idea of kissing him, an issue Tyler resolved three minutes into their first date when he parked his mom's minivan on the gravel part of Kent Road and pulled Caitlin into the back seat), my two best friends proceeded to have a seventeen-day, completely intense fling.

They spent every day together until they both left for school, Caitlin to Yale and Tyler to Michigan, without ever defining the relationship. Caitlin is refusing to call him her boyfriend, despite the fact that they talk on the phone every night and aren't seeing other people. Tyler, on the other hand, is using the *G* word and the *L* word every chance he gets. Playing it cool is apparently not in Tyler's game plan for this particular relationship. Last night, he left me a two-minute-and-forty-six-second voicemail in which he belted out the lyrics to a Caitlin-inspired rendition of Taylor Swift's "Love Story".

"Things with Ty are good," Caitlin says. "He wants to come visit at the end of the month, but I told him that's too early . . . it's too early, right?"

Before I can answer, there's a loud knock at my door. I peer through the peephole, expecting the maid. But Bret Woodward is standing in the corridor, wearing a blazer and holding flowers. He's the A-list actor who's generating all the buzz about our movie, the one whose face is on the cover of nearly every major magazine this month, promoting the *other* eighty-million-dollar action flick he's in, which opens this Friday. And he's at my door. With *flowers*.

"Crap!" I whisper violently into the phone. "Crap, crap, crap!"

"What?" Caitlin whispers back.

"Why are *you* whispering?"

"Sorry." Normal voice again. "Who's at the door?"

There's another knock.

"*Abby.* Who's at the door?"

"Bret," I manage to choke out.

"Bret *Woodward*?!?"

"Shhhh," I hiss. "I'm pretending I'm not here."

"Hey, Super Stealth," comes Bret's voice from the corridor. "I can see your feet under the door." My eyes drop to the floor: There's a three-inch crack between the door and the hardwood floor. *Damn old hotel.*

Caitlin cracks up. "I'll call you back," I mutter. I punch the end button and open the door.

"Hiding from me?" Bret asks with a wink. Yes, a *wink*. The Sexiest Guy Alive is standing at my door, holding flowers and winking.

"Hiding? HA! Why would I hide?" I hold up the phone. "I was just on the phone. My friend was in the middle of a story, and I didn't want to interrupt." I put on what I hope is an offhand, totally-at-ease smile. The opposite of how I'm feeling.

Bret grins. "Good. Then these are for you." He holds out the flowers. I take them, stepping back to let him inside the room.

A brief word about my gentleman caller. Officially he just turned thirty-three, which means in real life he's probably pushing forty. So, best-case scenario, the man has fifteen years on me. Worst case, he's old enough to be my father. "So what's the occasion?" I ask, admiring the eclectic bouquet. I'll say one thing: the man has excellent taste in flowers.

Bret rolls his eyes. "Very funny."

"But my birthday's not until tomorrow," I point out.

"I know that," he says. "But the celebration starts now. So go change."

"Celebration?"

"Yes. No arguing." He walks over to my wardrobe and opens it. It's empty. Bret gives me a quizzical look. I point at my suitcase, jammed into a corner with clothes spilling out of it.

"I haven't exactly unpacked yet," I say.

"You haven't unpacked? You've been here all summer!" Bret eyes the explosion of clothing. "How do you live like this?"

"I don't like to be tied down?" I offer. This isn't even remotely true, but it sounds less lame than any of my real reasons – all of which have to do with my obsessive fixation with getting out of here so I can start university on time and proceed with my Plan. Bret nods knowingly.

"I get that," he says in a low tone, which I think is supposed to be his meaningful voice. "Permanence is suffocating." I nod in what I hope is an equally meaningful way as Bret lifts my suitcase on to the bed and begins rifling through it, examining each article of clothing before folding it and setting it aside. Yes, folding. *Bret Woodward is folding my clothes.* "How about this?" he asks, holding up my black pyjama top. I laugh. Bret doesn't blink.

Oh. Right. He's serious.

"Uh, OK . . . with what?" I ask, afraid to hear his answer. Bret tosses me the pyjama top, then pulls a pair of cowboy boots out from under the bed.

"With these," he says, holding up the boots. "Now, go change," he instructs, steering me towards the bathroom. "We have to be somewhere in fifteen minutes."

To Bret's credit, the pyjama top sort of looks like a dress. A really, really tiny dress. If only it weren't a PYJAMA TOP. I contemplate telling Bret there's no way I can go out in this, but then, something in me gives way. My eighteenth birthday is less than five hours away. After that many years of model child behaviour, I've earned the right to bend the rules a little bit (in this particular case, the rule that says that a self-respecting girl should not go out in public wearing nothing but a pyjama top and boots). And it's LA; it's not like I'll be the most scantily clad girl on the street – not by a long shot. I strip out of my jeans, spritz on some perfume, say a quick prayer of thanksgiving that I shaved my legs, and slide the pyjam – er, dress – over my head.

Even though I've worn this top to bed a zillion times, I'm not prepared for the reflection that greets me in the full-length mirror on the back of the bathroom door. The "dress" is longer than I remembered, and it fits me in all the right places. Dressed like this, with my dark waves blown straight and make-up still camera-ready, I barely recognize myself. For the first time since I arrived in LA, I look like someone who belongs. Only my eyes – round and slightly panicked – give me away.

"You almost ready?" Bret calls from the other side of the door. "We're late."

"Just a sec!" I shout, gulping the contents of the travel-sized bottle of mouthwash by my sink.

When we emerge from the hotel, the valet attendant is waiting with Bret's pride and joy, a cherry-red Prius with imported calfskin seats. I wonder how much Bret paid to get the baby cow interior on his environmentally responsible ride. The attendant gets out of the car and hurries over to open the passenger-side door, but Bret beats him to it.

"Right on schedule," he says as I slide past him into the car, cringing as the slinky fabric slides up my thigh.

"But a few minutes ago you said we were late," I say when Bret joins me in the car.

"Necessary exaggeration," Bret replies, flashing an impish smile. "I find that women move more quickly when there's time pressure." He guns the accelerator, and we speed away from the kerb. *Women.* I think of the parade of females Bret has been linked with in the past: actresses, models, and most recently, a fashion designer. These women are, well, *women.* Suddenly, the fact that my not-yet-eighteen-year-old virgin self has just got into a car with this allegedly-thirty-three-but-probably-more-like-forty-year-old (wearing nothing but a pyjama top and boots, mind you) seems like a really, really bad idea.

Bret glances over at me as we whiz down Venice Boulevard. "What are you thinking right now?" he asks. "You have a funny look on your face." He slows long enough for us to turn on to Abbot Kinney, then speeds up again.

"I just can't believe I'm gonna be *eighteen* in a couple hours," I say, drawing out the word. "I still feel so young, you know?"

Bret just laughs. "You are young." He turns the wheel sharply and slams on the brakes. "We're here."

We're parked in a narrow alleyway next to a windowless black brick building with an electric-blue door. *A restaurant?* At first I think so, but there's no sign, no awning, no menu out front. Nothing to indicate what's inside.

*Oh, God. This isn't a restaurant. It's some weird sex club.*

"I hope you're hungry," Bret says, leaning across me to push open the passenger door. "Everything on the menu is amazing." *Not a weird sex club!* I am elated. Bret grins at me. "Welcome to your birthday party, Birthday Girl."

To my surprise, there are about twenty people waiting for us inside, exactly enough to fill the restaurant's private cellar. I recognize most of them, all from the movie. Bret steps away to talk to our server, and someone hands me a glass of champagne. I down it like I'm used to being handed glasses of champagne in super-swanky back rooms, hoping it'll help take the awkward edge off the evening.

"Abby!" Kirby, the youngest (and from the looks of it, drunkest) member of the cast beelines over to me, teetering in four-inch heels. "Can you believe this?" she breathes, clutching my shoulder for balance. *Whoa. Hello, vodka. I see you've met Kirby.* "This is, like, *ohmyGodlikeTHEplacerightnow,*" she gushes in a heavy Boston accent I didn't know she had. "You, like, can't even get a reservation unless you're somebody."

"Wow." I glance over at Bret, who's busy giving one of the servers detailed instructions. He catches me watching him and winks.

"We need cocktails," Kirby announces, letting go of my shoulder and grabbing my elbow. She drags me towards the bottle-laden table in the corner of the room and pours herself a Red Bull and vodka. I watch as she downs it, then immediately pours herself another. "RBV?" she asks, waving the vodka bottle in my face.

"No, thanks." I'm already feeling the champagne.

"Whatever." She shrugs, then ambles off, taking the bottle with her.

19

"So how'd I do, Birthday Girl?" I hear Bret ask, his voice at my ear. I turn to face him, immediately aware of how close his lips are to mine. "You know, you're not an easy read," he murmurs, brushing the hair off my face. "Not that I'm complaining." As his finger dances down my jaw, tiny beads of sweat prickle above my upper lip. I fight the urge to lick them away.

The moment is gaining intensity by the millisecond, but I can't bring myself to look away. Bret's eyes are SO BLUE (coloured contacts, no doubt), and he smells ridiculously good. How have I never noticed this before? I tilt my head forward to get a better whiff. Bret, decidedly less tipsy than me and thus still operating in the realm of normal behaviour, assumes I'm leaning in for a kiss. Because, really, who leans in for a *smell*? The crazy girl in pyjamas and boots, that's who.

So he kisses me. It's more of a prelude to a kiss, actually. His lips barely graze mine, and then it's over. A second later, I hear the distinct *click* of a camera phone. I don't even have to look to know whose it is. RBV #3 in one hand, mobile phone in the other.

"Smile!" Kirby calls in a sing-song voice, snapping another picture. It dawns on me that there's an excellent chance I'm going to end up in *US Weekly*, a notion that is both horrifying and thrilling. I grit my teeth and smile for the camera, already rehearsing rational explanations in my head. *Oh, that. We were just rehearsing a scene for the movie, Dad. No, we don't actually kiss in the movie, but the director wanted to see what it would look like if we did. . . Yes, he does play my uncle, but the screenwriter was toying with an incest storyline. . .* CRAP.

"Don't be worried about the picture," Bret says, putting his arm around me as Kirby keeps clicking away. "There's no service in here, so she can't send it to anyone until after we leave. And by that time, all incriminating photos will be long gone." He nods at the guy next to Kirby. His biceps are the size of my thigh, but he can't be older than twenty. "That's Seth, my trainer. Every time we go out with Kirby, she goes camera crazy. So Seth's been tasked with 'borrowing' her phone and deleting everything before she can do any damage." Arm still around my shoulders, Bret steers me towards a plush sofa at the other end of the room.

"So you didn't answer my question," he says as we sit. "How'd I do?"

"Are you kidding? This is great. Best birthday ever."

"But it's not your birthday yet." Bret points at his watch. "It's only nine thirty."

"Hmm. Good point. So I guess this is the best day-*before*-my-birthday ever. Which sadly, doesn't say much," I tease.

"Then I guess it's a good thing I've saved the real fun for tomorrow," says Bret with a mysterious smile.

I raise my eyebrows. "These people barely know me, and you're forcing them to celebrate my birthday twice?"

"Tomorrow night it's just you and me, kid. Dinner on the beach in Malibu." He sips his champagne. "Unless, of course, you have other plans. . ." He trails off, taking another sip as he waits for me to jump in and assure him that I don't. Expecting me to. But there is simply no way I am going to dinner with this guy. Sure, the idea of having an intimate dinner with the Sexiest Guy Alive is appealing, but he's (a) too old for me, (b) too famous for me, and (c) too likely-to-seek-sex-on-the-first-date for me. Besides, I still have a firm enough grasp on reality to know that this – the Hollywood scene, thirtysomething celebrities, private

21

cellars at trendy restaurants – isn't my world. I am merely passing through.

Bret is still waiting for my response when the first course arrives. "I'm starving," I announce, practically sprinting to the table.

"Let's eat!" Bret calls to the crowd, and everyone sits.

Three hours, four courses, and one very delicious molten chocolate cake later, I'm sipping my fourth glass of champagne and marvelling at the difference between this birthday and my last. A year ago, I celebrated the big day with a Baskin-Robbins ice cream cake and dinner with Caitlin and my parents. Now here I am, all the way across the country, partying with celebrities and drinking Cristal. Beside me, Bret Woodward – *the* Bret Woodward – is talking university football with the guy who plays my brother, his arm draped around the back of my chair as though it belongs there.

"Hey, BW!" Seth calls to Bret from the other end of the table. "I think it's time to put Hollywood Barbie to bed." He points at Kirby, who is now slumped down in her seat and snoring. "Mind if we take one of the cars?" Seth asks. At the word "bed", I'm hit with a wave of exhaustion. I've been up for twenty-one hours after having slept for only four.

"Do you mind if I go with them?" I ask Bret, suddenly overwhelmed by the weight of my eyelids. "I've got a six a.m. call time tomorrow."

"We'll all go," he says, fixing his blue eyes on my sleepy grey ones. I flush under his gaze but don't look away, emboldened by all the sugar, alcohol and endorphins. For a second, I let myself imagine kissing him – really kissing him. "Just say you'll have dinner with me tomorrow night," I hear him say.

"I'll have dinner with you tomorrow night."

"Really?" For a guy who seemed so confident, he looks awfully surprised.

"Hey, Jake, just hang for a minute," Bret tells the driver as the limo pulls up in front of the Culver. "I'm gonna walk Abby up."

"Oh, that's OK," I say. "I'll be fine. You should get Kirby home, anyway." I give her limp arm a friendly pat and quickly slip out of the limo, closing the door behind me before Bret can argue. Two seconds later, I'm knocking on the window, feeling like an asshole.

The sunroof slides open, and Bret's head pops up. "I forgot to say thank you," I say. "Tonight was awesome."

"You deserve awesome," he replies, raising his empty champagne glass in the air. Behind him, the night sky is an arresting shade of indigo. My first thought is that it's just light pollution. But then I notice the stars. They're so bright. Like, oddly bright. I tilt my head back for a better look. The wind picks up, making me shiver, but I can't stop staring at the stars, which are so brilliant they're almost blinding. "It's your night, Birthday Girl," I hear Bret say. I drop my eyes, forgetting the stars and my goosebumps, but Bret has already ducked back into the limo, disappearing behind the tinted glass as the car pulls away.

When I get up to my room, I don't even bother with the lights. I kick off my boots, think to myself how convenient it is that I'm already wearing my pyjamas, and fall into bed. And finally, effortlessly, I sleep.

I dream of earthquakes that night. Shaking so violent that the door rattles and the windows crack and the mirror over the antique dresser shatters on the hardwood floor. It only lasts for a second, though. Then the world goes black.

I'm jolted awake by a bright, searing light and a blast of cold air. Shivering, I open my eyes, then immediately close them, wincing at the brightness. It takes me a few seconds to realize that the blinding light is the sun.

*Shit, shit, shit.*

If the sun's up, I either slept through my five a.m. wake-up call or the front desk never made it. I feel myself start to panic. How late is it? I was supposed to be in hair and make-up at 6.05. Alain will be livid if I'm late. *Please don't let it be past six, please don't let it be past six, please don't let it be past six.* Eyes still adjusting to the light, I roll over towards the bedside table and force myself to look at the clock.

But there's no clock in sight. Where the bedside table should be is a wall. A poorly painted white one.

Fear grips my body. The walls of my hotel room are covered in textured gold linen. And the bed isn't this close to the wall. Heart pounding, I look down at the blanket I'm holding. A blanket that should match the pale ivory upholstery of the Victorian chair by the window.

The blanket is blue.

# 2
# (here)

## MONDAY, 8 SEPTEMBER, 2008
## (THE DAY BEFORE MY SEVENTEENTH BIRTHDAY)

"Abby? Abby, honey, wake up."

My eyes fly open. My mom, still in her pyjamas, is sitting on the edge of my bed, her face the picture of calm. I appreciate her effort, but I know instantly that something is wrong. There is much too much sunlight in my room.

"What time is it?"

"Five till eight."

I blink. For a moment I am still, calculating the exact number of minutes between now and the time the late bell rings. Thirteen.

"Abby?" My mom is clearly confused by my stillness. We both know there's no way I'm making it to school on time, which means I'll miss the beginning of the senior parking lottery. They start at the parking spot closest to the building and work their way towards the street, drawing names from a box at lightning speed. In order to claim your space, you have to be present at the drawing when they call your name. If you're not, game over. You're automatically relegated to the annex car park across the street.

I spring out of bed.

"Why didn't my alarm go off? And why is my alarm clock on the floor?" I point an accusing finger at the base of my bedside table, where my clock radio is lying face down on the carpet. My mom bends to pick it up.

"There was an earthquake last night," she replies, setting the clock back on my bedside table. It's blinking 12.00. "At least, they think it was an earthquake."

"There was an earthquake? In *Atlanta*?" I stare at her. "How is that possible?"

"Apparently, it's not the first time it's happened. And it wasn't just here, either." She presses the radio button on my clock. The familiar sound of my favourite morning news programme fills the room.

"*No significant damage or injuries have been reported, but people are reporting power outages in various parts of the city. This is the third earthquake to hit the Atlanta area since 1878. Seismologists are baffled by the quake, which, despite its relatively small size – only five point nine on the Richter scale – appears to have triggered seismic activity all over the globe.*"

I wonder briefly if I'm still asleep. An earthquake felt all over the world?

"Can I make you breakfast?" Mom asks, standing up.

I shake my head as I slide out of bed. "No time. But thanks." I pull the elastic from my hair, wishing I'd had the foresight to wash it last night, and wince as my fingers hit a tangle.

"Any chance school is cancelled?" I call after my mom. She reappears in the doorway and shakes her head.

"They've already announced that it isn't."

"What about aftershocks?" I ask as I give myself a once-over in the mirror over my dresser, trying to decide whether it's absolutely necessarily to bathe.

"I guess they figure kids will be safer at school," Mom replies. "Fewer windows."

I skip the shower and douse myself with lavender Febreze instead. I put my unwashed hair back into a ponytail, grab my bag and head down the back stairs to the kitchen.

"You excited about your big first day?" Dad asks when I appear.

"'Excited' is a strong word."

"Well, try to enjoy it." His voice is wistful. "You're only a senior once." I can tell by the look in his eye that he's remembering his own senior year of high school, hanging out in Andy Warhol's studio in midtown Manhattan after school (yes, *that* Andy Warhol), making silk screens and lithographs and probably doing massive amounts of drugs. He told me once that although his life got happier in the years that followed, he's never felt quite as alive as he did then.

"Don't forget your lunch!" Mom says, coming up behind me, brown paper bag in hand. As always, there's a colourful sticker holding it closed. I told her once, years ago, that the stickers were unnecessary because the bag just ended up in the rubbish. The next day, there was a note inside the bag, on exquisite handmade paper: *Dearest Abby, The Beauty of Life is in the beauty of life. Treasure the details. Love, Mom.* The stickers kept coming.

"Don't speed," my dad warns.

"I won't," I lie, and head for the door.

My school is exactly four miles and five traffic lights from my house. Over the past three years, I've learned that the time it takes me to get there varies dramatically depending on the time of day and the weather. Before seven o'clock on a clear day, it takes me four minutes. On rainy days during rush hour, it takes at least twelve. Today is the first "morning after an earthquake" I've ever experienced, so I'm not sure what to expect, but I'm definitely not prepared for the standstill I encounter as soon as I pull out of my neighbourhood. Nobody is moving. It's as if everyone within a ten-mile radius decided to hop into their cars at the exact same time. I glance at the clock on my dash and groan. It's 8.25 already, and I still have three and a half miles to go.

"If I'm late, then it probably means a lot of people are late. I'm sure they'll postpone the drawing." I say this out loud, confidently, trying to trick myself into believing it. Yeah, right. Our head teacher – a large, unfortunate-looking man whose arsenal of painful clichés and acne scars has earned him the nickname "The Cheese" – will no doubt relish the opportunity to wield his favourite catchphrase: "It's up to you to do what it takes." In other words, don't blame the earthquake – if being at school on time is important to you, get a battery-operated alarm clock (this was his response after a tornado wiped out a local power grid two years ago, delivered to the entire student body, sans irony, with a completely straight face).

At 8.54, I pull into the school car park. From the looks of it, the cars clogging the roads hadn't belonged to my classmates. There's not a single empty space. "A preview," I mutter, crossing into the annex car park across the street. "Might as well get used to it." I park in one of the few open spots and sprint towards the building. The second-period bell is ringing, loud and shrill, as I pull open the front door. I don't see any seniors in the crowded corridor, which I take as a good sign: the lottery must not be over yet.

As I approach the auditorium, I'm met with the muffled sound of the Cheese's voice. I slip through the doors and take a seat in the back row. Our state-of-the-art auditorium has stadium seating, so I have a bird's-eye view of the stage. Behind the podium, there is a giant diagram of the car park propped up on an easel. Although I can't read them from this distance, every space is filled with a name. Damn it.

"This is your year," Mr Cheese is saying. "Make it count." He pumps his fist for emphasis. From the sea of slumped bodies, it's obvious he's being wholeheartedly ignored.

I scan the crowd for Caitlin and Tyler. Ty is easy to spot. He's the only black head in a row of white ones (our golf team). I eventually spot Caitlin on the far left, one empty seat between her and the aisle, no doubt saved for me. My eyes are fixed on the top of her blonde head, willing her to look at me, but she's focused on something in her lap.

Two seconds later, my phone buzzes with a text.

Caitlin: WHERE R U???

I quickly write back. BEHIND U. FAR BACK. As soon as I hit send, she turns around. I wave and she smiles, looking relieved to see me, then turns back to her phone.

U OK?

29

YEAH. ALARM DIDNT GO OFF.

YIKES. SORRY.

TELL ME ABOUT IT. WHAT # DID U GET?

#27

Lucky her! Second row from the building.

NICE! ME?

Caitlin raises her eyes and gives me a sympathetic look. My phone vibrates in my hand.

A7 :(

A as in Annex. Lovely. "Sorry," Caitlin mouths. I shrug. At this point, it's not like I'm surprised.

I'm not sure I want to know, but I ask anyway:

WHEN DID THEY CALL MY NAME?

Another sympathetic look.

#19.

The very first row. Naturally.

"We expect each and every one of you to take ownership of

your future," the Cheese drones on. "Our guidance counsellors are a wonderful resource – use them – but the decisions are ultimately yours to make. Where you go from here is up to you. Don't get on a Road to Nowhere." There is a collective eye roll. His captives are reaching their Cheese threshold. Thankfully, he's wrapping it up. "It's nine-oh-five," he announces, pointing at the wall clock. "We expect everyone to be in their second-period classrooms, in their seats, by nine fifteen. You are dismissed."

I make my way to the left aisle to meet Caitlin. In skinny jeans, peep-toe heels and a cropped silk blazer, she looks like she should be on the cover of *Teen Vogue*, not cruising the halls of a suburban high school.

"Hey," Caitlin says as she saunters up the aisle. "Forgot to replace the batteries in your alarm clock?"

"How'd you know?" I fall into step beside her. "Did I miss anything important?"

She shakes her head. "Just pearls of Cheese wisdom. I know you're devastated to have missed those." Her phone buzzes with a text.

"Tyler?"

She shakes her head. "My dad. He's down at the USGS field office. I made him promise to send hourly updates."

"USGS?"

"US Geological Survey. They're worried about structural damage from the tremor."

"Have they figured out what caused it yet?" I ask. "Since when do earthquakes shake the whole planet?"

"Earthquakes don't."

Before I can ask Caitlin what she means, someone taps me

on my shoulder. "Abby?" It's Ms DeWitt, one of our guidance counsellors. I've been to her office so few times I'm surprised she even knows who I am. "Do you have a minute?"

"Uh, sure." I glance at Caitlin. "See you later?" Caitlin nods, then heads towards the lobby doors. I turn back to Ms DeWitt, who motions for me to follow her.

"I sent a note to Mrs Gorin this morning, asking that you stop by before the lottery," she says as we set off down the hall. "But I gather you didn't make it to form today?"

"Oh – no – I just got here. We lost power because of the earthquake," I explain. She's a few steps ahead of me, so I hurry to catch up. "Uh, is everything OK?"

We arrive in front of her door, and she ushers me inside. "Everything is fine," she says, gesturing for me to sit. "We just have to make a change to your class schedule."

I freeze. "What kind of change?"

"Mr Simmons has cancelled History of Music," she says, sitting down at her desk. There are photos of a mean-looking Siamese cat tacked to her notice board. "Which leaves you without a fifth-period class." Her voice is brisk, like she's in a rush. "This morning there were openings in a couple of electives, but since we've rescheduled twenty-two students since then, I'm afraid you don't have many options."

*Shit.* History of Music was a key component of my perfect schedule. The title sounds legitimate enough, but it's a total no-brainer. The final exam consists of listening to Mr Simmons's hand-selected "essentials" playlist while writing an essay on the importance of music to American pop culture.

"So, where does that leave me?" I ask, hoping she'll tell me that Mr Simmons has created a new class, something that'll make HOM look like rocket science.

"Principles of Astronomy." To her credit, she doesn't even try to make this sound like good news.

*I will not freak out, I will not freak out.* "That's my only option?"

"At this point, yes," she says apologetically. "If you'd been here when we first sent for you, you could've taken Ms Ziffren's drama class instead . . . but I guess that's neither here nor there at this point, isn't it?" She smiles reassuringly as she hands me my new schedule. "The good news is, astronomy will really stand out on your transcript." I glance down at the page, still warm from the printer.

*Yeah. Fs usually do.*

"Abby, stop freaking out." Caitlin stabs a cucumber with her fork and pops it into her mouth. "I took it freshman year. It's not a hard class."

"This coming from the girl who's spent the past two summers interning at NASA." We're sitting on the hill behind the cafeteria, our lunches next to us. The lawn is packed with seniors enjoying the sunshine and one of the few perks of senior year: outdoor dining.

Caitlin rolls her eyes. "Abby, it's not even a real astronomy class. I promise you, if there are sci-track kids in there, they'll all be freshmen."

"Great," I say sarcastically. "So a bunch of fourteen-year-olds can make me feel stupid. I feel better already."

"It's senior year, baby!" We look up. Tyler is grinning down at us, flanked by four guys from the golf team.

"What are you so happy about?" I grumble as Tyler plops down on the grass next to Caitlin, lunch bag in hand. The other guys sit down at a picnic table a few feet away, no doubt worried about wrinkling their pressed khakis.

Caitlin, Tyler and I have been eating lunch together every day since sixth grade. My parents met Tyler's parents – both classical musicians – at a fund-raiser for the National Endowment for the Arts two weeks after they moved here, so Ty and I have been spending cookouts and game nights together since we were babies. There was a period in primary school when we professed to despise each other, but by fifth grade we were inseparable. We didn't meet Caitlin until sixth grade, when her family moved here from San Francisco. The three of us have been best friends ever since. These days, Caitlin and I are closer than either of us is to Tyler, mainly because he spends all his time playing golf and hooking up with volleyball players. And cheerleaders.

Tyler shrugs out of his blazer and drapes it over the fence behind us. Yes, he's sporting a seersucker suit at school. That's Tyler. A walking contradiction. The choirboy who uses a fake ID to buy beer every weekend but refuses to jaywalk. The jock with an unyielding Carrie Underwood obsession. The black guy who wears seersucker and plays competitive croquet.

"We're seniors. What's not to be happy about?" Tyler turns his lunch bag over and dumps its contents on to the lawn. Four sandwiches, two apples, an orange, two bags of crisps, a pot of blueberry yoghurt and an entire sleeve of Chips Ahoy.

"Abby's freaking out because she has to take astronomy," Caitlin tells him.

"I am not freaking out."

Caitlin looks at me, eyebrows raised.

"Ugh, I'd be freaking out, too," says Tyler. Caitlin elbows him.

"Ignore him," Caitlin instructs. "You'll be fine. Mr Kang is a great teacher."

"He isn't teaching it," I tell her.

"What are you talking about? It's Kang's class."

"Not this term," I reply, handing her the printout of my new schedule. Caitlin glances down at it and immediately reacts.

"No way!"

"What?" I demand.

"Unless this is a different Gustav P. Mann, the guy teaching your astronomy class is a Nobel Prize winner."

Memories of tenth-grade Botany Basics come barrelling back. "Please tell me you're kidding," I moan.

"There's still room in all my classes," Tyler says sympathetically. "History of the Southern Narrative, Prop Design, Intro to Tempo and Beats, Practical Physics, Senior Maths and Conversational Spanish." Listening to him rattle off this laughable lineup, I am envious of Tyler and his utter lack of scholastic ambition. It's not that he's not smart, but when you're a golf star, the university application process goes a little differently.

"Are those even real classes?" I ask him.

"Barely," Tyler replies, polishing off the last of his sandwiches.

"What is he doing teaching here?" Caitlin is still staring at my schedule. "I know there was pressure for him to resign, but how did he end up down here?"

"Resign from where?" I ask.

"Yale," Caitlin replies. "He has tenure there." She frowns. "*Had* tenure."

"What, did he molest a student or something?" Tyler jokes. Caitlin glares at him.

"No, he did not molest a student. He published a book the scientific establishment couldn't stomach, mostly because it read like the plot of a sci-fi novel. When they weren't able to dismantle his theory, they laughed at it. And him."

"What's the theory?" I ask.

"It has to do with parallel universes," Caitlin replies. "Dr Mann claims it's possible for them to—"

"Hiii, Tyler!" Caitlin's expression instantly turns sour. Neither of us has to look to know who the voice belongs to. Ilana Cassidy, quite possibly the least likable and most genuinely mean-spirited person on the planet. Apparently, the fact that Ilana is the devil incarnate was not enough to keep Tyler from hooking up with her at Max Levine's annual end-of-summer party, giving Ilana the mistaken impression that she and Tyler are a couple now. Ilana is standing at the foot of the hill, hands on her bony hips, posing like she's on the red carpet.

"Is she expecting paparazzi?" Caitlin mutters under her breath. The only person who likes Ilana less than I do is Caitlin.

Ilana's eyes dart to Caitlin. In an odd twist of fate, the only person whose approval Ilana craves is Caitlin's, which has everything to do with Caitlin's runway-worthy wardrobe. Ilana

36

sees me watching her and glowers. "What are you looking at?" I know better than to respond.

"I'll catch up with you later, OK?" Tyler calls to Ilana. "We're sort of in the middle of something."

A look of annoyance flashes across Ilana's face, but she covers it with a plastic smile. "Yeah, OK!" she chirps. "Text me!"

Tyler gives her a non-committal wave, then turns back to his lunch.

"I still can't believe you hooked up with her," Caitlin says to Tyler when Ilana is out of earshot, her tone harsh.

"I don't know why you hate her so much," Tyler replies. "She's not that bad."

"Oh, yes. She is."

"You know, you guys kinda look alike," Tyler says casually, pulling the top off his yoghurt. He licks blue yoghurt off the little aluminium lid, then wads it up into a little ball and tosses it into the nearest rubbish bin, pretending not to notice that Caitlin is glaring at him.

"We do not."

"The blonde hair, the blue eyes. . ." Tyler grins. "You two could be sisters."

I can't help but laugh. It's true that Caitlin and Ilana are both blonde-haired and blue-eyed, but they look nothing alike. Caitlin is a replica of her mother – tall, lanky, beautiful in an I-just-rolled-out-of-bed-and-threw-this-on way. Ilana, on the other hand, always looks like she just spent two hours in the bathroom (and about four hours at the gym) trying to achieve Barbie-doll beauty. Her five-foot-two-inch frame has been spun and kickboxed down to kids' department size, and her frizzy brown hair has been bleached and straightened into submission, so that it now hangs limply at her bony shoulders.

Caitlin makes a face and punches Tyler in the shoulder. He catches her fist in his and holds it for a couple of beats longer than he has to. That's when it happens. Something passes between them. Something I've never noticed before. Something so slight, it's nearly imperceptible. . .

*Chemistry.*

The moment the thought pops into my mind, I'm certain of it. I can't explain how I know, I just do. It's like this intense gut feeling, an intuition so strong it almost feels like déjà vu. Is that why Tyler asked me yesterday if Caitlin had met anyone at the lab this summer? I assumed it was because he wanted to tease her about it (Tyler has no shortage of nerd jokes), but now I wonder if he had other reasons. And Caitlin has been disproportionately critical of the Ilana thing, catty when she's normally not.

"So you're saying Caitlin is your type, then," I say, keeping my voice casual. "You can't have Caitlin, so you're settling for Ilana."

Both Tyler and Caitlin look at me in surprise. We don't joke like this. Ever. *Is it me, or did Tyler's cheeks just get rosier?* It's awkward for an instant. Then Tyler smiles, and the awkwardness evaporates.

"Yeah, that's it," he says, tugging Caitlin towards him, playing into my joke. "Ilana is filling my Caitlin-shaped void."

"Last I checked, I wasn't shaped like a lollipop," Caitlin retorts, swatting him away. Her tone is sharp and bitchy and not like her at all. As soon as the words are out of her mouth, she winces. "Sorry. That was mean."

"The girl has pictures of Mary-Kate Olsen taped to the inside of her locker," Tyler points out. "I'm pretty sure 'lollipop' is what she's going for."

Caitlin looks at her watch. "I should go," she says. "I need to stop by DeWitt's office before class." Her mention of the guidance counsellor's name sends me back into panic mode. Astronomy starts in ten minutes.

"Please tell me you're switching into my class," I beg. "You can learn from your idol and tutor me at the same time."

"I wish," she replies. "But I already took it with Kang freshman year. There's no way they'll let me take it twice."

"So what're you switching?"

"Not switching. Just adding. I want to see if they'll let me double up sixth period."

"You want to take two classes at once?" I ask. I've seen Caitlin's schedule. It's intense.

"Neither is offered in spring term," she says nonchalantly. "So, yeah. Why not?"

I look over at Tyler. He just shrugs.

"News flash, Barnes. She's insane."

I get to fifth period a few minutes early, but the room is already full. Caitlin was right about the freshmen; about half the faces look young and scared. Another third are kids I know, probably other History of Music refugees. The rest I recognize as science-track brainiacs who will no doubt destroy the grading curve for the rest of us. I look around for an empty seat.

There's only one, in the very back row, next to a guy I've never seen before. Blond crew cut, dark brown eyes, average-looking features. Light blue T-shirt tucked into dark green cargo trousers that have about five too many pockets. White Converse One Stars (the low kind) that look like they just came out of the box. His vibe is definitely dorky, but cute dorky. The way Max Levine was before he grew his hair out and started smoking truckloads of pot. Since he looks too old to be a freshman, I decide he must be new.

Astronomy Boy sees me looking at him and smiles. He points at the empty seat.

"Hey," he says as I approach. "I'm Josh."

"I'm Abby." *Why am I suddenly nervous?*

"Popular class," Josh remarks, glancing around the crowded room. "That means it's either really good or really easy."

"Definitely not easy," I reply. "Unless you're on the science track, in which case 'easy' is a relative term."

"Oh, right," Josh says. "The whole magnet school thing. Are you in the science programme?"

"Ha. No. Nowhere close. I've never met a science class I didn't hate."

"So what're you doing in astronomy?"

"An unfortunate twist of fate," I reply, distracted by the tiny mole beneath his left eye, just below his lash line. It's infinitesimal, not more than a pinprick, but that little mark somehow elevates his face from average to adorable. Or maybe it's the smattering of pale freckles on his nose. Or the perfect shape of his bottom lip.

The mole does a little dance as his eyebrows shoot up. "Fate, huh? This must be a pretty important class for you, then." I can't tell whether he's teasing.

"What about you?" I ask. "Are you here by fate or choice?"

"Hmm. I guess I'd have to say choice. This was the first class I signed up for."

"Oh, so you're into self-torture, then."

Josh laughs out loud. His laugh, deeper than his voice, reminds me of the rich sweetness of my mom's gingerbread. I angle my knees towards him, wishing his were close enough to touch. "I mean, c'mon – what's cooler than the universe?" he says. "It's this great, big, never-ending mystery that astronomers and cosmologists spend their whole lives trying to solve. And after all that discovery and revelation, there's always more to figure out." His mouth widens into a boyish grin. "I love that."

I match his grin. "I take it you were one of those kids with a telescope in your bedroom," I tease. "And let me guess . . . glow-in-the-dark star stickers on your ceiling?"

"Guilty," he says, as the lights dim.

"Velcome to Prinzeeples of Astronomy!" a voice booms, the words flecked with German. "Let zee fun begin!" Dr Mann claps his hands together with glee, earning some muffled laughter from the back of the room.

Our teacher is shorter than I expected but otherwise looks like every photograph I've ever seen of Albert Einstein: wild grey hair, huge round eyes, unruly eyebrows. In his brown tweed suit with suede patches on the elbows, he's the perfect incarnation of a nutty professor. Would his colleagues at Yale have laughed at him if he'd looked a little less like one?

Dr Mann holds up a stack of papers. "This is the syllabus for this course," he says as he hands the stack to a girl in the front row. "Our task is not to master the topics on this list, although that is certainly a worthy pursuit and one well worth the discipline it requires." He pauses, surveying the room. He has our attention. "Rather, our work will be focused on the larger picture. The big questions. I just ask this: no matter what the concept, you commit yourselves to this principle." He turns on his heels and strides to the overhead projector, where he begins to write with sharp, definitive motions. When he's finished, he flicks on the light. Two words, all caps, appear on the white screen:

## LOOK DEEPER

"No cross-country practice?" My mom is at the kitchen table paying bills when I come through the back door.

"Coach cancelled it," I tell her, setting my bag and keys on the counter. "I think he was spooked by the earthquake. What are you doing home so early?"

"The museum was closed today," Mom replies. "We had a water main break." She takes off her reading glasses and rubs her eyes.

"Uh-oh. How bad was the damage?"

"Not nearly as bad as it could've been, thankfully. An entire wing flooded, but there was only an inch or so of water, so the collection wasn't affected. We're in a lot better shape than MoMA," she says. "They had an electrical fire and lost four pieces."

"Oh, wow. That's terrible."

"I know. But listen to this: the four pieces they lost were the two hanging on each side of Dali's *Persistence of Memory* – you know, the painting your dad and I were looking at when we met. The fire started behind that wall."

42

"But the Dali survived?" I can tell by her tone that it must have.

She nods. "More than survived," she says. "No damage at all. Not even from the smoke." She smiles. "Your dad, of course, thinks it means something. He just hasn't decided what yet." She stands up from the table and stretches her back. On the TV mounted beneath our kitchen cabinets, a news reporter is talking about the earthquakes. The banner at the bottom of the screen reads EARTHQUAKE ROCKS THE GLOBE.

"Do they know what caused it?" I ask, nodding at the TV.

"They're calling it a 'fluke', if you can believe it. Which I'd say means they don't have a clue." She pulls open the fridge and examines its contents. "Want a snack?"

"Sure," I say, suddenly ravenous. I hop up on the counter, then reach down to pull off my boots.

"So?" Mom asks, scooping hummus into the clay bowl my dad painted in Mexico last summer. We have a dozen dip bowls, but my mom always reaches for this one. "Am I allowed to ask for details?" She tosses me a bag of mini carrots.

"About my day? Sure." I crunch on a carrot. "I arrived just in time to miss the entire car park drawing. Good news is, I don't have to worry about exercise this year, because I'll get plenty of it hiking to and from the annex."

"I'm sorry, sweetie."

"Eh, it's OK," I reply, reaching for another carrot.

"How about the rest of your day?" Mom asks. "You're happy with that schedule you worked so hard on?"

I open my mouth to complain about my unwelcome astronomy class, and Josh pops into my head. Josh whose last name I don't even know. Astronomy Boy. My stomach does a little flip-flop at the thought of him.

"I had to change it," I tell her. "Goodbye, History of Music. Hello, Principles of Astronomy."

My mom is clearly puzzled by my smile. "Is this a good thing?"

"I dunno," I admit. "The teacher seems cool, and. . ." I hesitate, knowing that if I mention Josh, he will become the topic du jour.

"And. . .?"

My mobile phone rings from inside my bag.

"Tell Caitlin I said hello," Mom says, sitting back down at the table.

"I will." I grab one last carrot, then hop off the counter. "Thanks for the snack." I dig my phone out of my bag and answer it. "Hey."

"UGH. I literally JUST pulled out of the car park."

Bag and boots in hand, I wave to my mom and head up to my bedroom.

"I'm sure they'd let you switch your spot for one in the annex," I say, teasing, knowing Caitlin would rather sit in her car for an hour than walk the quarter mile to the annex, for two main reasons: she lives in four-inch heels, and she travels with about thirty pounds' worth of science textbooks in her bag.

"Very funny. So how was astronomy? What'd you think of Dr Mann?"

"The man used the words 'kerfuffle' and 'tomfoolery' with a straight face," I reply. "What's not to like?"

"Did he say why he's at Brookside?"

"A kerfuffle with the Yale administration."

"Seriously?"

"No. But it's an awesome word, right?" I drop my bag and boots on my bedroom carpet and sprawl out on my stomach on my bed. "I think you were right about the pressure to resign. All he said was academia is not what it used to be, and that he wanted to spend some time with 'unadulterated minds'. He picked Atlanta because his daughter lives down here."

"I wish I were his daughter," Caitlin says wistfully. "All that Nobel-worthy DNA."

"I'll be sure to tell your dad that." I roll over on to my back, propping myself up with the oversized Cheshire Cat pillow I've had since I was nine. He was supposed to go to Goodwill when I repainted my room last year, but he's still here, big and pink and frayed around the mouth, holding court in the centre of my blue-and-white-striped bed. "Hey, do you know where I can get some of those glow-in-the-dark stars?" I ask. "You know, the kind you can stick on your ceiling?"

"One day of astronomy and already you want stars on your ceiling?"

"This is me, embracing science. Go with it."

"Can your stargazing wait until Thursday?" Caitlin asks. "I'm going to Fernbank for this young scientists thing. I'll get you some from the planetarium gift store."

"Thanks! It can be my birthday present."

"Nope. Already have that, wrapped and ready to be brought to dinner tomorrow night with your cake." Caitlin's been getting me the same mint chocolate chip ice cream cake from Baskin-Robbins every year since seventh grade, and each year, we devour the entire thing in one sitting. It's a highly calorific rite of passage we refuse to abandon. The rest of the day is always pretty anti-climactic, since by the time my birthday rolls around, everyone else in my grade has already had theirs. Turning seventeen (or sixteen or fifteen) is much less exciting when everyone else has already done it. "Hey, I'm pulling into my driveway," Caitlin says. "Talk later?"

"Yup." There's a click, and she's gone. Phone still pressed to my ear, I stare up at the ceiling, envisioning my future neon galaxy.

That night, I have trouble falling asleep. At ten past midnight, I give up. Very careful not to wake my parents, I make my way through the kitchen to the door that opens on to our deck. Outside, it's both colder and quieter than I expect it to be. The wind picks up, icy against my bare legs, and I shiver in my thin T-shirt. I hug my arms close to my body. "Happy birthday," I whisper in the darkness.

Above me, the dark, moonless expanse is thick with stars. I can't remember the last time I noticed the night sky. When I was younger, I was enthralled by it, awed by its scale and mystery. On clear nights, I'd sit out here for hours, connecting the dots with my fingers, bringing animals and objects to life in my mind, while my dad sat beside me, sketching out my creations in his notebook, describing the exact location of each so none would be lost or forgotten. My creatures are up there now, right where I left them. Letting my head fall back, I trace their outlines with my fingertips, wishing I knew the real constellations.

My vision blurs as I stare, unblinking, at the starry sky. And then, out of nowhere, a strange sense of purpose overtakes me. Like a thunderclap, the words *THIS IS IT* reverberate in my brain. I blink – hard – and the sky comes into sharp focus. I blink again, trying to make sense of what I'm feeling. *What* is it? But the stars aren't giving anything away.

# 3
# (there)

## WEDNESDAY, 9 SEPTEMBER, 2009
## (MY EIGHTEENTH BIRTHDAY)

My heart is pounding so violently that my ribs ache.

I whip my head to the right and see a second twin-size bed a few feet away, pushed up against another white wall, this one decorated with a framed black-and-white photograph of the Seattle Space Needle. The bed is unmade and its flowered sheets look slept in, and the clock on the window sill next to it is blinking 12.00. There is no sign of the bed's owner.

*Where am I?*

I scan the rest of the small room: two identical desks, two identical dressers, two closed doors. I wonder briefly if I could be in prison before deciding that flowered sheets and arty photographs probably aren't government-issue. My mind careens through a parade of other horrible possibilities. Maybe those two doors are locked. Maybe I was drugged and kidnapped, and this is where my captors have been holding me. I think back to last night. *Did I remember to dead-bolt my door?* The flannel trousers and grey Brookside Cross-Country T-shirt I'm wearing are mine, but I don't remember having brought them to LA with me, and I definitely wasn't wearing them last night. I never changed out of my pyjama-dress. *What the hell is going on?*

There are voices outside. People talking. Someone laughing. I get out of bed and move towards the window, which, to my relief, is not barred or locked but halfway open and clearly the source of both the sunlight and the icy air. I push the glass all the way up and stick my head out.

The window is on the second storey of a U-shaped brick building, overlooking an enclosed courtyard. The voices I hear belong to a group of students, laden with rucksacks and messenger bags, gathered around a wooden bench. The room, the building, the kids outside. This has to be a university campus. *But where?* This doesn't look anything like the pictures I've seen of UCLA or USC. And besides, the air feels much too cool for this to be Southern California. My fear turns into panic. *I have to get out of here.*

I walk to one of the doors, say a quick prayer that it's not locked, and open it. It's a wardrobe. As I survey its contents, my forearms prickle with goosebumps. The clothes inside are mine.

On the other side of the other door is a short corridor leading to what looks like a living room. I see the end of a green sofa and the edge of a coffee table. An out-of-commission fireplace that's doubling as a pantry, stocked with a box of organic oats, two bags of cinnamon soya crisps and a jar of almond butter. A fancy-looking espresso machine on the floor. Purple Nikes by the door. And an ankle.

The ankle – attached to a small, delicate-looking, bare female foot – is suspended in the air, parallel to the ground, as if its owner is balancing on one leg. I take a step closer, trying to get a better glimpse of this person before she sees me.

"Abby?" The foot drops to the floor, and a pretty Asian girl comes into view. At first I think she's younger than me, but then I realize that she's just small. She can't be more than five feet tall, but she looks strong. Her tiny, muscular body is in yoga trousers and a vest top, and she's standing on a yoga mat. When she sees me, she smiles. "I didn't wake you, did I? I was trying to be quiet."

I want to scream, *WHO ARE YOU AND WHAT AM I DOING HERE????* But for some reason, I don't. I simply smile back and shake my head.

"Good," she replies, reaching for the bottle of water near her feet. "After last night, I figured you could use some sleep." *Last night?* She smiles again, bigger this time. "Happy birthday, roomie!"

*My birthday.* I'd forgotten. Which, considering the morning I've had, is not nearly as weird as the fact that this chick I've never seen before is calling me roomie. "Thanks."

The girl reaches for an opaque vitamin bottle sitting on the coffee table and dumps two pills into her palm. "Willow bark?" she asks me. I give her a blank, slightly bewildered stare, which pretty much sums up my mental state right now. "It's for headaches," she explains. "I woke up with a monster one."

"Um, no, that's OK," I reply. Considering the circumstances, it's probably better not to accept unmarked pills from strangers. Plus, remarkably, though my head is swimming, it isn't pounding.

Despite the gallon of champagne I consumed last night, I'm not the least bit hungover.

The girl pops the pills in her mouth and takes a swig of water. "Well, I guess I should get in the shower," she says. "I have econ at eleven." She steps past me towards the bedroom. A polite person would step out of her way, but I just stand there motionless, trying to come up with a reasonable explanation for all this. I'm still standing in the same spot when she emerges from the bedroom a few moments later, wrapped in a towel and carrying a shower caddy. "See you in a few!" she says brightly as she heads for the door. When she opens it, I get a glimpse of an octagonal entryway, surrounded by four dark wooden doors, all labelled with three-digit brass numbers. The door falls shut behind her, and I am alone.

I walk over to the sofa and don't so much sit as fall into it. My heart is racing, I'm ridiculously thirsty, and I have absolutely no idea where I am or how I got here. The clock on the cable box says it's 10.10, which means that in the span of the last eight hours I, and all my belongings, somehow managed to get from room 316 at the Culver Hotel to here. Wherever "here" is.

My eyes scan the room, looking for evidence, and land on a dog-eared blue book lying on the coffee table. It takes me a moment to process its title: *2009–2010 Yale University Programmes of Study.*

*I'm at Yale.*

I squeeze my eyes shut and will myself to wake up from what must be a dream. But when I open my eyes, I'm still here, on this velour sofa, holding the Yale course catalogue in my shaking hands. I take a deep breath, forcing myself to stay calm.

A phone rings, and I jump. Then I realize it's *my* phone, ringing in the bedroom. I leap off the sofa and hurry down the hall. My mobile is on the desk next to the bed I woke up in.

MOM AND DAD – HOME

They're no doubt calling to wish me happy birthday, but I can't deal with them right now. I won't be able to hold it together. I send the call to voicemail and immediately dial Caitlin's number.

"Thank God," I say as soon as she picks up.

"Happy birthday!" she shouts. I relax the moment I hear her voice. *Caitlin will explain this to me. She'll make this make sense.*

"You have to help me."

"Are you that hungover?" she asks with a laugh. "My head is throbbing, but other than that, I feel OK."

"I'm serious, Caitlin. I'm freaking out."

"What's wrong?" she asks in alarm.

"Where are you right now?"

"In my room. Why?"

"At Yale?" I hold my breath, praying. *Please let her be here, please let her be here.*

"Of course at Yale, silly. Where else would I be?" I experience a brief flash of relief. *Caitlin's here.* Caitlin, who has an answer for everything. She'll have an answer for this. Everything is going to be fine. "Abby?" Caitlin's voice is tinged with worry. "What's going on?"

I take a deep breath. "I know it sounds crazy," I begin. "But . . . I think I'm here, too. At Yale."

52

Caitlin laughs. "You had me worried there for a sec. I thought something was seriously wrong. It is sorta surreal though, huh? Our being here together." Her voice sounds breezy, like nothing is amiss.

"How long have I been here?" I whisper.

"What do you mean? We got here a week ago Friday. Hey, are you all right?" The worry is back.

I am reeling. Caitlin is acting like it's the most normal thing in the world for me to be here. Caitlin, the most rational person I know. My panic quickly becomes dread. *Something is very wrong.* Either that, or:

"Is this some sort of joke?"

"Is *what* a joke?" Caitlin sounds genuinely confused now. "Abby, what's going on? Are you OK?"

I am most definitely not OK. My mind charges forward, tearing through every imaginable possibility. The problem is, there aren't very many. Either I'm dreaming or hallucinating or crazy. Or everyone else is.

"I'm coming over there," Caitlin says. "I'll be there in five minutes."

"No!" I say quickly, louder than I intended. "I mean, no . . . that's OK. I'm fine," I lie. I want Caitlin's help, but first I need some time to think.

"You don't sound fine."

"I'm fine," I insist. "I just had a really weird dream, that's all." *One I can't wake up from.*

"Abby."

"I'm fine!" I repeat, struggling to keep my voice as light as possible. "I'll catch up with you later, OK?"

"We're shopping Art History at eleven fifteen, right?" She still sounds unsure.

"Yep!" I say this with all the enthusiasm I can muster.

"OK, cool." Her voice returns to normal. "There's a chem class I want to check out at ten thirty, so is it OK if I just meet you at McNeil?"

"Sure," I say, already distracted. It's ten fifteen now. That gives me an hour to figure out what the hell happened last night.

"'K, see you then."

As soon as I press the end button, a text pops up on my screen.

Tyler: HAPPY BDAY BARNES. WELCOME TO THE BEST YEAR OF YOUR LIFE.

Ten minutes in, "best" is not the word I'd use.

I grab what looks like my laptop and shove it into the satchel hanging on the back of the desk chair, along with my wallet and phone. I'm about to leave the bedroom when I realize I should probably get dressed first. After surveying my wardrobe, I go with the jeans I got for Christmas last year, my favourite white V-neck, and a snuggly brown cardigan I've never seen before. As I'm leaving the bedroom, my roomie returns from her shower.

"We're still on for dinner tonight, right?" she asks. "I was thinking I'd invite a friend of Ben's to come with."

"Sure, sounds great." I don't have time to make birthday plans. Or figure out who Ben is.

"Eight o'clock at Samurai Sushi? Ben's train gets in at seven thirty."

I nod distractedly, checking around the room to make sure

I have everything I need. My eyes land on a key card with my picture and a bar code on it. I grab it. "OK, awesome," the girl is saying. "I'll make a reservation. Oh! Before you go. . ." She retrieves a tan envelope from her desk drawer and hands it to me. "This is for you." I turn the envelope over in my hands. The words *For Abby, Love, Marissa* are handwritten in crisp black letters on the front. "Open it," says Marissa, nudging me with her elbow. "And please don't say I shouldn't have got you anything. So what if we've only known each other twelve days? By the time my birthday comes in February, we'll have been living together for five months, and even if we hate each other by then, you'll feel obligated to get me something. I'm just saving myself from the hassle of feeling like an asshole when that happens."

I return her smile, momentarily forgetting the fact that in the last seven minutes, I have somehow acquired an entirely new life, complete with autumn-appropriate attire and a gift-giving roommate.

Inside the envelope is a single black-and-white photograph of Caitlin and me, sitting side by side on the grass in front of an imposing stone tower, laughing at some unknown joke. The photograph looks like something you'd see in a magazine. "What a great picture! Did you take this?" I ask, looking up at Marissa. She gives me a funny look.

"Last weekend, remember? At the Freshman Picnic."

"Oh – right. Duh." I force a smile, willing my heart to slow down. *How does this girl I've never met have a photograph of me from last weekend?*

"Since it turned out so well, I figured you might want a bigger version to hang on your wall. So I printed an eight by ten and am having it matted and framed. It's supposed to be ready tomorrow."

"Wow . . . thanks! Such a cool present." I'm genuinely touched by the gift but itching to get out of here. I put on my best apologetic smile. "I really should get going. There's a class I want to check out that starts pretty soon." I move towards the door, hoping she won't ask what class.

"No worries," she replies. "See you tonight!" She waves, then disappears into the bedroom. I grab the course schedule from the coffee table and hurry out of the door.

When I reach the courtyard, I realize that I don't really have a plan. What I need is a place to think, preferably somewhere quiet with internet access. I flip through the course schedule and find a campus map on the inside back cover. It's not exceptionally detailed, but the words *Sterling Memorial Library* leap out at me. Perfect. *Now how the hell do I get there?*

The courtyard, like the building around it, is U-shaped. The open part of the U faces a busy street, but there's a high, wrought-iron fence stretching the entire length of the opening. *Who gives someone a view of a major street but no way to get to it?* I briefly consider yelling at someone through the bars but quickly decide against it. Probably wise to avoid crazy-person behaviour, at least for the time being. At the base of the U is a wide tunnel through the buildings, which appears to be my only way out.

The tunnel dumps me into a massive enclosed quad. A quick glance at my map is all I need to get my bearings. The layout of the buildings, the size of the courtyard . . . this has to be Old Campus, which means I've just come from Vanderbilt Hall, the

U-shaped building on the southern end. The library is just a couple of streets north-west of here, so I head for the arched gate at the far corner of the quad. As I'm passing through the archway, a group of girls emerges from a door a few yards away, carrying coffee cups and pastry bags. My stomach growls with envy. The sign above the door says DURFEE'S and has a picture of a coffee mug on it. I dig through my bag for my wallet, praying that there's money in it. I find four dollars and some change, enough for coffee and a bagel.

Durfee's is bustling with activity. No one pays any attention to me, which is great, and the place is dirt cheap. I buy a large coffee, a sesame seed bagel, a bottle of water and a granola bar for later, and still have a dollar left over. I'm a long way from LA, that's for sure.

As I'm walking out, two guys, both wearing polo shirts with the collar flipped up and smelling like day-old (OK, make that week-old) beer, walk in. They see me, look at each other and smile. "Hey, hey," one of them says to me. His shaggy red hair looks like it hasn't seen a shampoo bottle in quite some time. "You looked like you were having fun last night."

"Last night?"

The guys laugh. "Yeah, it's all a little foggy, huh?" the other one says. His blond hair is sticking straight up, like it dried while he was upside down.

Dirty Hair nods at my coffee cup and sack of goodies. "Lemme guess – coffee, water and a bagel." I stare at him. "Am I right?" I nod, not sure whether to be frightened or impressed. "Hangover essentials," he explains. "But you forgot the aspirin."

"Oh . . . right." I flash what I hope is a friendly smile, trying not to grimace as I feel my stomach churn. Standing this close to them and their beer-emanating pores is making me nauseous.

"They're out of aspirin," the blond one says, pointing to the empty box. "Man, something must be up with the barometric pressure. Everyone I've talked to has a headache." He nods at the line of people waiting to pay. All of them are clutching travel packs of pain relievers. "You want some paracetamol?" he asks me.

"Uh, no. I'm OK, actually. But thanks." Blond Spikes just shrugs.

"So, what're you up to today?" Dirty Hair asks, alcohol heavy on his breath. I seriously might puke. Right now.

"Uh, you know . . . nothing much. Hey, gotta run." I don't bother to wait for a response. Rude, maybe, but I figure a hasty exit is less socially scarring than dumping the contents of my stomach on their suede loafers.

A few minutes later, I'm flashing my ID card to the security guard at the entrance of Sterling Memorial Library, which I recognize from the photograph Marissa gave me. It looks more like a Gothic church than a library. The exterior is impressive, but the interior is breathtaking. The main entrance, adorned with symbols and writings in various ancient languages, opens into a cathedral-like nave with vaulted aisles, clerestoried lighting, and too many stained-glass windows to count. I head towards the circulation desk, which, fitting with the cathedral theme, looks like an altar. The librarian looks up as I approach.

"Hello there," she says. "May I help you?"

"Hi . . . I'm, uh—"

She politely cuts me off. "A freshman." *I look as clueless as I feel, apparently.* "Freshmen are the only students who come to the library during shopping period," she explains with a kind smile. "Is this your first time to SML?" I nod. She reaches under the desk and pulls out a library map. "Then you'll probably need one of these," she says, sliding the map across the desk. "Library policies are on the back."

I scan the map. "Where's the best place for me to go?"

"Depends on how much privacy you want," she replies. "There are five reading rooms on this level, a couple more scattered throughout the rest of the main building, and half a dozen study carrels on each level of the stacks."

"The stacks?"

The librarian points to the map in my hands. "Our fifteen floors of books. If you're looking for privacy, that's your best bet."

"And how do I. . ."

She turns to her computer and types a few keys. "All I'll need is your ID card to reserve a carrel," she tells me. I hand it to her. She scans the bar code, then gives it back to me. "All set. Carrel 3M-06." She leans over and draws a red $X$ on my library map, then points to her left, to another security guard station. "Just show the guard your ID."

"Carrel," I soon learn, is the library's euphemism for the ridiculously tiny cubicles with plastic sliding doors that line the interior walls of the building. While I'm waiting for my laptop to boot up, I close my eyes and go over the last twenty-four hours in my mind, attempting to recall every detail of last night's events. Could Bret have slipped me something? But why would he drug me and take me to Yale? And if I just got here last night, how does Marissa have a photo of me that was supposedly taken last week, and why is there a student ID card with my name and picture on it?

I sigh, opening my eyes just as my computer finishes booting up. Any uncertainly about whose laptop this is disappears when I see the home screen. The background image is a picture of Caitlin, Tyler and me, standing on the Brookside football field, wearing caps and gowns and grinning like we just won the Super Bowl. It's a graduation photo, obviously. *But where did it come from?* I missed graduation. I was already in LA by then, doing preproduction for the movie. Saturday, 6 June, 2009. I remember calling Caitlin that afternoon to see how it went.

*How is there a picture of me at graduation if I wasn't there?*

I stare at the photograph, trying to remember that moment, but I can't. I have absolutely no recollection of being there, which makes sense, because I WASN'T. All of a sudden, I'm annoyed. Annoyed that whatever is going on has made me doubt my sanity, made me doubt reality. I have been in Los Angeles, living at the Culver Hotel, shooting a movie with Bret Woodward since May. *That* I know. *That* I remember. *That's* what's real.

*Right?*

Confronted with inconsistencies I can't explain, I jump into journalist mode. I'll fact-check my life the way I'd fact-check a newspaper article, starting with the movie I've spent the last four months shooting. I launch my web browser, which redirects to a secure log-in screen for the Yale network, with boxes for my student ID number and password. Undeterred, I pull out my ID card and examine it. Under the bar code is a ten-digit number, which has to be my student ID number. I type the numbers into the top box. Now for the harder part: the password. I've been using the same password since we read *Through the Looking Glass* in seventh grade.

I type w-o-n-d-e-r-l-a-n-d into the password box and hold my breath as I click the log-in button. A few seconds later, the log-in screen disappears.

I'm in.

Buoyed, I type the words "Everyday Assassins movie" into the search bar and hit enter. The top hit tells me what I want to know. *Directed by Alain Bourneau and starring Bret Woodward,* Everyday Assassins *is a high-octane thriller about a renegade military sniper and his band of teenage assassins.* I scroll down. Bret's name is right where I expect it to be, at the top of the lengthy cast list. The next three names are all ones I recognize. So far everything is exactly as I remember it. I keep scrolling, looking for my name. There's Kirby. There's the guy who plays Bret's other sidekick. My name should be next.

*Please let it be there, please let it be there.*

It isn't.

I think back, remembering my audition. That tiny studio office. The loud hum of the window AC unit. The casting director's encouraging smile. Then I go back further, remembering the night of the school play . . . then even further, to the day I found out I'd been cast as Thomasina . . . then further still, to the first day of senior year, when Ms Ziffren handed out copies of *Arcadia* and told us auditions would be held the following week.

I squeeze my eyes shut, replaying my conversation with Ms DeWitt that morning. I remember her telling me that Mr Simmons had cancelled History of Music, and that my options for a replacement were Drama Methods and astronomy. But I also remember – just as vividly – Ms DeWitt telling me that astronomy was my *only* option . . . that there had been other classes available, but they'd been filled already . . . that because I was late, I was the last of Simmons's students to be rescheduled.

But I *wasn't* late. I'm never late.

*The earthquake.*

A stream of new memories floods my mind: sitting in traffic on my way to school, getting stopped by Ms DeWitt as I was coming out of the auditorium, complaining to Caitlin at lunch, pretending to listen to my astronomy teacher while staring at the new guy next to me.

*Same day, two completely different sets of memories.* It's as if my mind recorded two different versions of what happened that morning. I run through both versions again, struggling to make sense of the inconsistency. When I can't, I rack my brain for other duplicate days, but there aren't any. Just the one. Exactly a year ago yesterday. I remember, because it was the day before my birthday.

On impulse, I Google the words "Atlanta earthquake September 2008." The search returns over a million hits. The top one is a link to an article on CNN.com, dated 9 September, 2008.

*A rare earthquake measuring magnitude 5.9 shook the Southeast early yesterday morning. Scientists are baffled, as it appears there may have been more than seventy similar quakes at various sites across the globe. Theories about the cause of the quakes abound, but so far seismologists have been unable to isolate their origin.*

I close my eyes, again trying to summon more of these alternate memories. Other astronomy lectures, other conversations with the friendly new kid. *Nada.* Nothing beyond that first day. I've got one day of earthquake memories and a full year's worth of non-earthquake ones.

*DING!* My eyes fly open. It's another text from Tyler.

TELL C TO LET ME COME VISIT

I think for a sec, then quickly reply.

WHAT AIRPORT WOULD YOU FLY OUT OF?

He'll think it's super weird that I'm asking, but at least I'll know from his answer whether he's still at Michigan. My phone dings with his reply.

U GONNA BOOK MY FLIGHT FOR ME?

Damn. So much for that.

I'm crafting a response when my phone dings again.

DTW

Detroit. So Tyler's still at Michigan, Caitlin's still at Yale, and I'm three thousand miles from where I should be. And no closer to figuring out why.

I sigh, slumping down in my seat, wishing I could go back to sleep and forget this whole experience. But I'm supposed to meet Caitlin in six minutes, and according to my map, McNeil Lecture Hall is in the art gallery on the other side of campus.

I leave my laptop on the desk, lock the door to my study carrel and hurry back downstairs.

The blue sign outside 1111 Chapel Street welcomes me to the Yale University Art Gallery. I pull open the door and step inside the lobby. I'm so preoccupied with the fact that I'm late that I almost don't notice the banner hanging on the lobby's far wall.

THE ART OF HARMONY: SEURAT'S CHROMOLUMINARISM.
I SEPTEMBER–30 NOVEMBER AT THE YUAG.
COURTESY OF THE HIGH MUSEUM.

My mom's pointillism exhibit. I knew the collection was touring after its nine-month stint at the High, but it catches me off guard to find it here. A professor's voice, loud and crisp, reverberates through the thin walls of the lecture hall, reminding me that class started five minutes ago. Eyes still on the banner, I reach to pull open the auditorium door.

"I wouldn't do that if I were you," a male voice says. I look around. The only other person in the lobby is a guy in a grey Yale Lacrosse T-shirt, sitting on the wooden bench that runs the length of the auditorium wall. He's leaning back against the wall, his long legs stretched out in front of him. He has a notebook in his lap and a pen in his hand. I quickly take him in: dark, floppy hair, bright green eyes, skin that's been tanned in the sun, not in a booth. He's good-looking. Like, *really* good-looking. His T-shirt is snug on his biceps, which appear to get quite a bit of use.

"Why not?" I ask, pulling my hand off the door handle.

"Prof has a thing about punctuality," he says. "Every year,

he makes an example out of the kids who show up late during shopping period. Berates them, mocks them – it's not pretty. Good news is, he doesn't take attendance, so it's no big deal if you're not there. Especially if you have the notes." He holds up his notebook and nods towards the wall. "From here you can hear every word. I'm Michael, by the way," he adds, leaning forward to shake my hand. His palm is warm, dry, and slightly scratchy. A boy's hand. For a split second, I wonder what it would feel like running down my back.

"I'm Abby," I tell him, and quickly drop his hand before my thoughts go R-rated.

Michael scoots over, making room for me, so I sit.

"So, you're a freshman?" he asks.

"Is it that obvious?"

He grins. "Kind of. You have this sort of bewildered look on your face. It's cute." Bewildered and unshowered and, now, sweating. Cute is probably not the most appropriate word. I dig around in my bag for some gum but can't find any.

"What college are you in?" Michael asks. When I just stare at him blankly, he laughs. "Don't worry, I'm not gonna stalk you. I was just wondering. I'm in Pierson, but I live off campus at the Beta house."

*Oh. Right.* Yale has the whole residential college thing. Caitlin explained it to me when she got in. Freshmen get assigned to one of twelve residential colleges, where they live the entire time they're at Yale unless they move off campus. Each is its own little community, and the colleges compete against one another in intramurals and sit together at football games. But which one am I in?

Michael is still waiting for me to respond. "I must look especially menacing today," he jokes when I don't.

"Oh – no," I say quickly, "it's just. . ." *It's just that I had no idea what you were talking about because I wasn't here yesterday, have no idea how I got here, and know virtually nothing about this school.* "I live in Vanderbilt Hall?" It sounds more like a question than an answer, but Michael doesn't seem to notice.

"So you're in Berkeley," he says with a nod. "Cool." Now I'm even more confused, but since Michael is the only one of the two of us who knows what the hell he's talking about, I defer to him.

From inside the lecture hall, the professor gets louder. Michael and I both lean into the wall, listening. "Today we continue our discussion of prehistoric art," comes the voice through the wall. Michael and I both reach for our notebooks and pens, and we spend the next forty minutes scribbling furiously.

As soon as the lecture ends, Michael has to hurry to his next class. "Another professor with a punctuality mandate," he explains, slinging his rucksack over his shoulder. "But I'll see you Monday, right?" When I nod, he smiles. "Good."

Caitlin emerges from the auditorium a few seconds later. "I didn't see you inside," she says. She retrieves a bottle of water from her bag and pops two pills into her mouth. "Man, I can't seem to kick this headache."

"I took notes from out here. Hey, listen, are you busy right now?"

"Nope. Wanna get some lunch?"

"I need you to come with me to the library," I say.

"Why?"

"I'll explain when we get there."

When I unlock the door to my carrel, Caitlin looks surprised. "You already rented a weenie bin?" I slide open the door and motion for her to go inside, then close the door behind us and relock it. Caitlin drops her bag on the desk and crosses her arms. "Now will you please tell me what's going on?"

"Remember eighth grade, when Jeff Butler dumped me the week before the spring dance?"

"Of course. You didn't come to school for three days."

"Do you remember what you said to me?"

"He spits when he talks?"

I shake my head impatiently. "You said I shouldn't let it bother me, because in some parallel world, *I* was the one who broke up with him."

"Look how wise I was, even back then." Caitlin smiles, then immediately frowns. "Wait, is *that* why we're here? Because you're pining for Jeff Butler? Ab, the guy gives new meaning to the phrase 'say it, don't spray it'. Plus, didn't he chop off part of his pinkie in shop cla—"

I cut her off. "This isn't about Jeff."

"Then what is it about? Seriously, Abby, you're starting to freak me out a little here."

"I want to know if they really exist."

"If what really exist?"

"Parallel worlds. Are they real?"

Caitlin responds without hesitation. "Yes."

"Like, for *real* real?"

"Yes," Caitlin repeats. "I mean, it's not like we can prove it empirically, but quantum theory says there's a parallel world for every possible version of your life. And most mainstream physicists would probably stake their careers on it."

I feel my brain switching into sceptical mode. "But it sounds so crazy," I say.

"That's what they told Galileo. And Pasteur. And—"

"OK, fine. So is there any way a person could somehow . . . end up in one?"

Caitlin gives me a funny look. "No. Parallel worlds inhabit separate dimensions of space. There's no way for us to even see them, much less travel to one." She eyes me closely. "This is why you brought me up here? To talk about the multiverse?"

I take a deep breath, giving myself a five-second mental pep talk – the same pep talk I've been giving myself all day. *There's a rational explanation for this. Caitlin will explain it to me, and everything will make sense again.*

"Abby?"

*Here goes nothing.* "When I went to bed last night, I was in a hotel room in LA," I begin slowly. "The same hotel room I've been living in for the past four months. And when I woke up this morning, I was here."

Whatever Caitlin was expecting me to say, it clearly wasn't this. "Huh?"

"I'm not supposed to be here. At Yale. I'm supposed to be in LA, shooting a movie with Bret Woodward. And he and I are supposed to be having dinner tonight for my birthday, which I'm pretty sure is a date, because he kissed me last night. Well, technically, *I* kissed *him* . . . or at least he probably thinks I did, but I didn't mean to, and it was more of an almost-kiss anyway." I'm starting to ramble, but I don't care. At this point, I just want to get it out. "Except now I'm here, and everyone's acting like I've been here for weeks, and there are pictures of me doing things I never did – like graduation!" I point at the photo on my home screen. "Where did that picture come from? I wasn't at graduation. I wanted to be, but I was already in California by then. And my ID car—"

"Time-out." Caitlin does a T motion with her hands, silencing me. "You weren't at graduation?" I shake my head. "And you missed it because you were in *Los Angeles*, filming a movie. With *Bret Woodward*." Her voice is calm, but she's eyeing me strangely. I don't blame her. I sound like a lunatic. I exhale, forcing myself to relax.

"I know it sounds crazy," I say. "But, yes. A casting director saw me in the autumn show last year and thought I looked the part."

"The autumn show at Brookside?"

I nod. "I was the lead. I didn't *want* the lead. I didn't even want to be in the class. But Simmons cancelled History of Music, and I had to pick a replacement. Drama sounded slightly less brutal than astronomy, so—"

Caitlin's brow furrows. "But you took astronomy. I helped you study for the final, remember?"

"That's just it. I *don't* remember – not the part about you helping me study, anyway. I remember taking drama, getting the lead in *Arcadia*, giving a kinetic performance as Thomasina – the casting director's words, not mine – and then being asked to fly out to LA the week before Christmas to audition for *Everyday Assassins*."

"The Bret Woodward movie."

I sigh heavily. This is even harder than I thought.

"I know how it sounds," I say wearily. "Believe me, I know." I fight to keep my voice steady. "But I'm telling you, Cate, when I went to bed last night, I was in LA, at the Culver Hotel, where I've been living all summer."

"And you were there because some casting director saw you in the autumn play," Caitlin says this slowly, her eyes never leaving mine. "And this happened because you took drama, not astronomy, last autumn."

"Yes. Exactly."

"And because of this, you thought you might be in a parallel world?"

It sounds ludicrous. "I'm crazy," I moan. "That's the only rational explanation, right? Everything I remember from the last year, none of it really happened. I'm having some sort of psychological breakdown."

Caitlin rolls her eyes. "You're not having a breakdown."

"So you can explain this, then. You can explain what's happening to me."

"Well, no. Not yet."

"So how can you be so sure that I'm not crazy?"

"A crazy person wouldn't be so quick to call herself crazy," she says matter-of-factly, switching into scientist mode. She gets like this when she's trying to problem solve. "OK, so we know that one of two things is true: either your memories from the last twelve months are accurate or they're not. If they're not, then they have to be coming from someplace, whether it be your imagination – which still doesn't make you crazy – or some external source."

"An 'external source'? What, like mind control?" I might not be a crazy person, but my voice has taken on the frantic, high-pitched screech of one. "You think someone's messing with my memories?"

"Calm down. I don't think anything yet." She chews on her lip, thinking.

I lay my head on the desk, the wood cool on my skin. Someone has written CARPE DIEM in blue pen on the wall.

"Did they ever figure out what caused that earthquake?" I hear myself ask.

Caitlin stops chewing. "Why'd you ask that?"

"Because it's the only thing I remember from the last year that seems to have actually happened," I reply. "*And* it's the only memory I have that doesn't fit with the rest."

Caitlin's eyes fly to my face. "What do you mean, 'doesn't fit'?"

I sit up. "It's like my mind recorded two versions of the same day," I tell her. "The first day of senior year. In the regular version – the one that fits with the rest of my memories – there was no earthquake, and DeWitt called me to her office during form and told me History of Music had been cancelled. I had the choice between drama and astronomy as a replacement elective."

"And you picked drama."

"Right. And in the other version, the earthquake knocked the power out and I was late to school."

"That's the way I remember it," Caitlin says slowly. "You came in at the end of assembly, and by the time DeWitt tracked you down, Dr Mann's class was your only option. You spent the rest of the day freaking out about your GPA."

"I was *not* freaking out. I merely—"

"The tremor changed things." Caitlin starts chewing on her lip again, this time so hard I'm afraid it might bleed. "What does the tremor have to do with—" Suddenly, she stops. "What time is it?"

I glance at my phone. "Quarter till one. Why?"

"There's a train every hour. If we hurry, we can make it."

"A train? To where?"

Caitlin is already heading towards the stairs. "New London," she calls. "I'll explain on the way."

"After the tremor, a group of physicists in Japan came out in support of his theory. They thought it was at least possible that he was on to something. The Ivies still wouldn't touch him, but Connecticut College gave him a grant to continue his research at Olin Observatory. He's been teaching at Conn since January. A bummer for those of us who wanted to take his cosmology class in spring term, but a career-redeeming moment for him."

We're sitting side by side on a commuter train, sharing a stale chocolate muffin from the newsagent at the station.

"Westbrook!" comes the conductor's voice. "Westbrook is next!"

"So Dr Mann's theory was about earthquakes?" I ask, confused.

"No, his theory was about the interaction of alternate realities – something he calls 'cosmic entanglement'. Basically, the idea that it's possible for parallel worlds to collide." At her mention of parallel worlds, the hair on my arm prickles.

"That's what he thinks the earthquake was? A collision of parallel worlds?"

"The tremor," Caitlin corrects. "Not an earthquake. And yes. At least according to the article he published in *New Science* last month."

My heart begins to pound. "And if he's right?"

"I only skimmed the article," Caitlin says, and then pops the last bite of muffin into her mouth. "So we're going to the source."

We find Dr Mann in the F. W. Olin Science Centre, a contemporary grey brick building near the centre of campus, five minutes into an hour-long cosmology lecture. I drop my bag on a bench in the rotunda, prepared to wait, but Caitlin has already disappeared into the lecture hall. I slip in quietly behind her.

Dr Mann sees me come in and smiles with recognition. *He knows who I am.* I, on the other hand, have only a single image of him in my mind, one that doesn't do the man justice. I pictured his wild grey hair and ink-stained fingers, but not the intensity of his cerulean eyes. For someone who has to be in his seventies, Dr Mann has the gusto of a much younger man.

His lecture is surprisingly straightforward. He passes out

copies of the syllabus, then launches into what feels like a bedtime story, taking us through the evolution of modern cosmological thought. It's a compelling tale, made even more so by our storyteller's German-accented delivery. In fact, I'm so completely absorbed in the narrative that when he stops mid-sentence and says he'll see us on Friday, I'm startled. Have we really been sitting here for fifty-five minutes?

"Come on," Caitlin says. "Let's catch him before he leaves."

Dr Mann is erasing his whiteboard as we approach. "Professor?" Caitlin says politely.

The old man turns and smiles. Up close, he looks more like a sweet grandfather than a nutty professor, and he smells like butterscotch candy. I like him immediately.

"I'm Caitlin Moss," Caitlin says, extending her hand. "I was a student at Brookside—"

"*The* student, if the impression you made on the faculty is any indication," Dr Mann replies warmly, grasping her hand in both of his. "In four years as a student, you received top marks in more than a dozen science courses and won three national physics prizes, yes?"

Caitlin grins. "That's me."

The professor turns to me now, and his smile broadens. "Ms Barnes! What a pleasant surprise." He takes my hand in both of his. "What brings you to New London?" He winks conspiratorially. "Bored at Yale already?"

"We, uh. . ." I look at Caitlin for help.

"We were hoping you might walk us through the basics of cosmic entanglement," she says. The old man's eyebrows shoot up. This clearly isn't a request he gets often. "Specifically," Caitlin adds, "the concept of shared reality." Dr Mann looks delighted by her request.

"It's for a creative writing project," I blurt out. In my peripheral vision, I see Caitlin roll her eyes.

"It'd be my pleasure," Dr Mann replies. "Where should I begin?"

"The global tremor," Caitlin says.

"Certainly," Dr Mann replies. "I believe the tremor was caused by what I'll call an 'interdimensional collision'. Simply put, two parallel worlds crashing into each other."

"But *why*?" I ask. "Isn't it more likely that it was just a big earthquake?"

Dr Mann's blue eyes sparkle. "Ah, but we know for certain that it wasn't," he says. "Earthquakes cause a certain seismic wave pattern. What happened last September simply did not." I swallow hard, my throat suddenly very dry. "If the tremor was indeed a collision," Dr Mann continues, "then I believe the force of the impact may have created a link between our world and the parallel world with which we collided, resulting in an effect similar to the quantum entanglement of particles."

I gawk at him. "Huh?"

Dr Mann chuckles. "A perfectly appropriate reaction. It's one of the greatest oddities in quantum mechanics," he explains. "When subatomic particles bounce off one another with enough force, they become linked in a way that is not bound by space or time. Whatever happens to one particle begins to have an effect on the other." The old man smiles. "Einstein called it *spukhafte Fernwirkung*." His voice is quieter now, almost a whisper. "The 'spooky action at a distance'."

Though the room is warm, I shiver.

"And you believe the same thing would happen if two parallel worlds were to collide?" prompts Caitlin.

"Exactly," Dr Mann replies with a definitive nod. "I believe that the force of the collision would cause the physical reality of one world to overtake the physical reality of the other, leaving the worlds – and their inhabitants – in a permanently entangled state."

*Permanently entangled.* It sounds ominous, but what does it mean? My eyes dart to Caitlin for help. "A concrete example would be useful," she tells Dr Mann.

"Of course," Dr Mann says kindly. "I'll use the illustration I give my students." Caitlin pulls out a notebook to take notes.

"Unlike many of my colleagues," Dr Mann begins, returning to his whiteboard, "I believe that every world that presently exists was divinely created at a unique moment in history. If this is true, then the 'now' of our world must occur at a different moment in time than the 'now' of any other world." He uncaps a marker and draws two parallel lines. "In our world, 'now' is 9 September, 2009. But in a parallel world, 'now' could be 31 December, 2020, or 9 April, 1981. Or—"

"9 September, 2008," Caitlin interjects.

"Ah." Dr Mann looks impressed. "The date of the tremor. Of course." He writes the date beneath the top line and circles it. "That," he says, pointing, "is the parallel world. And this," he taps the bottom line, "is our world." As he scribbles today's date in shorthand beneath it, my eyes lock on the repeating numbers. 09/09/09. *Does the repetition mean something?*

"So what would happen – specifically – if these two worlds

were to collide?" asks Caitlin. Eager, as always, to get to the point.

"At the precise moment of impact, the reality of the parallel world would replace the reality of our world," declares Dr Mann, popping the cap on his marker with a snap.

Beads of sweat prickle on my upper lip. "*Replace?*"

Dr Mann mistakes my panic for fascination and prattles on. "I had the same reaction, when I realized the implication. To think that in a single instant, the reality of a parallel world could completely overtake the reality of our world, wiping out and replacing everything we know and believe to be true." He smiles broadly. "It's an exhilarating notion, yes?"

*Roller coasters are exhilarating. This, dear man, is terrifying.*

"Why can't it go the other way?" I demand. "Why does the parallel world get to win?"

"Because time only moves in one direction," Caitlin says before the professor can answer. "The present can't change the past. The past creates the present."

"The past of some *other world?*" I stare at them incredulously. "Come on. We're talking about the physical world here. Everything can't just change overnight." My voice has taken on an *I gotcha* tone, as if I've somehow bested the man with a Nobel.

The professor's lips curl into an amused half smile. "Are you familiar with Seurat's *Un dimanche après-midi à l'Île de la Grande Jatte?*" he asks.

I blink. *La Grande Jatte* was the centrepiece of my mom's pointillism exhibit. It was reproduced in miniature on the banner I saw this morning. "Uh, yeah," I reply, rattled by the synchronicity. "I know the painting pretty well, actually."

"Is that the big one with all the little dots?" Caitlin asks. I swallow a smile. As soon as Dr Mann starts speaking my language, he stops speaking hers.

"Hundreds of thousands of them," Dr Mann replies. "Arranged in a very particular way to create a very particular image. But if one were to rearrange those dots, that image would become unrecognizable and a new one would take shape. Same dots, same canvas, different picture." The old man looks at me. "Reality is the same way, I think."

Somehow, this metaphor strikes me as more concrete than all the science-speak. Maybe because I'm accustomed to this vocabulary – it's the one my parents spoke at the dinner table every night when I was growing up. Reality as a pointillist painting. *That* I can wrap my brain around.

"But how could it happen without anyone noticing it?" I ask. "You said this entanglement thing affects everyone. So why does no one but me—" I stop short as the professor's eyebrows shoot up. "Why does no one realize it?" As much as I like this man, I'm not about to become the lab specimen for his wacky theories, even if they happen to be true.

"Shared reality," Caitlin says before Dr Mann can respond. "We're getting our parallel selves' memories, and our brains are processing them as our own." She looks to Dr Mann for confirmation. "Right?"

"Exactly right," he replies. "If our world has indeed collided with a parallel world, then as your parallel self moves forward in time, your memories are continuously being erased and replaced with your parallel's memories, causing you to remember her life experiences as though they were your own. Not only the things she has already experienced, but also the things she *will* experience over the course of the next year," Dr Mann explains. "These experiences have yet to happen, but we remember them as though they already have. It's the way our brains make sense of the gap."

"And my *real* memories?" I ask. "The things that actually happened to me. . .?"

Dr Mann snaps his fingers. It's a loud, jarring sound. "*Ausradiert!* Gone."

Relief washes over me. *This can't be the explanation, then.* If our worlds were really entangled, then I wouldn't remember the movie, or Bret, or my summer in Los Angeles. And I wouldn't have just one day's worth of new memories, I'd have the whole year.

"But there could be anomalies, right?" Caitlin interrupts my thought as if reading my mind. "People who've kept their old memories, for example. Or who haven't got a complete set of new ones."

"I'm counting on it," Dr Mann says enigmatically, fixing his eyes on me.

My eyes bolt to Caitlin, but she's scribbling furiously in her notebook.

Another student approaches Dr Mann with a question about the lecture. "Excuse me for a moment," the professor says to us, turning away.

"If my past has been overwritten, why do I remember the way things were before?" My whisper sounds like a hiss.

"You heard what he said," Caitlin replies, not bothering to keep her voice down. "There are always anomalies."

I shake my head, unable to accept it. I wanted an explanation, but this is too much. Lunacy would've been easier to digest.

"Where were we?" Dr Mann asks in a booming voice, startling both of us. The student he was speaking to is halfway up the aisle. *How much did he overhear?*

"Anomalies," Caitlin replies, holding my gaze.

"To recap," I say, staring the good doctor down. "You're telling me that if my parallel self and I are *entangled*" – I spit the word out like it tastes bad – "then right now I should remember not only the stuff she's already experienced, but also everything she *will* experience in the time between her present and mine?"

"You should, yes." He's looking at me strangely again. This time, I don't look away.

"So her future, it's already determined, then."

"Ah – good! The very heart of the matter." The professor grins at me like a schoolboy. "Of course, it's hard to be certain of these things," he says, "but in my view, the answer is both yes and no. I believe that at every moment, whether in our world or another, each person's future is, to some degree, already mapped out. Because each of us is naturally inclined to make certain choices and to go a certain way, there is, in a sense, a default trajectory to our lives."

"A 'most likely' path," Caitlin offers.

"A most likely path," Dr Mann agrees. "Which isn't to say our fates are sealed. In fact, I believe the very opposite is true. At every moment, each person has the freedom to choose a different path, thereby changing the trajectory of his life. Nothing is set in stone."

My mind jumps to my own life path. The series of choices that led me to LA, starting with my decision to take that drama class last autumn. That single moment – the seemingly innocuous choice between two electives – radically altered the direction of my life. But I didn't know that then. I had no idea what hung in the balance that day.

*Did she?*

"Are our parallel selves real people?" I hear myself ask. "Like, living, breathing human beings?"

"Absolutely," replies Dr Mann. "They inhabit a different world, but it and they are no less 'real' than we are." He pauses thoughtfully. "I find that this concept is often the most difficult for students to grasp," he says then. "If our world has indeed been entangled with a parallel world, you have not *become* your parallel self. Nor she, you. You haven't switched bodies or travelled through space. You remain separate and distinct beings, living in two distinct physical worlds. Those worlds have simply become linked."

"But what does that mean for me?" I ask. "What happens if my parallel self makes some crazy life-altering decision tomorrow? Where will I end up?" I am fighting to keep the panic out of my voice. I am failing.

"That's the beauty of it," Dr Mann muses. "There is no way to know how her choices will manifest in your life until she has already made them. A decision that appears 'life-altering' might ultimately not be. Often it is the choices that seem inconsequential that uproot us." His voice is light and laced with delight, as if he were describing the rules of his favourite card game. "A great deal depends on what sort of person your parallel is," he says then. "Some people carve a new path daily. Others stay the course for a lifetime. If your parallel is the former sort, it is quite possible you could end up somewhere new every day."

He looks at me strangely. "It's an exhilarating notion, but I'd imagine it'd be quite disconcerting to experience it first hand."

My limbs go to pins and needles. *He knows.*

My pulse starts to race as I envision myself pinned under a gigantic microscope, locked in the back of a lab somewhere. *I need to get out of here. Right. Now.*

Beside me, Caitlin puts on a breezy smile. "Well, we should probably be going, if we want to make our train. Thank you so much for your time, Dr Mann."

I'm halfway up the aisle. Caitlin practically has to run to catch up with me. "Abby!" she hisses, grabbing my elbow. "Will you slow down?"

"Alcohol. Where can we get some?"

"It's four thirty in the afternoon."

I shoot her a look and push through the double doors. "I just found out that my life is being controlled by a parallel version of me LIVING. IN. A. PARALLEL. WORLD. I'd say that warrants an afternoon cocktail." A guy in the rotunda gives me a funny look. "You know, it'd be a whole lot easier if we just decided I was crazy," I mutter. "We could just lock me up and be done with it."

Caitlin puts her arm around me. "Hey, crazy girl, there's a new pizza place on Crown Street, and word is they don't card. How about I buy you a pitcher for your birthday?"

"Yes, please."

Caitlin lays her head on my shoulder. "Whatever happened – or is happening – we'll figure it out," she tells me. "Promise." And for a moment, I believe her.

A pitcher and a slice of pizza later, I feel much better. And relatively normal. It's my second week of university and I'm tucked in a corner booth with my best friend, eating white clam pizza and drinking slightly flat beer while scoping out the cute lacrosse players two tables over (well, I'm scoping. Caitlin is pretending to scope while texting Tyler under the table). This doesn't feel like some parallel person's "potential future". This feels like my life. Or a version of it, anyway. *But how long will this version last?*

"Hey. This is supposed to be fun. No thinking about astrophysics at the table," Caitlin commands, her voice slightly slurred.

"Wow. Did you ever think you'd be the one saying those words to me?"

"Ha! Definitely not." Caitlin takes a sip of her beer. "Maybe this is God getting back at you for being such a science-hater." She's joking, but part of me wonders if maybe there's something to that . . . if maybe I'm like Ebenezer Scrooge or George Bailey, being punished for not fully appreciating my life.

"You don't believe in God," I point out. But my voice wavers a little.

Caitlin hears it. "Abby, I was kidding. If this is happening, it has nothing to do with you. Or God."

"If this is happening, then I shouldn't *know* it's happening," I remind her. "I shouldn't be aware of the incredibly freaky fact that things are dramatically different than they were yesterday. But I am. There has to be a reason for that."

"Not necessarily," Caitlin replies. "It could just be a fluke."

"A *fluke?*"

She shrugs. "Maybe your mind is just different. Like the guy in England who can recite pi to the twelve hundred and fiftieth place."

"Yeah, thanks," I retort. "That's encouraging." I stare down at my half-empty beer, turning my cup in my hands. *Maybe your mind is just different.* Not exactly the answer I was looking for.

"I know you want to make sense of this," she says gently, "but sometimes science doesn't give us the reasons we're looking for. We can theorize about how things are supposed to work, but like Dr Mann said, there are always outliers."

"You think he knew why we were really there?" I ask. "He kept looking at me, and then he made that comment at the end. . ."

"But you had that really awesome and totally believable creative writing cover story," Caitlin deadpans. "How could he possibly have figured it out?"

"I'm serious, Caitlin. What if he tells someone and they lock me up or something?"

"Who's 'they', Abby? The government officials Dr Mann has in his back pocket? The man's been ostracized, stripped of tenure and relegated to the fringes of mainstream cosmology. Even if he did tell someone, who would believe him?"

"But you do?" I ask. "Parallel selves. Entangled worlds. Shared reality." The words are barely audible when I speak them. "You really believe that's the explanation for all this?"

Caitlin hesitates, then nods. "I can't explain why, exactly, and I doubt anyone could ever prove it, but, yeah. I do. So far, anyway," she adds.

"OK, so here's what I don't understand, then," I say. "If our world is really entangled with a parallel world, then it's not just affecting me – it's affecting everyone. Which means that right now, your memories of the past aren't your own."

"Right. They're my parallel's." Her tone is matter-of-fact. "I remember things that happened to her – and things that *will* happen to her over the next three hundred sixty-five days – as though they happened to me." She balances the saltshaker on a grain of salt.

"But they *didn't* happen to you," I point out. "They happened to the parallel you. Which means your memories are false."

"Technically. Yeah."

"Caitlin!"

"What?"

"You're acting like it's no big deal that the last year of your life has been erased!"

"Not erased," she corrects. "Modified."

"Rewritten."

"Rewritten," she agrees.

"And that doesn't freak you out?" I demand. "The idea that your memories are being *rewritten* by someone else?"

"That 'someone else' has the exact genetic make-up that I do," Caitlin points out. "She's me, under different circumstances." She shrugs like we're talking something trivial. "So, no, it doesn't freak me out."

"She's not you!" I insist. "For all you know, she could decide tomorrow to drop out of school and join the circus."

"But the overwhelming odds are she won't," Caitlin replies. "Odds are, she'll do exactly what I would have done in her situation."

"Says who? Mine certainly didn't."

85

"That's because the collision made the path you took impossible," Caitlin says calmly. "Your parallel self *couldn't* take that drama class last year because it was already full by the time she got to DeWitt's office. If she'd had the choice you had, she would've picked drama, just like you did."

I'm not convinced but don't have the energy to argue. "If you say so," I say. I drain the rest of my beer and stand up. "Another round?"

Caitlin looks at her watch. "Our reservation is at eight o'clock, right?"

*Dinner.* I'd completely forgotten. "Ugh. Can't we cancel?"

"Marissa will be devastated. She's dying for you to meet Ben."

"Seriously? On top of everything else, I now have to make small talk with a stranger?"

"Two strangers," Caitlin corrects. "Ben's bringing a friend."

"Right." I sigh. "Who's Ben?"

"Marissa's boyfriend. A junior at NYU. They met in New York two summers ago – Marissa was doing a summer session at Pratt and Ben was interning somewhere, I think. And the other guy is Ben's best friend from high school who goes here. Purportedly super hot."

It dawns on me that I haven't showered today. Or looked in a mirror. Caitlin sees the panic on my face. "Relax. It's not even six yet. You have plenty of time to get ready. But maybe we should forgo the second pitcher."

"How about we get the pitcher and forgo the dinner," I suggest, sliding back into the booth. "I mean, is this really the best time for me to be meeting super hot upperclassmen?"

"Is that a rhetorical question?" Caitlin signals the waitress for our bill. "Now for wardrobe . . . what about that Marc Jacobs top my mom gave me for my birthday – the greyish purple one – with my straight-leg Hudsons? I wear them with flats, so if you wear heels they should be fine."

I picture my reflection in the bathroom mirror last night, my expression equal parts fear and delight. A girl in a pyjama top and crew socks, ready for anything. Or trying to be.

"Earth to Abby . . . did you hear what I said? Marc Jacobs top. Jeans."

"Yeah, I heard you. But that's OK," I tell her. "I already have an outfit in mind."

It's amazing what a hot shower and some caffeine will do. By the time seven forty-five rolls around, I've relaxed into something resembling normal. Marissa sent me a text about an hour ago telling me that she and "B & M" would meet us at the restaurant, so I have the suite to myself. The pyjama top looks even better than it did last night, probably because it hasn't spent the past four months wadded up in a suitcase. I add a pair of black tights and a boyfriend blazer to the ensemble (my attempt to make the outfit East Coast–friendly) and slip into my cowboy boots. The look on Caitlin's face when I step outside is priceless.

"Whoa! You look amazing! Where did you get that dress?"

"I got a crash course in wardrobe versatility from Bret Woodward last night. Where I saw a pyjama top, he saw a dress." I shrug. "So I went with it."

Caitlin looks impressed. "It totally works."

We set off for the restaurant, which Caitlin tells me is only a couple of streets away. Now that I'm not in MacGyver mode, I notice things I didn't this morning, like the Old Campus architecture and how distinctly urban the city of New Haven feels. There's an audible energy on the pavement – students talking animatedly as they walk, music blaring from inside cars and dorm rooms, the hum of a crowd inside a nearby sports bar. *This is what university sounds like.* Something in me rises and swells.

"So," Caitlin says, linking her arm through mine, "I'm thinking there's probably a good chance this is going to be our reality for a while."

"Don't get my hopes up."

"Think about it," she says. "My parallel certainly isn't going to change her mind about Yale, and yours won't decide definitively about universities until she gets her acceptance letters in the spring."

"Yeah, but she could decide not to apply here at all," I point out.

"She won't," Caitlin replies, sounding very certain.

"How do you know?"

"Because I'm the one who filled out the application."

I stop walking. "You did not."

"With your permission!" she says quickly. "Your mom was bugging you to apply, and I knew the only reason you weren't was because you thought she'd be disappointed if you didn't get in. So I convinced you to let me fill out the application for you, and we submitted it without telling anyone. That way, if you didn't get in, no one would have to know."

"But how *did* I get in? My grades were good, but it's not like I had a genius-level SAT score or anything." *It wasn't you who got in,* the voice in my head reminds me. *It was the parallel you.*

Caitlin rolls her eyes. "Abby, you spent the entirety of high school crafting the perfect university application. You scream well-rounded."

"So what about the essays? Did you write them?"

"Of course not. I wanted you to get in, remember?" Her expression darkens for a split second, so quickly I wonder whether I imagined it. Caitlin's always been self-conscious about her writing, and predictably self-deprecating. But the look I just saw was more like annoyance. "I used an editorial you wrote for the *Oracle* as your personal statement," she tells me, "and an email you sent me as the five-hundred-word supplemental essay. All your words. Or, your parallel's words," she says, correcting herself. "Not that the distinction matters at this point."

*Says who?*

"Well, thank you," I say. "Or, thank her. If I'd woken up at Northwestern this morning, I'd be catatonic by now."

"I doubt that."

"I'm serious, Caitlin. I couldn't do this without you."

"You'd never have to," she says. "Even if you were at Northwestern. You'd still have me." She points to a small, dimly lit restaurant with Japanese lanterns hanging out front. "We're here."

The place is crowded, but Marissa is easy to spot (largely because she starts waving like a maniac when she sees us). The guy sitting next to her is cute(ish) in a skinny-jeans-and-horn-rimmed-glasses sort of way and has his arm around the back of her chair. "M" has his back to the door, so at first, all I see is a green shirt collar and a dark-haired head. "Keep it moving," Caitlin whispers from behind me, nudging me forward. Just then, M turns his head towards us. Our eyes meet, and we both smile.

M for Michael. And he's even cuter than he was this afternoon, if that's possible.

"The guest of honour arrives," Marissa says as we approach the table. The guys stand to greet us. "Abby and Caitlin, meet Ben and Michael."

"So you're the birthday girl," Michael says, pulling out the chair next to him. "This saves me the trouble of stalking you," he whispers when I sit, then flags down the waiter to order a round of "s-bombs" for the table. "And bring a tall glass for this one," he adds, pointing at me. "It's her twenty-first birthday today." There's no way the waiter believes this, but he doesn't question it.

"What's an s-bomb?" I ask when the waiter is gone.

"Sake bomb," Michael explains. "A shot glass of hot sake, dropped into half a glass of beer, and then chugged as fast as possible." He laughs at the disgusted look on my face. "It doesn't taste as bad as it sounds. Promise."

"He's lying. It tastes exactly as bad as it sounds," Ben says. "But after the first one, you won't notice any more."

Ben is right. By the second round, I couldn't care less about the taste: my sole concern is mastering the art of the shot glass drop so as to minimize beer splash (I gave up on being the fastest drinker during the first round – even teensy Marissa can chug faster than I can, although the comparison isn't really fair, since she's dropping her sake into sparkling water. Something about beer causing "accelerated amino acid catabolism", which, yes, she said with a straight face). Marissa, Michael and I are in the midst of a pretty heated competition. Meanwhile, Ben and Caitlin aren't really participating in the frenzy. They're leaning back from the table, talking in a way that doesn't really invite group participation. I glance over at Marissa to see if she's annoyed by it, but she's too focused on improving her chug time to notice that her boyfriend appears to be totally taken with another girl.

"Whatcha guys talking about?" I ask them, adding a slight slur to my words so I sound drunker than I am and thus less like I'm calling them out.

"Caitlin's telling me all about astroparticle physics," Ben replies, looking decidedly un-guilty. He smiles at her. "Well, maybe not all about it, but the parts my pea brain can understand."

"Ben's a journalism major," Caitlin announces. "He interned at the *Huffington Post* last summer." I shoot her a look. I'm probably supposed to know that already. Thankfully, Marissa jumps in before I have to respond.

"I told her that," she says with a dismissive wave of her hand. "But what I didn't tell her is that Michael is *really* good at lacrosse. And he's in a fraternity. Right, Michael?"

"Uh-oh," Michael says as our waiter arrives with the food. "If those are my two best selling points, I'm in trouble."

After the waiter distributes the plates, conversation pretty much comes to a standstill as we collectively inhale an obscene amount of sushi. The food helps balance the alcohol, and by the time Ben signals for the bill, I'm feeling really good. Full, slightly buzzed, and more than slightly enamoured with Michael, who seems to be enjoying himself just as much as I am. Right now he's leaning back, arm around the back of my chair, lightly rubbing my shoulder with his thumb. I close my eyes and lean into him, soaking this moment in, thankful that my brain malfunction (because, really, let's call a spade a spade) will allow me to remember this tomorrow even if no one else does.

"Abby?" Michael sounds concerned. I don't blame him. His sake-bombed date is sitting at the table with her eyes closed. I open them and smile.

"Hi."

"You OK?"

"Uh-huh. Best birthday ever." Bret's face pops into my head. I said the exact same thing to him last night. *Was that really less than twenty-four hours ago?*

Michael points at his watch. "And it's only ten o'clock. Whaddya say we make this an unsurpassable standard of birthday excellence?"

"Does that involve more drinking?" Ben asks.

"Most definitely," Michael says, nodding. "Significantly more drinking. And quite possibly some dancing."

"Some" dancing is a vast understatement. Turns out, Ben knows a guy who knows a guy who's the bouncer at Alchemy, a townie club east of campus (how the guy from New York has the hookup in New Haven, I have no idea). It's old-school hip-hop night, and the cramped space is already crowded with white people trying to bust a move. The five of us spend the next two hours on the dance floor, stopping only for two-dollar kamikaze shots and increasingly frequent pee breaks.

"What's next?" Ben asks when the house lights come on. As if on cue, I yawn.

"Looks like the birthday girl is partied out," Michael notes.

"No, I'm not!" This is a lie. I am completely partied out. My hair is plastered to my forehead, and my tights are damp with sweat. I yawn again, giving myself away. "OK, maybe a little."

"I'm sleepy," says Marissa, leaning against Ben and closing her eyes.

"Yeah, I should get home," Caitlin says. "I have class at eight. And Ab, aren't you shopping that poli-sci class at nine?"

Yikes. Classes.

Michael drapes his arm across my shoulder, his skin as sticky as mine. "Looks like we're outnumbered," he says to Ben. "Should we call it a night?"

By the time we walk the ten streets back to Old Campus, I am basically asleep on my feet. Once we pass through the main gate, Caitlin hugs me goodbye. "Call me tomorrow," she whispers, giving me a squeeze. "Wherever you are."

"Let me walk you," Ben says casually. "You shouldn't walk alone." I glance quickly at Marissa to see if she looks annoyed, but she doesn't – she just looks sleepy. Out of the corner of my eye, I see Caitlin hesitate.

Just then, her phone rings. Her face lights up when she checks the caller ID. "Hey!" she says, answering it. "I was just about to call you." Caitlin mouths, *I'm fine* to Ben, then sets off across the quad.

"Boyfriend?" Michael asks.

"Yep. He goes to Michigan." I watch for Ben's reaction, but he doesn't have one. He just puts his arm around Marissa and steers her towards our building.

When we get back to our room, Marissa and Ben disappear

inside, leaving Michael and me in the hall. I'm in the midst of trying to decide whether to invite him in when he says, "I had a really great time tonight."

"Me, too," I say, as I silently will the parallel me to stay on whatever life track will bring her to this precise moment. For the first time in a long time, there is nowhere else I'd rather be.

*I want this. This moment. This reality. This life.*

These thoughts scare me, because there's no guarantee that everything won't change again tomorrow. Anger and gratitude compete inside my brain. I hate that my parallel could erase this, but I also know that she's the reason it's happening at all. I focus on the tiny flecks of amber in Michael's green eyes, illuminated by the warmth of the yellow bulb above us.

"Happy birthday, Abby," Michael says, right before leaning in to kiss me. His lips are soft but firm as they move against mine, his palms gently cupping my face. My eyes flutter shut, quieting everything but the sensation of Michael's mouth on mine.

"I'll call you tomorrow," I hear him say. I just nod, not trusting myself to speak coherently at this moment, my lips still warm from his. Michael kisses me once more lightly and turns to leave. I watch until he disappears down the stairwell, then let myself inside.

Ben looks up from the pillow pallet he's making on the floor. Marissa is sprawled out on the sofa, already asleep.

"So you like him," Ben says.

"I just met him."

"So? You can still like him." Ben finishes with his makeshift bed and lies down on top of it.

"I don't even know his last name," I point out.

94

"Carpenter," Ben replies, and closes his eyes. "And he likes you back." Smiling, I head to the bedroom.

As I climb into an unfamiliar bed, a wave of dismay sweeps over me, replacing the fatigue. *This could be it. This could be my last moment here.* The thought makes my stomach churn. I don't want things to change again. I want to stay on this path long enough to see where it leads. I want it so badly I can taste it on my sake-numbed tongue. My phone lights up with a text, and I reach for it in the dark.

Michael: SWEET DREAMS, BIRTHDAY GIRL.

I can see it so clearly in my head, but I pull up the photo anyway, the only one I have from tonight. Michael's on the dance floor, belting out the lyrics to a Salt-N-Pepa song, and even with his eyes squeezed shut and his mouth wide open, he looks ridiculously cute. Marissa and Ben are in the background, barely visible in the dim light, dancing and laughing with their arms around each other. The tip of Caitlin's elbow is at the bottom corner of the frame. I was laughing when I took it, so hard I couldn't keep my phone still, and forgot to use a flash. But though it's dark and blurred a little, it captured the moment I didn't want to lose.

"Let me stay here," I whisper in the dark. The closest thing to a prayer I've said in a while. My phone goes dark, and I slide it under my pillow, wanting it close. If the photo is there in the morning, I'll know reality hasn't changed overnight.

From where I'm lying, I can see a sliver of the night sky through the window. It's cloudy, so the sky has this greenish tinge to it. I think back to that night, a year ago yesterday, when I stood on my parents' back porch, staring at the stars, feeling as though I was hovering on the brink of something significant. But then, that wasn't really me who stood there. And those stars weren't of this world, but hers.

I close my eyes, finally giving in to the fatigue.

# 4
## (here)

"As a general policy, I don't turn down free beer," Tyler says, dipping a crisp in ketchup and popping it into his mouth. "Makes these decisions easy." He takes a swig of chocolate milk. Caitlin makes a face.

"This is Ilana we're talking about," she points out. "She won't even have beer."

I'm only half listening to their conversation. Astronomy starts in nine minutes, and I still haven't finished last night's reading assignment.

"It's a party. Of course she'll have beer."

"The girl lives off Diet Coke and peppermints," Caitlin replies. "She carries Splenda packets in her purse."

"So?"

"White wine and vodka. Sugar-free jelly shots if you're lucky."

"You're crazy. There's no way she's throwing a party without a keg," Tyler replies. Caitlin just smiles. *Whatever you say.*

Tyler looks over at me. "What are you doing?"

"Astronomy homework," I reply without looking up. Two more pages to go.

"Waiting till the last minute. Nice. Glad to see my study habits are finally rubbing off on you, Barnes." I ignore him and keep reading.

"So what's the occasion, anyway?" Caitlin asks. "Don't her parents go out of town all the time?"

"She got the lead in the school play," Tyler answers, mouth full. "This is her victory bash." Caitlin makes a gagging motion, then returns to her salad.

"So, what time are you ladies picking me up tonight?"

"Sorry," Caitlin replies. "We are otherwise engaged."

"Oh, yeah? Doing what?"

I glance up at Caitlin. We have no plans.

"Movie," we say in unison.

Tyler just shakes his head. "Lame."

"You realize there's no way the cops aren't coming to that party," I say, speed-reading through the last few paragraphs.

"Man, you guys are a complete and utter buzzkill today. Even more than usual." There's a pause, then I hear Tyler say, "But you look especially hot, so maybe it's a wash."

*Whoa.* I look up and see Tyler smiling at Caitlin in a very un-Tyler way. Scratch that. It's a very Tyler smile, but it's the one he reserves for girls whose trousers he's trying to get into. I glance over at Caitlin, expecting her to look as uncomfortable as I feel. But she just makes an adorably flattered but still demure face and smiles in his direction.

*What is happening right now?*

Just then, the bell rings, and the moment is over. Tyler grabs his rucksack and is gone, so unceremoniously that I wonder if I was reading too much into their exchange. Maybe it was nothing. Maybe he was just paying her a friendly compliment. Tyler wouldn't blatantly hit on Caitlin while he's hooking up with Ilana, and Caitlin has a very strict rule about flirting with guys who are taken. (Two summers ago, Caitlin spent six weeks in Huntsville interning with NASA, where she fell in love with this guy, Craig, who she thought was a student intern. She found out after she slept with him – her first and only time – that he was a twenty-six-year-old postdoc *with a wife*. She was different after that, in ways I'll never fully grasp. So when I say she has a very strict rule about flirting with guys who are taken, I mean she doesn't do it. Full stop.)

"You coming?"

Caitlin is standing a few feet away, clearly wondering why I'm sitting at the lunch table thirty seconds after the bell. My textbook is still open on the table. I run my eyes over the last paragraph of the chapter, then shove the book in my bag and follow her out.

Astronomy is different from any class I've ever taken. We have at least thirty pages of reading every night – sometimes closer to fifty – but there aren't quizzes or questions to complete at the end of each chapter, forcing us to keep up. Dr Mann seems to just assume that we will. And it's not like he walks us through what we're supposed to have read. His lectures are more like philosophical discussions in which he asks more questions than he answers. It's actually kind of fun. I just wish our teacher had better face-name recall. He insists on calling us by our last names, but he can't remember all of them. So he makes us sit in alphabetical order and uses the class roster as his cheat sheet, putting me five rows and two seats away from Astronomy Boy Wagner.

Why couldn't Josh's last name have been Barney or Barr or Bartlett?

I get to class a few minutes before the warning bell rings. Most of the seats are already filled, their occupants scrambling to get through the reading before class starts. Josh's seat is empty as usual. He always slips in right before the late bell, carrying nothing but his notebook and a pencil. No rucksack, no textbook. Just the notebook and a pencil. I'd assume he was a total slacker were it not for the fact that he's fairly vocal in class, always raising his hand and participating, but only when no one else is. It's like he waits to make sure that the rest of us aren't going to answer, then puts his hand in the air just before Dr Mann becomes Mr Hyde (the man is a teddy bear, but does *not* like it when he asks a question and no one responds).

Smart and cute and considerate. And totally not interested.

Things seemed promising the day we met. Pointing at the empty seat next to him, all that talk about fate and the stars. It felt like the start of something. But I must have misread it, because Josh hasn't made any effort to talk to me since then, despite the fact that I've casually lingered at my desk every day after class.

I am That Girl.

More evidence? The fact that I am now completely turned around in my seat, blatantly staring at the classroom door, just waiting for him to walk through it. Less than a minute later, he does. Pencil behind his ear, textbook under his arm, brown T-shirt tucked neatly into khaki shorts. He meets my gaze and smiles. I quickly drop my eyes, mortified that he caught me looking at him again. It's the third time this week.

OK, seriously, it's getting to be kind of ridiculous. All he has to do is look in my direction, and my insides gets all fluttery and my eyes go hot, and all I can think about is how badly I want to touch him. The inside of his forearm, the mole under his eye, the place where his earlobe meets his neck. It's borderline creepy how preoccupied I am with this boy's body. He, meanwhile, doesn't seem at all preoccupied with me. Right now he's thumbing through his notebook, looking for a blank page.

The late bell rings, and Dr Mann appears. "Parallax," he begins. "Miss Watts, define it for us, if you would."

The smiley blonde girl behind Josh scrambles for the definition. She's flipping pages so fast I'm surprised she hasn't ripped one.

"Uh . . . parallax is, like, the difference in how you see something," the girl stammers, hiding behind her blonde curls. "Like, when a star seems like it's in one place, but then you look from another angle, and it's somewhere else."

"Correct!" Teacher and student look equally surprised that she got it right. Dr Mann turns to the rest of the class. "As Miss Watts has explained, parallax is the difference in the apparent position of an object viewed from two different angles. The name – 'parallax' – and the fact that we use terms like 'arcsec' and 'parsec' to determine it – makes the concept sound more complicated than it is."

"What the hell is an arcsec?" someone behind me mutters.

"How is our perspective skewed? That's the deeper question

101

we must ask," Dr Mann declares. "Let's begin with an illustration. Please select someone at least two rows away from you. Make sure you choose someone you can see clearly from where you sit."

I force myself not to look at Josh. Instead, I focus on the girl Dr Mann called on.

"Now close one eye," the old man instructs. "With your hand in a thumbs-up position, move your arm until your thumb blocks your view of your subject's face." Smiley blonde girl disappears. "Now open the closed eye and shut the open eye. Your subject should appear to have moved from behind your thumb." *Voilà.* Smiley blonde girl reappears.

I slide my thumb up the aisle until Josh comes into view. He's looking right at me, one eye closed, arm outstretched, face obstructed by his upright thumb. When our eyes meet, it takes considerable effort not to grin. There are forty-two people in our class, and he picked me.

Smiley blonde girl is forgotten. I close my left eye and inch my thumb forward until Josh's face disappears behind it. I close my right, then slowly open my left. There he is again, left ear just grazing my thumb. I watch as he mirrors me, aligning his thumb with mine. We stay like that for a moment, right eyes closed, arms outstretched, just staring at each other. At this distance, I can just make out the mole on his left cheek. I inch my thumb towards it.

"It is all a matter of perspective," I hear Dr Mann say. I switch eyes again, and Josh's face disappears. *Why do you assume he's not interested?* the voice inside my head asks. *He smiles at you every day.*

"Miss Barnes?" Dr Mann's voice jars me back to reality. *Crap!* I have no idea what he just asked.

"Um, would you mind repeating the question?" I ask, bracing for the old man's reaction. I hear several sniggers.

"I have yet to ask one," our teacher replies. "I was simply going to invite you to put your arm down."

The sniggers turn to chuckles.

My still-closed left eye flies open as I quickly drop my arm. With Josh's face hidden behind my thumb, I hadn't noticed that he'd looked away. Or that the rest of the class had started staring at me, the only person in the class still facing backwards.

I spin in my seat. "Sorry, I was just. . ." With no coherent way to end that sentence, I trail off, dropping my eyes to the metal surface of my desk and feigning preoccupation with the two boobs someone has scratched into it. Fortunately, Dr Mann quickly resumes his lecture, so the collective attention soon moves on. I, however, remain mortified. *So you were staring at him for an inordinate amount of time. So what? For all he knows, you were looking at the guy in front of him.* I steal a glance at Josh's row. The guy in front of him has cystic acne and a unibrow. And I'm pretty sure he's wearing eyeliner.

When the bell rings at the end of the period, I shove my textbook into my bag and beeline for the door, desperate not to make eye contact with Josh.

"Abby!"

No such luck.

Josh is a few steps behind me when I turn around. As I wait for him to catch up, my heart goes from steady beating to wild pounding. Thrown off by his nearness and by my own jitters, I

103

forget that he's the one who called out to me and immediately start talking.

"I just wanted to see what you were up to tonight," I say. A perfectly normal thing to say when you're the one initiating the conversation. A little weird when you're not. Josh just goes with it.

"Oh, you know," he replies. "The usual. Back-to-back reruns of *CSI*. Maybe some Pringles."

"Are these your preferred weekend plans?"

We step aside as the room clears. "'Preferred' implies a preference among several choices," Josh points out. "I'm the new guy, remember."

"Why don't you come to Ilana's party?" The words pop out without my planning them. Never mind that I'm not actually going to the party I've just invited him to. This is what happens when I don't have a plan. I cannonball into disaster.

"A party, huh?"

Not: "Sure, I'd love to!" or "Yeah, sounds great!" Just: "A party, huh?" *How does one even respond to that?* Is it a question? A stall tactic until he can figure out how to let me down gently? I backpedal.

"Yeah, a bunch of us are going," I say quickly. "It's a group thing."

"Cool," he says. "Sounds fun."

"OK, great! We'll pick you up around eight." I turn to go, expecting him to follow me out. But he just stands there. I look back at him, not wanting to be rude but not wanting to be late to journalism either. Our adviser is super laid-back, but not about lateness, especially not when the tardy staffer is her editor in chief.

"Don't you need my address?" he asks.

"Oh! Yes. Duh. Your address." I rip a piece of paper from my notebook and hand it to him just as the warning bell rings.

"So who all is going?" he asks. He, unlike me, appears to be in no hurry to get to his next class.

"The whole senior class, practically," I tell him, willing his pencil to move faster. "Well, except the hermits."

"The hermits?"

"The people who never go out." I watch the clock on the wall behind him. Forty seconds till the late bell. Forty seconds to get from the A Hall all the way to the newspaper lab at the end of G. If I don't leave now, I'm going to be late.

"I meant with us," Josh says, finally handing me the paper. "You said 'we'll' pick you up. Who's the 'we'?"

"Oh. Right. I don't think you know any of them," I say distractedly as I move towards the door. *When is it acceptable to break into a run?* "So I'll see you later?" I'm out of the door before he can respond.

Despite the fact that I haul ass to get there, I'm still late to sixth period. I mumble some excuse about having to stay after class for astronomy (not technically a lie), then slide into my seat, where I spend the rest of the period mentally rehashing my conversation with Josh while pretending to review page layouts for the *Oracle*'s next issue.

As soon as class is over, I sprint to Caitlin's car. She emerges from the building a few minutes later, balancing a ridiculous stack of textbooks. "Don't you have cross-country practice?" she asks when she sees me.

"I wanted to talk to you first. About tonight."

"Can we ride and talk?" She drops the books into her boot,

105

then nods at the growing line of cars waiting to exit the car park. "Keep in mind that I use the term 'ride' loosely."

"Sure."

We get in. Caitlin pulls out of her primo parking space and joins the stalled exit line, then looks over at me. "So, tonight. What's up?"

I try to sound casual: "I invited Josh to go with us to Ilana's party."

"Who's Josh?"

"Josh Wagner. Astronomy Boy."

"You invited Astronomy Boy to go with us to a party we're not actually attending. Interesting strategy. Shall I bring the boyfriend I don't actually have?"

I shoot her a look. "Ignoring that. So will you drive? And can we take Tyler, too?"

"Why do *I* have to go?"

"Because I told him a bunch of us were going." Caitlin just looks at me. "He hesitated when I invited him! I wasn't sure what it meant."

"Of all the things you could've invited him to, you picked this?"

"I don't know where it came from!" I moan. "I opened my mouth and . . . *blah*. There it was."

We've finally reached the main road. The crossing guard stops us to let street traffic pass. "Am I taking you to the field house or are you getting out here?" Caitlin asks.

"Getting out here," I say, already pushing open the passenger door. "We don't have to stay long. We'll go, we'll see how lame it is, and we'll leave. OK?"

"You realize how ridiculous you are, right?"

"See you at seven forty-five!" I blow her a kiss and shut the door.

Cross-country practice is predictably brutal. Our first meet is next Thursday, so we started fast-paced runs yesterday. Which means unless I want to sit through Coach P's annoying Tortoise Only Wins in the Fairy Tale speech, I have to really push myself.

It's a rough six miles, especially in twenty-five-degree weather, but it feels good to turn my brain off for a while, to focus on nothing but my breath and the steady, calming sound of my trainers hitting the asphalt. Running is the one thing I can count on to quiet my unceasing inner monologue. If I couldn't run, I'd probably overthink myself into a nervous breakdown.

The mental quiet never lasts. By the time I pull into the driveway after practice, my brain is cluttered again. Astronomy Boy. Astronomy homework. AP Calculus test on Monday. Northwestern application. Northwestern application essays. The SAT. Astronomy Boy. Astronomy Boy. Astronomy Boy.

My mom is in the kitchen, sorting the mail.

"You're home early again," I say, dropping my bag on the table.

"Am I?" she says distractedly. "I was up to my eyeballs in flooring bids for the damaged wing. I had to get out of there." She looks up. "How was your day?"

"Good," I tell her. "Except for the part where I blatantly asked the new guy out on a date."

Mom's eyebrows shoot up. "Lucky new guy."

"Yeah, I'm not so sure he thinks so," I reply. "When I asked him, he didn't answer right away."

"But he eventually said yes?"

"Only after I made it sound like it wasn't a date."

"It sounds very complicated," Mom says. "But promising! So where are you taking him?"

"Oh, just this get-together a girl from school is having at her house." I keep my voice casual, but not too casual. I don't want to sound evasive, but I am, in fact, being evasive, because of course Ilana's parents are out of town, and of course there's no way my parents will let me go to the party if they know that.

"Tonight?"

"Yep. Hey, are those for me?" I ask, pointing at the stack of oversized envelopes on the table.

"They are," she replies, sliding them towards me. University application packets. I quickly flip through them – Vanderbilt, Duke, University of Georgia and Yale – then drop the whole stack in the rubbish. "You know, it might not hurt to have some options," she says. I can tell she's treading carefully. "Not that I don't think you'll get into Northwestern, because I know you will. But why limit yourself now? Why not give yourself some choices?"

"I am giving myself choices. By also applying to Indiana and NYU." My dismissive tone earns me a pointed look. "Sorry," I tell her. "I just don't want to go to school in the South, OK? We've talked about this."

"Fine. That covers three of the four." Mom walks to the rubish bin and pulls out the blue-and-white Yale envelope. "Connecticut is definitely not the South. And Yale has one of the oldest and most widely read university newspapers in the country." We both know she only knows this because Caitlin said it at my birthday dinner.

"But no journalism programme," I point out. "Which would matter if we were talking about a school I could get into, which we're not." This earns me another look. "Mom. It's *Yale*. Nine-per-cent-acceptance-rate Yale. Normal people like me do not get into places like that."

"Who says you're normal?" She smiles, making a joke, but this conversation is irritating me, because it's the same one we've been having since I was a kid. Mom thinks I underestimate myself. I know she overestimates me. Despite her conviction that I'm Someone Special, history has proven that I am merely average. Which I'm fine with – I just wish she'd get on board. "At least think about it," Mom urges, holding out the envelope. "Will you do that for your annoying mom?"

I take the envelope. "Only because she's being particularly annoying right now."

Mom winks. "She tries."

At quarter to eight, having tried on nearly every item of clothing in my wardrobe in every possible combination and promptly dismissed each one, I'm digging through my mom's top drawer. My skinny jeans work with this slouchy top and heels, but the whole ensemble still feels a little blah on its own. As I'm wrapping a sparkly linen scarf around my neck, the doorbell rings. I grab a pair of earrings from her jewellery box and head downstairs.

Caitlin and my mom are standing in the foyer, talking, when I appear. They get quiet when they see me.

"What?" I ask suspiciously. I hate when they talk about me. Which is often.

"Nothing," my mom says with a breezy smile. "Enjoy your non-date date."

As usual, Caitlin looks amazing. Her faded jeans and thin hooded sweatshirt give the impression that she just threw the outfit on, but the details – gold accessories, her grandfather's watch, dramatic metallic platform sandals – pull the whole look together. I wonder briefly if it's a mistake to let Josh meet her. Not that anything would ever happen between them, it's just that I know how she looks and I know how I look.

"You're being ridiculous," Caitlin says as we walk to her car. For a second I think she's read my mind. "You should just apply."

"Huh?"

"To Yale. Your mom told me they sent you an application packet. Would it really be so horrible if you and I were at the same school?"

I roll my eyes. "Yeah, that's why I don't want to apply. I'm afraid you and I will both end up there." Caitlin unlocks the doors to her Jetta, and we both get in.

"So what is it, then? Why not apply?"

"(A), I won't get in, so it's a waste of energy. And paper."

"The application is electronic."

"And (B), Yale doesn't have a journalism programme."

"That's because it's a liberal arts school."

"Exactly. And while that's great, and while it might be true that I could get a job at the newspaper of my choice if I graduated from there, it doesn't change the fact that I do not want to spend four years taking art history or poli-sci classes. I actually want to learn how to be a journalist. In a classroom. Preferably at Northwestern."

Caitlin glances over at me as she starts the car. "Or, (C), you're just afraid you won't get in."

"No, I *know* I won't get in. So there's nothing to be afraid of."

"But unless you apply, you won't know that for sure."

"Can we drop it, please?" I snap. I know she means well, but I get enough of this crap from my mom. Caitlin backs off.

"Yes. As long as you promise to edit my personal statement as soon as I'm done with it."

"Haven't I promised that, like, forty times already?"

"Ugh, I'm just nervous about it," she says. "I've heard that the essays matter a lot – more than at other schools." Her words are tinged with worry. We both know writing is not her forte – she's struggled with it since being diagnosed with dyslexia in fifth grade. Caitlin is great at expressing herself, but her dyslexia causes her to use the wrong word a lot, something spell-check doesn't catch. "I can't even imagine what I'll do if I don't get in." Her voice falters slightly. It's uncharacteristic of Caitlin to be so set on something like this – unlike me, she doesn't have tunnel vision when it comes to her future. But getting into Yale is not just about academics for her. Her grandfather worked as a shipping clerk in the Port of New Haven when he first arrived in the United States from the Ukraine in the 1960s, and from then on was determined that a member of his family would go to Yale. He started calling Caitlin "my little Yalie" the day she was born (he'd already given up on his daughter, who dropped out of school when she got her first modelling contract). Caitlin idolized him. He died three days after her sixteenth birthday.

111

"You'll get in," I assure her. "And your essay will blow their minds. We'll make sure of that." Her expression goes from worried to relieved.

We pick up Tyler first. As we pull into his driveway, the garage door goes up and Tyler emerges carrying a rucksack. He walks quickly to the car, holding the bag close to his body, obscuring it from view. His beer stash.

"You decided I was right," Caitlin says as Tyler slides into the back seat.

"Wrong. I decided it was worth the precaution on the off chance that you were," Tyler corrects, tucking the bag under his feet.

"Uh-huh." Caitlin starts to back out of Tyler's driveway, then stops. She looks over at me. "Wait, where are we going? You never told me where this guy lives." I hand her the piece of paper with Josh's address on it, noticing for the first time his cute, boyish handwriting. Caitlin types the address into her GPS.

"Remind me how the new kid knows Ilana?" Tyler asks, fiddling with Caitlin's iPod. "Do you have any normal music on here? 'Elliott the Letter Ostrich'? FYI, indie bands should be barred from naming themselves."

"If by 'normal' you mean crappy pop, then no," Caitlin replies. "And the new kid doesn't know Ilana. Abby just thought it'd be a good idea to invite him to her party. You know, 'cause we were so excited about it."

"Again, I don't understand why you two are so anti," Tyler says. "So she's a little temperamental. So her head outweighs her body. She does have some redeeming qualities."

"Such as?" I ask. I'm not just being catty. I've tried to come up with reasons to like her. Or at least tolerate her. And I've come up blank.

"She's fun," Tyler replies, his euphemism for slutty. "And she's talented."

I snigger. "*Talented*, huh?"

"I'm serious," Tyler says. "I saw her audition for the play she's so amped about. She was really good." He sounds disturbingly sincere.

"Please don't tell me you have legitimate feelings for her," I say. "Caitlin, help me out here. Tell him he's not allowed to actually like her."

"I don't care who he likes," Caitlin retorts, a little too quickly. Her eyes are focused on the road. "We're here," she announces.

I look up, startled. "Already?"

Caitlin points at a two-storey brick house at the end of the street. There's a beat-up Jeep with Massachusetts plates parked in the driveway. "Looks like Astronomy Boy is Ty's neighbour," she says. I glance out of the side window. We're stopped in one of the newly developed cul-de-sacs near the new back entrance of Tyler's subdivision. There was a party back here in junior year, a few streets over, before the asphalt was poured on Poplar Drive. The "Poplar Party", which was quickly renamed the "Popular Party". There were rumours of a guest list, but none materialized.

"Wait, don't pull in yet." I yank down the visor and survey my reflection. I look exactly the same as I did fifteen minutes ago. A little wild-eyed, but otherwise fine.

Tyler is busy humming the theme song to *Mister Rogers*. "So what's the new guy's story?" he asks between bars.

"Dunno," I say. "He's in my astronomy class. I think maybe he's on the crew team?"

"We have a crew team?"

"It's new, I think."

"Can I pull into the driveway now?" Caitlin asks. We're still idling in the middle of the street.

"Yes. Ready." Caitlin pulls forward. "Wait!" She hits the brakes. I turn to Tyler. "No mention of how little Cate and I like Ilana. Or how much we hate her parties."

Tyler looks at Caitlin. "She realizes how weird this is, right?"

"Yes," I mutter. "Now shut it. And give me some gum."

Caitlin pulls into the driveway and parks. "Are you going to the door?" she asks me. "Or do you want me to just honk?"

"You can't honk," Tyler says. "What kind of signal does that send? His parents will think you're some sort of parent-fearing freak."

*His parents.* I didn't even think about the fact that I might have to talk to parents. Yikes. Thankfully, two seconds into my internal *parents love me!* pep talk, the front door opens and Josh emerges. *Wait, should I be offended that he didn't want me to come to the door?*

Tyler leans forward to get a better look. "He's got kind of an accountant-on-holiday vibe to him, doesn't he?"

I shoot him a look. "Be nice."

"I'm always nice." He leans over to open the door for Josh, then slides over to make room for him in the back seat. "Hey, man," he says as Josh gets in. "I'm Tyler."

We cover introductions and then lapse into moderately awkward silence. I chew nervously on my gum, willing Tyler to say something. He can make conversation with a fire hydrant.

114

"So, Josh. . ." Tyler says finally, "what brought you to Atlanta?"

"My stepdad was offered tenure at Emory," Josh replies

"What does he teach?" I ask, turning around in my seat.

"Astrophysics." *Aha*. So that explains his astronomy savvy.

Caitlin perks up. "I wonder if I know him," she says. "What's his name?" Josh just laughs.

"Oh, she's serious," I tell him. "Physics professors are to Caitlin what celebrities are to normal people. She started salivating when she heard Dr Mann was at Brookside."

"Well, in that case, my stepdad's name is Martin Wagner," Josh tells Caitlin. "He specializes in—"

"—dark matter," Caitlin says, finishing his sentence. "I read his book." Josh looks impressed. I remember the stupid comment I made in class today and cringe.

"You got all the way through it?" Josh asks her.

She smiles. "Twice. "

"Wow. No offence to my stepdad, but you should get some sort of prize for that."

Caitlin laughs. "Well, I did have ulterior motives. He's on the Yale alumni committee," she explains. "Since he's the only committee member with a hard sciences degree, I requested him as my interviewer." She smiles. "I figured if all else fails, I'd tell him how brilliant I think his book is."

"A solid strategy. A cute girl with an affinity for astrophysics? He'll beg the admissions committee to let you in."

It's objectively true – Caitlin is, in fact, a cute girl with an affinity for astrophysics – so it shouldn't be a big deal for the guy I like to point it out. Still, I bristle.

Caitlin laughs again. "Let's hope so. Remind me, where'd he

teach before this? In Massachusetts somewhere, right? But not Harvard or MIT . . . Brandeis?"

"Clark," Josh replies. "In Worcester."

"So, Massachusetts," Tyler says. "What's it like up there?" Before Josh can respond, Tyler adds, "This is my attempt to steer the conversation into non-boring territory."

Josh laughs. "Nicely done. Massachusetts is great. It's the only place I've ever lived, so I don't have a lot to compare it to."

"Is rowing a big thing up there? Abby mentioned you're on the crew team."

"You were wearing a Brookside Crew T-shirt yesterday," I say quickly. "That's how I knew. I mean, I didn't really know, I just assumed. You know, because of the shirt." *Please, make the crazy girl stop talking.* Caitlin and Tyler exchange a look in the rear-view mirror.

"So . . . rowing," Tyler says. "That's cool. Are we any good?"

"I think we're pretty decent," Josh replies. "But ask me again in a couple weeks. Our first regatta is next weekend."

Tyler and Josh move on to golf and make small talk about the PGA tour until we arrive at Ilana's. Her pink stucco house is nearly identical to the one next to it, except that hers has a deep bass beat emanating from inside. There are cars everywhere.

"So this girl," Josh says. "Is she a good friend of yours?" Caitlin snorts.

"More like a friend of a friend," I say, ignoring Caitlin.

We head inside. The living room is packed. Tyler spots the golf team in the kitchen, holding pink plastic cups and huddled around what looks like a keg. Tyler shoots Caitlin a told-you-so look and heads towards it.

It's not a keg. It just looks like one. Sort of. It's an aluminium barrel filled with red liquid. "'Splenda Punch,'" Josh says, reading the bubble-letter label. The word "Splenda" is outlined in bright pink marker. "Looks lethal."

"It is," Efrain, the most soft-spoken of Tyler's golf buddies, pipes up. He's cute in a Latino boy band kind of way, but he's a total wallflower. Sometimes at lunch I forget he's at the table. "I saw her make it," Efrain says. "Grain alcohol, diet cherry soda, and about fifty packets of Splenda." He nods in the direction of the living room. "She only started drinking an hour ago." Ilana has her arms around a girl I don't recognize, and the two are swaying to the beat. Or trying to. With the amount of alcohol coursing through their bodies, they're not exactly in sync (with the music or each other). I laugh at the sight of them.

"Ouch. She's gonna be feeling that in the morning," Josh says. He sounds legitimately concerned. Meanwhile, I'm the bitch who laughed. I'm feeling a wave of remorse when I hear, "Hey, Abby, nice *scarf*," followed by a high-pitched cackle. Ilana points at me and whispers something to the girl next to her, and they both crack up. *Yeah, I hope she is feeling that in the morning. And all week.*

"So I have six beers," Tyler announces. "Efrain's drinking girly punch, Caitlin's not having any 'cause she's driving, and Abby never finishes more than one." He opens a bottle and hands it to me. "So that leaves five for you and me to split," he says to Josh.

"Oh, that's OK," Josh says.

"Nonsense," Tyler tells him. "Beers are meant to be shared." Before Josh can argue, Tyler puts the bottle in Josh's hand. Josh holds the beer awkwardly, like he's not sure what to do with it.

Tyler stashes the rest of his beer in the fridge, then heads towards the makeshift dance floor.

"How long have they been dating?" Josh asks me.

"Who?"

"Caitlin and Tyler," Josh replies. "They seem like a good couple."

"Oh! They're not a couple," I tell him. "The three of us have been friends for ever. Tyler's kind of with Ilana." The word "unfortunately" hangs unspoken on my lips.

Someone cranks the music and Ilana shrieks with glee. The kitchen-cabinet doors rattle on their hinges.

"Which one is Ilana?" He practically has to shout, the music is so loud. So loud, and so painfully bad.

I point.

"Huh." Josh studies Ilana, who is now slapping her friend's butt in time with the music and laughing hysterically. "I wouldn't have put them together."

Again, I'm tempted to add something witty and bitingly mean but refrain. "Yeah, it was a surprise to us, too," is all I say.

"What about Caitlin?" he asks then. "Does she have a boyfriend?"

"Nope." Then, even though it's not really true, I add, "She doesn't want one. She's too focused on school for that."

"Yeah, she seems really smart," Josh remarks. *Why do I suddenly feel the need to announce my GPA?* I look over at Caitlin. She's standing by the keg, making small talk with the guys, keeping her distance so that Josh and I can be alone. She's my biggest ally. Why am I acting like she's a threat?

"She's the best," I say, and leave it at that.

We're quiet for a minute as we survey the sardine can that was once Ilana's living room. People are jammed into the oversized space, their voices reverberating off the vaulted ceiling above. Tyler is out on the dance floor now, twirling our slaphappy hostess. I glance back at Caitlin and see her watching them out of the corner of her eye. She doesn't look like a girl who doesn't care who Tyler dates. She looks like a girl who cares very, very much.

Josh touches my arm. I jump, as if electrified.

"Wanna take a walk?" he shouts.

"Outside?"

"Nah. I figured a stroll around the living room might be a good way to spend the next thirty minutes," Josh teases, still shouting to be heard. "Yes, outside. Where I'll actually be able to hear you, instead of just pretending that I can." He sets his beer down on the coffee table and nods at the door.

My heart has sped up again at the thought of being alone with him. I put my half-empty bottle down next to his full one and follow him out of the front door.

The air outside has cooled off quite a bit, and the sky is perfectly clear. "Which way?" Josh asks when we reach the street.

"Left?" I suggest.

"Left it is."

We walk in silence for a few minutes, but it's not awkward silence. It's more like this-moment-is-going-so-well-I-don't-want-to-ruin-it-by-talking silence. On my end, at least. I glance over at Josh. He has his head back, looking up at the night sky. His hair is damp, and there's a tiny piece of soap tucked under the top rim of his ear. It strikes me how recently he must've showered. How recently he was naked. *Get ahold of yourself, Barnes.*

"We're about three days too early for a good moon," I hear Josh say. I tilt my head back. There's a thin sliver of light hanging low in the sky.

"But in three days, there won't *be* a moon," I point out.

"Exactly. No light pollution." He looks over at me and smiles. "This probably isn't something you're supposed to say at a moment like this, but I think the moon is seriously overrated." *A moment like what?* I bite my cheeks, taming the grin that threatens to take over my face.

"And the stars?" I ask, once the smile is under control.

"Wildly underrated," he declares with a grin. He looks up again. "The sky is a storybook," he says then. "Every constellation's like its own fairy tale."

"Do you have a favourite?" I let my arm drift away from my body, until my elbow grazes his forearm. It's awkward to hold my arm like this, but I do it anyway, liking how it feels to be touching him.

"Cygnus," he replies, pointing. "The Swan." I squint, trying to make it out.

"Here, stop for a sec." Josh comes around behind me and puts his hands on my shoulders, turning me slightly. "OK, now look up. See that really bright star right there?" I nod, so rattled by being this close to him that I don't trust myself to speak. "That's his tail," he says, pointing, his arm just inches from my cheek. His skin smells like Irish Spring. I inhale deeply, letting my eyelids flutter closed for a just a second as I breathe him in. "Imagine him diving at a forty-five-degree angle, facing down, his wings outstretched," I hear Josh say. His breath is warm on my ear. "There's his neck, his beak . . . and those are his two wings." I force my eyes open, and the figure he's describing leaps out at me.

"Wow," I whisper. "He's big."

"He's huge. See that star there, at the tip of his beak?" Josh points. "That's Albireo. You can't tell without a telescope, but it's actually a double."

"A double?"

"Two stars orbiting around the same centre of gravity," he explains. "All double stars are pretty cool, but this particular one is especially cool because of its colours. Albireo A is bright gold and Albireo B is sapphire."

"I don't think I knew that stars could be different colours," I say, turning to face him.

"Hang out with a stars guy and you'll learn all sorts of stuff." We're standing really close now, just inches apart. I suck on my gum, trying to extract whatever remains of its original mintiness. Josh, meanwhile, has delicious cinnamon breath. How can a person smell so manly and so sweet?

"So what's the swan's story?" I ask. "What's he diving for?"

"His best friend," Josh replies, his eyes still on the sky. "Phaethon was a mortal like Cygnus, but his father, Apollo, was the god of the sun. Somehow, Phaethon convinced his dad to let him drive the sun chariot. Phaethon, a typical teenager, drove recklessly, nearly destroying Earth, so Zeus, angry in a typical Zeus way, hurled a thunderbolt at him, and Phaethon fell from the sky into the Eridanus River. Cygnus was devastated. So, determined to give his friend a proper burial, he dived into

121

the water to retrieve Phaethon's body. But he couldn't find it. So Cygnus kept diving and diving, refusing to give up. Eventually, the gods took pity on Cygnus and changed him into an immortal swan."

"How sad," I say. "And beautiful."

Josh drops his eyes to my face and smiles. Neither of us says anything then. As we stand there, inches apart, neither of us moving, it crosses my mind that this would be a perfect first kiss moment. He just needs to lean in ever so slightly. . .

A car taps its horn. I look over, prepared to be annoyed at the interruption, then realize that we're standing in the middle of the street. We quickly move to one side to let the car pass.

"So how'd you get into astronomy?" I ask when we start walking again. "Through your stepdad?"

"Nah, I was into it before Martin. I think it started with a really bad episode of *Futurama* when I was nine. And an old cosmology textbook my dad gave me for my tenth birthday."

"Is he a scientist, too?"

Josh shakes his head. "He was an English teacher," he says. The "was" hangs heavy in the air.

"And what about you?" I ask. "What do you want to be?"

"I'm not sure yet," he says thoughtfully. "I've got time to figure it out." *But what about picking a university and choosing a major and getting ahead?* I can't ask these questions, of course, so I just nod in assent. "What about you?" he asks then. "Do you know what you want to be?"

"A journalist."

"You sound very sure," he notes.

"I am. It's the only thing I've ever wanted to be."

"My older brother's like that," Josh says. "He always knew he wanted to be a lawyer." He looks back up at the sky. "I don't have that clarity of vision. Not yet, anyway."

We've reached the end of Ilana's street. Josh points at the unfinished house at the centre of the cul-de-sac. "What's your guess about Ilana's future neighbours?" he asks, stepping up to what will eventually be their driveway. "An ageing entrepreneur and his trophy wife? Two lesbian doctors? No, wait – an ex-NFL player and his three pit bulls." I examine the house, which is essentially just foundation and studs at this point. Tyler and I used to play this game in primary school, guessing who his future neighbours would be when his subdivision kept expanding and expanding.

I examine the house. "Easy," I say. "A rapper and his baby mama. He bought her the house to convince her to keep the baby. Unfortunately, it's not his, but he doesn't know that yet. He'll find out the day they move in."

"Poor guy," Josh says, playing along.

"Oh, don't feel too bad," I tell him. "After they break up, he'll write a song about the experience. And couple of years from now, he'll win a Grammy for it."

Josh laughs. "Are you sure you want to be a journalist? Maybe you should write fiction instead."

We step to the side as an SUV pulls into the driveway where we're standing. The driver, Eleanor, is the photo editor of the *Oracle*. She rolls down her window and waves. Led Zeppelin's "What Is and What Should Never Be" is blaring from her speakers, a song I only know because my dad sings it in the shower.

"Hey! Which house is it?" Eleanor asks.

I point. "Just follow the horrible hip-hop," I tell her.

Eleanor turns down her music to hear it. "You weren't kidding," she says with a grimace. "See you guys in there?"

"Yep!" I reply, eager for her to leave.

Eleanor backs out of the driveway and parks on the street just a few yards away. The line of parked cars is nearly four houses long now, in both directions. Either Ilana is more popular than I thought or tonight is a particularly lame Friday night.

The mood of our moment now broken, Josh and I just stand there, watching Elena make her way towards the party, which is beginning to spill out on to Ilana's front lawn. "So should we head back?" Josh asks me. *Back to the overcrowded house, too-loud music, and disproportionate number of annoying people? Why would we do that?*

"Sure," I say, waiting for him to suggest that we stay. He doesn't. He just puts his hands in his pockets and turns back towards the party.

I take two steps and stop. *I don't want to go back.* It's a beautiful night and a really lame party. I don't want to be there. I want to be here.

"Let's go inside," I say suddenly. Josh looks confused.

"I thought we were."

"No. I mean here." I point at the house-in-progress. "Let's see what our baby daddy is getting for his money." Josh gives me a sceptical look. "C'mon. It'll be fun."

"You're wearing heels," he points out.

"So I'll take them off," I say, pulling them from my feet as I walk. "C'mon!" I'm already halfway up the driveway. Josh is still at the street, hanging back. I can't tell if he thinks I'm cute or crazy. I keep walking, determined not to look back again.

I'm almost to the wooden plank leading to what will become the front porch. *Please let him follow me, please let him follow me, please let him—*

"Barefoot on a construction site. I can't believe I'm authorizing this." Josh is standing just a couple of feet away, my shoes in his hand. My grin is back with a vengeance. I do my best to rein it in.

"This way, sir," I say, stepping on to the plank. It's wobblier than it looks. Josh puts his hand on my hip, steadying me. My entire body goes to liquid. I force myself to keep moving forward.

The house seems even bigger from the inside. We wander around, guessing which room is which. "Our house in Worcester would fit inside this one room," Josh says as we make our way through what we assume is the living room. "No joke. The whole thing."

"The stairs are done," I say, pointing at the grand spiral staircase in the centre of the room. "We should go up. From outside it looked like there was a balcony off the bedrooms. I'll bet the stars are awesome from up there."

"Only if you let me go first," Josh says. "If one of us has to fall through the stairs, I want it to be me."

"OK . . . but be careful!"

He points at the ground. "Says the girl with bare feet."

I look down at my toes, which are now covered in sawdust. "Yeah, the no-shoes thing seemed like a better idea out on the driveway," I admit.

"Nah, it seemed like a pretty terrible idea out there, too," Josh says, starting up the stairs. "But you were too cute to stop."

Fighting it is futile. The grin takes over.

He climbs the stairs slowly, testing each step before putting his full weight on it.

I'm two steps behind him, texting Caitlin as I ascend.

W JOSH. DONT LEAVE WITHOUT US.

"Watch out for those nails," I hear Josh say. Slipping my phone into my back pocket, I sidestep the two-by-four lying across the staircase. There are four nails sticking out of one end, pointing straight up.

"Talk about an accident waiting to happen," I remark. "Someone could step on that."

"Hence the 'Authorized Personnel Only' sign on the fence at the end of the driveway," Josh replies. He reaches the top of the stairs and looks around. "I think this is the end of the road, boss."

I step up beside him. Although we couldn't tell from down below, only the landing has been floored: the rest of the second floor is still just beams and rafters. So much for our romantic rendezvous on the balcony. I look over at him, willing him closer, but he's already headed back down the stairs.

As I'm following him down, my phone vibrates with Caitlin's response.

WHERE R U GUYS?

I'm looking down at my phone, writing her back, when the nails pierce my skin. The sensation catches me off guard. I inhale sharply, bracing for the pain. A moment later, it comes. Sharp, swift, intense. Crying out in agony, I jerk my leg up, but the nails – and the two-by-four – are still attached to my left foot. I reach for the railing to keep from losing my balance, then realize there isn't one. The next thing I know, I'm lying in a heap at the base of the stairs, free from the offending two-by-four, which clatters to the ground beside me.

"Abby!" Josh leaps to my side.

"Stepped. On. The nails." The pain is radiating up my leg, and there is sawdust in my eyes. "I'll be fine, I jus—"

Before I can finish my sentence, Josh has pulled me up into his arms and is carrying me towards the front door.

"Really, I'm f-fine," I manage. "You can p-put me down."

"Abby, you're bleeding all over the floor. I'm not putting you down. I'm taking you to the hospital."

I consider arguing with him but decide that I don't have the mental stamina. The pain is all I can think about right now. It's blotting out everything else.

I force myself to look at the wound, then immediately regret it. The nails went all the way through the ball of my foot, leaving four ragged holes beneath the knuckle of my big toe. Blood is seeping out from the bottom of my foot, leaving a trail in our wake. Looking at it, I get light-headed.

When we reach Ilana's house, Josh sets me down on the kerb next to Caitlin's car and sprints inside to get her. I close my eyes and lie back in the grass. The music from inside is even louder now, so loud that the yard vibrates beneath me. My foot throbs in sync with the thumping bass. I focus on that instead of the pain radiating up my leg. It hurts so much it's hard to breathe.

"I shouldn't have let her take off her shoes," I hear Josh saying.

"My guess is she didn't ask for permission," Caitlin replies.

I open my eyes. Josh and Caitlin are standing over me. "You weren't kidding about the blood," Caitlin says to Josh, inspecting my foot.

"I'm calling her parents," Josh says.

"Do it from the car," Caitlin says, opening the boot. "We're going to the hospital. Someone has to clean those holes out, and it isn't going to be me." She walks around to the back of the car and disappears from view.

"What about Tyler?" I ask as I try to stand up, which isn't impossible so much as really awkward. With one leg out of commission, I have to sort of heave all my weight forward, then push up with my good leg to get to standing. I possess neither the coordination nor the leg strength to pull this off gracefully. Fortunately, Josh grabs me before I topple over.

"Tyler can fend for himself," Caitlin retorts, still hidden behind the boot door. *There's that catty tone again.* A few seconds later, the door slams, and Caitlin emerges with a stack of textbooks, all business now. "Here, prop your foot on these."

"You're letting me bleed on your books?" I joke, then grimace from the effort of smiling.

"Let's not get crazy now," Caitlin says, slipping out of her sweatshirt. She wraps it tightly around my foot, then uses the sleeves to tie it off. Only Caitlin would ruin a Helmut Lang hoodie to save a stack of books. "Hand me those," she instructs, pointing at the wad of plastic grocery bags tucked into the pocket behind the driver's seat. She drapes the largest one over my foot, knotting it loosely at the ankle. "There," she says. "Now elevate."

I obey, propping my foot up on top of a worn copy of *Advanced Quantum Mechanics*.

"Give me your phone," Josh instructs as we pull away from the kerb. "I'm calling your parents. We'll need their insurance information when we get to the hospital."

"I'll call them," I say, knowing that Josh will tell them the truth about what happened and wanting to give a more parent-friendly version instead. I'm dialling my home number when we pass a police car with its lights on, headed towards Ilana's house. Followed by three more. Josh and I turn in our seats, watching as the first two pull into Ilana's driveway and park. The third one turns into the driveway of the unfinished house and turns on its spotlight. Josh and I look at each other. "Looks like we left at the right time," he says.

Unless Northwestern's definition of a well-rounded applicant includes a police record for trespassing, then yes. We certainly did. I feel a momentary surge of gratitude for the four holes in my foot, but the feeling is quickly replaced by the dull throbbing that has taken over my whole body.

"So there was a two-by-four in the middle of the street?" my dad asks when I tell him the censored version of what happened. "Just lying there? With nails in it?"

"Yeah, it was crazy," I say, keeping my voice casual. "They're building a house next door, so maybe it fell off a truck or something." Josh watches me as I relay this concocted story, then looks away. *Does he think less of me for the lie?* I can't tell.

My parents are understandably concerned, especially since none of us can remember when I had my last tetanus shot. They agree that I need to go to the hospital and say they'll meet us there.

"Drop Josh off," I tell Caitlin. "It's on the way." This outing has already taken a weird turn. No need to cap it off by spending hours in an ER waiting room. Plus, it really is on the way – we'll literally pass his house. Still, I expect Josh to protest, to insist on coming with me, but he doesn't.

"So should we assume Tyler's sleeping at Ilana's tonight?" I ask, munching on a pretzel. I really mean "with" not "at" but for some reason the euphemism feels necessary.

Caitlin and I are sitting on a bed at Emory University Hospital, waiting for the doctor to return with my discharge papers. My nurse gave me a shot of "the good stuff" (her words, not mine) before cleaning the wound – thank God, because I swear they were using steel wool – so the pain has subsided to a subtle ache and my mood has radically improved. My parents left to track down the doctor, who said he'd be back in ten minutes an hour ago. Caitlin and I are sharing a bag of vending machine Chex Mix while she paints my toenails Fire-Engine Red (another gift from Nurse Nina).

"Who knows," Caitlin says, her tone dismissive. She focuses on my big toe.

"Do you have feelings for him?" The question just pops out, catching even me by surprise. Apparently, my thought filter switched off when the painkillers kicked in.

"What? No. Why would you think that?" She's believably adamant, but her voice sounds edgy. Like she's nervous. Her face is angled down, her hair covering her eyes, so I can't tell if she's doing that rapid blinking thing she does when she's lying.

"Just had a feeling you might," I say. "If you don't, you don't."

"I don't," she says.

"But if you did—"

She looks up at me. "I don't." The look on her face tells me she means it.

"Right. Of course you don't." I say this convincingly, but I am not convinced. My gut feeling is too powerful, too strong. There's something between them, even if neither of them will admit it. "But can I just say I think you'd be a *really* good couple?"

"Abby. Drop it."

Just then, the door opens and my parents reappear with the doctor, a perky little Argentinean man with giant hands.

"I guess I'll take off," Caitlin says, screwing the cap back on to the bottle of nail polish.

"Thanks for being here." I squeeze her hand. Caitlin's calm kept me calm. It always does.

As soon as she's gone, the doctor starts in on his spiel. I'm only half listening. My eyelids are beginning to droop. I could probably fall asleep right here, while he's talking. I will him to finish his speech.

". . . immobilized for at least four weeks. No running or strenuous activity for at least eight."

"*Eight weeks?*" I interrupt the man mid-sentence. "I can't run for eight weeks? But I only have eight stitches. And it doesn't even hurt any more."

The doctor chuckles like I've just made a joke. I give him a death stare. His brow furrows.

"Honey, it doesn't hurt because they gave you a morphine shot," my mom says gently. Ugh. Sometimes I loathe the soothing voice. My dagger eye shuts her up.

"Four nails went through your foot," the doctor says, his voice almost as patronizing as the look he's giving me. *Yes, thank you, jackass, I'm aware of that.* "You chipped two bones. You're lucky they didn't shatter."

"What about cross-country?" I direct the question at my dad, the only person in the room who's not irritating me right now. "Eight weeks is the whole season." My voice sounds strained. Panicky.

"Ab— ," he begins. I don't let him finish.

"I'm the captain of the team! There's no way Coach P will let me keep the title if I'm not competing."

"It sucks," Dad says simply. "I get that. We all do. But it is what it is." And with that bit of banality, he takes the air right out of my rage balloon.

"So," the doctor says, smiling like we're at the circus. "Pink gauze or white?"

I'm quiet on the drive home. Annoyed at myself, annoyed at Josh for not making me put my shoes on, annoyed at the construction worker who left nails on that step. Most annoyed at the universe for allowing a momentary lapse in judgement to have such a massive effect. Not running with the team this season means I now have only one extracurricular for my university applications:

EIC of the *Oracle*. Without cross-country as a counterweight, I'll seem tunnel-visioned and one-dimensional, which aren't exactly qualities admissions officers look for. The worst part is, I have no back-up plan. I'm on crutches for three weeks, so every other sport is out, and it's not like I can just join some random club three weeks into the term. I mean, I'm sure I *can*, but it'll seem like I'm just doing it for my university applications. Which I am, but it's not supposed to look that way.

My dad was right. This sucks.

To their credit, my parents leave me alone. They know me well enough to know that I am not in the mood to hear how it could have been worse or why having four nail-sized holes in my foot isn't the end of the world. No doubt they'll lay it on thick tomorrow, but tonight they're kind enough to hold off. I spend the duration of the car ride glowering at the cocoon of pink gauze on my foot and wishing I could rewind my life.

As we're pulling into the driveway, my phone rings. JOSH– MOBILE.

"You answered," he says when I pick up. "I figured I'd get your voicemail. Are you still at the hospital?"

"Nope. Just pulled into my driveway."

"What's the damage?"

"Eight stitches. Crutches for three weeks. No cross-country for the rest of the season." I say this mechanically, as if the diagnosis belongs to someone else.

"Oh, no. Really? You're out for the whole season?"

The sympathy in his voice pushes me over the edge. Blinking back tears, all I can do is nod.

"Abby?"

I clear my throat. I read somewhere that coughing physically prevents you from crying. *Is once enough, or do you have to keep doing it?* I don't want to take any chances, so I cough a few more times for good measure. My mom glances back at me, eyebrows raised. I wave her away.

"Are you OK?" Josh asks.

"Fine," I say, relieved that the throat clearing seems to have done the trick. "Bummed. But fine. I'll get over it." As untrue as this may be, it sounds good. "Well, I guess I should probably go," I tell him. "My parents are sitting in the car, waiting to help me into the house since we don't have my crutches yet."

"OK, well . . . I'm really sorry about tonight. I feel like it's my fault. I never should've let – I just should've known better." He sounds annoyed. I can't tell whether it's with me or himself.

"Next time we'll stay indoors," I say.

Josh is quiet on the end of the line. No suggestion for when "next time" might be. No offer to stop by tomorrow to check on me. Just an awkward ten seconds while I absorb the fact that any interest Astronomy Boy had in me evaporated along with my cross-country career.

"I should go," I tell him. My voice sounds flat. My parents look at each other, no doubt noticing my abrupt change in tone.

"See you Monday?" he says.

"Yep," I say dully and hang up on him.

"Everything OK?" Mom asks.

"You mean other than the fact that I spent the last three years busting my butt to be captain, only to have it snatched away by a stupid nail?"

"Technically it was four nails," my dad points out.

134

I glare at him. "Thank you. Can we go inside now?"

Dad sighs. "Sure." He gets out of the car and opens the back door.

"I know you're upset," my mom says sympathetically. "But things'll look better in the morning. They always do."

*Yeah. Except when they don't.*

135

# 5
# (there)

Daylight is pressing against my eyelids, but I resist the urge to open them. Not yet. Not until—

*BEEEEP. BEEEEP. BEEEEP. BEEEEP.*

Like clockwork: the campus rubbish truck, backing up to the skips on the other side of the courtyard wall. The sound I wait for every morning. I won't open my eyes until I hear it.

It's a ritual that serves no purpose. Just my way of preserving the illusion that I am exactly where I was the night before. As long as my eyes are closed, I can assume that reality hasn't changed again. And once I hear the campus rubbish truck's now-familiar beep, I know for certain that it hasn't. I haven't thought through what would happen if I were to wake up somewhere other than this room. How long would I keep my eyes shut, waiting for that sound?

Let's hope I never have to find out.

I open one eye and look around. The photograph Marissa gave me for my birthday is on the wall. The jacket I wore last night is slung over my desk chair. There is a tiny mound of crust crumbs on my floor. In other words, my room looks exactly the way it did five hours ago when I fell into a food coma after inhaling three slices of double pepperoni on my walk home from Toad's, the most popular place for Yalies to drink, dance and make bad decisions. (None for me so far – I forced myself to write CAN'T TONIGHT! in response to Michael's 11.57 p.m. text request that I "stop by" his house on my way home. When does BE RIGHT THERE become an acceptable response to a booty call from a guy who hasn't taken you on a real date yet? Doesn't the fact that this guy could wake up tomorrow with no clue who you are warrant some bending of the hook-up rules?)

Continuing my morning ritual, I retrieve my phone from under my pillow and begin scrolling through my recent photos. I've taken dozens since I got here, logging every potentially erasable experience. These photos are my security blanket. As long as they look the way I remember them, I know that things haven't changed too dramatically overnight. I breeze through them quickly today, skipping over one of a group of girls in blue vest tops that Caitlin must've taken, eager to get to the one I care most about: the photo I took of Michael on my birthday. When I see it, I relax, satisfied that everything is the way it's been for the past two and a half weeks. At first it seemed silly to hope that reality wouldn't change again, but each day, the possibility gets a little easier to imagine, and my life in LA gets a little more distant, like something that happened a long time ago, or in a dream.

As of this morning, I have nineteen days' worth of alternate memories. As Caitlin predicted, I seem to be getting my parallel's memories as she lives them, which means that right now, I have everything up to September 26, 2008. I've been trying to write down my new memories as they come, but the task is harder than you'd think. It's not like the new stuff is top of mind when I wake up, so remembering takes effort. And even then, I can't always tell what came from the parallel world. Sometimes a detail will stand out, but most of the time, my parallel's memories just blend in with my own, making it difficult to tell them apart. Did I bring my lunch that Wednesday or buy it? Did I wear boots that Friday or my red ballet flats? Does it matter? The one notable difference between my real memories and the new ones is how sterile the new ones are. I remember things my parallel has done as though I did them, but I have no sense of how she felt in the moment. That's how I know these memories don't belong to me – I don't feel anything when I replay them in my head.

The journalist in me is still sceptical that entanglement is the explanation for all this, but Caitlin has gone from pretty sure to totally convinced. She's now read every book, magazine article and academic paper on the subject and says she no longer has any doubts. It's hard to argue with her, and I'm not sure I want to anyway. What she's proposing is hard to wrap my head around, but it makes my life make sense, and right now, that's reason enough to accept it.

If our world *is* entangled, it looks like I'm the only person who remembers the way things were before. Every day I scour the internet for evidence that there are others like me out there, but I have yet to find any. Plenty of people have written about the collision – "the earthquake that wasn't an earthquake" – and theories about its significance abound, but few appear willing to accept Dr Mann's explanation, and no one has drawn a connection between the tremor on 8 September, 2008, and the global headache on 9 September, 2009 (though people have lots to say about each). Apparently, millions of people woke up on my birthday with pain at the base of their skulls. Among the myriad explanations offered online, I haven't found a single one that has linked the headaches to the tremor. Even the conspiracy theorists haven't contemplated that their memories may have been wiped out and replaced by the memories of their parallel selves. Dr Mann has his theories – and after our visit to see him, surely his suspicions – but no real evidence. Not so far, anyway. Caitlin wants to tell him about me, but I'm still not sure we can trust him. What better way to restore his damaged reputation than to go public with my story? I'm all for scientific progress, but there's no way I'm becoming some physicist's lab specimen. Or ending up in a padded room somewhere.

Light is streaming in through the crack between my curtains, which is surprising because it was supposed to rain today. I tug at the panel closest to me, pulling it to one side. The sky is bright blue, dotted with puffy cotton-ball clouds. *I guess the weatherman was wrong.*

I slide the curtains closed and snuggle down under my sheets. I'm supposed to meet Caitlin and Tyler for brunch at Commons before his flight back to Michigan (all the talk of impermanent realities convinced Caitlin to let him come visit), but that's not until ten, giving me at least another hour of sleep. The delicious, semiconscious, edge-of-wonderland kind of sleep, where I'm awake enough to control my dreams but asleep enough to forget that I'm doing it.

"Abby?" I peer out from under my covers. Marissa is at my doorway, dressed in yoga gear and holding a yoga mat. "It's quarter to. Aren't you going to be late?"

*Late?* Late for what?

It is at this moment that I realize the previously overlooked flaw in my morning ritual. Just because the events I've photographed haven't been overwritten doesn't mean my reality hasn't changed in other, undocumented ways.

I feign sleepy confusion. "Wait, what day is it?" Fingers crossed that whatever I'm late for isn't an everyday thing.

Marissa looks at me like I'm crazy. "It's Sunday. Don't you have to be at the boathouse at eight?"

*The boathouse?*

"Oh, right. . . Yeah. Thanks for reminding me! I'd better get up." I flash a smile and throw off the covers.

"OK, well, I guess I'll see you later, then," she says, still eyeing me. "I have Bikram at eight, then I'll probably head to the library for a couple hours." She makes a face. "I have two chapters of *Ulysses* to finish before tomorrow."

I nod distractedly. "Good luck with that." I'm anxious for her to leave so I can call Caitlin. As soon as the door clicks shut, I lunge for my phone.

My call goes straight to voicemail. I start talking before the beep.

"Why is your phone off?!? When your best friend is suffering from some freaky astrophysical phenomenon – is astrophysical even a word? – you're supposed to keep your phone on. At all times. Who else can tell me why I'm supposed to be at the boathouse at eight in the freaking morning on a Sunday? I didn't even know Yale *had* a boathouse. Call me as soon as you get this."

I toss my phone on the bed and sit down in front of my computer. According to the Yale website, Gilder Boathouse is in Derby, nearly ten miles from campus.

I contemplate bagging the whole thing, but know that I can't. Not if I'm committed to keeping up the appearance of normalcy. What if it's something important? What if it's class-related? What if I'm writing a story on the sailing team for the *YDN* and I'm supposed to meet someone for an interview? Usually freshmen have to go through a term-long "heeling" process before they can become full-fledged reporters for the *Yale Daily News*, but since I – OK, my parallel – wrote more than half of the articles published in the *Oracle* last year, I got to skip that step and last week became the *YDN*'s newest staff reporter, an opportunity I'm not about to screw up.

*Ooh.* Could that be it? Could my parallel self have done something to earn me a spot on the coveted sports beat? That would rock. I need to learn how to cover sports. Plus, it'd give me an excuse to go to Michael's lacrosse games without feeling like a stalker.

Newly motivated, I fly out of my chair and start getting dressed. Since I'm going to a boathouse, I opt for sporty layers, figuring that if I'm underdressed, I'll just pretend I'm on my way to the gym. As I'm lacing up my running shoes, I realize with a start that these aren't, in fact, my running shoes. Yes, they're running shoes, and yes, they were in my wardrobe, but they're not mine. Mine are old and worn in, practically falling apart from use.

These fit, but they're a different brand, and they look like they've barely been worn. *Where is my old pair?* I glance at the clock on my computer screen: 7.51. Boathouse now, shoe mystery later.

Outside, the sun is blindingly bright, making me wish I'd brought my sunglasses. I squint at my campus map, trying to pinpoint the closest shuttle stop. There's a little blue *S* on the corner of College and Elm, two streets from where I'm standing.

Jogging down the pavement, I rack my brain for my newest memory. If something has changed today in our world, then that means Parallel Abby must have done something yesterday in her world to cause it. Since her yesterday is a year behind mine in time, I need to remember what happened on September 26, 2008.

A blue-and-white school bus turns from High Street on to Elm. I pick up my pace to catch it and am surprised at how quickly I'm winded from the effort.

There are a handful of people on the bus, scattered among the first few rows. I go all the way to the back. Sliding down until only my chest is upright, I pull my knees up and press them against the scratched brown leather seat in front of me, the way I used to do in primary school. Mobile phone balanced carefully on my stomach in case Caitlin calls back, I squeeze my eyes shut, trying to summon the memories I need. The memories that will make this all make sense.

*Think, Abby.* 26 September, 2008. It would have been a Friday. That makes it easier. I only have three Friday memories so far, so this one would have to be—

My phone rings. *Thank God.* I slide further down in my seat, out of view.

"Please don't tell me I joined the sailing team," I say, answering.

"You didn't join the sailing team." I can hear Caitlin smiling.

"Then why am I supposed to be at a boathouse at eight o'clock on a Sunday morning?"

"You really have no idea?" she asks.

"I really have no idea."

"Wow! So reality changed again!" she exclaims. "That's—"

"Where's Tyler?" I ask, annoyed that she's not whispering. "And Muriel?" Muriel, Caitlin's roommate, rarely leaves their room.

"Tyler's asleep on our futon, and Muriel's in Pennsylvania for the weekend," she replies. "So what else is different? And how'd you figure out you were supposed to be at the boathouse?"

"Marissa told me. She was worried I'd be late." I glance out the window and see a sign for Gilder Boathouse, two miles away. "We're almost to the boathouse," I tell her. "Please just tell me what's there."

"You should try to figure it out," Caitlin says. "What's your latest alternate memory? That should tell you—"

"Caitlin! I don't have time for this!" *This isn't a freaking science experiment, Caitlin. It's my life.*

"Fine. You're a coxswain on the crew team."

My shoes hit the floor with a loud thud. "A *what*?"

"A coxswain," she repeats. "The person who sits in the stern of the boat and steers it."

I press my forehead against the window, trying to process this. "Since when?"

"Since Yale recruited you," Caitlin says matter-of-factly. "Well, you'd already been accepted, so maybe 'recruited' is the wrong word. But, yeah. A scout saw you at a regatta last spring."

"Last *spring*? I was a coxswain at *Brookside*?"

"Well, yeah. When you couldn't run cross-country, you panicked that you didn't have anything sports-related for your university applications," she says. "The crew team needed a coxswain."

*When you couldn't run cross-country.* My breath catches in my throat.

"The nails," I murmur as the memories come flooding back. *So my parallel is smart enough to get into Yale but dumb enough to walk around a construction site barefoot. Awesome.* "Well, I guess that explains the trainers," I mutter. I bought my running shoes after our first meet last year, when I decided my cross trainers were too heavy. The ones I'm wearing suddenly feel like lead.

"That's what's different?" Caitlin asks. "Your foot?"

"Yeah," I say distractedly, running though a highlight reel of cross-country memories in my mind. I ran an 18:36, my best time ever, at the state meet last autumn. And now it's as if it never happened. It seems so unfair that she could've erased such a hard-won accomplishment. Did someone else from Brookside take my place at the meet?

"Hey, Abby!" a voice calls. A girl I've never seen before is waving at me from a few seats up. She's wearing jogging bottoms and a maroon Andover Crew sweatshirt, her auburn curls tucked into a baseball hat. A teammate. I smile and wave back, grateful for the phone to my ear.

"So are you going to practice?" I hear Caitlin ask.

I slide back down in my seat, out of view. "You're kidding, right?"

"I think you should go."

"Yeah, that's a great idea," I say sarcastically. "Who cares that I have absolutely no idea how to do whatever a coxswain does? I should just wing it."

"But maybe you do."

"Do what?"

"Know how to cox."

"But I don't," I say, confused. "I didn't even know what a coxswain was until you told me."

"Just go to practice," she urges. "Act like you know what you're doing and get into the boat."

"Why would I do that?"

"Because I think there's a decent chance that the moment you get out there, you'll realize that you *do* know what to do. But since you don't remember learning how to do it, the only way to know for sure is to put you in a circumstance where your procedural memory will be forced to kick in."

"My what?"

"Procedural memory. The type of memory that lets you do something without consciously thinking about it, like swimming or driving a car," she explains. "Which is different from declarative memory, which lets you consciously recall facts and events. Don't you remember AP Psych?"

"You're seriously asking me that right now?"

"The point is, by the time your parallel gets to where you are right now, she'll have both an unconscious, procedural memory of how to cox a boat – well enough to be on a Division I team, no less – and a set of conscious, declarative memories associated with doing it. We know you don't have the conscious memories yet, but that doesn't mean you don't have the unconscious ones."

"Are you getting off or not?" a gruff voice barks. I jerk up. The bus driver is turned around, looking at me expectantly. I'm the only one still on the bus, which is now stopped in front of a sprawling wooden complex. I nod distractedly and stand up.

"Are you listening to what I'm saying?" Caitlin asks.

"Yes. Procedural and declarative memories. Got it." I sling my bag over my shoulder and hurry towards the impatient bus driver. "Sorry," I mumble on my way past him.

Kids in sports gear and anoraks mill around the boathouse, looking purposeful and busy. A group of guys in spandex carry a boat painted in Yale blue over their heads, while two middle-aged men wearing matching white visors – coaches? – consult wooden clipboards. Waves lap against the deck in a steady rhythm as people perform their various tasks. Things are orderly here. Organized. I breathe in the calm. My life may be chaotic, but this crew practice is not.

"Abby!" The girl from the bus is standing at the boathouse door, which is framed on each side by a row of fibreglass oars. The entrance cuts through the building and opens on to an expansive deck overlooking the silver blue of the Housatonic River. "Want me to wait for you?" she calls.

"No, that's OK!" I yell back. "I'll be in in a minute." The girl nods and disappears inside. "So what am I supposed to do?" I ask Caitlin. "Just get into the boat and hope it all comes back to me?"

"Pretty much."

"And if it doesn't? If I make a total fool of myself?"

"Feign amnesia."

"Funny," I retort. The deck is beginning to clear. "OK, if I'm going to this practice, I need to go now."

"Go," Caitlin urges. "Consider it research."

Despite the very real risk that this will result in my looking like a complete idiot in front of the entire crew team, I have to admit I'm curious.

"Fine. I'll go."

"Yay!"

"Wish me luck," I say, not optimistic that I'll have any.

"Who needs luck?" Caitlin replies. "You're a freak of nature. You're the definition of luck!"

I hang up on her and head inside.

What happens on the water is beyond surreal. One minute, I'm sitting at the stern of a wobbly wooden boat, facing eight excessively tall female rowers (seriously, one of them is six foot two and the shortest is five foot ten), waiting for our stone-faced head coach to blow his whistle, praying that I'll somehow be able to fake it when he does.

Half a second later, autopilot kicks in, and I'm steering the boat and barking into my headset like a pro. For the first few minutes, I struggle to get the calls out fast enough. But once I'm in a rhythm on the water, my motions become instinctive, and it stops being so much work. It's unnerving how natural it feels. Unnerving, but ridiculously cool. The cox is literally the boss of the boat – it's my job to decide where we go and how quickly we get there. A task the planner in me was made for.

As we're running through our second warm-up drill, my mind wanders back to the night that got me here. Ilana's party. The terrible music, the crowded living room, the mini barrel of artificially sweetened punch. Standing in the street in front of that unfinished house, willing that guy from my astronomy class

147

to kiss me. Running inside barefoot to give him another shot. As if a guy like that would ever make the first move. How could my parallel not have seen that? Even *I* can see that, and I've only got a handful of memories of him. I mean, c'mon. The boy wore pleats.

"Ugh. You reek," the gorilla of a girl sitting in the seat closest to me grunts between strokes. "Next time you decide to come to practice hungover, do us all a favour and take a shower first."

I stare at her. "Excuse me?"

She ignores me. Rattled, I pull up on the little handle thingy and the boat jerks to the right. I yank the rope in the other direction, trying to correct the error. The boat rocks violently, prompting a string of profanity from a girl resembling a stalk of celery (no hips, greenish complexion, lots of unruly hair). The beast in front of her gives me a death stare.

"Barnes!" Coach booms, shouting through his megaphone from the dock. "Is there somewhere else you'd rather be? Get it together or get off the water!" he bellows.

And there we go. The novelty of this little adventure has officially worn off.

It's cold. It's wet. My legs and back feel like they've been stuffed in the overhead compartment of an aeroplane, and I've been staring at a girl's camel toe for over an hour.

Instantly, my mood sours. If my parallel wants to spend what little free time she has crouched in a tiny space, shouting commands at unnervingly tall women, then by all means, she should. I, however, can think of several ways I'd rather spend my Sunday mornings, and none of them involve a hoarse voice or frozen fingers.

*If she and I are so freaking similar, then how did she end up on a path I never would have taken?* If *I'd* had a crush on the new kid, I wouldn't have invited him to an objectively lame party just to spend time with him. And if I had, I certainly wouldn't have suggested we tour a construction site barefoot. If she's supposed to be my genetic equivalent, then shouldn't she possess at least a modicum of my common sense?

OK, so there was that one incident a few years ago. The first night of spring break sophomore year. Caitlin and I were in Florida with her parents, and we'd ditched them for a bonfire on the beach. A boy named Roy with buck teeth and a peach fuzz moustache was handing out hot dogs. The "night hiking" was his idea, but going barefoot was mine. I didn't see the broken bottle lying in the sand until after I'd stepped on it. The cut wasn't very deep, but Redneck Roy disappeared when Caitlin's parents showed up, leaving me with a bloody big toe and an overwhelming sense of relief.

Fine. I may have had my own lapses in judgement when it comes to ill-suited boys and bare feet. So perhaps it's *possible* that I would've been as careless as my parallel was that night. But if I'd stepped on those nails, eight stitches and a tetanus shot wouldn't have been a game changer for me. I busted my ass for three years, staying late after practice every single day, doing everything I could think of to prove to Coach P that I was captain material. How could she have given up so easily on the goal she'd worked so hard for? Didn't she know better?

*Like you knew better than to pursue an acting career you didn't even want?*

149

I don't know if that voice belongs to me, or Caitlin, or God. Either way, I'm ignoring it.

Back on dry land, Coach rattles through administrative details while we wipe down the boats. I stay busy, trying not to make eye contact with anyone.

"Next week's practice schedule," Coach tells us, holding up a stack of papers. "Take one before you leave. Two-a-days start tomorrow, with a breather on Friday afternoon. Bus leaves at six for Providence." He clips the papers to his clipboard and sets it on the wooden railing.

"What's in Providence?" I whisper to Celery Girl. She gives me a funny look.

"Our regatta."

"Oh, he meant Providence, *Rhode Island*," I say casually. "I thought he was using the word metaphorically."

Celery Girl narrows her eyes. "Are you on drugs?"

"No!" I reply, forgetting to whisper. Everyone looks at me. "Sorry," I mumble, to no one in particular.

Coach shoots me a look and keeps talking. "I'll make final boat assignments by Thursday morning. If you want me to consider you for the A boat, you better bring your A game to practice this week." He pauses for dramatic effect, as though he's just said something exceptionally clever. "OK, people, that's it. See you tomorrow morning, not a minute after five."

Is he kidding? Five in the morning?

The group disperses. Most of the girls head for the locker room, while a few linger on the deck, enjoying the morning sun. I move towards the building, hoping for a stealthy exit.

"Hey, Ab, wait up."

I turn, smile ready. It's the girl from the bus again. The hat is gone now, her curls loose, and her sweatshirt is stuffed into the bag slung over her tanned shoulder. "We still on for brunch?"

"Oh. I, uh—" Mentioning my brunch with Caitlin and Tyler feels risky. Without knowing how good of a friend my parallel is with this girl, I can't be sure how bailing on her for plans with someone else would go over. Would she be majorly offended? Would she invite herself to join us? I close my eyes and grimace. "Sorry. I've just had this headache all morning." I wince and press my temples. "It's so weird, every time I talk, it gets worse."

"Oh, no. Maybe we should scrap brunch?"

"Yeah, maybe so," I respond, my voice thick with disappointment. *Dial it back, Barnes. It's just brunch.*

My fake headache works like a charm. I get out of brunch and avoid the risk of an awkward conversation on the ride back to campus. As a bonus, I get to listen while Britta (the girl from the bus) and Annika (Celery Girl) gossip about nearly everyone on the team. I now know that Ginger, another coxswain, doesn't shave her legs, and that Bobbi, our team captain, is sleeping with her history TA. They ask about Michael, leading me to believe that I must be decently close with these girls, but other than that, they seem generally uninterested in the details of my life, perhaps because the other girls on the team provide more than enough fodder for discussion.

As soon as I step off the bus, I head for Caitlin's room.

"I can't live like this," I announce when she opens the door.

"So I guess this means I was wrong," she says, stepping aside to let me in.

"Oh, no, you were right. Turns out I rock the cox box." I look around. "Where's Tyler?"

"In the shower. So, what was it like?" she asks excitedly. "Was it so super cool?" When I don't react, her enthusiasm fades. "Why don't you look happy?"

"Because this isn't my life," I say simply. "*She* might want to spend her mornings – and her afternoons, by the way – freezing her ass off, not getting any real exercise, crouched in a space designed for small children. But, I, Abby, elect not to spend my free time staring at some girl's camel toe."

Caitlin wrinkles her nose. "Spare me the visual, please."

"Whatever you're picturing, it was worse in real life." I toss my bag on the floor and fall back on to her bed, sinking into navy silk. The sheets were a gift from her mom, who's convinced that cotton causes wrinkles. "Never again," I vow. "The madness stops today."

"Meaning what?"

"I'm getting my life back. *My* life."

"Abby, this *is* your life."

"How can you say that? Someone else is deciding what happens to me!"

"Yes, but that 'someone else' is doing exactly what you would've done in the same situation."

"You're acting like she and I are the same person," I scoff, staring up at the ceiling.

"That's what makes her your parallel. She's you, in different circumstances."

152

"No," I said, shaking my head so emphatically that my cheeks brush silk. "She and I may be sharing brain waves, but she's not me."

"I know it freaks you out," Caitlin says gently. "But Abby, that's what our parallel selves are. By definition. You can't keep separating 'you' from 'her' and 'us' from 'them'."

"That's not what Dr Mann said."

Caitlin sighs. "Dr Mann needs you to be distinct from your parallel in order to preserve free will."

"You don't believe in free will?" I gape at her.

"Free will is an illusion, Abby. Our actions are determined by our biological make-up. That's what I've been trying to explain."

I refuse to accept this but know better than to debate with Caitlin about science. *If you can even call this science.* I put on a plastic smile. "So I guess that means my parallel self will quit crew next September. You know, if she's just like me."

Caitlin sighs. "Abby. I get it. You feel powerless and it bugs you. But quitting the crew team won't give you your old life back."

"I know that," I snap. "But if I do something she would never do – like quitting a sport she apparently loves, or at least, pretends to – then at least she won't be calling the shots any more."

"Oh, yeah? If you quit just to spite her, then what's changed? Her actions are still dictating yours." Caitlin's voice is matter-of-fact, the way she gets when she's convinced she's right.

As irritated as I am by her tone, her words give me pause. If I quit the team just to prove a point, then on some level, Parallel Abby will still be running the show. But what's the alternative? Letting my life be a carbon copy of hers? Unacceptable.

"You might be right," I tell her. "But if I stay on this path, my entire university experience will be affected by her decision to become a coxswain. My schedule, my time, my friends, my resume. All of it." I shake my head, resolute. "No. This path ends today."

Caitlin sighs. "Fine. Quit the team. But don't expect everything to change just because you do."

Just then, the door to Caitlin's common room opens and Tyler appears, wearing nothing but boxers and holding a pink shower caddy.

"Ah! My eyes are burning!" I shriek, quickly looking away.

"I know. A body this hot should come with a warning label and some protective glasses."

"Trousers! Please!" I yelp.

"I didn't realize you were such a prude, Barnes," Tyler says, grabbing a pair of jeans from the open suitcase on the floor.

"It's *you*," I say, making a face. "Ew." Caitlin laughs out loud.

"Thanks," Tyler says dryly. He pulls a shirt over his head. "How was practice?"

"Practice sucked," I tell him. "I'm quitting the team."

"Yeah, right," Tyler replies. "You've never quit anything in your life."

I'm looking at Caitlin as I answer. "I guess I'm not as predictable as you thought."

After brunch, Caitlin takes Tyler to the airport, and I head back to my room. As I'm passing through the High Street gate, a fluorescent green flyer tacked to the outdoor notice board catches my eye:

**Open Auditions for**

**Mary Zimmerman's *METAMORPHOSES***

**Yale's 2009/2010 Freshman Show**

**Monday, 12 October, 2009**

**2 p.m.–5 p.m.**

**@ 301 Crown Street**

**Sign-up sheet on the door at 222 York Street**

In my mind, I'm there again, standing on the stage in the Brookside auditorium, struggling through my audition piece. Ms Ziffren is smiling. Ilana is sniggering. The stage lights are hot on my face. I'm thinking, *Why am I up here? This isn't me.* Yet somehow my name ended up at the top of that cast list. It seemed like such a small thing – just a silly school play – but it turned out to be such a big thing. The doorway to something huge. The opportunity to discover a talent I never imagined I had.

Parallel Abby won't get to experience any of that. She's not taking Ziffren's class, so she won't be forced to overcome her stage fright for the sake of her grade, surprising herself and everyone else in the class by getting the lead. Which means she won't get Ms Ziffren's crash course on method acting. Which means she won't be able to wow a Hollywood casting director with her "kinetic" portrayal of Thomasina Coverly on opening night. Which means she won't get the chance to spend four months on a movie set. Which means no matter what happens in the parallel world, she'll never acquire the skills I now have. She's already missed her chance for that.

*I have something she doesn't.*

The hair on my arm prickles. The fact that I kept my old

memories is more than an oddity of science – it's a gift. Unlike everyone else in the world, I haven't forgotten who I was before the collision. Which means I can become that person again. A person my parallel will never be.

My mind starts to race, leaping ahead, connecting the dots. Parallel Abby can have my beloved Plan. She can have all the writing classes, and my subscription to the *New York Times*, and all the nights and weekends I spent in the Brookside newspaper lab. She can have the *YDN*, the prestigious internship, the impressive job, the fancy byline that I always imagined I'd have. She can be the person I was going to be.

I'll be someone else.

The thought is exhilarating.

I see it so clearly now. Caitlin is right: trying to undo what my parallel has done won't give me autonomy. To prove my independence, it's not enough to do things my parallel wouldn't do; I have to do things she *couldn't* do, things only I can. Like acting. Like getting cast in the Freshman Show.

I pull the flyer off the board. Open auditions. All I have to do is sign up. With my background, I should at least have a shot at getting cast.

A smile stretches across my face. *Metamorphoses.* Exactly.

Still smiling, I slip the flyer into my bag.

My phone rings then, and my stomach dips a little when I see Michael's name on the caller ID. We've seen each other six times since my birthday (four times in class and twice on the weekend, one of which was planned in advance) and text almost every other day, but I'm still not used to him yet. Probably because I'm not sure what I should be getting used to, or whether I should be getting used to him at all. As much as I like him, my parallel could so easily ruin this relationship (assuming that sitting together in in art history, standing side by side at a fraternity toga party, and kissing behind a U-Haul at the Yale-Dartmouth football tailgate constitute a relationship). I shouldn't get attached. My head knows this, but apparently my stomach and knees do not.

"What're you doing tonight?" Michael asks when I answer.

"Nothing," I answer, then wince. *Lame.*

"Wrong. You're going out with me."

"Where are we going?" I ask casually, determined to keep all traces of *ohmigod-he's-finally-taking-me-on-a-real-date!* from my voice.

"It's a surprise," he says mysteriously. "Can you be at my house at eight thirty?"

"Sure," I reply, only moderately annoyed that he didn't offer to pick me up. Maybe this date requires preparation. *He's making dinner!* I picture us sharing a bowl of spaghetti by candlelight, feeding each other tiny bites of home-made meatball.

"Oh, and eat before you come," he says.

Or not.

"What am I supposed to wear?" I ask Marissa over takeaway from Thai Taste that night. "What if we're going somewhere dressy?"

"He would've told you," she says, twirling noodles with her spoon. "Since he didn't say anything about wardrobe, I think you should assume it's casual."

"Outdoor casual or indoor casual?"

"Hmmmm." She chews on a chopstick, thinking. "Since he already did the outdoor date, this one is probably indoor, right?"

"You mean the tailgate last weekend? I don't think that counts as a date."

"No, silly. The kayak yesterday. Wait, is it called a kayak? Whatever – two-man crew boat. Or does that not count because it was your idea?"

This is why having a year-long memory gap really sucks. I'm always in the dark. My friends have memories of stuff my parallel will do next September that I don't have yet. When I'm with Caitlin, it's not a big deal; she just fills in the details I'm missing. But how do I handle my roommate, who right now is looking at me like I'm an Alzheimer's patient? "Oh, I thought you said something about last weekend," I say lamely, pretending her question about the boat was rhetorical. "You were saying something about Ben?"

Marissa looks at me funny. "I was?"

"You were about to tell me about your best date." I stuff a huge wad of noodles into my mouth before I make things worse. Lucky for me, my roommate is slightly spacey and prone to losing her train of thought, so she doesn't doubt me here.

"Oh. Right." Marissa thinks for a minute, then smiles. "Summer after junior year, about two weeks into our relationship. Ben planned a picnic dinner in Central Park. He bought all these locally made meats and cheeses and baked a loaf of French bread."

"Ben *baked*?"

She nods, her face bright with the memory. "It was super romantic. The sun was shining when he picked me up – on his bike – and we rode through the park with the picnic basket balanced on the handlebars, me in a white linen sundress and Ben in a khaki suit. It was like something out of an old movie, you know?"

"It sounds perfect," I tell her, picturing it.

"It was," she agrees. "Until about ten minutes after we got to our picnic spot, when it started *pouring*."

"Oh, no!"

She nods, still smiling. "Both the bread and my dress were soaked. We tossed the food, bought "I Heart NY" sweatshirts from a street vendor, and went for pizza instead."

"So you're saying I should bring an umbrella tonight," I say as I reach for a fortune cookie.

"I'm saying even when you know what you're in for, you never *really* know what you're in for," she tells me, crunching on a bean sprout. "So dress accordingly."

If I learned anything in LA, it's that with the right accessories, you can go anywhere in jeans and a white V-neck. Tonight I add an oversized cardigan I bought on eBay and a pair of brown leather riding boots I found at Cinderella's Attic in Guilford last weekend. Since my parallel self's definition of "style" appears to have been limited to Gap jeans and tops from J. Crew (which, admittedly, aptly describes the contents of my own pre-Hollywood wardrobe), I've had to do some wardrobe supplementing since I got here. Unfortunately, my bank account is quite a bit smaller than it was when I was in LA, so I'm making do with what I can find second hand.

"You look great," Michael says when he opens the door. "Cool boots."

"Thanks," I say as I survey his attire. Jogging bottoms and a Yale Lacrosse T-shirt. And here I was worried about being underdressed. *Is that a grease stain on his chest?*

"I was just about to change," he tells me, and holds out the red plastic cup in his hands. It's empty. "Can you get me a refill?" he calls, already halfway up the stairs. "Beer's in the fridge."

"Uh, OK," I call back. "Sure."

I turn the cup over in my hands. Not exactly how I thought the first thirty seconds of this date would go. Which, now that I'm here, doesn't even feel like a date.

By the time I reach the kitchen, I'm officially pissed off. *"Can you get me a refill?"* I mutter. "Seriously?" I grab the handle of the fridge and yank it open. Bottles on the door clang against one another, and it crosses my mind that I wouldn't mind if they all broke.

And then I see them. A bouquet of pink peonies spilling out of a trumpet-shaped beer stein. I reach for the bright yellow Post-it stuck to the front of the glass. *For Abby.*

"The refill was just a ruse."

"Oh!" Startled, I jump at the sound of Michael's voice and knock a family-sized bottle of Heinz off the refrigerator door. The flip top flies open when it hits the ground, squirting ketchup all over the linoleum. I look down at the ketchup, then up at Michael, who's now dressed in khakis and a very wrinkled blue button-down that, despite the fact that it looks like it was retrieved from the bottom of his laundry pile, is definitely date appropriate. "You scared me," I say sheepishly.

"I noticed," he replies, laughing as he bends to pick up the ketchup bottle. I grab a roll of paper towels off the counter to wipe up the mess. Clearly not standard procedure around here. The floor is disgusting, and wet with something that isn't ketchup. *Is that puke?* I dab at the linoleum, trying not to gag, then toss the wad of paper towels towards the giant rubbish bin next to the stove. It lands on the floor with a wet slap. Michael, meanwhile, is busy exchanging the Heinz bottle for two beers. "A drink before we go," he explains, twisting the caps off and dropping them in a bucket next to the fridge.

"Thanks," I say, eyes on the paper towel heap, trying to decide if I'm obligated to pick it up. A puddle of what looks like pee is saturating its edges.

"But we have to drink it fast," Michael is saying. "We're leaving here in five minutes."

*No time to worry about nasty paper towel wads, then.* Excellent. I gulp my beer.

"So do you like the flowers?" he asks between sips. "After what we talked about yesterday, I wanted to surprise you."

Yesterday. The boat ride. The most romantic thing Michael and I have ever done, and I don't remember it. I'm not sure what I could've said to prompt a surprise bouquet, but whatever it was, I'm glad I said it.

"I love them," I say. "Where'd you get peonies in New Haven?" I've been to the Safeway near campus. Their flower selection is limited to carnations and roses, each with a healthy dose of baby's breath.

"The farmers' market in Edgewood Park," he says, then grins. "According to the guy I bought them from, they're an aphrodisiac."

Heat floods my cheeks. Embarrassed that I'm embarrassed, I turn an even deeper shade of red.

"So what else did you do today?" I ask, quickly changing the subject before my face catches fire.

"Not a whole lot," he replies. "Went to the gym. Watched some baseball. What about you?"

"I quit the crew team," I tell him, tasting the Thai noodles I had for dinner and wishing I'd brought gum. I take several more swigs of beer, hoping to drown out the persistent peanut.

"Ha. Very funny."

"I'm serious," I say. "I sent an email to the coach right before I came over here." It strikes me that someone who's been on the team for weeks probably wouldn't say "*the* coach", but Michael is too busy looking flabbergasted to notice.

"You quit the team? Over email?"

His reaction throws me. "Well, yeah," I reply, suddenly self-conscious. "What's the big deal?"

"Did something happen at practice today?" he asks. "Is that where this is coming from?"

"Why does it have to be 'coming from' anywhere?" I ask, getting defensive. "Can't a person just decide she doesn't like something any more?"

"Overnight?"

"Why not?"

"I dunno, maybe because that's not how people are? People don't just abandon whole parts of themselves," he says. "You're a

162

coxswain," he declares, as though he's telling me the sky is blue. "It's part of who you are. A part I happen to like. You're this little bossy ball of energy."

*Subtext: I will like you less if you're not a coxswain.*

"I love that you like that about me," I begin, and then swallow hard when I realize that I've used "I", "love", and "you" in close proximity to one another in the same sentence. Thankfully, he doesn't flinch. I barrel on. "But it's not really part of who I am. Even if it seems like it. I only started coxing because I hurt my foot and couldn't run cross-country," I explain. "Since I didn't want to obsess over the fact that I couldn't do what I *really* loved, I told myself I loved crew, and after a while, I started believing it." I'm making this up, of course, because it wasn't really me who did any of this. But as I'm talking, I wonder: *Is this how it happened for my parallel?* Because if it is, then I sort of get it. Even if I want to believe I never would've given up so quickly on cross-country, I can imagine how it might've been easier to throw myself into something else than to suffer the disappointment of not being able to run.

"Sounds to me like something happened at practice today," Michael says.

"Nothing happened at practice today," I insist. "I just don't want to do it any more."

Michael takes a sip of his beer, considering this. "So I guess that means you can sleep over tonight," he says, all nonchalant. "No crew practice in the morning."

I freeze. I didn't shave my legs. Or my bikini line. My underwear has a hole in the crotch, and not in a sexy way. For these and a wealth of other reasons, I AM NOT READY TO

HAVE SEX. Flustered, I put my bottle to my lips and tilt it back, my cheeks warm again. This is one of those moments – and there have been several since Michael and I met – when I'm reminded of how totally and completely out of my league I am. It's not like I'm a total neophyte when it comes to the opposite sex – I've dated and made out with and almost-seen-naked a respectable number of them. But those were regular guys. Michael Carpenter is a different species altogether. He's gorgeous. He's smart. He's athletic. And he's cool. Like, really cool, without even trying. I, meanwhile, am of lesser calibre. I'm cute but not gorgeous, more hardworking than smart, fit but not athletic, and while I have moments of cool, those moments are surrounded by hours of carefully planning how to execute them.

Michael sees the look on my face and laughs. "I'm kidding," he says. "I intend to walk you to your doorstep after our date, where I will kiss you chastely goodnight." He pauses, then adds, "Unless, of course, you *want* to sleep over. . ."

"It's a school night," I say, and smile. My attempt to sound coy and flirty and not completely unhinged by this conversation.

"Then we should probably save the sleepless night for another time, then." Acting all blasé, he drains the rest of his beer and sets it on the counter. "Ready to go?"

"Mm-hmm," I manage, as casually as I can, as the words "SLEEPLESS NIGHT" reverberate in my head. Michael's eyes are lit up with laughter.

"So have you figured out where we're going yet?" he asks as we set off down the street. His elbow grazes the back of my arm, sending a ripple to my fingertips. If our conversation in the kitchen was just a ploy to get me naked, it might have worked. My legs aren't *that* hairy, and the beer I just downed has made me decidedly less self-conscious about my holey underwear. I'm not talking sleepless-night-level nakedness, but it's possible that *some* articles of clothing could be removed in a couple of hours. "C'mon," Michael says with a playful nudge, jolting these thoughts from my mind. "Not even a guess?"

"Hmm. A movie?"

"Nope."

I see the lights of the Yale Bookstore up ahead. "Uh . . . a poetry reading?"

"Nope." He points at the red-brick building on the corner. "Church."

"Church," I repeat. "Like, a church service?" My grandma Rose is always asking if I've been to church since I got to Yale, and she makes this *tsk* sound when she hears I haven't.

"Sort of," he says. "But sort of not." He slips his hand into mine. "You'll see." He whistles softly as we walk, his warm hand dry and rough against my clammy palm. We've made out in a coat cupboard and kissed on his doorstep, but this is the first time we've ever held hands.

The whistling stops when we step inside the building. The cross-shaped sanctuary is dark and cavernous, with Gothic arches and impossibly high ceilings, the kind of room that looks like it should be freezing cold. But this one isn't. Dozens of candles line both sides of the sanctuary, which might have something to do with the warmth and are definitely responsible for the sedating scent. I inhale deeply, trying to place it. Juniper? But something else, too . . . something more familiar. Rose? An inscription in

165

the stone of the eastern wall catches my attention. The words glow in the candlelight. WE MAY IGNORE, BUT WE CAN NOWHERE EVADE THE PRESENCE OF GOD. THE WORLD IS CROWDED WITH HIM. – C. S. LEWIS.

"C'mon," Michael whispers, tugging me further inside.

A handful of other people are scattered among the pews, but not enough of them to convince me that we're in the right place for whatever it is we came for. I glance at Michael, expecting him to look confused or uncertain, but he's grinning. He points at an empty row.

We slide all the way in, to the very centre of the pew, where it's much darker than it was along the edges. I don't know whether it's the placement of the massive stone columns or the sheer size of the room, but, though the candles are visible from where we're sitting, their glow is distant. Michael's face is almost entirely shrouded in darkness.

"It's called Compline," he tells me, in a voice so low it's hard to hear. "It's a time of reflection and meditation at the end of the day. This one happens every Sunday at nine."

"Oh," I whisper, because I'm not sure what else to say. Or do, for that matter. I glance around the room, looking to see what other people are doing, but the closest person is at least twenty feet away. Everyone is so *quiet*. There are no whispers. There is no motion. *Are we just supposed to sit here in the dark?*

Then, out of the darkness, I hear a lone tenor, chanting in Latin, coming from one of the alcoves near the front. The voice is quickly joined by many others, all singing in beautiful, haunting harmony. I listen, trying to determine which side of the sanctuary the sound is coming from, but I can't. The acoustics are too perfect to pinpoint the origin, and the choir is completely out of sight.

The words of the inscription come drifting back, as though carried by the music. Right now, the word "thick" feels more appropriate than "crowded". The air feels thick with something divine. And in this one moment, any feelings of fear or confusion about my circumstances have been replaced by an overwhelming appreciation of the here and now. I say a quick, wordless prayer, thankful for a fleeting thought that has brought more clarity than any other. Grateful for this moment I so easily could have missed.

When the song ends a few minutes later, the room is completely silent. Then another song begins. Halfway through the third song, Michael leans over and puts his lips to my ear. "Like it?" he asks, his voice barely audible. His breath on my neck sends a shiver down my spine. I turn, finding his ear.

"Yes," I breathe. And though I want to say more – how magical and significant this feels, how deeply I'm moved by the music, how honoured I am that he shared this with me – I don't, in part because I don't want to interrupt the silence but mostly because I know words won't be enough. So I touch my lips to his cheek in a soundless kiss – a silent thank-you – then sit back against the wooden pew, letting the music and the darkness envelop me. He finds my hand and squeezes it. Neither of us lets go.

# OCTOBER

# 6
# (here)

SATURDAY, 11 OCTOBER, 2008
(OPENING NIGHT FOR MY MOM'S EXHIBIT)

"There are a couple of calls you need to know before you get on the water," she tells me, pulling her blonde curls into a ponytail. We're sitting side by side on a picnic table near the river's edge, watching the rowers run laps around the boathouse. "You obviously shouldn't push off until everyone is ready, so your first call will always be 'number off from bow'. The bowman will call, "Bow!" and then the rest of the rowers will shout out their seat numbers. Once you hear 'stroke', check to see that it's clear, then push off."

"Number off from bow," I repeat. *Does it matter that I don't know who the bowman is?*

Turns out the smiley blonde girl from astronomy (whose name I now know is Megan) is a coxswain for Brookside's crew team. I didn't even know what a coxswain was until three days ago when Josh told me the crew team was looking for one and suggested that my gimp foot and I would be perfect for the job. They needed a coxswain, and I needed a varsity sport for my Northwestern application. Lacking other options, I decided to give it a shot. The coach was so elated that he didn't even make me try out. Say hello to the newest member of the Brookside crew team.

I'm making an effort to stay positive – about this and everything else. The effort is necessary, because without it I succumb to sulking and pouting and generally feeling sorry for myself, which isn't the way I normally react to setbacks, but appears to be my default response to this one. For the first couple of days, I moped around like Eeyore, stuck under a giant cloud of gloom, until Caitlin finally shook me out of it (literally, took me by the shoulders and shook me, practically giving me whiplash in the process).

"I know it's a lot to take in," Megan is saying. "But you're doing really great for your first day." She smiles encouragingly. "Before you leave, I'll give you a handout that lists all the calls with a little picture that tells you when to use them."

"That'd be awesome," I say with a grateful smile. "Thanks."

"I'm the one who should be thanking *you*!" she gushes. "Because we only had one cox for the men's team – me – Coach had to split practice so I could run both boats. I had no life." She leans back on her elbows, arching her back to let the sun hit her face.

*How can such a small girl have such big boobs?*

"How long have you been on the team?" I ask. "I didn't even know we had one until I met Josh."

"He's great, isn't he?" Megan says, flashing a smile at Josh as

170

he runs past us. He returns her smile, then waves at me. "Are y'all a couple?"

"Oh – no," I say quickly, shaking my head. "Just friends." In reality, I'm not sure you can even call us that. We haven't hung out outside school since the night I hurt my foot. And we don't really hang out *at* school, either. The polite "Hey!" we lob at each other across the room during fifth period is pretty much the extent of our social interaction. His suggestion that I join the crew team was the longest conversation we'd had since Ilana's party, and it was only two sentences long. How pathetic is it that talking to him was the highlight of my week? Fortunately, I've been doing a better job of keeping my feelings to myself. I've been polite but aloof. No more stalkerish staring in astronomy. No more asking him out. If there's gonna be a next move, it'll have to come from him.

So far he hasn't made one.

Caitlin thinks I secretly like the fact that Josh is so enigmatic. That the uncertainty keeps it interesting. It does, but that's not why I find him so appealing. I like him because when he's around, I feel really, really awake, like I've just drunk a Venti Red-Eye and chased it with Red Bull. It's not an adrenaline rush, exactly (the boy wears crew socks with loafers), it's just that when he's around – even if he's on the other side of the room and not paying any attention to me – I stop thinking about all the things I normally obsess over, i.e., the Things That Matter: my grades, my university applications, my future, my Plan. When Josh is there, wherever "there" is, the only moment that matters is the present one. The rest of it just falls away.

"So you're not a couple then?" I hear Megan ask.

171

"Not a couple," I reply, resisting the urge to add the word "yet".

Megan's eyes light up. "Could you talk to him for me, then?" she asks. "Be subtle, of course. If he doesn't like me, I don't want him to know that I like him. . ." Megan smiles self-consciously. She's pretty. I-can't-help-it-that-I'm-adorable pretty. Ugh.

"Uh, sure," I reply. "No problem." What was I supposed to say? *No, sorry, I can't talk to him for you because I'm still hoping he's secretly in love with me?*

"Thanks!" She hops off the picnic table and turns to face me. "Let's head down to the water," she suggests, handing me my crutches. "I can explain the rest of the calls on the way."

When we reach the water's edge, Megan climbs into a boat mounted on wooden blocks a few feet from the dock. "This is our practice shell," she says. "Hop in!" As soon as she says it, she giggles. "I guess you're not doing a lot of hopping, huh?" she says. "Do you need help getting in?"

"No," I say irritably, laying my crutches on the ground next to the boat. "I can put weight on it, just not for long periods of time." I swing my leg over the edge and ease down on to the seat facing Megan, my knees at her nose.

"Where you're sitting, that's the stroke seat," she tells me. "So depending on what boat you're in, that's either Josh or Brad." Megan prattles on about the various boat positions, but I don't hear her. I'm too busy fixating on the fact that I'm supposed to remember what to call, when to call it, *and* how to steer the boat with my face at Josh's thighs.

"To steer to port, pull the cord on your right towards you, like this. To steer to starboard, pull the cord on your left. Just remember that it'll take a few strokes for your actions to take effect – the worst thing you can do is—"

"The stroke seat, is that a good position?" I ask, interrupting her. "Is that where the best rower sits or the worst, or does it not work like that?"

"Oh, definitely the best," Megan replies. "From a technical standpoint, at least."

"So, Josh . . . he's pretty good, then?"

"Like, ridiculously good," she says. "His team got the gold last year at the World Rowing Junior Championships in France." Megan glances over at the rowers, now huddled together for a team meeting. I follow her gaze. Josh is listening intently to whatever the coach is saying. "I wonder what else he's good at?" she whispers, then starts giggling uncontrollably.

*She did not just say that.*

"So how'd you and Josh meet?" I ask, steering the conversation to less nauseating ground.

"Here," she replies. "I was supposed to give him a tour of the boathouse before practice, but we never made it past the locker room. Not that anything like *that* happened. Not yet, anyway." More giggling. The sound is really getting on my nerves. "We just started talking and the next thing we knew, it was time for practice. We, like, totally clicked." She looks past me to where the rowers are gathered and brazenly stares at Josh's butt.

"Megan!" Coach Schwartz calls. "Need you over here!" He motions for her to join the group.

"He means you, too," Megan tells me, climbing out of the boat. "He's just forgotten your name. He forgets everyone's name, so don't take it personally." She picks up my crutches and hands them to me. "His bark is also worse than his bite, so if you mess up out there and he yells at you, don't let it bother you too much."

"I'm going out on the water?" I assumed I'd get to watch today from the safety of dry ground. "Isn't it a little too soon for that?"

"Don't worry, you'll be great," she assures me. "I'm sure Coach will put you with the M8A, which means you won't have to do much, anyway. With the water being as calm as it is, you won't even have to steer. Josh can handle the calls."

"Megan!" Coach bellows. "Now!"

I follow Megan over to where the team is gathered, trying not to look like a total gimp in the process. When she introduces me as the team's newest coxswain, everyone cheers and claps. When I count how many of them I've met before, I'm startled to discover that it's less than half. *How do I not know these people?* Brookside isn't *that* big. Then again, I've been hanging out with the same crowd since freshman year and haven't exactly made the effort to branch out beyond Caitlin, Tyler, the golf team and some girls from the *Oracle* staff. These kids seem nice. And super serious about their sport. As Coach Schwartz runs through the plan for practice, they hang on every word.

Megan was right about the M8A, which I soon learn stands for the men's eight A, the team's fastest boat. They barely need a coxswain, which is great, since having me onboard is basically the same thing as not having one at all. She was also right about Josh. He's ridiculously good.

He doesn't let me off easy, though. "The only way to learn the calls is to do them," he tells me as he helps me into the boat.

174

"So I'll tell you what to call, but you've got to call it. As loud as you can."

"I thought I got to wear a little microphone," I say, pointing at the headset Megan has on.

"You will," he replies, and smiles. "Eventually. The cox box does a lot of the work for you, but the best coxes don't need one."

"How about the no-clue-what-they're-doing coxes?"

"Eh. They don't know how to use 'em, anyway."

"So, Wags, we actually gonna get in the water today or what?" It's Phillip Avery, the bowman, who, if Josh's body language is any indication, is Josh's least favourite person on the team. Phillip also happens to have been my date to Homecoming freshman year, which ended with my leaving him on the dance floor and walking home after he tried to stick his hand up my dress during Coldplay's "Fix You". We haven't spoken since.

"Since this is Abby's first day," Josh says evenly, "I thought, being *captain*, I might explain to her what she'll be doing before she does it. That OK with you, *Phil*?" Phillip hates to be called Phil.

I look down at the dock, swallowing a smile. *Astronomy Boy is a badass in spandex.*

Phillip mutters something unintelligible.

Josh carries on, undeterred by the seven impatient rowers standing behind him. I glance over at the B boat, already fifty yards down the river. Megan's voice echoes in the air.

"Come on, guys! Put it in clean!"

"I'd like to put it in clean," Phillip says under his breath.

"Wouldn't we all," the guy next to him says wistfully. "She's so freaking hot."

Josh looks past me to Megan. He's still talking about steering technique, but his eyes are on her. And her big, perfectly perky boobs.

"I think I'm ready," I say suddenly, cutting him off midsentence. "Now."

His eyes snap back to mine. "Yeah?"

"Sure." I shrug, feigning confidence. "How hard can it be?"

Turns out, even when you have someone telling you what to do and when to do it, coxing is still hard. Really. Freaking. Hard.

By the time practice ends two hours later, I'm exhausted. My butt aches, my throat hurts and my brain is approaching overload. It takes every ounce of my remaining energy to hobble to my car. So much to remember! So much to do! Cross-country is effortless compared to this. All you have to do is run. Coxing is so much more work, and it's not even a workout. But at the same time, it's oddly exhilarating. Being out on the water. Being in charge. Being six inches from Josh.

"Abby!" I jump when I hear my name. I turn to see Josh jogging towards me, his hair wet from the shower. "I was worried you were gone already," he says, coming up beside me. "I'm glad you're not. Here, let me take these." He reaches for the keys dangling from my pinkie finger.

I smile, dropping the keys on to his outstretched palm. *Megan who?* I feel a flash of guilt for agreeing to talk to him for her. But it's not like she gave me much of a choice.

"You really rocked out there!" he says enthusiastically.

"Ha. Yeah, right."

"I'm serious. You just need to get more comfortable with the commands," he tells me. "Your instincts were great."

"I'm not sure I believe you, but thanks. It was fun. More fun than I thought it'd be," I admit.

We reach my car. Josh unlocks the doors and opens the driver's-side door for me. "Big plans tonight?" he asks, sliding my crutches into the back seat.

"Oh, just this museum event," I say. "With my parents," I add, just to be clear.

"Cool," Josh says, and hands me back my keys. I just stand there, smiling, waiting for him to suggest that we get together some other time. That's why you ask someone about their Saturday night plans, right? Because you want to ask them out?

"Have fun tonight," is all Josh says. He gives me a little wave, then heads to his Jeep. Defeated, I plop down in my driver's seat.

He must like Megan. That's the only explanation. OK, it's not the *only* explanation, but it's the only one I want to accept. I'd rather believe that he fell for the smokin' hot girl on the crew team than think he just doesn't like me.

There's only one way to find out.

I grab my mobile phone from the glove compartment and quickly dial his number, saving the last digit until he's in his Jeep. He answers on the second ring.

"Hey," he says, looking my direction.

"Hi. I was wondering what you thought of Megan."

"Megan Watts?"

"Megan the coxswain."

"Megan the coxswain is Megan Watts," Josh says. "What do you mean, what do I think of her? I think she's a good coxswain." I lean forward in my seat to get a better look at his face, but there's a glare on his windscreen.

177

"I meant, are you interested in her? As a girlfriend."

"Why?"

"Because I think you'd be a great couple," I lie, fiddling with the zip on my rucksack.

Josh is silent on the other end of the line. When I look up, his Jeep is pulling away. I wait for him to say something, but he doesn't.

*This is awkward.*

"I just didn't want you to feel weird about it," I say quickly. "If you like her. Because I'm fine with it. If you do."

"Great," Josh says, his voice totally void of anything for me to latch on to and analyse. "Thanks." There is a sinking feeling inside my chest.

"OK, well. . ." How does one end a conversation like this gracefully? *Hope it works out!* Obviously not, but somehow the equally ridiculous words "Good luck!" spring from my lips. Then, before it can get any worse, I hang up on him.

"I am a lunatic," I say to the phone in my hand. Now what? Do I call him back? Send him a text blaming a bad connection?

Caitlin calls before I can do either.

"Hey," I say, answering. "I think I just set Josh up with Megan Watts."

"Who's Megan Watts?"

"The other cox. Curly blonde hair, big boobs. The guys on the crew team thinks she's really hot."

"Why would you try to set Josh up with another girl?" she asks. "Wait. Lemme guess. It was some twisted plan to see if he liked you, and it backfired."

I sigh. "Something like that."

"How'd I know? Listen, I want to help you overanalyse every detail of this, but I only have a minute before I have to be at the lab."

"No problem," I tell her. "We already have our conclusion, anyway. I'm a loser."

"A loser who *must* read my Yale essays this weekend," Caitlin says. "I emailed the latest drafts to you an hour ago. My application is due November first, and I need time to revise it before sending. Knowing me, lots of time."

"Sure," I say, still thinking about Josh. "He said *why* when I asked him if he liked Megan. That definitely means he likes her, right? Otherwise he just would've said no."

"Do you make these rules up as you go along? Or are they from the same relationship manual that recommends asking the guy you like if he likes the hot blonde girl?"

"She asked me to talk to him for her!"

"Ohhh. So *that* was your motive. It was philanthropic." I can picture her rolling her eyes. "Hey, I gotta go," she tells me. "We'll obsess about Astronomy Boy later. Just read my essays, OK?"

"Of course I'll read your essays," I reply. "But *no*, we will not obsess later. Or ever. I'm officially over Astronomy Boy." As I say it, I am certain, but I delete his number from my phone just to be safe.

"Your mom sure knows how to throw a party," Dad remarks, looking around the crowded room. We're standing in the High

179

Museum's Grand Lobby, which has been transformed into a nineteenth-century French salon. Mom is holding court nearby, stunning in royal blue silk. The gown belongs to Caitlin's mom, a remnant from her ten-week stint as the lead in *Madame Bovary: The Musical!* six months before Caitlin was born. Thanks to the fifteen pounds Mrs Moss put on in her first trimester, and with the help of some full-body Spanx and a pair of five-inch heels, it fits my mom perfectly.

"No one would believe she's almost fifty," I muse, watching her.

"Just don't let her hear you call her 'almost fifty'," Dad replies, swirling his Scotch. "She's convinced that forty-eight still qualifies as mid-forties."

"Not too shabby, Barnes." Tyler's voice cuts across the dull adult chatter. He strides over to us, wearing a tuxedo that looks like it belongs in the 1970s. "You don't look bad either, Ab."

I stick my tongue out at Tyler as he shakes Dad's hand. "What happened to the crutches?" Tyler asks me. "Don't you have another week left?"

"Yeah. But crutches plus a floor-length gown equals Abby face-planting in front of hundreds of people. So I left them in the car."

"See, now *that* would be fun," Tyler says. He looks at my dad. "Not that this party isn't *super* fun already, Mr B."

"Of course it is," Dad replies between sips. "We're surrounded by boring old white guys in ill-fitting tuxes. How could it not be fun?" He tilts his glass, finishing his drink.

"Don't be so hard on yourself," Tyler deadpans. "Your tux fits OK."

My dad laughs, but since he has an ice cube in his mouth,

180

it comes out as a snort. The sound earns a few looks from the people around us. Dad doesn't notice. Chuckling, he ambles off to get another drink.

"So where's Ilana tonight?" I ask when he's gone, trying not to scowl as I say her name.

"Play rehearsal," Tyler replies. "She's all worked up 'cause some big casting director is coming to see it opening night."

"Ooh. Can Cate and I come heckle her?"

"She's been acting weird," Tyler says.

"News flash. She *is* weird."

"I meant Caitlin," he says.

"Oh." I think about it. *Has she been acting weird?* I haven't noticed anything, but between my foot and the SATs and the feelings Josh doesn't have for me, I've been sort of preoccupied lately. "Weird how?"

"I dunno. Skittish."

*Skittish.* Not a word I've ever used to describe my best friend. She's the opposite of excitable. But just as I'm about to tell Tyler that I don't know what he's talking about, I remember how she reacted when I asked her if she had feelings for him. Uncharacteristically cagey. Perceptibly off-kilter.

*She's acting weird because she likes him.* All at once, I know for certain that I'm right. I don't know how I know, I just do. Caitlin likes Tyler, and Tyler likes her back.

"You haven't noticed?" Tyler asks.

I hesitate. If Tyler and Caitlin do have secret feelings for each other, then until one of them actually does something about it, they'll both be miserable. OK, so maybe not *miserable*, but less happy than they otherwise could be. And what if the year passes and we graduate and they miss their chance altogether? That has to be worse than any fallout from my playing Cupid. Besides, Caitlin needs this. She hasn't dated anyone since Craig, and I know it's because she's afraid of getting her heart broken again. Ty would never hurt her.

I choose my words carefully. "It's the Ilana thing," I say, keeping my voice light. "It's hard for her." I make it sound like this is no big deal, when Tyler and I both know it is. There's only one reason Tyler's relationship with Ilana would be "hard" for Caitlin.

Tyler's face stays neutral. "She told you that?"

"She didn't have to tell me," I hedge. "I'm her best friend." It strikes me that Caitlin might take issue with that statement at this particular moment.

"So she never said it explicitly?" he asks.

"She did," I lie. "I just wasn't supposed to tell you." *What am I doing?* I open my mouth to take it all back, but Tyler cuts me off.

"I'm in love with her," he says in a voice that doesn't sound like his. Maybe because he's using words I've never heard him use before. At least, not with a straight face. "I didn't think I had a shot," he says then. "You're saying I do?"

OK, whatever I was expecting, it wasn't this. I mean, I thought he had feelings for her, and *I* might've used the word "love", but I've known Tyler since nursery school, and I've never heard him use the *L* word except when talking about golf clubs. Yet here he is, throwing it around and sounding all heartfelt and sincere. As I stand here, looking into his open and honest eyes, I'm startled by the depth of emotion I see. He's really in love with her. And I've just hinted that she feels the same way.

My mind keeps reeling *Caitlin is going to kill me.*

"Depends on how you play it," I try to backpedal. "You can't come on too strong." *If you do, she'll know I said something to you.*

"Yeah. OK." He's trying to play it cool, but he's failing. The boy is beaming, which is good, because the look on his face removes any doubt that I did the right thing. Not that I even did much at all – my words were nothing more than a nudge in the direction he was already heading. At least, that's what I'm telling myself over and over again right now, trying to mitigate the rising swell of guilt. "Think she'll be at the party tonight?" Tyler asks a few seconds later.

"What party?"

"Cul-de-sac party in that new neighbourhood off Providence Road. Football team got a keg."

"Oh. No. She's working at her dad's lab tonight." *Thank God.* Caitlin is scarily intuitive. She'll take one look at Tyler's dopey grin and know something's up. He needs to recover from his euphoria before their next encounter. And figure out what to do about Ilana.

Across the room, someone is waving. I'm not sure if the gesture is directed at me – all I see is a man's hand flailing in the air. Whoever the hand belongs to is blocked by two obese women in silk taffeta. The women shuffle away and Dr Mann comes into view, looking rather dapper in a grey suit. His smile widens when we make eye contact.

"Ms Barnes!" he calls across the crowd.

"Who's that?" asks Tyler, clearly amused by the wild-haired old guy moving towards us.

"Dr Mann," I reply. "My astronomy teacher."

"*That* guy won a Nobel Prize?"

"Shhh." I look past Tyler to my teacher, who's balancing a plate of meatballs on a can of Dr Pepper. His other hand is extended to shake mine.

"They didn't give you a glass for that?" I ask, nodding at the soda can as I shake his hand. The old man laughs.

"They offered me one, but I declined. It's harder to spill on oneself from a can." Dr Mann smiles and takes a careful sip.

Tyler looks at me. Again: *That guy won a Nobel Prize?*

I ignore him. "Dr Mann, this is my friend Tyler Rigg. He goes to Brookside also."

"It's a pleasure, Mr Rigg," says Dr Mann, shaking Tyler's hand. "Perhaps I'll have you in class next term."

"I wouldn't count on that," Tyler says pleasantly.

"So what brings you to the museum?" I ask Dr Mann.

"My daughter is on the board," he tells me, and points at a woman who looks to be in her early thirties, wearing a demure black dress. She has an Audrey Hepburn quality and her father's striking blue eyes.

"So you got dragged here, too," Tyler says. He stops a man carrying a tray of lamb chops and heaps six on to a cocktail napkin.

"I'm afraid it was me who did the dragging," Dr Mann says. "Greta just flew in from Munich this afternoon and was planning to stay home, but I insisted that we come. I am a great admirer of '*le petit jeune chimiste qui accumule des petits points*.'" His French is perfect.

"Hmm. . . Something about a chemist and small dots?" I say, trying to parse it out.

"'The young chemist who puts together little points,'" he translates. Then explains, "It's how Gauguin described Seurat.

184

He missed the artistry of the pointillist method, I'm afraid. Saw only the science."

"And you see both?" I ask.

"In my view, the science *is* the artistry," the old man replies. He looks past us to Seurat's A *Sunday on La Grande Jatte*, the painter's most famous piece and the centrepiece of the exhibit, on loan from the Art Institute of Chicago. "With his '*petits points*', Seurat invited the viewer to participate in a transcendent experience instead of thrusting one upon him." He points his Dr Pepper can at the painting. "The inherent order you perceive in that image has not been constructed on that canvas; rather, it is *being* constructed as we speak, in your mind."

This, of course, is not the first I've heard about pointillism. When you're the only child of an art curator and a retired painter, you get more art theory at the dinner table than would fit in a term on the subject. But for the first time, the theory resonates on a grander scale. Up close, all you see are the pieces, strewn about, heaped on top of each other. Total disarray. But step away, and a picture takes shape. When you make sense of the chaos, the chaos disappears. Or maybe, what looked at first like chaos never was.

*In an ocean of ashes, islands of order.*

It's a line from *Arcadia*, a play we read in AP English last year. (I wouldn't have remembered it except for the fact that I flubbed it when I read it aloud in class. "In an island of ashes, oceans of order," I'd said, and someone made a joke about Oceans of Order being a great band name.) The original line is a reference to the patterns that emerge out of chaos. The phrase captures Seurat's masterpiece perfectly. By themselves, the dots are just little circles of colour. But in the right arrangement, they become so much more.

Before I can get too far with this idea, Tyler interrupts it. "Is that a monkey?"

"It's supposed to be satirical," I say vacantly. "The word for female monkey in French – *singesse* – was a slang word for prostitute." My comment earns an impressed look from Dr Mann. "It's an equation," I say then, still thinking about *Arcadia*. "The dots are the variables. The coherent image we see from far away is the solution."

"*Et l'artiste est le mathématicien*," Dr Mann says.

"The artist is the mathematician," I translate, liking the idea. But how much control does the artist have over the solution? I imagine my life as a painting and wonder the same thing.

My left foot begins to throb, so I shift all my weight to my right one.

"Papa!" Greta is calling to her father, gesturing for him to come meet whoever she's talking to. Dr Mann gives us a little bow before departing.

"So how long till we can get out of here?" Tyler asks, clearly not interested in discussing my philosophical ideas about life and maths and pointillist painting. "I'm bored."

"We've only been here an hour."

"An hour in museum time is, like, five hours in regular time," he replies. "How about we stay until nine, then hit the keg?"

"Fine. This ends at ten, anyway."

"You should call Caitlin," he says. "Tell her to stop by the cul-de-sac after the lab."

I'm debating whether to shoot this idea down or pretend

to call her when I hear my phone buzz from inside my clutch. Tyler hands it to me. He's looking at my screen when I read the incoming text:

Caitlin: C U AT THE PARTY?

I look from the text to Tyler.
*Shit.*

By the time we get there, the "party" has dwindled to more of an intimate gathering.

Everyone is standing around the fire someone built in a metal bin. Some football players are roasting marshmallows on a stick. Andy Morgan, our star running back, whistles when he sees us.

"Lookin' good, kids!" Andy calls out. Tyler twirls me, and I do a little curtsy in my dress, careful not to put too much weight on my bad foot. Across the cul-de-sac, Ilana is giving me the death stare. She's standing away from the fire with a group of drama girls, drinking a diet soda and looking pissed off at the world. Tyler heads towards her.

"S'more?" Andy asks, pressing a charred marshmallow between two graham cracker squares and holding it out for me. "There are Hershey bars around here somewhere."

After a truckload of salty hors d'oeuvres, a melted marshmallow is hard to resist. "Sure," I tell him. "Thanks." I nibble on the corner of the graham cracker, waiting for the insides to cool.

"How long have you guys been here?"

"About an hour," Andy replies. "Long enough for Ilana to get pissed that Tyler hadn't shown up yet." I feel a flash of sympathy for Ilana. She and Tyler are standing off to the side, away from the rest of Ilana's friends, in the midst of what looks like a heated discussion. I try not to stare. "Hey, there's Caitlin," Andy says, shoving another marshmallow into his mouth. "She's so hot."

I look up and see Caitlin parking her Jetta down the street. My eyes dart back to Tyler. Ilana has his forearm in a vice grip. *It doesn't look like he'll be having any alone time with Caitlin tonight.* I feel myself begin to relax. I'm not really worried that Tyler will rat me out, but he's been known to get chatty when he's been drinking, which, thanks to his flirtatious banter with the bartender at the museum, includes tonight.

"You look amazing!" Caitlin says to me as she walks up. "How was the gala?"

"Really great," I tell her. "You should've seen my mom—"

"Are you *kidding* me?" Ilana's voice, even more high-pitched than normal, stabs me in the eardrum, stopping me mid-sentence. All heads swivel in her direction. She's staring at Tyler, her face contorted in disbelief. Tyler mutters something indecipherable.

"Keep my voice down?" Ilana shrieks. "You break up with me – at a *party*, in front of my *friends* – and then you have the *audacity* to tell me to keep my voice down? Who do you think you are?"

My eyes dart to Caitlin. Hers are glued to the drama unfolding across the street. I brace myself, waiting for Ilana to come screaming towards me.

*This is not how I expected this to go.*

Yes, I assumed Tyler would probably break up with Ilana at some point. But I didn't think he'd do it *tonight*. Or in front of a crowd.

"If that's all it took to put him over the edge, their relationship was doomed anyway," I murmur.

"If what was all it took?" Caitlin asks.

"Whatever made him break up with her. Not that I know what that is," I quickly add. "Because I don't." Caitlin gives me a funny look.

"And . . . she's out." Andy points his roasting stick at Ilana's retreating figure. She flings open her car door and gets in. I look over at Tyler. He's looking at Caitlin.

*This is bad. This is very bad.*

"Hey, I'm pretty tired," I say to Caitlin, feigning a yawn. "Can you take me home?"

"Right this second?" Caitlin asks. "I just got here. Besides, didn't you drive? I saw your car when I drove in."

"I'm not feeling well." Out of the corner of my eye, I see Tyler heading towards us. "I don't think I should drive."

"I can take you," Andy offers, skewering another marshmallow with his stick. "I told my dad I'd be home early tonight."

"Oh . . . that's OK," I say. "I'll just wait for Cate." Caitlin eyes me. She knows something is up. I pretend not to notice.

"You OK?" Caitlin asks as Tyler joins our little circle. She puts her hand on his forearm. There are nail marks on the inside of his wrist.

"I'm great," he tells her and smiles. "Although I think she

may have shattered my eardrum," he adds, tugging on his earlobe.

"That girl does have quite the set of lungs," Andy muses as he watches his marshmallow burn. "Want a beer?"

"Nah, I think I'm done for tonight." Tyler tells him. "I had about a quart of JB at the museum. I should probably quit while I'm still standing."

"I'll drive you," I say before Andy can offer. There's no way I'm staying to make small talk with Caitlin. She and I don't do small talk. And we don't do fake talk either. So unless I'm prepared to admit that I'm freaking out about the fact that I told our best guy friend that she has a thing for him after she told me unequivocally that she doesn't, it's time to call it a night.

"A minute ago you were too sick to drive," Caitlin points out.

"I got a second wind," I say.

"In the last sixty seconds?"

"Ty, you ready?" I ask, pretending not to hear her. He's busy shoving marshmallows on to a stick.

"One sec," he says. "I'm making a roadie."

Caitlin pulls me aside. "What's going on with you?" she asks, lowering her voice. "You're acting bizarre."

"Nothing!" I say brightly. A little too brightly. Caitlin eyes me suspiciously.

"I don't believe you. Is this about my essays? Did you read them and hate them?"

"If I hated them, I'd tell you," I reply. "I haven't read them yet. But I will," I promise. "Tomorrow."

"So why are you being weird?"

"I'm not being weird," I insist, careful to avoid Caitlin's gaze. "I'm just tired."

"'K, let's go," Tyler declares, his mouth full of chocolate pieces. There's a burnt marshmallow stuck to each pinkie. "Bring the graham crackers."

"OK, bye!" I announce, to no one in particular. Then beeline to my car.

As soon as we pull away from the party, I slump down in my seat, visibly relaxing.

"Why are you being weird?" Tyler asks. At least, I think that's what he said. With the two marshmallows he has jammed in his mouth, it's hard to be sure.

"You can't tell Caitlin what I told you."

"I can't?"

"I'm serious, Tyler. She'd freak if she found out. Promise me you won't tell her."

"I won't tell her," he says. "But if you were so worried how she'd react, why'd you tell me in the first place?"

"Because I wanted you to do something about it," I say. "*Subtly.* And I knew you wouldn't make a move unless you knew you had a shot."

Tyler doesn't answer right away. "Nah," he says after a minute, his words slurring just a little. "I would've done something either way." He glances over at me, then out of the passenger-side window. "I mean, don't get me wrong: it's definitely easier knowing she feels the same way. But I wouldn't have let the year go by without telling her how I felt."

I glance over at him, his profile illuminated in the moonlight. He looks older, somehow. Sure of himself. "So you didn't even need me," I joke.

That's when I hear the sirens. Approaching from the other direction. At least, that's what I think until we come around the next corner and see the red lights. Traffic is stopped in both directions.

"That's Ilana's car," I hear Tyler say. He's staring at the mangled white Mercedes on the shoulder. There's an empty red pickup truck in the ditch across the street. Firemen and paramedics surround what's left of the Mercedes.

"Where's Ilana?" I hear myself whisper.

Tyler just points as a paramedic lifts a limp body through the broken windscreen of her car.

# 7
# (here)

**MONDAY, 12 OCTOBER, 2009**
**(MY AUDITION FOR THE YALE FRESHMAN SHOW)**

*I scream as they wheel the stretcher past me, but no sound comes out. I run after them, but they close the doors in my face. I look back at the car and see Ilana lying on the pavement, her tiny frame bent like a rag doll. "Wait!" I yell as the ambulance pulls away. I try to run after it, but my feet are frozen in place.*

"Abby." The voice is urgent. "Abby, wake up."

I squeeze my eyes shut. *You're dreaming,* I tell myself.

"You're dreaming," another voice says.

"No," I hear myself mumble. And then I'm awake.

I blink my eyes open, and my bedroom comes into view. Marissa is kneeling beside me, her hands on my shoulders. Her eyes are wide with concern.

"You were screaming," she says.

I just nod. My throat is like sandpaper.

"What were you dreaming about?" she asks me.

I just shake my head, unable to push the image of Ilana's broken body from my mind. "My phone," I whisper hoarsely. "Could you get me my phone?" I point at my desk, where I left it plugged in.

"Sure." Marissa gives me another concerned look, then gets to her feet. She disconnects my phone from its charger and hands it to me. "I'll be in the common room." She closes the door softly behind her as she leaves.

For the first time, I want less information, not more of it. I don't want to know that Ilana was in a horrible car accident the night Tyler broke up with her out of the blue. Or that my parallel is the reason he did it. But I already know those things. The memories are seared into my mind, bright and unflinching. What I don't know is whether my parallel's attempt to play Cupid cost Ilana her life.

With trembling fingers, I make the call. It goes straight to voicemail.

It's Monday. Caitlin is in class until twelve forty-five. It's only ten fifteen now.

Staring vacantly at my screen, I scroll through my photo log. All the pictures are there. I should feel relieved. But seeing them only makes me feel worse. What if Ilana is dead? What if I'm here smiling for photos while she's—

*Please, God, don't let her be dead.*

I contemplate calling Michael, but I don't have the energy to pretend that my dream was just a dream when I know that it wasn't. Even if I don't tell him about it, he'll try to cheer me up as soon as he hears how upset I am, and I don't deserve to feel better. Not until I know what happened to Ilana. I move from my bed to my desk, intending to Google the accident, but my fingers just hover above the keyboard. I can't. I can't see photographs of the wreckage. I can't read some reporter's sensationalist spin on the facts. The images in my mind are harrowing enough.

My vision blurs as I picture Tyler throwing up in the grass as Ilana's ambulance pulls away. The look on that police officer's face as he tells us what happened. Ilana was coming around the curve when a pickup truck crossed over the centre line going nearly twice the speed limit and hit her head-on. The driver was handcuffed in the back of a police car when we got there, passed out against the window glass, his only injury a broken hand.

Another memory springs to the surface. One that feels like mine, even though I know it isn't. Standing in the Grand Lobby of the High Museum, lying to Tyler's face.

*Why did she do it? Why would my parallel make something like that up?* So what if she had good intentions. Didn't she realize what was at stake? "Don't play Cupid," is right there below "Don't lie" in the BFF code. Cardinal don'ts, especially if your best friend is Caitlin Alexandra Moss. Things are black or white with her. Right or wrong. True or false. She doesn't live in shades of grey. She also has a ridiculously strict moral code for someone who thinks religion is a crutch for the lonely and stupid.

Fresh air. I need fresh air.

I quickly change into running clothes, then grab my phone and keys. Marissa is waiting for me in the common room with a mug of something frothy. She doesn't drink coffee or milk or anything else they sell at Durfee's, so she's set up a little barista bar by our bay window where she brews, steams, and froths her decaffeinated non-dairy creations with the espresso machine her parents gave her for graduation. She makes a very tasty vanilla rooibos soya latte. Her hemp milk green tea cappuccino, on the other hand, tastes like the inside of a lawn mower.

"Chamomile with soy and stevia," she says, handing me the mug. "I thought you could use something calming."

"Thanks." I try to smile.

"Are you OK?" she asks gently. "That dream seemed pretty gnarly. Want to talk about it?"

I shake my head. "I think I'm gonna go for a run," I say, setting the mug down.

"But I thought . . . I skipped econ so we could run lines. Your audition's today, right?"

*Crap.* I'm supposed to be at the drama school at two o'clock. I nod distractedly, too preoccupied with the awfulness of the accident to feel relieved that I still *have* the audition – part of me was sure it'd be erased with the next reality shift, which is why I've put off quitting the *YDN*. But it appears my decision to try out for the Freshman Show belongs on the growing list of recent events that haven't yet been overwritten. Caitlin says the list makes sense; that because I kept my memories, there are certain things I've done since the collision that my parallel can't undo as easily. "There's a causal disconnect," Caitlin said when I asked her to explain it. "Your parallel can't undo the fact that you kept your memories, so she can't undo the things that have happened because you did." I'm still not clear on the nuances of this rule, but I'm not arguing.

"Actually, I think I'm good," I tell Marissa. "I've been over it so many times, I think going through it again will jinx me."

"Whatever you need," she says. But a hint of annoyance flashes across her never-annoyed face.

I take another step towards the door, then stop. Of all the roommates I could've ended up with, I got the girl who is kind and funny and generous and willing to skip class to run lines with me. Meanwhile, she got stuck with the forgetful, spacey girl who makes lame excuses for her increasingly odd behaviour.

"I'm really sorry to bail like this," I say, turning back around. "I think I'm just rattled from that dream."

The annoyance disappears. "I get it, Ab. Do what you need to do. Just remember – it was only a dream." She smiles reassuringly, her brown eyes wide and warm.

*Oh, Marissa. How I wish you were right.*

Fighting back tears, I jog up Hillhouse Avenue towards Sterling Lab, where Caitlin's chem class meets. Lined with nineteenth-century mansions and shaded by towering oak, Hillhouse is one of the most beautiful streets on campus. This morning I barely notice it, though. All I see is Ilana.

*Please let her be OK.*

When I get to Sachem Street, I turn down Prospect and do the loop again, faster this time. By the time I get back to Sachem, I'm heaving and sweating and still thinking about the accident. So I do it a third time, and then a fourth. After the fifth, my lungs are burning and my heart feels like it might burst through my rib cage and my brain is still locked on Ilana.

Sweaty and spent, I park it on a bench to wait. I try to focus on my breath, counting each inhalation, but the exercise is pointless. My mind is on an unrelenting loop, replaying those awful moments over and over again in garish detail.

My phone rings, jarring me back to the moment. I haven't moved in over an hour.

"Hey!" Caitlin's voice is bright. Cheery. It fills me with hope. "Isn't your audition—"

"Ilana."

The line goes quiet.

"What – what happened to her?" The words are like sand in my throat, but I force them out. I have to know. "After the accident. Is she. . ."

Caitlin doesn't say anything.

"She's dead," I whisper. "Oh my God, she killed her."

"Wait, what? Who killed her?"

"My parallel," I choke out. "It was her fault. And now Ilana is dead."

"Abby, Ilana's not dead. She was in a coma for a couple of weeks, but she didn't die."

My body floods with relief. Then my brain registers what Caitlin just said.

"But she was in a coma? Did it . . . does she—"

"There was some damage to her brain," Caitlin says carefully. "We should talk about this in person. Where are you?"

"Corner of Hillhouse and Sachem," I manage, tears streaming down my cheeks. *Damage to her brain.*

"I'll be right there," Caitlin says.

I'm still holding the phone to my ear when Caitlin arrives, out of breath from running.

"Damage to her brain," I repeat.

"It could've been much worse," she says, sitting down next to me. "Speech or movement problems, long-term memory loss, personality changes. But she doesn't have any of that."

"Then what does she have?"

"Her short-term memory is impaired," Caitlin says. "She can remember stuff that happened before the accident, but she has trouble remembering things that have happened after it."

I'm quiet as I process this.

"It's not debilitating," Caitlin continues, trying to sound upbeat. "I mean, it made taking tests pretty impossible, so finishing school was a challenge. And she had to give up acting." I blink back fresh tears, unable to imagine Ilana doing anything else. As unpleasant as she was in real life, she was captivating onstage. "But last I heard, she was doing really well," Caitlin adds. "Living with an aunt in Florida. Tyler keeps up with her, I think."

The "I think" gets my attention. Caitlin should know if Tyler still talks to Ilana.

"I don't understand why you thought your parallel killed her," Caitlin is saying. "Why would you—"

"When was the last time you talked to him?"

"Who, Tyler?" Caitlin looks at me strangely. "I dunno, right before we left for school?" I can literally feel the colour drain from my face, trickling down my neck.

"Oh, no. No, no, no."

"Abby, what?"

"You're supposed to be together," I say. "You're supposed to—"

"Whoa. *What?* Like, a *couple?*" Caitlin blinks in surprise. "Since when?"

"August." I stare at the backs of my hands. "Max Levine's party. Ty got up on a chair and told everyone he'd been in love with you since ninth grade."

"Seriously? He used the word 'love'?" Caitlin is staring at me, slack-jawed.

199

"So did you," I say softly, sorrow like a dead weight inside me. "Not then. But two weeks ago, when he came to visit."

"He came to visit me *here*? We were that serious?" She shakes her head in disbelief. "Wow."

I just nod, too sad to tell her what she said when he left. That she could see herself with him for the rest of her life. Or what he told me the night he arrived. That he was a better version of himself when she was around.

"Wow," Caitlin says again.

"She's the reason you're not together," I say glumly. "It's my parallel's fault."

"Why?" Caitlin doesn't sound upset. Just curious.

"She told Tyler you liked him. The night of my mom's – *her* mom's – gala at the High. It's the reason he broke up with Ilana." The words come tumbling out. "If he hadn't, Ilana wouldn't have left that party when she did, angry and upset, and the accident—" My voice breaks.

"Abby, Ilana was hit head-on by a drunk guy going seventy in a thirty-five. The accident was nobody's fault but his." I look away, knowing it's not that simple. "Listen to me," Caitlin says, grabbing my hand. "Your parallel didn't cause that accident."

"But why did she have to lie to him?" Anger swells inside me. "Screw her motives. You told her you didn't like Tyler. But she just had to trust that stupid hunch—"

Caitlin's eyes light up. "What hunch?"

"She was convinced that you and Tyler were supposed to be together," I tell her. "*Convinced*. It sounds crazy, but it's almost as if—"

"—she knew." Caitlin and I just look at each other.

"But that's impossible, right?" *Do I even believe in impossible any more?*

Caitlin stands up and starts pacing, her stiletto boots click-clacking on the pavement. "Why couldn't it go both ways? Why couldn't she be getting your memories the same way you're getting hers? Not all of them, obviously – but fragments." The excitement in her voice is mounting. She paces faster. "It makes sense that she wouldn't recognize that information as memory – how could she, since it relates to something that hasn't happened in her world yet? So her brain is storing it as something else. Premonition. Intuition."

"But that premonition was wrong," I point out. "You and Tyler *don't* end up together. Not in her world."

"The premonition wasn't wrong," Caitlin replies. "You said it yourself: Ty and I *would've* ended up together if your parallel hadn't tried to orchestrate it."

I picture the photograph taped to the back of Caitlin's phone, taken two days before she left for school. She and Tyler are on a roller coaster at Six Flags, grinning like idiots. Idiots in love. That picture is gone now, the moment along with it. *Who knew fate was so fragile?*

"Maybe it's not too late," I offer. "Maybe you and Tyler could give it a try now. He could come visit and you could—"

Caitlin just laughs. "Yeah, I think that ship sailed about a year ago."

"But you guys are meant to be," I say. The words sound silly, even to me. I expect Caitlin to laugh again, but she just looks at me thoughtfully.

"I said I loved him?" she asks. I nod. She's quiet for a few seconds. "I've thought about it before," she admits, her cheeks flushing just a bit. "What it would be like." Her face reddens, and she looks away.

"Call him!" I say, holding out my phone.

She waves the phone away. "Don't be silly," she says. "What's done is done. Besides, it's not like it would've lasted anyway." She pulls out her own phone to check the time. "I should probably go," she says. "I don't want to miss my train."

"Train to where?"

"New London," she replies. "I'm meeting with Dr Mann to convince him he needs a research assistant." She points at the clock on her phone. "Isn't your audition at two? It's one fifty-two."

"Ah!" I leap up from the bench, nearly twisting my ankle on the uneven pavement.

"Break a leg!" Caitlin shouts as I sprint down Science Hill.

"Name, please?" A short guy holding a clipboard is checking people in at the door.

"Abby Barnes," I tell him, heaving from my run.

He marks my name off. "Just take a seat inside. They'll call your name when they're ready for you."

A quick scan of the theatre gallery leaves my palms sweaty and my throat uncomfortably dry. There must be a hundred people here, and at least two-thirds of them are girls, all of whom *look* like actors. Long scarves, vintage hats, funky boots.

I, meanwhile, am wearing running shorts and a sweatshirt with bleach stains on the sleeve. So much for my perfect audition outfit. Since *Metamorphoses* is a series of eleven vignettes from Greek mythology, my plan was to channel Aphrodite in understated Greek-chic. But the gauzy white dress I scored at Goodwill yesterday is still hanging on the back of my bedroom door, and I am in butt-huggers. A girl in gladiator sandals and a peasant blouse smirks as I pass. Butterflies swarm my stomach.

*Breathe, Abby. Just breathe.*

Actors get nervous before their auditions. It's perfectly natural and not something to freak out about. Jitters are just part of the process. Bret told me once that he still pukes before every one of his (then again, he hasn't actually *had* an audition since his first big movie). The fact that I'm anxious doesn't mean I'm going to choke.

*I'm totally going to choke.*

It's happened before. Sixth-grade play. My part was tiny: I had two lines. And on the night of the performance, I forgot them both. If Ms Ziffren hadn't made auditioning for *Arcadia* a mandatory part of our grade last autumn, I never would've set foot on a stage again. Everyone was shocked when she gave me the lead. We all expected Ilana—

My stomach squeezes. *Oh, Ilana.*

"I've been sitting here trying to figure out whether his balls are that colour," the voice beside me says. Its owner is sitting cross-legged in the seat next to mine, the latest issue of *US Weekly* balancing on her knee. Her jet-black hair is cropped boy short, and she's wearing black fishnets and combat boots under a flowery dress that looks like it belongs on someone's grandma.

I glance down at the magazine in her lap and see Bret smiling up at me. Despite the ubiquity of publications with his face on the cover, I haven't seen a picture of him in over a month. I made the mistake of Googling him the day after my birthday and spent the next four hours gorging on celebrity gossip and Nutella. Even though I was ambivalent about the experience while I was living it, it was hard to see pictures of my cast mates – especially Kirby, who was an unknown just like me before she was cast in *EA* and now is *everywhere* – and not feel a pang of regret for my old life.

"I mean, there's no way that tan is real, which means someone had to spray it on him," the girl next to me is saying. She holds up the magazine to give me a better view. "Can you imagine that conversation? 'Sir, please lift your junk so I can chemically enhance the shade of your nutskin.'" She laughs. "I'm Fiona, by the way," she adds, sticking out her hand. There's a tattoo of a leaf on the inside of her wrist.

"Abby," I say.

"So what other plays are you going out for?" Fiona asks, closing the magazine and slipping it into her bag. Just like that, from testicles to theatre.

"I only know about this one," I admit, feeling like a fraud.

"You need this, then," she says, pulling a printed blue flyer out of the bag. "It's a list of all the shows this term. And if you're serious about the acting thing, you should totally join the Dramat," she tells me.

"That's a drama club, right?" I should just tape a sign on my forehead that says I AM AN IMPOSTER.

"Abby Barnes?" a male voice calls.

"That's me," I say, standing up. *Don't be nervous, don't be nervous, don't be nervous.*

"Kill it!" Fiona whispers, making bullhorns with her fists.

Legs shaking, I climb the steps to the stage, joining a guy with man-boobs and wire-framed glasses. He wears an over-confident smile aimed squarely at the third row, where the director (an Indian guy wearing a bright pink Team Jolie T-shirt) and the producer (a hefty blonde in lavender barrettes) sit clutching coffee cups and iPhones.

"Ready when you are!" my stage mate bellows.

The director smiles serenely. "We are not deaf, and the characters we're casting aren't deaf," he says. "Inside voices are fine."

"Great!" Still shouting.

The director and producer exchange glances. Fiona gives me double thumbs-up.

"Anytime you're ready," the producer calls. "And again, no need to shout."

Unfortunately, the shouting is either his normal speaking voice or a stage affectation. Either way, he maintains it for the duration of the audition.

I do my best not to let him throw me off. He's reading the part of Erysichthon, which actually is quite fitting, given his size. Cursed by the gods with an insatiable hunger after cutting down a sacred tree, Erysichthon eventually eats himself.

When the director thanks us for our time midway through the scene, I resolve not to obsess. They're on a tight time schedule. It doesn't take that long to get a sense of someone's ability. Their impatience had nothing to do with my performance and everything to do with Shouty McShouterson's grating voice.

Or, I sucked.

"We'll post the cast list on the theatre door at seven," Lavender Barrettes tells us with a bland smile. "Thanks for auditioning."

"Thank *you*!" Shouty shouts.

There is no way I'm not a casualty of this disaster.

Fiona and I walk back to Old Campus together. "You were amazing," I tell her, meaning it. She went right after me and knocked it out of the park as Ceres, the goddess of the harvest. We stayed till five to watch the rest of the auditions, and none of the other girls were anywhere near as good.

"So were you!" Fiona enthuses.

"Ha. Hardly."

"I'm serious," she says. "You totally kept your cool, even as flecks of spit ricocheted off your face."

"Fiona!" a male voice calls. A hulk of a guy in a shirt that could double as a bedsheet is waving from across the courtyard. His forearm is the size of my thigh.

"Be right there!" Fiona shouts. "My boyfriend," she explains. "And yes, the size thing is an issue in bed. I once tried to straddle him and pulled my hamstring. Hey, you wanna eat with us? We're going to the Doodle for burgers."

The idea of making small talk with Fiona and her boyfriend while I mentally obsess over my audition is even less appealing than the thought of eating a greasy hamburger right now, both of which are infinitely more appealing than the mental image of her straddling him, now seared into my brain.

"I'd love to," I lie, "but I promised my roommate I'd have dinner with her."

"Right on," Fiona says. "Another time then. Here." She digs

through her bag and pulls out an index card with the lines from her audition scene written on the back. "My email," she says, scribbling it down on the blank side. "In case I don't see you later."

"We'll hang out!" I say enthusiastically, imagining us bonding over arty movies and obscure literary references.

When I get back to my room, there's a note from Marissa on the coffee table. *Dinner @ Commons w/ girls across the hall. Meet us!*

I drop my bag on the floor and plop down on the sofa, too revved to eat. What I *should* do is catch up on my philosophy reading. I have a midterm on Thursday, and I haven't even cracked open my course pack. It's remarkably easy to procrastinate when you're not sure you'll be around to take the test you're supposed to be preparing for.

I flip through the first section of the packet, a collection of essays on free will, predestination and foreknowledge, and scan over the sample questions at the end. *What did John Calvin mean when he said that God "did . . . freely and unchangeably ordain whatsoever comes to pass"?* Ugh. Philosophy of Theology seemed like a good choice when I was picking classes, but now the subject matter hits a little too close to home. *Did God know Ilana would get into that accident?*

*Did all this — the collision, the entanglement, the fact that I kept my memories — happen for some specific purpose, or is it all just a crazy cosmic fluke?*

I want to believe there's a reason behind it all, but it's hard to come up with one. If God had something he needed help with, I'm guessing he wouldn't pin his hopes on the girl who can barely remember to pray (except, of course, when she's studying for a super-hard theology midterm. *Please, God, don't let me fail*).

Feeling my eyes glaze over, I abandon my theology reading for DVRed episodes of *The Hills*. An episode and a half later, Marissa comes through the door, carrying a plastic cup full of dining hall frozen yoghurt, layered with Cap'n Crunch and Oreos. "I figured you might need a snack," she says, handing it to me.

"Thanks," I say, suddenly starving.

"How'd the audition go?" she asks as I shovel a heaping spoon of yoghurt into my mouth. She kicks off her shoes and plops down on the sofa next to me.

"Eh," I say between bites. "I couldn't tell. Hey, this is really tasty. Want some?"

She shakes her head. "No, thanks."

"HFCS?"

"The trifecta," she replies, making a face. "High fructose corn syrup, trans fats and aspartame."

"Mmmm. Yum." I take another massive bite.

"Hey, can I ask you something?"

"Sure," I reply, crunching on an Oreo.

"Does Caitlin like Ben?"

I stop mid-bite. My mind jumps to the night of my birthday dinner. In the version I remember, Caitlin was with Tyler, but she and Ben were acting awfully cosy at the table. Marissa didn't act like she noticed it, though. But things have changed now. Because of what happened in the parallel world yesterday, Caitlin was single on my birthday. Was the flirty banter between Ben and her even more intense? Marissa is still waiting for me to answer her question. When I don't right away, her face falls.

"She does, doesn't she? She likes him and you're afraid to tell me. I knew it."

"What? No! Caitlin does *not* like Ben," I assure her. After unwittingly ruining Craig's marriage that summer, Caitlin has adopted a zero-tolerance policy for guys who are taken. It's the reason she felt the need to wait four days after Tyler broke up with Ilana to go out with him. Relationship boundaries mean something different to her than they did before. Falling for someone who failed to mention his wife (at least, not until that wife called Caitlin, demanding to know why her husband had Caitlin's number in his phone) shattered something inside her, and there was nothing I could do to put it back together again. She wouldn't even let me try. After sobbing through the gory details the day after it happened, sick with sadness and regret, Caitlin made me promise never to bring it up again, and I haven't.

Marissa looks relieved. "I didn't think so, but I figured it couldn't hurt to ask."

"You have nothing to worry about," I say firmly. "Caitlin would never like a friend's boyfriend. Ever."

Marissa smiles. "Speaking of friend's boyfriends . . . how's Michael?"

"What did Ben tell you?" I demand.

"Nothing!" she insists. I raise my eyebrows, not buying it. "OK, fine. He said that Michael told him you guys were an official thing now. I was surprised you hadn't mentioned it to me, that's all."

"That's because it's news to me!" Things with Michael are going well, but I didn't think we'd reached label-level yet. "An 'official thing'? What does that even mean?"

"I'm pretty sure it means he's your boyfriend," Marissa replies.

"But we've only been on two real dates," I point out, then flinch. *Boat ride.* "I mean three."

"So?"

My phone rings. "See?" Marissa points at my phone, the screen lit up with Michael's name. "He's calling to see how the audition went. Total boyfriend move. Accept it, Ab. You're a couple." My heart flutters a little at the thought of it. What it would be like to let myself get attached, to stop worrying that a new reality will sweep him away. Maybe I'm overthinking it. In every relationship there's a risk that it'll end before you want it to. That's the nature of love.

*Love.* My heart flutters again.

"So? How'd it go?" Michael asks when I pick up.

"Eh."

"You realize that's not an actual response, right?"

"I'm not sure I *have* an actual response," I tell him. "The guy I read with shouted and spit his way through the scene. I'm not optimistic."

"Well, I'm sure you nailed it. What time are they posting the cast list?" he asks.

"Not till seven," I say

"It's seven-oh-five."

"Ah!" I fly off the sofa. "I'll call you back!" Without waiting for a response, I toss my phone on the table and dash out of the door.

"Good luck!" Marissa calls.

Although I didn't really expect to see my name on the cast list, I'm still bummed when it's not there. Not even an understudy role. The chatter of the crowd gathered around the theatre intensifies and blurs, the voices melding into one indecipherable chorus. The words on the cast list are hazy, as if I'm seeing them through warped glass. My eyes fall to the pavement and a drop of water appears there, barely visible in the weak yellow glow of the bulb above the stage door. I study the wet spot, resisting the bodies that push against me, vaguely wondering where it came from. Someone murmurs, "She's crying," and it's not until I touch my cheek that I know.

*Get it together, Abby. It's just a stupid play.*

But it isn't. Not to me. This was supposed to be my big identity-defining moment. My breakaway move. Getting cast in this particular play – one whose name means "transformation" – was supposed to be the beginning of *my* metamorphosis, from pathetic take-whatever-I'm-dealt Abby to powerful define-my-own-future Abby.

*It wasn't supposed to go like this.*

I had the exact same thought three months ago, the night I found out the studio had extended production a third time, eliminating any remaining chance of my starting university on time. I was sitting on a stoop on the backlot, watching two men change the facade of the building across the street from a bank to a bakery. I'd walked off set and just ended up there, on a street I'd seen in a hundred movies but never in real life. Of course, in the movies, you never see that the road just ends. It doesn't go anywhere or connect to anything. I remember thinking that as I watched the men across the street mount a giant cupcake over the building's fake door. *People think this road goes somewhere. They don't realize it's a dead end.* I hadn't realized I was crying until my phone rang. When I pressed it to my ear, the keys were damp.

The moment I heard my dad's voice, I started bawling. "This isn't the path," I kept saying, my words garbled with tears and snot. "It wasn't supposed to go like this." I remember feeling as though everything I had worked for had been snatched away. Dad saw things differently.

"Well-worn paths are boring," he said. "Embrace the detour."

*But how can you tell a detour from a dead end?*

The crowd around the theatre is beginning to thin. I blot my tearstained cheeks, grateful for the dark, and look around for Fiona, wanting to congratulate her on her part (cast as "Eurydice and Others", she essentially got the lead). But she must've come and gone.

As I'm making my way through the handful of people still gathered on the pavement, trying not to appear dejected, a male voice calls out to me.

"Abby!" The show's director is sitting on the theatre's main steps, away from the hullabaloo, smoking a cigarette. He waves me over.

"Hey," he says as I approach. "Great audition today."

Unsure if he's sincere, I respond with a vague "Thanks."

"I had ulterior motives for not casting you," he says then, his words punctuated by little puffs of smoke. "I want you to audition for the Spring Mainstage, and rehearsals overlap by a couple of weeks."

"Oh," I say, trying to process this. I don't really know what the "Spring Mainstage" is, but the words "main" and "stage" lead me to believe it's a big show. "Are you directing it?"

He shakes his head. "I'll be busy with this one. But you'd be perfect for the part of Thomasina."

"As in Coverly?"

He smiles. "You know the play."

I'm too rattled by the coincidence to form a coherent response.

"So I was right about your being perfect for it," he says. "Auditions are the week before Thanksgiving. I'll tell the director to look out for you." He drops his cigarette and stamps it out. "Have a good one," he says, then slips around the corner of the building, disappearing into the shadows.

"Thanks," I say, even though he's not around to hear it. Then I raise my eyes to the sky and say it again.

*Arcadia.* Of all the plays he could've suggested, he picked that one. The play that changed my life. A story about the connection between past and present, order and chaos, fate and free will.

*You'd be perfect for the part of Thomasina.*

A young girl who believed that everything – including the future – could be reduced to an equation.

Maybe this is part of the formula.

# 8
# (there)

## THURSDAY, 30 OCTOBER, 2008
## (THE DAY BEFORE HALLOWEEN)

"Ugh, hurry up!" I shout at the red brake lights in front of me. Of course, the day I have to be at school super early, there's a torrential downpour. I left my house six minutes ago, and I still haven't made it through the first intersection. The traffic lights must be out. Up ahead, lightning zigzags across the sky. I brace for the thunderclap, but still jump when it comes a few seconds later.

The clock on the dash clicks from 7.16 to 7.17. *Crap.* Dr Mann's review session started two minutes ago. With our mid-term exam just over five hours away, this is my last chance to get a handle on the two concepts I still don't understand before I have to write about them. I accelerate, riding the bumper of the black Toyota in front of me, willing its driver to go faster.

"C'mon, c'mon, c'mon—"

The Toyota stops short and I slam on my brakes to avoid it.

My bag flies into the dashboard, spilling its contents on to the passenger-side floor. The car behind me leans on its horn.

And . . . standstill. Again.

"Could this day be any crappier?" I mutter, then instantly feel guilty for it. Yes, this day could be much crappier. Ilana could still be in a coma. I could be the one in that hospital bed surrounded by machines, my face swollen and bruised. And I'm bitching about a little traffic?

The first three days after the accident were the worst. The doctors weren't sure Ilana would ever wake up, and they warned that even if she did, there was a good chance she'd spend the rest of her life in a permanent vegetative state (a phrase I made the mistake of Googling). Yet despite the scary medical speak, the idea that Ilana might not be Ilana any more just wouldn't compute. I kept waiting for her to saunter into the waiting room and make some snide remark about my outfit. *She was fine at the party,* I kept thinking. *She was fine, she was fine.* She was fine until she came around that curve on Providence Road at the exact moment a speeding pickup truck crossed into her lane.

When she squeezed a nurse's hand on day four, the crowd gathered in the waiting room cheered. I overheard her mom telling Ms Ziffren that she never knew Ilana had so many friends. I went to the bathroom and threw up. We aren't her friends. The four girls huddled in the corner wearing pink rubber "Awaken Ilana" bracelets are her friends. The rest of us are spectators to a disaster we can't comprehend.

*Thank God she woke up.* Exactly a week ago, on day twelve. She couldn't have any visitors for a few more days after that, but as of yesterday, non-family members are allowed between four

215

and six o'clock. I was the first person in. Ilana took one look at the flowers I'd brought and pronounced them "grocery-store ghetto". I was elated.

But then she started asking me how long I'd been there. Every ten minutes, as if she hadn't already asked. Her doctor told me that was normal for someone with hemorrhagic damage to her medial temporal lobe. I just looked at him. Nothing about this was normal.

The Toyota in front of me starts moving again, and I finally get through the first traffic light, which, as I suspected, is dark. After that, the pace picks up.

So does the intensity of the storm. By the time I reach the annex car park, the rain is coming down in sheets. As I'm slowing for the turn, another bolt of lightning rips across the sky, this time with a crack of accompanying thunder. The sky is the colour of a bruise.

I flick off my turn signal and speed up again. There's no way I'm walking all the way from the annex in this. I make a left into the senior car park, gunning it for the front row. Right by the side door there's spot with a RESERVED – HANDICAPPED sign, where I parked for a few days after I hurt my foot. I used to think that you'd get towed if you parked there, but now I know that it's not an official handicapped space. Those are in the visitor's car park on the other side of the building. The one in the senior car park isn't blue and doesn't have a wheelchair painted on the asphalt, which is good, because no one who parks there is actually handicapped. Any athlete with an injury is eligible for a permit to park there. But handicapped privileges are not a first-come-first-serve situation – mine were revoked when Gregg Nash tore his ACL in the Homecoming game last weekend. Star kicker trumps former cross-country runner. The fact that Gregg's regular parking spot is four spaces away from the handicapped spot appears not to have factored into the analysis.

"Thank you, Gregg," I say as I pull into his regularly assigned space. The car park is only about a quarter full, which isn't surprising, since school doesn't start for another forty-five minutes. Caitlin's here, of course (she comes early every day to get ahead on her lab assignments), and Josh's Jeep is in its regular spot. I don't know whether it should be encouraging or terrifying that he came early for the review. If he needs help with the material, then I'm a lost cause.

When the term started, I fantasized about the two of us studying for this test together, laughing as we quizzed each other with home-made flash cards. But that scenario would require us to be dating, or at the very least, to be friends. Josh and I are neither. We're still cordial, but I'm pretty sure he's dating Megan now, and apparently that means our permitted interactions are limited to polite smiles and the occasional wave. Not that I've had time for lengthy conversations. The last two weeks have been a series of identical days: home to school to crew practice to the waiting room at Piedmont Hospital, then back home again. Sleep. Then repeat. I still catch myself thinking about Josh – every time I see him or my astronomy textbook or the stars on my ceiling – but I've stopped pining over him.

OK, I'm pining less.

Lightning flashes, followed by another crack of thunder. I see a girl from my class battling with her umbrella as she darts across the front garden towards the main entrance, splashing mud with each soggy step. If I'm going to this study session, I should go now.

Rucksack over my head, I make a mad dash for the side door. Thankfully, it's unlocked. I take a moment to collect myself before continuing down the hall to our classroom, peeling off my raincoat and fluffing my damp hair. The corridor is still semi-dark, and most of the classrooms along it are completely black behind their closed doors. Only our room and the chem lab look inhabited. Dr Mann's door is swung open, light streaming out from inside along with the distinct sound of our teacher's voice.

I'm not sure why I do it. Maybe because there's a light on inside. Maybe because the door is slightly ajar. But as I'm passing the chem lab, I glance in through the vertical window and see them. Caitlin is talking. Josh is smiling. Alone in a half-lit room.

My breath catches in my throat, even though I know instinctively that it's not what it looks like. There's nothing going on between them. Nothing scandalous, anyway. They're bent over a piece of paper, intently discussing its contents. My mind calmly considers the possible reasons for this early morning meeting. They're doing homework. (*For what class? They're not in any together.*) Caitlin is helping Josh study for our midterm. (*Why didn't she offer to help me?*) They're partners on some extracurricular science project. (*Like what? And why hasn't either of them mentioned it?*)

None of these explanations makes sense. And none of them makes me feel better about the fact that if I hadn't come in through that side door, I never would've discovered what Caitlin obviously doesn't want me to know: she's been hanging out with Josh.

Even if it's totally innocuous, why hasn't she told me?

And why is Josh smiling at her the same way he smiled at Albireo, the breath-catching blue and gold double star at the tip of Cygnus's beak? (Annoyingly, my test-prepped brain now proceeds to rattle off the facts I've learned about Albireo in the weeks since Josh pointed it out to me, like an idiot savant on amphetamines: *three hundred and eighty light-years away from the Earth. Thought to be a gravitationally bound binary system with an orbital period of seventy-five thousand years. Loved by astronomers for its striking beauty, which is easily seen at low telescopic power.*)

Move. Away. From the door.

Part of me wants them to see me, because it'll force them to explain what they're doing. But do they owe me an explanation? Josh has made it clear that he's not interested in me, and even if he were her type (which he isn't), Caitlin would never go after a guy I liked.

Then again, we've barely spoken to each other since the accident. We talk at lunch, of course, but not at all after school. I've been blaming crew practice, university applications, and a fictitious new mobile phone plan with fewer minutes, but the truth is I'm hiding from her. If Caitlin knew how much time I've been spending at the hospital, she'd want to know why, and I can't tell her why. Mostly because I know how she'd react if she ever found out what I did, but also because I can't bear to say the words aloud. The refrain in my head is excruciating enough; speaking it would put me over the edge. *If I hadn't, Ilana wouldn't. If I hadn't, Ilana wouldn't.*

I pull myself away from the door and hurry down the hall to G103, where a dozen kids from class are gathered, listening to Dr Mann describe the phases of stellar evolution. Most of them look as panicked about our test as I feel. Megan is sitting by the window that overlooks the car park lot, her yellow rucksack propped up in the vacant seat beside her. Saving it for someone. She keeps glancing outside at Josh's Jeep, no doubt wondering where its owner is. She obviously doesn't know he's with Caitlin, either. *So they're hiding it from both of us.*

I slide into an empty seat and pull out my notebook, resolving to focus on nothing but astronomy for the next twenty minutes.

"We have time for one more question," I hear Dr Mann say.

My head snaps up. *Already?* I've absorbed about ten per cent of what's been said since I arrived and written all of three sentences in my notebook. The rest of the page is covered with doodled stars and lines connecting them.

My hand shoots up. "Hubble's law," I call out, before he can call on someone else. Dr Mann meets my gaze and nods for me to continue. "I understand that the universe is receding from us," I say, "and that we're receding from the rest of the universe at the same rate . . . right?" While I said I understood this, the truth is I'm only half-sure of what I just said. But Dr Mann nods. "But how is that possible? Everything can't be receding from everything, can it?"

"Ah," Dr Mann replies. "Excellent question. And one I came prepared for." He roots around in his pocket, coins clanging against one another, and pulls out a red balloon. "Imagine that this is our universe," he says, holding up the balloon. It's covered in black marker dots. "And that each of these dots is a cluster of galaxies within our universe." I hear Megan giggle. There's a half-eaten piece of butterscotch candy stuck to the old man's sleeve. "Hubble's law says that the distances between these clusters are continuously increasing and, most significantly, that our universe is itself expanding." Dr Mann puts the balloon to his lips and begins to inflate it. As the balloon fills with air, the dots get further and further from each other. The butterscotch candy dangles from a strand of tweed.

"You said *our* universe." Josh's voice catches me by surprise. I turn to see him standing in the doorway, holding his notebook, a folded piece of paper on top.

Dr Mann stops blowing and smiles.

"Ah. An observant listener." The old man's smile is enigmatic. "Ms Barnes asked about Hubble's law, which refers to the behaviour of galaxies within our universe."

"Wait, there's more than one universe?" I ask, confused again.

"Of course," Dr Mann says, as though this is the most obvious thing in the world. "Haven't you seen *Star Trek*?" There's a smattering of laughter from the class. Dr Mann ties off the balloon and volleys it to me. It lands in the centre of my desk. "But let's focus on this one for today," he says, just before the bell rings. "Our universe has enough troubles of its own." He says something else after that, but the shrill sound of the morning bell drowns it out.

I catch up with Tyler on D Hall. Except for a short bout of hysteria the night of the accident, Tyler has been his steady, pragmatic self since Ilana got hurt. Shaken, but not completely derailed by what happened to her. And why should he? He didn't orchestrate the chain of events that put Ilana in that truck's path. It was what I said to him that lit the fuse.

"You look like crap," Tyler says when he sees me. "When was the last time you washed your hair?"

"Shut it. I've been in study mode." Tyler doesn't know how much time I've been spending at the hospital, either, or how little sleep I've been getting since the accident. "Hey, has Caitlin said anything to you about Josh?"

"Your Josh?"

"He's not my Josh any more," I tell him. *Because he's Caitlin's?* It's just a tiny kernel of doubt, but it's there, lodged in my brain. *Does she like him? Does he like her?*

"What happened?" Tyler asks.

I shrug. "He wasn't interested."

He rolls his eyes. "Are you an idiot? Wait, don't answer that. Of course you are. Barnes, the guy got all googly-eyed every time he looked at you."

"He did not."

"Yeah, because I would make that up."

"If he was so interested, why didn't he ever do anything about it?" I challenge.

Tyler stops walking and looks at me. "Why are girls so ridiculous?"

"What's so ridiculous about wanting a guy to make the first move? And not some subtle, maybe-you-like-me-maybe-you're-just-being-nice crap, either. What happened to the grand romantic gesture?"

Tyler considers this. "How grand are we talking here?"

"It's too late," I tell him. "He's with Megan now." *That's not what it looked like this morning.* The kernel becomes an acorn of envy and fear.

"Hot Megan?"

I glare at him.

"I meant, 'Megan who looks like a troll?'"

"Nice try," I say, punching him in the arm. "I'll see you later. Gorin hates when I'm late." I pick up the pace to get to class. "Oh," I say, stopping again. "Don't tell Caitlin I asked about Josh," I tell him.

"I'll add it to the list," he says.

I'm so preoccupied with the Caitlin/Josh mystery that I forget about my looming midterm until the lunch bell rings. My plan to sneak my lunch bag into the library for a last-minute cram session is thwarted by the throngs of kids with the same idea. All those wild-eyed people frantically turning pages threaten to throw me off my game, so I opt to study in the cafeteria instead. Caitlin and Tyler are at our regular table, with a couple of guys from the golf team. I slide in next to Caitlin and open my textbook. *WHAT WERE YOU AND JOSH DOING THIS MORNING?* my brain screams.

"I saw your car here early," I say casually, keeping my eyes on the page. Beside me, Caitlin bristles.

"Could you move your book, please?" she snaps. "It's digging into my arm."

"Sorry. Jeez." I scoot my book over and try again. "So, were you—?"

"I thought you were going to study in the library," Caitlin says, not looking at me.

"I tried. But everyone else from my class was in there. Their stress was stressing me out."

"Your stress is stressing *me* out," Tyler says, not looking up. "I'm in the middle of a very important word battle here." He and Efrain are sitting side by side, playing Words with Friends on their phones.

"Fine," I reply, shutting my book. "I'll go back to the library."

"And . . . BAM. Toenail. Seven letters *and* a triple word." Tyler waves his phone in Caitlin's face. "Tell me I'm not a Scrabble genius."

"You're not a Scrabble genius," Caitlin parrots. Something across the room catches my eye. A cheerleader, doing some sort of signal with her hands. She's looking right at our table. I see Tyler see it, too.

"Oh, yeah?" Tyler's voice is grander than it was a second ago. More dramatic. I see him glance in my direction, hesitating for a moment before continuing. "Let's take a poll," he says then, and stands up. When he does, his voice gets even louder. "Listen up, y'all!" he shouts as he mounts his chair. "I only have a few seconds before some nice, hardworking faculty member will force me to get down." There's a ripple of laughter as the cafeteria gets quiet. Tyler steps from his chair on to the blue-and-white-checked table, crunching a half-eaten chocolate chip cookie with his heel. *What is he doing?*

"Raise your hand if you've played Words with Friends with me," Tyler calls to the crowd. At least thirty people raise their hands. "Keep your hand up if you've ever beat me!" The hands go down. "I think that qualifies me as a Scrabble genius, don't you?" There's some cheering and scattered applause. "Well, my

224

friend Caitlin here disagrees," Tyler shouts. Jovial boos fill the room. Caitlin leans back in her chair, smiling serenely, waiting for the punch line. Through the walls, I hear a rumble of thunder from outside.

My eyes search Tyler's face. *Where is he going with this?* Ms Kirkland, our ornery deputy head, hurries towards our table. I scoot my chair forward and make room for her, willing the old broad to hurry.

"How am I gonna prove her wrong, you ask? With a *fifteen-*letter word." Tyler has the crowd captivated, expecting the joke. He looks over at a table of cheerleaders outfitted in blue and orange for today's pep rally. "Can I get an *I*!" he calls to them.

"I!" they shout, clearly prepared for this.

"L!"

"L!" comes the echo. Pom-poms materialize. A couple of the girls are standing on their chairs, making Ls with their arms.

"O!"

"O!" Arms go overhead. More of them are standing on their chairs. Ms Kirkland yells for them to get down, but everyone ignores her.

On the "V", Tyler's voice breaks just a little.

*There's no way he'd—*

He ploughs through the next eleven letters, not waiting for his echo.

"– E-Y-O-U-C-A-I-T-L-I-N!"

*Oh, yes. He would.*

Caitlin's eyes widen. Her smile disappears.

*This is a disaster.*

"What's that spell?" Tyler shouts. The crowd has reached fever pitch, hooting and hollering and banging their fists on the tables. Tyler raises his hands above his head, ready for the grand finale.

"I! LOVE! YOU! C—"

Before he can finish, I grab his leg and dig my fingernails into his calf.

"Ouch!" he yelps. "What was that for?"

"What are you doing?" I hiss, sharply aware of the fact that everyone in the cafeteria is staring at us.

"What?" Tyler replies. "You said she wanted a grand gesture." His eyes go from me to Caitlin. He sees immediately that this has not gone how he hoped.

"What did he mean?" Caitlin's eyes are boring into the side of my face, while mine are pinned on Tyler, willing him to jump in and help me out. I'm not sure how exactly he could fix things at this juncture, but some effort would be nice. "Abby," Caitlin repeats, her voice like ice. "What did Tyler mean?"

The cafeteria is completely silent. Ms Kirkland just stands there, clearly at a loss for her next move.

"Can I talk to you in the hall?" I ask meekly.

"No. Answer the question. Why did Tyler say, 'You said she wanted a grand gesture'?"

"I was talking about Josh," I tell her, keeping my voice down. "What he would've done if he'd been interested in me. Tyler must've taken it the wrong way." I shoot a how-could-you-be-so-stupid look at Tyler, who's still standing on the table.

"That's all you said?" Caitlin asks. In the fluorescent lights, the skin under her eyes looks greenish grey, the way it looked at the Young Leaders brunch the morning after prom last year, after we stayed up all night watching *Sex and the City* reruns and eating

226

Twizzlers while our dates were passed out in garden chairs by her neighbour's pool. She's wearing concealer now, just like she did that morning, which she must've borrowed from her mom because Caitlin doesn't own any. There's a dot of skin-coloured goo stuck to the inside corner of her left eye. "Abby."

For a split second, I consider saying yes. *Yes, that's all I said.* Omitting the rest of it, the worst of it. Feigning ignorance and innocence. *No, Caitlin, I have no idea why Tyler would've told you he loved you in front of two hundred people. I was as surprised as you were.* I know Tyler would back me up, because that's the kind of friend he is. *What kind of friend am I?*

"I told him you liked him," I say quietly.

Caitlin doesn't react, as if what I've said didn't compute. "What?" she says evenly.

"I told him you had feelings for him but didn't want him to know." I close my eyes as I'm saying it, bracing for her reaction. There isn't one. When I open my eyes, Caitlin is walking away.

"Caitlin!" She ignores me. "Caitlin!" I yell, no longer caring who hears me (which is good, since everyone can). "Can I just explain—"

Caitlin spins on her heels. "Explain what?" she shouts. Her eyes are blue icicles. "How mind-blowingly self-absorbed you are? How it's all about Abby, all the time?"

"So she doesn't like me?" Tyler asks, sounding about as confused as I feel. *Caitlin thinks I'm self-absorbed?*

"This didn't have anything to do with me," I protest. "I just thought—" She doesn't let me finish.

"God, Abby, you're such a cliché," Caitlin spits. "*Ohmigod!*" She lifts her voice, mocking me. "*Do you think Astronomy Boy likes me? Ohmigod, I can't run cross-country any more! Ohmigod, what about my precious Plan!*" Behind me, someone giggles. "God forbid some stupid detail doesn't turn out exactly the way you planned it. How would you ever recover?" Her words drip with sarcasm and disdain. "You want to know why Josh wasn't interested in you?" Caitlin asks coldly, her voice authoritative, like she knows something I don't. "It's not a big mystery, Abby. You're just too self-involved to see it." She looks me in the eye then, her gaze like steel. "You're more work than you're worth."

Something in me snaps.

"Ohhhh. So we're talking about who's *easier*?" I fire back. "I guess you win then."

"Excuse me?"

I raise my voice and address our audience. "You'd think that amazing brain of yours might've picked up on the fact that he was married," I say derisively. The cheerleaders look at one another with arched eyebrows, wondering what I mean, but of course Caitlin and I are the only ones who know about Craig. The thing she's most ashamed of. Her greatest regret. "But I guess you just couldn't be bothered to worry about that stupid detail?"

Caitlin's mouth drops.

It's as if the room expands in that moment, like the surface of Dr Mann's red balloon. My stomach clenches and unclenches like a fist.

*What did I just do?*

"You're a bitch," Caitlin says, her voice hollow. "A self-absorbed bitch." She doesn't spin on her heels the way I would. She simply turns and walks out of the cafeteria. Tyler steps down off the table and follows her out. Heads turn, watching them go, then the attention snaps back to me. It occurs to me that I should do something – blink, sit down, leave the cafeteria – but the effort of those actions feels overwhelming. I can't move.

The bell rings and the gawkers disperse. Efrain appears in front of me, holding my bag. "C'mon," he says, his voice startling me out of my stupor. "I'll walk you to class." I nod weakly and follow him out.

Efrain steers me to my classroom and leaves me at the door. "Good luck on your mid term," he says, holding out my bag. I choke on a laugh. *I'm supposed to take an astronomy test right now?* Poor Efrain just stands there, not sure what to do. There are flecks of dried hair gel on his ear.

The warning bell rings.

"Hey, guys." Josh is walking up, pencil tucked behind his ear as always. When he sees the look on my face, his smile fades. "What's going on?"

"Caitlin and Abby just had a blowout in the cafeteria," Efrain explains, keeping his voice low. "I gotta go," he tells us. "I can't be late for bio." He hands Josh my bag, pats me awkwardly on the shoulder, then takes off down the hall.

"We should probably get in there," Josh says. His voice sounds distant, like he's talking from behind a pane of glass. I stare vacantly into the classroom. Everyone is in last-minute cram mode, flipping frantically through their notes. All except Megan. Her eyes are glued on us. When she sees me see her, she quickly looks away. *You want to know why Josh wasn't interested?* Caitlin's words slice through me. *You're more work than you're worth!* My throat tightens.

229

"Abby?"

"Yeah, OK." I force myself to put one foot in front of the other, shuffling towards my desk, when what I really want to do is run screaming from this room. From my life. From myself.

I reach my seat. I sit. Every motion mechanical. Every gesture forced.

I tell myself to focus. I tell myself to stop thinking about the fight and start thinking about this test. A test that's worth forty per cent of our grade. A grade that could single-handedly destroy my GPA.

This test. My grade. The weight of their importance is barrelling down on me, crushing me, overpowered only by the roar in my brain. A sound like static is screaming in my ears, drowning everything else out.

I can't breathe.

I can't think.

The roar intensifies.

"Astronomers!" Dr Mann announces as he comes through the door, carrying a stack of blue exam booklets. "The time has come to see what we've learned!" Grinning like he's handing out candy, Dr Mann begins to distribute the test booklets.

*I can't do this.* I squeeze my eyes shut, forcing myself to take slow, deep breaths. In. Out. In. Out. *Just breathe, Abby.* I try to envision myself calmly taking this test, steadily answering multiple-choice questions and filling in blanks. I try to recall the things I know. But all I see is Caitlin's face. The hurt. The anger. The disgust. All I hear is static.

A couple of years ago, two days before Christmas, a commuter plane crashed just off the coast of Charleston, killing fifty people onboard. Knowing that Caitlin and her parents were on their way to Charleston, I panicked. When she didn't answer her mobile, I assumed the worst. My best friend was dead. I spent the next three hours in the fetal position on my bedroom floor, unable to imagine my life without Caitlin. I'm close with my parents, but Caitlin is the sister I never had. The voice I trust more than my own. It wasn't just that I had lost my best friend; I'd lost a part of myself. Or so I thought. At five o'clock, Caitlin finally called me back. They'd got on an earlier flight, and Caitlin had taken her grandmother out for the afternoon, without her mobile phone. I still remember how it felt to hear her voice. The relief, the gratitude, the joy. The sense of wholeness I experienced in that moment, the profound sense of peace. I also remember how I felt before she called, when I thought I had lost her for ever. It's how I feel right now.

"OK, class." Dr Mann's voice sounds far away. "You may begin."

I look down at the typewritten test booklet, but the words might as well be in German. Caitlin's voice echoes in my head. *You're a self-absorbed bitch.* I earned the bitch comment by bringing up Craig in front of a room full of people, but where'd the self-absorbed part come from? *You're too self-involved to see it.* Is that really what she thinks?

My classmates scribble furiously as the wall clock counts minutes with an audible tick. I blink repeatedly, but everything is a blur. The page. My thoughts.

The bell rings.

I haven't written a word.

*There goes my future.* The thought doesn't faze me. Like a

robot, I write my name on my exam and pass it forward, where Dr Mann stands collecting them. Not wanting to be anywhere near here when he notices that mine is blank, I'm out of the door before he dismisses us, headed straight for the car park. I can't go to newspaper right now. I have to get out of here. If I go quickly, no one will notice. I'll probably get written up for skipping, but I'll deal with that next week. Say I got sick or something. As long as no one sees me leave—

"Abby!" My hand is on the side door when he calls out to me. It's Josh, of course, looking all gentlemanly and concerned. I let go of the handle as he walks towards me. So much for a stealthy exit.

"How'd it go?" he asks.

"I left it blank," I say. Then, inexplicably, I laugh. It's a joyless, bitter sound.

"Do you want to talk about what happened at lunch?" Josh asks. His brown eyes search mine, as if the answers to other, unspoken questions are hidden there. I don't answer, and he doesn't press me. The warning bell rings.

"Am I too much work?" It comes out ragged and rough, and the second the words are out, I want to take them back. "Never mind," I say quickly, looking away, trying to swallow the tears that went surging up from my chest as the words fell out. Josh catches my hand in his.

"Anything worth having takes work, Abby," he says softly. The noise in my head quiets as my eyes meet his. My next breath is easier.

"Do you want to maybe hang out after practice today?" I hear myself ask. "Maybe see a movie or something?"

"Oh, I, uh. . ." Josh breaks our gaze, glancing down the hall to where Megan is trying to look busy at her locker. Is it that transparent when I do it? *Note to self: when feigning preoccupation with bag packing, don't put your textbook in your rucksack, then take it back out again.* "I'm supposed to hang out with Megan," he says apologetically.

"Of course," I say, trying to sound breezy. "Duh."

"Maybe the three of us could do something?" he offers.

"Nah, that's OK," I tell him, practically pushing him out of the way. "I'll probably be working all night tonight anyway. The November issue of the *Oracle* comes out next week, so things are crazy. See you at practice!" I wiggle my fingers at Megan as I pass her (my attempt at a friendly, I-didn't-just-ask-your-boyfriend-out wave), then bolt for the main hall.

By the time I get there, my left foot is throbbing. The punctures healed without infection, but I'm still not supposed to put my full weight on it. I slow to a hobble. *So much for ditching sixth.* Now that I'm on the main hall, I won't be able to make it out of the building before the bell rings.

With next Wednesday's deadline looming, the editorial staff is working in overdrive to get everything done, making me feel guilty for almost bailing on them. Sixth period passes quickly as I field questions and review layouts, all while trying not to think about the fact that in the span of the past ninety minutes, I have (a) lost my two best friends, (b) blown my astronomy exam, and (c) asked out a guy who is dating someone else. How quickly a person can implode.

I leave newspaper a few minutes before the bell with the excuse of needing to stop by Ms DeWitt's office before the end of the day. Instead, I go straight to my car. Caitlin's Jetta is already gone.

Scattered leaves and wet pavements are the only signs of this morning's storm. Now the sky is dotted with white puffy clouds. I squint as the sun beats through my windscreen, irritated by its persistent brightness.

When I get to the boathouse, I put myself to work checking the nuts on the outriggers and greasing the seat slides while the rest of the team trickles into practice. Once out on the water, I discover a major advantage crew has over cross-country: the distraction factor. When you're running, all you can do is think. When you're coxing, you don't have *time* to think. Since I'm the one in charge, I have no choice but to give the guys my full attention as I steer the B boat down the river and back, grateful that Megan and Josh are fifty yards away in the A. Before I know it, the sun is fading, and Coach is blowing his whistle for us to return to the dock. *Thank God this day is almost over.*

As I pull into the garage, I can see my mom through the kitchen window, peeling carrots over the sink. The last thing I want to do is rehash the fight. Or the exam. Or listen to my mom reassure me that everything will be OK. A positive outlook is her default response to adversity, and right now, I'm content with keeping my bleak one.

"Hey! How was the exam?" she asks the instant I open the back door.

"Horrible."

Her face falls. "That bad?"

"Worse." I move towards the back stairs before she can ask whether I want to talk about it. "I'll be in my room."

"Your SAT score came," she calls after me, sounding hesitant. "Envelope is on the table."

I turn and look. A single white envelope stands out against the dark cherry of the kitchen table. I walk back to the table, pick it up and turn it over in my hands. "I wasn't expecting this till Monday," I say.

"I know."

We both stare at the envelope, at the small white rectangle with my name on it. "I don't want to open it now, OK?"

Mom nods. "Just wanted you to know it was here, honey."

I carry the envelope with me upstairs. What a fitting finale to what might actually be the worst day of my life. It seems crazy that a person's future could depend so heavily on one number. But without a solid SAT score, the top schools won't even look at you. Unless, of course, you give them one of those "this is why I suck at standardized tests" essays to explain it all away, but that generally requires having or feigning some sort of learning disability. For a second, I'm envious of Caitlin.

Envelope still in my hands, I kick off my shoes and climb under the covers. I lay the envelope beside me and stare up at my star-covered ceiling. My plan was to recreate Cygnus, but what I ended up with looks less like a diving swan and more like a deformed cross. I draw my left knee up to my chest, feeling for the scar on my foot. So much has changed since that night. I'm not running cross-country any more, Josh and I barely talk, and as of four hours ago, I no longer have a best friend.

A lot can happen in five weeks.

*You're a self-absorbed bitch.*

A lot can happen in five minutes.

235

I sigh and roll over on to my side, curling my body around the envelope. The contents of this innocuous-looking rectangle will determine my future. For a girl whose practice scores are all over the map, that's terrifying. If my score isn't within the median, I'm screwed. Panic starts to creep in. It sprouts in my stomach, then spreads to my chest. I've wanted to go to Northwestern since Career Day in seventh grade, when Brandon Grant's mom, a features reporter for the *Atlanta Journal-Constitution*, came and spoke to our English class. Ava Wynn-Grant. She was so stylish in her navy trousers and cropped blazer, and so articulate. I literally wanted to be her. She was a journalist, so I wanted to be a journalist. She went to Northwestern, so I wanted to go to Northwestern. And every scholastic decision I've made since then has been with those two goals in mind.

I wonder what path I'd be on if Ava Wynn-Grant had been an attorney or an actress instead.

Heart pounding, I slide my finger under the envelope's white flap and slowly inch it open. When I see how I did – not a Caitlin-level performance, but better than I was expecting – my eyes well up with tears. The only person I want to share this with isn't speaking to me. I tuck the envelope under my pillow and lay back against it, squeezing my eyes shut. The noise is still there, that sharp static from this afternoon. I give in to it, letting it drown everything out.

There's a soft knock at my door. When I open my eyes, my dad is standing in the doorway, holding two bowls of ice cream. What daylight was left is now gone.

"What are you doing home from work?" I ask, rubbing my eyes.

"It's seven thirty already," he replies, nodding at the clock on my nightstand. "I brought you a snack," he adds, holding up one of the bowls. "Cookies 'n cream."

I manage a smile, scooting over to make room for him on the bed. "Did Mom authorize this?"

"Your mother is busy making some very complicated-looking chicken dish that will likely not be ready for consumption until next Saturday. I figured we needed something to tide us over." He sits down next to me and hands me a bowl. We eat in silence for a few minutes, both flipping our spoons over before each bite so the ice cream lands squarely on our tongues.

"I heard you had a rough day," he says, pecking at a big chunk of Oreo with his spoon. "Wanna talk about it?"

"Caitlin and I got in a fight."

He looks surprised. "That's not like you two."

"I know."

"What happened?" he asks me.

"I told Tyler that Caitlin liked him. Things just kind of snowballed from there."

"I take it she didn't want you to?"

"Worse," I say miserably. "It's not even true. And I knew that, but at the same time, I had this feeling that maybe she liked him, even though she didn't know it yet." I shake my head, appalled at my own carelessness. "I'm an idiot."

"Maybe not your finest moment," Dad concedes, "but it certainly doesn't sound unforgivable."

"Caitlin was really upset," I tell him. "She said some pretty awful things to me." My eyes fill with fresh tears.

"Well, if I know Caitlin, there's something else going on." He pauses, then adds, gently, "And if I know *you*, dear daughter of

237

mine, that isn't how the fight ended. So what'd you say that you now wish you hadn't?"

"Am I that predictable?"

"Predictable? Not in the least. Prone to impulsive emotional outbursts?" He smiles. "On occasion."

I look down at my striped comforter. There's a black pen stain next to my big toe. "I was so mean," I whisper. "She'll never forgive me." A tear begins its descent down my cheek.

"You won't know that until you apologize," he says.

I want to tell him he doesn't know Caitlin as well as I do, but instead I just nod. The tear drips from my chin to the duvet, forming a perfect wet circle.

"Well, I better go check on your mother," Dad says then, standing up. "Make sure she hasn't ruined any more appliances." I giggle through my tears. Two weeks ago she killed our blender trying to puree a duck.

"I'll be down in a few minutes," I say. He nods, then bends to kiss my forehead.

"You two will work this out," he whispers. "It might take some time, but you will." I nod, blinking back the tears hovering on the edge of my eyelids. Dad straightens back up and heads for the door.

My mobile phone is lying next to me on the bed. I don't really expect her to answer, but I dial Caitlin's number anyway. It goes straight to voicemail. I try Tyler next. To my surprise, he picks up on the second ring.

"I get it," he says after my profuse apology. "You're you."

"What does that mean?" I prepare to be offended.

"You thought you could micromanage this the way you try to

238

micromanage everything else," he replies. "You thought we'd make a good couple, and you figured you could make it happen. But you can't plan a relationship like you've planned your career path, Barnes. Doesn't work that way." I hear him smile. "But good try."

"I shouldn't have lied," I say. "If I'd just kept my mouth shut, you wouldn't have broken up with Ilana, and—"

"Hold up there, chief. I'd been planning to end things with Ilana all week. Why do you think I got so blitzed at the gala?"

A thin layer of guilt melts away.

"So you don't hate me?"

"I don't hate you. I might be planning a very public humiliation as payback, but I don't hate you."

I smile too now, relieved that I haven't lost both of them. "Have you talked to Caitlin?" I ask then.

"Only for a minute," he says. "She had a meeting with DeWitt right after lunch."

"What for?"

"Dunno," he says. "She wasn't exactly chatty." His attempt to sound casual about it makes it worse. Behind the words, his voice is heavy with disappointment.

"I really am sorry I messed things up for you guys," I say for the fifth time. Downstairs, our home phone line rings.

"Not all's lost," Tyler says. "Elmo told me afterwards that if Caitlin didn't want me, she'd take me." "Elmo" is Eleanor Morgan, Andy Morgan's little sister, a perma-bubbly redhead who I suspect might sleep in her cheerleading uniform.

Before I can remind him that Andy would kick his ass if he ever even *attempted* to hook up with Eleanor, there's a knock on my bedroom door. My dad is back.

"Phone's for you," he tells me. "It's your astronomy teacher."

"Really?" Dad nods. He sets the cordless phone on my dresser and disappears again. "Call you later," I tell Tyler.

"Tell Dr Pepper I said hello."

We hang up, and I reach for the cordless. I don't know what I'm going to tell Dr Mann when he asks why my test was blank. The truth, I guess.

"Hello?"

"Ms Barnes! Gustav Mann here." I smile. As if, with that accent, it could be anyone else.

"Hi, Dr Mann. How are you?"

"A little concerned, my dear. What happened this afternoon?"

"I got in a fight with my best friend right before the test," I say, aware of how juvenile it sounds. But if Dr Mann thinks it's childish, he doesn't let on. "I was prepared for our exam, but I just couldn't. . ." My voice wobbles.

"Ah. I thought it might be something like that. I'm very sorry to hear it."

"I'm willing to do extra credit," I tell him. "As much as I can. I know it probably won't be enough to make up for the zero, but I'd like to do it, anyway."

"Let's see how well you do on the mid term first," he replies.

"You're letting me retake it?"

"Of course. Tomorrow morning, if you're up for it. Now, there will be a penalty, I'm afraid. School policy is explicit about that. Your test will have to be graded out of a total of ninety possible points, instead of a hundred."

A ten-point deduction. *That's it?* With the curve, there's a decent chance I could still get a B. A respectable, Northwestern-worthy B.

"I just ask that you refrain from further study," the old man is saying. "What you knew today is what you should know tomorrow."

"Yes, of course," I tell him. At this point, I'd eat a cockroach if he asked me to. "You have my word."

"Excellent," he replies. "I'll see you tomorrow at seven, then."

"Dr Mann?"

"Yes, dear?"

"Why are you giving me a second chance?"

Inexplicably, the old man chuckles. "I've learned, Ms Barnes, that a person rarely gets just one chance at anything. There are second chances everywhere, if you know where to look for them. Look deeper, remember?" He pauses for a beat. I imagine him smiling on the other end of the line. "I'll see you in the morning, dear."

Before I can thank him, he's gone.

Buoyed by this unexpected bit of good fortune, I head down to the kitchen, where Dad is snacking his way through our pantry while Mom braises onions. I tell them about the retest but opt not to share my SAT score. Caught up in her coq au vin, Mom doesn't ask about it.

As we're finishing dinner, the doorbell rings. "Are you expecting someone?" Mom asks, taking in my coffee-stained jogging bottoms and ratty T-shirt. I shake my head, making eye contact with my dad. It has to be Caitlin.

"I'll see who it is," I say.

I make it to the door and stop. *Should I apologize first? What if she doesn't apologize at all?* I'm still trying to decide on a strategy when the doorbell rings again. Not wanting her to leave, I fling open the door.

"Hey."

I blink in surprise. "Josh! Hi." I step back, suddenly intensely aware of the fact that I am wearing jogging bottoms that haven't been washed in a week. "What are you doing here?" I ask. His face falls a notch. "I just meant . . . I thought you had a date with Megan?"

"It wasn't a date. We were just hanging out."

"Oh," I say, stepping on to the front porch and closing the door for some privacy.

"So . . . how are you? You seemed pretty shaken up this afternoon." His forehead crinkles with concern. "Did you and Caitlin work things out?"

"Not yet. I'm sure we will, though." My plan was to convince him with a winning smile, but now it feels like too much effort. So, I burst into tears instead. "No . . . we . . . won't," I manage between sobs. "She . . . hates . . . me."

Josh steps forward and envelops me in a hug. At first it feels awkward, like the hug doesn't quite fit, but then he slides his left arm up a few inches and I tilt my head to the right, and suddenly it works.

"Fights suck," he says simply, his voice right next to my ear.

"She's my best friend," is all I can think to say.

"I know."

"I don't know what to do," I tell him, my face pressed against his shirt. "I'm so sad, but I'm angry, too, you know? Like I'm not sure I want to make up with her."

"You don't have to figure everything out tonight," he says softly.

I pull back, sniffling, and eye him with mock suspicion. "Why do you look like a teenage boy when you're clearly not one?"

"Glad I have you fooled," he says, and smiles. "Hey, do you want to go somewhere?"

"Right now?"

"Right now."

"I need to change first. . ."

"No, you don't. Grey sweats are perfect for where we're going. Go tell your parents you'll be back in an hour and grab a jacket." He looks down at my bare feet and smiles. "And don't forget shoes."

"But—"

He doesn't let me finish. "Do you want to come or not?"

"Yes! I'll be right back." Through the door and halfway up the front stairs, I realize I've left him standing on the front porch. "Come in if you want!" I call over my shoulder. "My parents are in the kitchen!" It dawns on me that he's never met my parents, making it a little weird for both of them if he were to just stroll in. As I'm entering my bedroom, I hear the front door close. *Did he come in or go out?*

I grab my trainers and hoodie, splash some cold water on my tearstained cheeks, and head for the back stairs, at which point I hear my dad bellow, "So *you're* Astronomy Boy!" I bound down the stairs before he can inflict any more damage.

"Josh and I are going out," I announce when my feet hit the linoleum. "We'll be back later." Before my mom can comment on my wardrobe selection, I grab Josh's hand and pull him out the back door.

"So where are we going?" I ask as Josh opens the passenger

door of his Jeep. The interior smells like fresh-cut grass and Ivory soap. There's a beach towel in the back seat.

"To visit Cygnus," is all he says.

A few minutes later, we pull up beside the pond in his neighbourhood and park. "The streetlight is burned out," he says, and points. I press my face to the window, peering out into the darkness. My breath fogs the cool glass. "Come on," he says, pushing open his door. "It's a near-perfect moon."

I follow him down the little dirt path to a wooden swing by the water's edge. The ground is still soft from today's storm. As many times as I've driven past this pond on my way to Tyler's, I've never noticed the swing.

"I figured Cygnus could commiserate," Josh says as we sit. "He knows what it's like to be separated from his best friend." The wooden seat is cold beneath my sweats, but not wet. Someone must've dried it after the rain. We tilt our heads back and look up. Dozens of pine trees form a horseshoe around the water, blocking the light from nearby houses, the closest of which is at least a hundred yards away. The moon, low in the sky, is barely a sliver. With so little light pollution, the sky is thick with stars.

"Did he ever get him back?" I ask, slipping out of my muddy shoes and pulling my bare feet up under me. "I know he went looking for Phaethon, but were they ever reunited?"

"Absolutely."

I look over at him. He's staring intently at the sky. "You're totally lying to me right now, aren't you?"

"Absolutely," he says without missing a beat. We both laugh, and an ease settles over the moment. Even after the day I've had, I feel oddly at peace right now. The world seems bigger, the universe infinitely more vast. As if there's room for everything that happened today. Enough space. I inhale, letting the crisp night air fill my lungs, feeling my rib cage expand. When I exhale, the only sound I hear is my breath. The static is gone.

"So, I keep thinking about something you said today," Josh says then. "It's been bothering me since you said it." He's looking at me now with the same intensity he'd previously directed at the sky. "You asked me if you were too much work. Why would you ask that?"

"It's something Caitlin said," I tell him. "Today, during our fight. She said it was the reason you weren't interested in me." I look down at the still-wet grass, barely visible in the darkness. "I'm more work than I'm worth."

"Who says I'm not interested?"

I nearly swallow my gum.

"As I remember it," he says, "you informed me that I should date another girl, which I – quite reasonably, I think – took to mean that *you* weren't interested."

"You never asked me out," I say defensively. "You had, like, a zillion opportunities."

"A zillion, huh? Like the night you told me you already had plans with friends? Or how about the night you said you had to go to your mom's museum opening? You're a very busy girl, Abby Barnes."

"Yes, but you could've suggested another night," I point out. "Either of those times. But you didn't."

"I wasn't aware that I was being timed," he teases.

"You weren't being *timed*," I reply, heat creeping up my neck. "But if you were so interested, then why'd you say 'thanks' when

245

I told you about Megan?" I demand. As I'm asking, I realize I don't care about his answer. I just want him to kiss me. *Kiss me, kiss me, kiss me.*

"How's a guy supposed to respond when the girl he's crazy about tells him he should date another girl?" Josh keeps talking, not even pausing to gauge my reaction. *Who is this person and what has he done with the dorky guy in spandex and boat shoes?* "Wait, don't answer that," he says. "I think I know now. I'm supposed to say, '*Don't be silly, Abby. I want to date you. Are you free tomorrow night?*'"

"You weren't *supposed* to say anything," I tell him. "You could've just been honest."

"I can do honest," he replies. "*Don't be silly, Abby. I want to date you. Are you free tomorrow night?*"

It takes me a few seconds to realize that he's waiting for a response.

Astronomy Boy just asked me out on a date. I'm still staring at him when he says, "Just so you know, I will be forced to treat silence as acceptance."

And just like that, this day that went from bad to worse to the worst day ever redeemed itself with one perfect moment.

"Halloween might sound like a weird night for a first date," Josh is saying, "but I think it's appropriate for the girl who took me trespassing the last time we went out."

"What about Megan?" I ask, when what I want to say is, *Kiss me, kiss me, kiss me.*

Josh shakes his head in mock disapproval. "See, here I thought *I* was the clueless one, because I've never had a girlfriend before. But it turns out you're even more clueless than I am." He turns to face me, and this time, I meet his gaze. "I like *you*, Abby," he says softly. "I have from the beginning. Ever since the moment you told me you were fated to be in Dr Mann's class." His face, so close to mine, blurs slightly. "There have definitely been some moments when I've doubted your sanity," he says with a laugh, wrapping his hand around my bare left foot, his palm covering the tender flesh of my scar. "But oddly, those moments only made me like you more." I look at his hand, imagining what it would feel like on my calf. My thigh.

"So maybe *you're* the crazy one," I say.

"Crazy about you," he says, with an uncharacteristic confidence that makes my cheeks flush. His face gets serious. "I was never uncertain. I just wanted to get to know you first, so I'd know exactly what I was getting into if I ever got the chance to do this." Cupping my chin with his hand, he kisses me. The kiss is gentle, but not tentative. I close my eyes, tasting his cinnamon-sweet breath, feeling the softness of his lips. His hand slides off my cheek to my shoulder and then down my left arm, leaving a trail of goosebumps in its wake. My whole body is drumming with pleasure. When his thumb reaches my elbow, he wraps his fingers around the crook of my arm and pulls me gently towards him. "So is that a yes?" I hear him whisper, right before he kisses me again.

I pause long enough to smile. "Yes."

# 9
# (there)

## SATURDAY, 31 OCTOBER, 2009
## (HALLOWEEN)

"BOO!"

My eyes fly open at the sound. I'm lying on forest-green plaid in a bed that isn't mine, staring at a chipped navy wall. The air smells like jalapeño peppers and processed cheese. Somewhere nearby, a girl squeals with laughter.

The fact that I've been preparing for this moment doesn't make it any less terrifying. Panic floods my body, pounding through my veins. I'm somewhere else, somewhere new, somewhere I've never been before. Yale is gone, Marissa is gone, Michael is gone. I put my hand on the wall, as if to steady myself. *I can handle this.*

"Morning, Sleepy."

I let go of the breath I didn't know I was holding, the panic melting away as I realize. Reality hasn't changed again. I've just never seen Michael's bedroom in daylight before.

"Hi," I say, rolling over. Michael's face is now inches from mine. I'm careful not to exhale too deeply, not wanting to ruin the moment with morning breath.

"I've been waiting for you to wake up," he tells me. "You're so cute when you sleep."

I am mortified. *Have I been snoring? Drooling? Making weird sleep noises?* This is precisely why I've never slept over at a guy's house (well, this and the fact that I had an eleven o'clock curfew and parents with a pretty expansive no-sleeping-anywhere-near-boys policy). There are too many ways to embarrass yourself in your sleep.

"How long have you been awake?" I ask, subtly checking my pillow for drool.

"Oh, ages," he teases as he touches his nose to mine. "Ten seconds, at least." He clearly does not share my concern about morning breath. Michael looks me up and down and laughs.

"What?" I demand.

"You're still wearing your shoes," he says, pointing. I am, indeed, still wearing my shoes. And every other article of clothing I came with, including my jacket and scarf. I think my purse is in the bed somewhere, too. "Were you afraid I'd get the wrong idea?" he asks. I look down at his bare chest and am instantly flustered. *Holy pecs.*

"It wasn't that," I say quickly. "It's just. . ." Every excuse I can think of is creepier than the real reason. "OK, yeah. I didn't want you to think that just because I was sleeping over, it meant that you and I would. . ." Heat creeps up my neck. *I can't even say the word without blushing.*

"Well, in the future, if you'd like to remove your outerwear before sleeping, I won't take it as a signal that you're asking for sex."

I squirm under his gaze, suddenly very uncomfortable with all the sex talk. *If you can't handle the sex talk, probably not ready for sex.*

My phone rings from inside my purse, buried under Michael's shirt at the foot of the bed. I scramble for it, glad for the distraction.

"Ben and I found the most amazing costumes!" Marissa squeals before I can even say hello. "Power Rangers!" In the background, Ben belts out a very off-key version of the theme song. "She has green, pink, red, blue and yellow," Marissa says. "Which ones do you guys want?"

"She?"

"We're at some lady's house in Hamden," Marissa replies. "Ben found her on Craigslist." When he heard we didn't have costumes yet, Ben appointed himself costume master for tonight's activities, which consist of a pre-party at Michael's house, a few hours at Inferno (the infamous banned-for-five-years-but-now-it's-back Halloween party in the courtyard of Pierson College), then on to the midnight symphony at Woolsey Hall.

"Which Power Ranger do you want to be?" I ask Michael.

"Green!" he shouts, flinging off the covers and leaping to his feet. "Go, go, Power Rangers!" With his hair all messed up, he looks like a little kid. With underwear-model abs. "I'm gonna get some water," he tells me, then pads out of the room in his jeans and bare feet.

I hear the beep of an incoming call. "What about you?" Marissa wants to know. "Which colour?" The line beeps again. I pull the phone away from my ear to check the number. It's an LA area code, but I don't recognize the number. *Who could possibly be calling?* It's six in the morning on the West Coast, and none of the people I know in California remember knowing me.

"Abby?" I hear Marissa say. "Did I lose you?"

"No, no, I'm here," I say. "Sorry. I was getting another call. Did you ask me something?"

"Just what colour you wanted."

"Oh! Yellow, I guess?"

"Yay! OK, we're buying them. See you guys tonight!"

As soon as we disconnect, it dawns on me that Caitlin probably doesn't have a costume yet, either. She's been spending so much time at Dr Mann's lab (and on the train *getting* to Dr Mann's lab) that I doubt she even knows it's Halloween. I text Marissa to tell her to get all five suits, just in case. As I'm putting my phone back in my bag, it vibrates with a new voicemail.

"So what're you up to today?"

Michael has reappeared, holding two glasses of water and sucking on an Atomic Fireball. His face is damp, like he just washed it. I, meanwhile, can feel dried drool on my cheek. I grab a slice of gum from my bag, eager to mitigate the effects of last night's beer pong. My tongue feels like it's coated in cotton.

"Library," I say. "I have a *YDN* article to write and two hundred pages of reading to finish before my Philosophy of Theology mid term on Monday."

"Let's study together," he suggests, handing me one of the glasses. "I loved that class."

"You took Hare's class?" I ask between gulps.

He nods. "Freshman year. After twelve years at a Christian school, I figured it'd be an easy A."

"You went to Christian school?" I'd pictured a prestigious

251

East Coast prep school, somewhere with a Latin motto and its own coat of arms.

"Yup. Kindergarten to eleventh grade." Michael turns away and starts digging through the pile of clothes on his desk chair.

"But not senior year?"

"Nope. Senior year was public school." He pulls out a Red Sox T-shirt, smells it, then puts it on. "Clean," he declares, and grins. "You want some breakfast?"

There is so much I want to know about this guy whose bed I've just slept in. Despite the amount of time we've spent together over the past six weeks, I can still count the things I know about him on one hand: he's from Massachusetts. His middle name is Evan. His parents are divorced, and he's never mentioned any siblings. And now, this latest titbit: twelve years of parochial school. It's not that he's evasive about personal stuff – he just doesn't offer it up. And I, not wanting to pry, don't ask.

"So?" Michael says as he walks me to the door. Knowing the contents of the Beta pantry, I passed on the breakfast offer. "You up for a study date tomorrow?"

"Sure," I tell him. "Sounds great." Actually, the idea kind of terrifies me. Maybe if I spend today studying but act like I didn't, I'll know enough to seem believably but not embarrassingly unprepared. Just as I'm turning to go, he pulls me into a kiss. Grateful for the gum in my mouth, I kiss him back, tasting the cinnamon heat of the Fireball on his lips. I close my eyes and inhale, breathing in the scent of him, sugary cinnamon and soap. There's something so familiar about the combination. I inhale again, deeper this time. And all of a sudden it's not Michael I'm kissing but Josh.

I snap my head back, caught off guard by the memory. Michael gives me a quizzical look. "Everything OK?" he asks.

"Yeah, uh, everything's fine," I say. "I should get going, that's all. See you later!" I peck him on the cheek and hurry down the steps.

The crowd at Starbucks is pretty small for a Saturday morning, which is incentive enough for me to stop. It takes all my will power not to think about Josh and that kiss as I'm waiting to order. The memory just keeps popping up, taunting me with its movie-moment perfection. The blanket of stars, the cool night breeze. *Don't be silly, Abby. I want to date you. Are you free tomorrow night?*

An impatient homeless man in tattered army fatigues stands uncomfortably close to me in line, jingling coins in his hand. "It's your turn!" he yells gruffly, inches from my ear. I step up to the counter and quickly order my latte.

"That'll be five eighty-five." The cashier looks bored.

As I dig through my bag for my wallet, the guy behind me taps his foot loudly and impatiently, still jingling his coins. Frazzled, I start taking stuff out and putting it on the counter. Mascara . . . keys . . . mobile phone . . . a travel pack of plasters . . . a package of highlighters . . . yesterday's *YDN*. *Where is my wallet?* The coin jingling intensifies. When I was in LA, I bought this great vintage messenger bag with five compartments – my consolation prize for having to put university on hold. Now I'm back to using my old slouchy black satchel, a bag with a mind of its own. Invariably, whatever item I need has disappeared to the very bottom. Like my wallet has done at this particular moment. By the time I find it, my latte is already ready and the guy behind me is about to lose it. "I'll pay for his, too," I whisper to the cashier, handing

253

him an extra five-dollar note. Feeling like I've broken the social code by taking too long in the Starbucks line, I keep my head down as I grab my coffee and bolt out of the door.

Marissa and Ben are still gone when I get back to our room, which is good, because I want to be at the library by ten, and there is no such thing as a five-minute conversation with Ben Blaustien. He's so well-read and well-watched and well-listened that he's always just read/seen/heard some super-fascinating story on CNN.com or NPR that he assumes you'll find equally fascinating and want to hear all about and then discuss at length. Great if you're stuck in a lift or standing in line for pizza at Yorkside. Not so great when you're in a time crunch because you need to cram for a study session with the guy you're pretty sure is your boyfriend even though neither of you have called him that yet.

I drop my bag on my bed and step out of my boots. As I'm unbuttoning my jeans, my eyes wander to the wall above my desk, to the spot where I hung my birthday present from Marissa. The photograph of Caitlin and me at the Freshman Picnic.

Only . . . it's gone.

There's a framed photograph there, but it's of me by myself, sitting cross-legged under an oak tree on Cross Campus. It's a cool, arty shot – obviously Marissa's handiwork. But it's not the picture she gave me.

Beads of sweat prickle on my upper lip. *Where's the other photo?*

The memory of my fight with Caitlin comes barrelling back.

"Oh, God," I breathe. *There's no picture of us because Caitlin and I aren't friends any more.*

No. That can't be right. That fight was last October. Sure, it was awful, but there's no way Caitlin and I stayed mad at each other for an entire year.

Frantic for answers, I dump the contents of my bag on my bed, but my phone's not there. *Crap.* I must've left it at Michael's.

With shaking hands, I reach for my laptop. If Caitlin and I stopped being friends last October, then my screensaver picture of Caitlin, Ty and me at graduation doesn't exist any more. My screen lights up. The graduation photo is gone.

I click on the camera icon and quickly scroll through the rest of last year's photos.

After October, Caitlin's not in any of them. Not a single one.

I have to talk to her. Now.

I sprint from Vanderbilt to Silliman in my socks, colliding with four different sets of passersby and nearly taking out a man on a bike. When I get to Caitlin's door, I bang on it. Her roommate, Muriel, opens it, still half-asleep.

"Abby?"

"You know who I am!"

"Of course I know who you are," Muriel replies, looking at me like I have three heads. "But Caitlin's not here. She's at the lab."

"Whose lab? Dr Mann's?"

Muriel nods, rubbing her eyes sleepily.

Grinning like a madwoman, I throw my arms around her. "Thank you!" Out of the corner of my eye I see the keys to Muriel's Civic, hanging on a hook by the door. The next train doesn't leave for an hour. "Can I borrow your car?"

Muriel shrugs. "Sure. It's in the car park on Sachem."

"Thank you!" I throw my arms around her again.

"Wait, you're not high, are you?" Muriel eyes me suspiciously.

255

"No!" I grab the keys from the hook before she can change her mind. "I'll bring it back this afternoon!" I call as I sprint down the stairs.

I make excellent time. Since it's a Saturday, I ignore the PERMIT HOLDERS ONLY signs in the car park at Olin Observatory and park next to the only other car in the car park, a bright-yellow Smart Car with Connecticut plates and an EXPECT THE UNEXPECTED window sticker. At least I know I'm in the right place.

According to the directory by the main entrance, Dr Mann's office is on the sixth floor. Once I'm up there, it's not hard to find. His door is the only one covered in newspaper headlines about last year's earthquake. Next to this door there's another one, marked LAB. The knob turns easily in my hand.

I push open the heavy metal door and step inside. On the far wall, an oversized digital clock declares the time down to the millisecond. Beside it, there is a giant magnetic calendar with a movable red $X$ on today's date. Dr Mann is standing in front of a floor-to-ceiling chalkboard that runs the length of the eastern wall, studying a string of equations, his shirtsleeves rolled up to the elbow. Caitlin is nowhere around.

Quietly I turn to go, hoping to slip out without being noticed. But the door clangs shut before I can catch it.

"Good morning, Ms Barnes!" Dr Mann calls.

"Hello," I reply, suddenly feeling very awkward. "I'm so sorry to disturb you."

"Nonsense! It's not a disturbance at all. Come in!"

I find a smile and step further inside. "Is Caitlin around?"

"She's at the library, trying to track down an old manuscript for me," he replies. "Friedrich Schiller's *Vom Erhabenen*. Are you familiar with it?"

"Uh, I don't think so, no." I glance back at the door, wishing I could will my way back out of it.

Dr Mann motions for me to sit, then turns back to the long string of variables, symbols and numbers on the board, tapping his nose thoughtfully as he examines his handiwork.

"What is it?" I ask.

"I've been calling it the destiny force," he says.

I wait for him to elaborate, but he doesn't. "The destiny force," I repeat.

Dr Mann nods. "I am attempting to calculate the force – the pull, if you will – of a person's predestined future."

"So you believe in fate," I say.

Dr Mann pauses thoughtfully before answering. "I believe each of us was uniquely created for a specific purpose designed by the Creator, and that, because of that, there are certain things in our lives that we are destined to do. The rest, I think, is soft clay: left entirely to the defining influences of choice, chance and circumstance. And luck! Don't forget luck." He touches the capital $L$ in his equation with his fingertip, leaving an imprint in its base. "The trick," he says then, "is how to determine which is which." He smiles. "But I'm afraid there's no equation for that."

Staring at the blackboard, I let my gaze blur. Every life, an equation. *Who's writing mine?*

I look at Dr Mann. "Chance and luck and all that aside. . ."

The old man's eyebrows shoot up at my wholesale dismissal of his variables, but I forge on. "Can a person *avoid* her destiny? Or refuse it?"

The professor's blue eyes sparkle with delight. "That's what I'm trying to figure out," he tells me, turning back to his equation. "The force of one's destiny, in mathematical terms. And, most particularly, whether that value varies from person to person."

"So if my parallel and I are sharing a reality, then is our equation the same?" Dr Mann gives me a curious look. "Theoretically, I mean," I say quickly, feigning breeziness with an awkward wave of my hand. "If we were to become entangled with a parallel world, you know, like your theories suggest."

"You ask exactly the right question," he says, his eyes alight with understanding. "What is your sense of the answer?"

I falter. "I don't know," I admit. "I'd like to believe I have my own destiny, but I guess if my life weren't entirely my own any more. . ."

"Your life is *always* your own," Dr Mann says sharply. "You are a uniquely created being with a transcendent soul. A new set of memories or an altered sense of reality cannot change what is fundamentally true." He's watching me closely now, measuring my reaction. "Your path will change," he says then. "Your destiny never will."

"But what if I'm on the wrong path?"

"There is no wrong path," he explains. "Not when it comes to destiny. There are only detours, you see." He studies me for a moment longer, then adds, "You said something curious when you came to see me back in September. I've been puzzling over its meaning ever since."

I try my best to keep my expression neutral. "Oh?"

"I believe your words were, 'Why does no one but me. . .'" He trails off, his gaze unblinking and pinned on mine. "You stopped abruptly, as if you'd said too much."

It takes everything I have not to look away. My palms are damp with sweat.

"A few moments later, Ms Moss asked about anomalies." Dr Mann cocks his head to one side, like a bird. "It was a very specific question, if I recall, about the possibility that someone might keep their knowledge of the way things were before the collision." He pauses as if waiting for my reaction.

"Oh," is all I say.

He smiles sympathetically, as if we're discussing a bout of indigestion, or a tooth that needs repair. "Is that 'someone' you?"

I expect to feel panic, but instead I'm washed in relief. Still, I can't bring myself to nod.

Dr Mann doesn't press it. "When you're ready," he says kindly. "I'd be happy to help, if I could." Then he looks past me and beams, the way a proud father might. "But I'd say you're in good hands already."

"Abby?" I turn to see Caitlin standing at the door, holding a stack of photocopied pages. She takes in my socked feet and the rim of slept-in mascara around my eyes. "Everything OK?"

"Everything's great!" I say brightly. "I just stopped by to say hi." Caitlin doesn't buy this, and clearly, neither does Dr Mann. But he just bows politely and reaches for his jacket. "I could do with a cup of tea," he announces, moving towards the door. "Would you girls like one?"

"No, thanks," we say in unison.

As soon as the door clangs shut, Caitlin beelines over to where I'm standing. "What are you really doing here?"

"Dr Mann just asked if I kept my real memories," I whisper, even though we're alone in the room. "I didn't say no." Caitlin's face lights up.

"So we're telling him?" she asks excitedly.

"I don't know. Maybe. But that's not why I came."

"Abby, if he knows anyway, why not just—"

"I remember the fight."

Caitlin gets quiet. "Oh." She fiddles with her grandmother's bracelet. "It was awful," she says softly.

"It wasn't really us," I remind her, as though it'll make a difference now. "It was them."

"Those bitches." It's a joke, but her voice is sad.

"How did it end?" I ask. "Please, fast-forward to the happy ending. How did we make up?"

"We didn't," she says. "Not officially, anyway. You called me on your birthday and acted like it never happened. That was the first time we'd spoken since the day of the fight."

But 30 October to 9 September is nearly eleven months. The longest Caitlin and I have ever gone without talking is three days. Memorial Day weekend 2003, after she didn't save a seat for me on the bus to the aquarium for the sixth-grade field trip (I found out later that Ms Dobson told her she couldn't).

"We stopped being friends over a *guy*?" I say. "Over *Tyler*?"

Caitlin hesitates for a second, then says, "The fight wasn't about what you told Ty. Not really. I was upset about that – and embarrassed about what he did in the cafeteria, and horrified about what you said about Craig—" Her voice breaks a little at his name.

"Oh God, Caitlin. I can't believe I – I'm so sorry."

"It's OK," she says. "I said some awful things, too. I was just so angry at you already."

"Angry at me for what?"

She looks away, but not before I see the hurt in her eyes. "You promised to edit my essay for Yale."

*Her personal statement.* The one thing Caitlin asked me to do for her last year. The one thing. How many times did I promise to edit it? Half a dozen, at least. I remember being annoyed that she felt like she had to keep asking me after I'd already said I'd do it. As if I needed to be reminded how important it was to her. I knew how self-conscious she is about her dyslexia. How much she was relying on my help. *And I never even read it.* The worst part is, I didn't even realize I'd forgotten until now.

My armpits tingle with shame. I can blame my parallel self for lying to Tyler and for saying what she did about Craig, but this broken promise is on both of us, because I forgot, too. Between classes, play rehearsal, cross-country practice and my own university applications, there wasn't a lot of space left in my own brain last autumn. I remember feeling frazzled and overwhelmed for most of the semester, just trying to keep track of everything I had to do. How many other promises did I break? Who else did I let down?

*I'm a jackass. A* self-absorbed *jackass.*

Now it all makes sense.

"Cate, I'm so sorry," I tell her, my eyes welling up with tears.

"I'm sorry, too," she says, hugging me as my tears spill over. "I should have just told you why I was upset . . . or reminded you again. I knew you'd just forgotten. But you were so busy with your own stuff, and I figured the essays wouldn't even matter that much if my SAT score was high enough. When it wasn't, I freaked."

I pull away and look at her. "What are you talking about?"

"I choked," she says. "Two hundred points lower than my lowest practice score."

"Oh, Caitlin. Why didn't you tell me?"

"I was embarrassed," she replies. "I didn't tell anyone." My chest aches at the thought of her going through that alone. How disappointed she must have been. How anxious and afraid. "When I didn't get in, it was easy to blame you for that, too," she explains. "I was so mad at you already. I told myself that if my essay had been better, the score wouldn't have mattered as much."

"Wait, *what*? You didn't get into Yale early?"

Caitlin shakes her head. "Wait-listed till February," she says. "That's not how you remember it?"

"No! In my version, you got your acceptance letter the day before Thanksgiving."

Caitlin looks puzzled for a moment. Then something clicks. "Martin Wagner," she says. "I'll bet he was the reason I got in early."

The name is familiar but I can't place it. "Who's Martin Wagner?"

"Josh's stepdad," she replies. "He was supposed to do my Yale alumni interview. Josh was helping me prepare. After our fight, I requested a different interviewer. The woman I ended up with was a total nightmare."

"So that's what you were doing," I say. "My parallel saw you and Josh in the chem lab that morning." At the mention of his name, another memory comes to mind. Sitting with him on a wooden swing, feeling his fingertips on the inside of my arm as we kiss. "Wait, were we a couple?" Even before Caitlin responds, I know the answer is yes. There is no way that kiss wasn't the beginning of something. The muscles around my rib cage contract, like a corset. "For how long?"

"I'm not sure," she replies. The corners of her mouth form a small, sad smile. "You and I weren't exactly dishing relationship details. All I know is it ended before prom."

*Prom.* In the real version of things, I was in LA and didn't get to go. At the time, I told myself it was no big deal, but deep down, I regretted missing it. "Did I still go, though? With someone else?"

She nods. "You went with Tyler. As friends."

"After he asked you, and you said no."

Caitlin looks surprised. "You remember that?"

"No, I just know Ty. And you." I look down at the floor, willing myself not to cry. That wasn't the way things were supposed to turn out. Tyler should've been at that dance with Caitlin, not with me.

"Hey," Caitlin says softly, touching my shoulder. "It's OK. We're OK. In the end, everything turned out the way it was supposed to."

I meet her gaze, the eyes I know better than my own, and nod. "We're OK," I repeat.

"We're OK." Her voice is unequivocal, as if she's never been more certain of anything in her life. A deep, ineffable gratitude washes through me. Her forgiveness is more than I deserve and yet I have it, completely. I grab her hand, my throat suddenly tight.

"I couldn't do this without you," I whisper.

She squeezes my hand. "Yes, you could," she says. "But you won't have to." She lets go of my hand and unlatches her bracelet, a delicate gold chain with an antique clasp. "Here," she says, putting it on my wrist. "As long as you wake up wearing it, you'll know we're OK."

I smile, running my finger over the tiny gold loops. "Why'd you pick up?" I ask. "On my birthday. If you thought we were still fighting, why'd you answer my call?"

"I dunno," she says thoughtfully. "I wasn't going to at first. But it'd been so long, and it was your birthday. . . I guess I figured if you were making the effort, I could at least hear you out." She shrugs. "Then when I answered, you acted like it was totally normal that you were calling me. I knew something was up. So I met you at the library, heard what was happening, and brought you here to see Gustav."

"You never told me about the fight?"

She shakes her head. "I didn't want to," she admits. "Since you didn't remember it, and no one here knew anything about it, I could pretend like it never happened."

Metal clangs against metal as Dr Mann comes through the lab door carrying a cup of tea and a half-eaten scone. He's wearing at least a fourth of it on the front of his shirt. Dr Mann sees us watching him and smiles mid-bite. Another chunk of scone lands on his tie. I stifle a giggle.

"I should probably get back to work," Caitlin says, hopping off her stool. "Gustav is leaving for Munich on Tuesday, and he wants me to finish his grant application before he goes."

"Well, then. I'll leave you and *Gustav* alone."

She sticks her tongue out at me, and I am hit with a wave

of relief that despite the fight and everything else, Caitlin and I are OK. I throw my arms around her. "I love you," I whisper, hugging her tight.

"I love you, too," she whispers back.

"Soulmates," comes Dr Mann's voice. "The most enduring of human relationships." He's staring thoughtfully at his chalkboard, munching on the last of his scone. "That's what we're missing." He brushes the crumbs off his shirt and steps up to the board. With the sleeve of his jacket and a broken piece of chalk, he makes several quick revisions to his equation.

When he's finished, he returns the chalk to its dusty ledge and takes a step back. His eyes remind me of an old-fashioned typewriter – up, down, over, up, down, over – as he studies the complicated string of numbers, symbols, and signs. "You asked if you could miss your destiny," he says then, with a nod at the board. "Not if you find your soulmates first."

"Soulmates, plural?" I ask him. "How many does each person have?"

The old man smiles at his equation, as if the answer is right in front of us. "Exactly as many as she needs."

Caitlin's hand catches mine. "One down," she whispers.

"Hey, Abby, who'd we get the fifth costume for?" Marissa asks. She's hunched over her laptop, watching the Power Rangers opening sequence on YouTube while Ben watches the World Series on our TV.

"Caitlin," I tell her, putting down the bio textbook I'm not really reading. "But I forgot to ask her if she even needs it." I dig through my bag for my mobile, then remember I don't have it. "Hey, can I borrow your phone?" I ask Ben. "I left mine at Michael's."

"Sure," he says, and tosses it to me.

Michael answers on the second ring. "Why is Nick Swisher such a d-bag?"

"Huh?"

"Abby?"

"Who's Nick Swisher?"

"Such a douche bag!" Ben shouts from the sofa.

"He plays for the Yankees," Michael explains. "Why are you calling me on Ben's phone?"

"I can't find mine. Did I leave it over there?"

"I don't think so, but I'll look. Where would you have left it?"

"Your bed," I reply, forgetting my audience. Ben sniggers. Blushing, I step into the hall, letting the door shut behind me.

"Nope," Michael says. "Don't see it. Are you sure you left it here?"

"I think so . . . I realized I didn't have it as soon as I got back, and I didn't go anywhere befo—" *Starbucks.* I must've left it on the counter when I bought my coffee. "Crap."

"Uh-oh. Where'd you leave it?"

"Starbucks. I stopped for coffee."

"Call it," he tells me. "Maybe someone picked it up."

I do, but no one answers. As I'm hanging up, I remember that I never listened to the voicemail I got from that 310 number. I quickly dial my mailbox to retrieve it.

266

"Please enter your password," comes the automated voice.

3-7-7-3.

"I'm sorry," the voice says. "You have entered an incorrect password."

I enter it again, slower this time, making sure to get it right.

"I'm sorry. You have entered an incorrect password. Please hang up and try again."

I stare at the keypad, puzzled. 3-7-7-3. The last four digits of Caitlin's home phone number. That's been my voicemail password since I got my first mobile phone in ninth grade. Could whoever has my phone have changed the password? Don't you need the original password to do that?

*The fight.* My parallel self must've changed it.

I try the last four digits of my parents' phone number and the last four digits of Tyler's, but neither work. Equally annoyed at myself, my parallel, and the thief who's commandeered my phone, I punch out Caitlin's number. As soon as I hit the call button, her name appears on the screen. I stare at it uncomprehendingly. This is Ben's phone. *Why does my roommate's boyfriend have Caitlin's number?*

The phone is still in my hands when Caitlin's voicemail picks up.

"Hey, it's Abby," I say after the beep. "Why does Ben have your number in his phone? I'm calling to see if you need a costume for tonight and if you want to walk over to Inferno with us. Lemme know." I start to hang up. "Oh – I lost my phone. So call my landline."

"Did you find it?" a male voice asks. Ben is standing in our doorway.

"Nope." I hand him his phone, then step past him into the common room. "I called Caitlin," I announce to Marissa, louder than I need to.

"Is she coming with us?" Ben asks casually.

"I got voicemail." I want to ask him why the hell he has Caitlin's number saved in his phone, but not while Marissa is in earshot.

Our landline rings, and Marissa reaches for it. "Hey, Caitlin!" she says a moment later. She listens, then nods. "OK. We'll just meet you there then." I glance at Ben, but he's fiddling with his phone. "Yep," I hear Marissa say, just before she hangs up. "I'll tell her."

"She doesn't need a costume?"

"No," she replies. "And she told me to tell you she's probably going to skip Inferno. Said she'd catch up with you at the concert."

"Did she say why?"

Marissa shakes her head. "But she sounded stressed. Work maybe?"

"Yeah. Maybe." I glance back at Ben, but he's still busy with his mobile. "I guess I'll walk over to Starbucks to see if they have my phone."

On my way there, I run through reasons why Ben would have Caitlin's number. Marissa gave it to him. Marissa called Caitlin from his phone and he saved it.

*Ben and Caitlin have a thing.*

I push the thought from my mind. Caitlin wouldn't do that to Marissa. Not after Craig. There's just no way.

My phone, of course, is not at Starbucks. Annoyed, frustrated, and suddenly very tired, I treat myself to a caramel latte with extra caramel and take the long way back to my room. Ben passes me as I'm coming up the entryway stairs. "Going to buy vodka," is all he says. He doesn't slow down.

Marissa is standing on her head in the common room. "Ben's acting weird," she announces.

Dread pools in the pit of my stomach. "Weird how?"

"I dunno. Just weird. Antsy." She bends her legs, lowering them until her knees are resting on her triceps. "Has he said anything to you?"

"To me? No."

In one fluid motion, she dismounts from the headstand and stands up. "I'm probably overthinking it," she says. "People act weird sometimes. It doesn't always mean something. Right?"

"Not always," I agree.

*Just usually.*

"*Wow.*"

I follow Michael's gaze over the rowdy crowd to the back of Woolsey Hall, expecting to see another elaborate costume. Instead, I see Caitlin, wearing plastic lab glasses, a form-fitting white lab coat, and five-inch magenta Louboutin stilettos . . . and not much else. Her long blonde hair is tied back in a low ponytail, and her face is bare except for the five coats of black mascara layered on her lashes. She looks amazing. I suddenly feel very dowdy in my yellow uni-suit.

"I'll be right back," I say, leaving Michael by himself in our overcrowded row. "Don't lose our seats."

"I'll try my best," Michael replies, sliding over to the centre of the three seats we've claimed. Marissa took Ben to "Haunted Yoga" at the Elm Street cemetery, so it's just the two of us trying to hold three seats in a room that would give the fire marshal a heart attack. "But hurry. I'm not sure how long I can fend off the seat vultures."

I make my way through the costumed crowd to where Caitlin is standing.

"Sexy cops, sexy nurses . . . why should scientists get the shaft?"

"My thoughts exactly," she replies, curtsying a little.

"Why didn't you come to the party with us?" I ask her as we weave back through the crowd towards our seats.

"Oh, I just had some work to do," she says, keeping her voice breezy.

"At ten o'clock on Saturday night?"

"Yup."

Caitlin does not use words like "yup".

"Why don't I believe you?"

She sighs and looks me in the eye. "Ben."

I stop walking. A fat guy dressed as Buzz Lightyear crashes into me from behind, nearly knocking me over.

"Sorry!" he slurs. Caitlin pulls me out of the way as he barrels past us.

"Nothing's going on," she tells me in a low voice.

"He has your number saved in his phone."

"He asked for it when he walked me home after your birthday dinner. He did it so casually, it didn't feel like a big deal."

"He walked you home after my birthday dinner?"

Caitlin nods. "Michael went with you and Marissa back to Old Campus, and Ben walked with me. I told him I was fine by myself – I think I was the least drunk of all of us – but he insisted. We got to talking, and before we knew it, it was three thirty."

"Those are alternate memories," I tell her, keeping my voice down. "In the real version, Tyler called you right after Ben offered to walk you home, and you left. The four of us walked back to my room together."

"Why was Tyler calling me at two in the morning?" Caitlin asks.

"It was your thing. You talked every night before you went to bed."

"Every night? Did he also wear a lock of my hair around his neck?" Caitlin makes a gagging motion. "Why do relationships make otherwise cool people act like morons? And I can't even make fun of him for it."

I don't respond.

"Abby!" Michael motions for us to hurry. A guy in a rubber Bill Clinton mask hovers at the end of our row, stalking the empty seats.

"Coming!" I call to him, then turn back to Caitlin. "What else?"

"There's nothing else. A few phone calls and emails. That's it."

"He's Marissa's boyfriend, Caitlin."

"I know that, Abby."

"Do you like him?"

"He has a girlfriend."

"You didn't answer the question."

271

"Yes, I did," she says firmly. Then, looking past me: "We should sit, the show's about to start."

"Does he like you?"

I see her hesitate and have my answer.

"Poor Marissa," I say then. She's the one whose heart will be broken here, and she hasn't done anything wrong. She's just another casualty of the chain reaction my parallel started when she tried to play Cupid.

Caitlin looks hurt. "I didn't mean for this to happen, Abby."

"I know," I tell her, giving her hand a squeeze as we inch down our row towards Michael. "It's not your fault."

*It's mine.*

The Yale Symphony Orchestra's annual Halloween show is more than just an orchestral concert. The musicians play the soundtrack to a student-made silent film, complete with several live-action sequences and a crazy pyrotechnic finale (there's no way the fire marshal is on board with this). With three thousand university students stuffed into an auditorium that seats twenty-five hundred, it's a raucous, borderline chaotic affair. By the time the house lights come on afterwards, I'm both hoarse and deaf from all the screaming.

"Should we go to Toad's till close or skip it and get pizza instead?" Michael asks us as we're inching towards the door after the show. Getting thousands of people into the building was a lot easier than getting them out.

"Pizza," I reply. "I'm too tired to dance."

"Ooh, pizza sounds good," Caitlin says.

"Yorkside or Wall Street?" Michael asks, pulling out his phone.

"Yorkside," we say in unison.

"Cool. I'll text Ben."

Caitlin and I exchange a glance. She feigns a yawn. "Actually, on second thought, I think I've passed hunger and descended into sheer exhaustion. I'm just gonna head home."

"You sure?" Michael asks, slipping his hand into mine as we descend Woolsey's front steps. Throngs of costumed revellers spill out on to the pavement and into the intersection of College and Grove as uniformed campus security guards try in vain to break up the crowd, which moves towards York Street in a Toad's-bound mass. "All roads lead to Toad's!" I hear someone shout.

"Yeah, I'm sure." Caitlin puts on a smile. "You guys have fun."

"Brunch tomorrow?" I ask.

"Definitely." She squeezes my hand and heads off down the pavement.

Michael's phone buzzes with a text. "Looks like it's just you and me," he says. "The lovebirds are calling it a night."

Yorkside is packed when we get there, so we split up. Michael goes to the counter for our pizza, and I claim a booth near the back.

"I hope you like pepperoni," Michael says as he approaches the table, balancing two paper plates and a pitcher of beer. He's holding our cups between his teeth.

"Who doesn't like pepperoni?" I lift a slice off the plate and take a bite. Hot, gooey mozzarella sticks to the roof of my mouth.

"So what'd you think of the show?" he asks, biting into his own slice.

"I thought it was awesome. You?"

He nods as he chews. "Loved it. It's one of those quintessentially Yale things, you know?" He takes another bite, and a glob of pizza sauce sticks to his upper lip. "I used to make fun of that stuff," he says. "A capella groups, theme parties, singing at football games. But then I got here and realized how cool all of it is." Then, with a laugh: "Utterly dorky, but cool."

"I didn't even know any of it existed until I got here," I say as I try not to stare at the sauce on his lip.

"So what sold you?" he asks.

"Sold me?"

"On Yale," he says. "What convinced you to apply?"

"Oh. . ." I falter. The reasons I *didn't* want to apply pop into my mind, reasons that seem more like excuses now. "Academics, I guess." *When in doubt, go with the lamest, most generic reason ever.* "What about you?"

"Lacrosse. And the fact that it was a hundred and one miles from my house."

"Lucky number?"

He laughs. "I had a minimum distance requirement. I had to be at least a hundred miles from home. Lucky for me, now it's more like a thousand."

"What do you mean?"

"My mom moved the summer after my freshman year." Then, casually: "To Atlanta, actually."

I blink. "Your mom lives in *Atlanta*? Where?"

"Lilac Lane," he says, drawing out his vowels. His attempt at

274

a Southern accent sounds like Crocodile Dundee on sedatives.

"I meant, what neighbourhood? And why didn't you tell me before?"

"I don't know anything but the street address," he replies. "And I haven't mentioned it because I generally don't." His tone doesn't invite a follow-up question, but for once I don't let that deter me.

"But you know I'm from there, right?" As I say this, it crosses my mind that he might, in fact, *not* know that. What else have I assumed he knows that he actually doesn't? *Ohmigod, he doesn't even know my last name.* I rack my brain, trying to come up with a single instance where I've heard him use it, and can't come up with one. *Mortifying.*

"Yes, silly. Of course I know you're from there. I was planning to mention it eventually, I just hadn't yet." This explanation is laughably lame, but I opt not to point it out.

"How much time do you spend there?" I ask him.

"Last year, I only went home for Thanksgiving," he replies.

"And this year?"

"Same. Arriving Wednesday night at eight fifty-two p.m., departing Friday morning at eight forty-eight a.m.," he says. "Same flights as last year."

"Short trip."

"It's a long thirty-six hours," he says flatly, and reaches for the last slice. He doesn't elaborate.

I pick at a piece of pepperoni, not sure what to say next.

We sit in silence for a few minutes as Michael works on his second piece of pizza and I play with the rest of mine. *Should I change the subject? Wait for him to say something?* After a few bites, he smiles. "You know what'd make those thirty-six hours better this year?" he asks me. His tone is lighter now, his eyes brighter. "A turkey dinner at the Barnes house." He takes another bite, watching my reaction. I'm so elated that he just used my last name that it takes me a second to realize that he's just invited himself over for Thanksgiving.

"You have pizza sauce on your lip," I say coyly. He licks his lips. "Still there," I tell him. He smiles and reaches for a napkin.

"You're just gonna leave me hanging, huh?"

I lean forward, my thumb reaching his upper lip before his napkin does. "Pretty much," I tease.

"No sympathy at all for the poor, lonely guy who can't bear to spend Thanksgiving away from his girlfriend?"

"Nope." My voice sounds tight. Airless. Probably because sometime between his use of the word "girlfriend" and this moment, I stopped breathing. It's the first time he's said it. Suddenly, intensely, I want to be exactly that. His girlfriend. For as long as fate will let me.

*Parallel Abby, please don't screw this up.*

"That's a shame," Michael says, leaning across the table until his face is inches from mine. My eyelids flutter as I breathe in the spicy-sweet scent of mint, pepperoni and aftershave. *Who knew the smell of cured meat could turn a person on?* My lips tingle in anticipation. I've been thinking about that kiss my parallel self got from Josh all day, unable to shake the memory of it. This is exactly what I need: an even more amazing kiss to take its place. I let my eyes close, feeling his lips touch mine, wishing we were in his bedroom instead of this crowded restaurant.

"Abby?" a small voice says. My eyes pop open. A tear-stained Pink Ranger is standing next to our table, holding a plastic pumpkin.

"Marissa? Are you OK?"

"Ben broke up with me."

"What?" My eyes dart to Michael. His eyebrows are arched in surprise, but the expression strikes me as false. The face you'd make at your surprise party, when it's not a surprise at all. *He knew.* I look back at Marissa. "When?"

"Right before I puked in this pumpkin," she says miserably, holding out the orange plastic container, which is, indeed, filled with vomit. Michael recoils. I take the pumpkin and set it on the floor beneath the table.

"Sit," I tell her, sliding over to make room. "How much have you had to drink?"

"Too much." She puts her forehead down on the table.

I look at Michael.

"Uh, I'll get some water," he says, and stands.

"What happened?" I ask as soon as Michael leaves.

"I don't know." She looks at me with red-rimmed eyes. "He just started acting weird. I kept asking what was wrong, and he kept saying he was just tired. But he didn't seem tired, you know? So I told him that, and his face got all twisted, and he said he'd wanted to wait until tomorrow to tell me, but he felt like he was lying by not saying anything. And then his voice broke, and I knew." Her eyes well up again. "He said he didn't want to hurt me, but he just didn't feel the same way about me any more. And that's when I puked."

"Where were you?"

"On our way back from the cemetery."

"You did yoga like this?"

She nods miserably. "I don't know where I got the pumpkin. Someone must have given it to me." She nudges it with her shoe. "There's candy at the bottom."

I look down and instantly regret it.

*Don't throw up, don't throw up, don't throw up.*

Michael returns with a pitcher of water and some breadsticks, which he sets on the table in front of Marissa. She stares at the cup vacantly.

"Should I. . ." Michael looks from Marissa to his empty seat as if not sure what to do with himself.

"I think we're good," I tell him. I doubt Marissa wants her ex-boyfriend's best friend listening to her sob about their break-up. Plus, although I don't think I can reasonably be mad at Michael for not ratting Ben out, it feels a little like he's on Team Ben right now when I've just become captain of Team Marissa. Neither of us is neutral. "Call you tomorrow?"

Michael looks relieved. "Hang in there," he tells Marissa, giving her shoulder a squeeze. "Let me know if you want me to punch him in the face."

Marissa's eyes well up with fresh tears. "I love his face," she says miserably. I give Michael a you-should-leave-now look, and he gets the hint.

"You should eat something," I tell Marissa when we're alone. "A breadstick at least." I break off a piece and hand it to her. "I think it's whole wheat," I lie. But she reaches for the rest of my pizza instead.

278

"That has peppero—"

"I keep replaying it in my mind," she tells me, midbite, either unaware or unconcerned that she's breaking about ten of her food rules right now. "It's like something happened today . . . but nothing happened. He was with me the whole time. I just don't get it." She shoves the last of my slice into her mouth and reaches for what's left of Michael's.

I, of course, know exactly what happened. Ben realized that his secret wasn't a secret any more. He felt like he had to pick between Marissa and Caitlin, and he picked Caitlin. He doesn't realize that he just lost them both.

But the thing is, he never should've thought Caitlin was an option. She was supposed to be off-limits the night they met, wholly and happily unavailable. But she wasn't because my parallel tried to play cupid, destroying not just Caitlin's relationship with Tyler but, ultimately, Marissa's relationship with Ben.

Of course, my parallel didn't know how powerful her words were, how far-reaching the consequences of her lie.

We never do.

*Everything is a cause.*

It's not a new idea, but still, I am stunned to stillness by its truth.

*Everything we do matters.*

I reach for Marissa's hand. "I'm sorry," I tell her, knowing these words are insufficient but wanting – needing – to say them anyway.

# NOVEMBER

# 10
# (here)

## THURSDAY, 26 NOVEMBER, 2009
## (THANKSGIVING DAY)

"You're missing the parade."

I peer out from under the covers and see Dad standing in my doorway, still in his dressing gown, holding a coffee mug. His thinning hair is all mussed up from sleeping on it.

"So are you," I point out.

"That's because I don't have anyone to watch it with. Your mom is busy playing Martha Stewart in the kitchen."

My grandma usually does all the cooking on Thanksgiving, but this year she and my grandpa are spending the month of November on a seniors' tour of South America. Determined not to let this year feel Less Than, my mom has planned an elaborate Thanksgiving meal involving excessively complicated recipes she found online.

"Meet in the living room in five?"

"Avoid the back stairs," he warns. "If she sees you, she'll put you to work. And then I can't save you."

I giggle. "Front stairs. Got it." He nods, then disappears down the hall. I hear him shuffling down the steps. A few moments later, the TV comes on.

I spend another few minutes in bed. *My* bed. With all that's been happening, I'm relieved to be home, in my room, where even the smells are familiar. Except for the blue Yale pennant hanging above my door frame and the graduation photos tacked to my notice board, everything is the way I left it when I moved to Los Angeles last May. It's amazing how dramatically life can change while your bedroom decor stays exactly the same.

It's been twenty-six days since my last reality shift, which is good, because the last one left me rattled. I haven't been sleeping well, and when I'm awake, I'm distracted and uneasy. Replaying the horrible things Caitlin and I said to each other in the cafeteria that day is nowhere near as chilling and awful as reliving the night of Ilana's accident (which I still do, at least once a day), but the memories of the fight and its aftermath haunt me in a different way. I used to think that waking up someplace else was my greatest risk. Now I know that there are far bigger things at stake. We're all just a decision or two away from destroying the relationships that are most important to us and to the people we love. And most of the time, we never even know it.

Now I do. Now I see.

But this new awareness isn't the only thing that's throwing me off. There's also the Josh factor. Against my will, my brain has stored that kiss from the day before Halloween in its Best Kiss Ever file, despite my attempts to replace it with one from Michael (who, it's worth noting, is objectively the better kisser).

But it's not just the kiss that won't go away. It's every memory of Josh I've got since. Holding hands in the hall, sharing Skittles at the movies, watching him from across the room in astronomy. There's nothing particularly significant about these moments, but that hasn't kept my mind from making a freaking highlight reel out of them. Meanwhile my real memories, the new ones, the moments with Michael that I actually *want* to keep, have been relegated to Oh, That Happened status.

*Michael.* At the thought of him, my heart flutters a little and my stomach sinks. Joy competing with fear. The more serious we get, the more I dread our inevitable end. Thankfully, it doesn't look like that end has come today. I haven't run through my morning checklist yet, but with the blue pennant over my door and Caitlin's bracelet on my wrist, I feel good about my odds. But I grab my phone off the bedside table to make sure.

The one perk to losing my phone on Halloween was the discovery that I was due for an upgrade, which meant I could get a fancier one for half the regular price. Since taking advantage of the offer required me to re-up my contract, I decided to get a new number, too. It's silly, but having a 203 area code makes me feel rooted to New Haven, like I've somehow staked a claim to my existence there. Like I truly belong.

The truth, of course, is that I don't. I belong in LA, or maybe at Northwestern, and no matter how many times I wake up to my current reality, I know that it won't last. It can't, now that Caitlin and my parallel aren't speaking. Yale's regular admission application deadline is a week away, and without Caitlin to talk her into it, there's no way my parallel will apply. Truth be told, as thankful as I am to have got a few extra weeks with Michael,

I can't figure out why I'm still at Yale now. The way I figure, the fight with Caitlin erased any chance my parallel had of ending up here. Maybe she'll decide on her own to apply? She'd better hurry. She only has a week till the deadline and, as of right now, she's determined not to apply.

I tap the camera icon and scroll through the latest entries in my photo log, skipping over the one Caitlin took of Michael looking at another girl's butt (I'd delete it, but it's the only one I have from 22 November) and pausing on a shot of him and me at the Yale-Harvard Game last Saturday. We're standing with our arms around each other in front of the Beta tailgate, holding Styrofoam cups of hot cider, our noses red from the cold. The next photo is from the night before, five seconds after Michael told me he loved me for the first (and so far only) time. We were in his kitchen, making microwave popcorn at three in the morning, when out of nowhere he said it. "You know I love you, Abby Barnes." Just like that, as if he were stating the obvious. Yes, it was weird when I asked him if I could take a picture of him right after, but the weirdness was worth it for the proof.

I continue scrolling until I get to the picture from 13 November, the morning they posted the cast list for *Arcadia* with my name at the very top. This one gets a grin every time. Rehearsals don't start until the first week of next term, but the Dramat held auditions early to get them out of the way before exams (which, unfortunately, start two weeks from Monday).

Of all of them, the tailgate photo is my favourite. My hair is down and wavy around my shoulders, and my eyes look almost silver in the midday sun. Michael's green eyes are on me, and his mouth is open in a laugh. Neither of us looks particularly great, but there's something so hi-we're-a-happy-couple about the image.

Caitlin asked me yesterday if I'm in love with him. She knows Michael told me he loves me last Friday, and she also knows I didn't say it back. I wanted to, but then the microwave dinged and one of his roommates came in and we all started eating popcorn. Not exactly an I-love-you-too scenario. Caitlin knows that part, too. So her question caught me off guard, surprising me enough to give me pause. Am I in love with him? How is a person supposed to distinguish between Love and Very Strong Like? Is the distinction all that important? Here's what I know: I like being with him. I like the way he makes me feel. I like waking up next to him, fully clothed, and that being OK with both of us, on his flannel tartan sheets. Do those things add up to love? I think so, but I'm not sure. Which is exactly what I told Caitlin. She responded with some cryptic "trust your instincts" comment and wouldn't elaborate.

*Ding!* A new text appears on my screen.

Michael: HAPPY T-DAY. CANT WAIT TO C U LATER.

I'm smiling as I reply: DITTO. DONT FORGET TO TEXT ME UR ADDY!

The next text I send is to Tyler. He's been acting weird the last few weeks, enough to make me wonder if he's mad at me for something. He and I talked for over an hour the day after Halloween, but since then, I haven't been able to get him on the phone, and when he responds to my texts, it's always with a one- or two-word reply. Not that Ty is a particularly loquacious texter, but I can usually count on him for some dry wit or not-so-veiled sarcasm.

U HOME? I write. CAN WE HANG OUT TOMORROW?

"Abby!" my mom is calling from the kitchen. "I need your help down here!"

"Coming!" I shout. I toss my phone on the bed and head down to the kitchen, where Mom is up to her elbows in turkey (literally). Dad is holding the bird while she stuffs it.

"She tricked me," he declares. "Used the ole 'come here a sec' routine."

"This turkey has to bake for six hours. It's already eight twelve." Mom is rapidly shoving handfuls of celery and onion into the hollow chest cavity. "Abby, there's a ball of twine somewhere in the pantry. Can you see if you can find it, please? And there's a bag of lemons in the fridge. I need those, too."

"Sure."

"So what time's the boyfriend coming over?" Dad asks.

"Not sure yet. He doesn't have a car, so I'm picking him up." I emerge from the pantry with the twine. "How long a piece do you want?"

"I don't know, check the recipe," Mom replies, wiping away an onion-induced tear with her sleeve. "It's on the counter over there."

"So are things serious with this guy?"

"Dad."

286

"What? You've never invited a guy for Thanksgiving before. It feels like a big deal."

"Well, it's not," I insist, even though it feels that way to me, too. "He's not that close with his family and doesn't have any friends here because his parents moved after he was in university. So I invited him to eat with us. That's it."

"Why isn't he close with his family?"

"I don't know. But let's not ask him that over dinner, OK?"

"Maybe you should give me a list of approved talking points before he arrives."

I stick my tongue out at him. "Don't you have a parade to watch?"

"Have you talked to Josh?" Mom asks when I hand her the twine. The question stops me cold.

"Uh, no," I tell her, suddenly very interested in the burlap bag of cornmeal on the counter. "I should call him," I say, because that's what people say.

"You should," Mom is saying. "I obviously don't know what happened between you two, but he was always such a nice guy. If you can save the friendship, you should."

"And next time you sever ties with an ex-boyfriend," my dad pipes up, "clue us in, would ya? I had to hear from Josh that you stopped speaking to him. Over email, nonetheless."

My head jerks up. "What?"

"When I sent you both that article about Lewis Carroll writing *Alice in Wonderland* in a rowing boat," he says. "A couple of weeks ago. I asked if we'd see him while you were home, and he wrote back and said you'd stopped returning his calls."

My heart begins to pound. A couple of *weeks* ago? My reality hasn't changed since Halloween, so if my dad sent me an email, I should remember getting it. "I don't think I got an email from you about *Alice in Wonderland*," I tell him.

"Hm," he says, puzzled. "That's weird."

"Will you forward Josh's email to me?"

"Sure," he replies.

"Done!" my mom announces, stepping back from the turkey. "Put that sucker in the oven," she instructs, then walks to the sink to wash her hands. I open the oven door for my dad, and he puts the bird inside.

"Could you do it now?" I ask him as soon as the oven door is closed.

"What time is it?" my mom yells from the sink.

"Eight nineteen," Dad and I say in unison.

"Could I do what now?" he asks.

"Forward Josh's email. I really need to see it."

"Sure," Dad says. "Lemme just go get my BlackBerry." He disappears into the living room.

"What *did* happen between you two?" Mom asks as she studies her to-do list. "Was it the distance?"

I feel nauseous. If my mom is asking about the distance, it means Josh and I must've still been together when I left for Yale. Never did I consider that Caitlin might have been wrong, that Josh and I might've lasted beyond prom, and definitely not past graduation. OK, maybe I considered it, but I told myself it wasn't possible. Only a certain calibre of high school relationships last past high school. The word "LOVE" is pressing in on me, but I will it away.

"Uh, yeah," I tell her. "The distance." Too bad I don't even know what kind of distance we're talking about. I rack my brain, trying to remember where Josh said he wanted to go to school. West Coast somewhere. For crew.

"Does he know about Michael?" Mom asks as she disappears into the pantry.

Another wave of nausea. The idea that there might've been an overlap makes my chest hurt. *Is it still considered cheating if you don't know you're dating the guy you're cheating on?* "Not yet," I manage.

"Well, he'll hear about it eventually," she calls from the pantry. "I'm sure he'd rather it come from you."

Dad reappears with his BlackBerry. "Where am I sending it?" he asks.

"Hotmail," I tell him, surprised that he's even asking. He knows I only use my Yale address for school stuff.

"Done," he says, and sets his BlackBerry on the counter. "Now back to Michael. What's he studying? Am I allowed to ask him about that?"

"Sure," I say, distracted by the email that's now waiting in my inbox. "I should get into the shower. I'm supposed to pick him up in an hour, and I still don't know how far away he lives."

Taking the stairs two at a time, I book it to my bedroom. My dad's email is the only unread message in my inbox. The subject line is "Alice in Coxswainland". I click on it.

Josh's second reply message is the first one I see, sent from Josh.Wagner@usc.edu.

University of Southern California. Yes, distance would definitely have been an issue.

Hey Mr Barnes,
Abby stopped returning my calls and emails a few weeks
back. So no, I don't think I'll see you over Thanksgiving.
Hope you and Mrs Barnes are doing well.
Take care,
Josh

Holy terse. No pleasantries, no euphemisms. Just: your
daughter is a bitch. I keep reading. The message right below that
one is from my dad.

Josh – Glad you enjoyed it! I thought you might. Will we
see you at Thanksgiving? Anna is already scouring the
internet for recipes.
Hope you're doing well.
Best,
RB
P.S. Tell that daughter of mine that it's rude not to respond
to witty emails from her dad.

I keep scrolling. At the very bottom is my dad's original email,
addressed to Josh and to me at abigailhannahbarnes@gmail.com,
an address I've never seen before today.

My heart is pounding as I type abigailhannahbarnes into the
Gmail username box. Holding my breath, I type w-o-n-d-e-r-l-
a-n-d in the password box and hit enter. Two seconds later, I'm
staring at my sixty-eight unread messages. At least half of them
are from Josh. I hover over the earliest one, sent 31 October,
2009 at 7:08 a.m. PST.

I take a breath and double-click.

Abby,
I just left you a vm. I really need to talk to you. I have a
plan! Call me when you can. My mobile's not working, so
call my landline. 310-555-1840.
J

My rib cage contracts. *Those calls on Halloween were from
him.* He's the LA phone number I couldn't place, the voice
message I couldn't retrieve. Even though I've only ever heard
his voice in my head, I imagine how it would've sounded
on my voicemail that morning, asking me to call him back
and expecting that I would. But of course, I didn't call him
back. Not that day or since. I'm struck with a deep, hollow
pang of regret. If I hadn't lost my phone that morning, I
would've eventually listened to his message. I'm not sure
how I would've handled it, but I certainly wouldn't have frozen
the poor guy out. But now I have. Not for a day or a week, but
for nearly a month.

Chest tight and getting tighter, I click on a more recent
message, dated 10 November, 2009. Ten days later.

Abby,
Not that it matters any more, but the coach at UConn
offered me a spot on their team. I was going to transfer.
That's what I wanted to tell you. That was my big plan.
I was going to leave a school and a team I love to be
closer to a girl I love even more. But I guess it's a good

291

thing I didn't, since clearly she doesn't give a shit about
me.

— J


I stare at my screen as if staring at a train wreck, unable to look away.

*He hates me now.*

This awareness affects me more than I expect it to. I've never even met Josh – not in person anyway. He exists only in fragments, as mere memory, void of the emotion of experience. But in this moment, I remember more of him than I thought I possessed. Images pop into my head, new but familiar. Alternate memories I've been struggling to ignore. Josh carrying my bag for me. Josh singing along to the radio in his Jeep. Josh running his hands through my hair. The caramel corn sundae we split on our first date, and the slow kiss on my doorstep when he dropped me off, his lips still sweet from the ice cream and candy. The giant blue teddy bear he won for me at the Georgia Fair. The self-portrait we took with his phone at the top of the Ferris wheel. The way he looked in the moonlight on the drive home.

All of a sudden, I wish I could switch places with the parallel me. Not permanently. Just . . . for a day. An hour, even. Just long enough to know what it's like to hold Josh's hand, to kiss him, to feel his breath on my neck. My eyes flutter shut and I'm back there again, on that bench by the pond in his neighbourhood, my lips on his, tasting cinnamon and Ivory soap, willing the clock to stop so I won't have to go home. I give in to the memory, soaking in every detail. I haven't let myself do this, not once, afraid of where it might lead. What I might feel. But that was a mistake, because there is truth in these memories. Raw and bright. Of course Josh and I were still together after we left for school. That's not the surprising part. The surprising part is that we broke up. From these memories, it seems impossible that we could.

I scroll down, past the unread messages to the ones marked READ, clicking on one dated August 29, 2009. The day I left for Yale. There's a sweet I-miss-you-already message from Josh and a reply email from me. I stare at my screen, marvelling at the fact that, because of some freaky cosmic accident, I'm reading an email exchange my parallel self will have with her boyfriend nine months from now.

I click on the next message and the message after that, needing to read every one. The first few are brimming with *I love yous* and *I miss yous* and talk of upcoming visits and holiday breaks. But it doesn't take long for the tone to shift, for anxiety and doubt and fear to take hold. My parallel starts writing things like, *Maybe it was crazy to think we could do this*, and Josh starts writing things like, *Let's not make any decisions right now, OK?* But he should've known better than that. The Abby he loves isn't a wait-and-see kind of girl. The Abby he loves doesn't know how to handle uncertainty, so she runs from it, the way I used to, before.

Subject line: Tonight. Sent 25 September, 2009.

Abby,
I'm sorry I reacted the way I did tonight. I just wish we
could've had that conversation in person. I know the

distance is a lot. But we knew it would be, and we won't
always be three thousand miles apart. Please, don't do
this. What we have is worth fighting for. Let's figure this
out, together. I love you.
Josh

I sit, unmoving. Unhinged. Seeing the words in black
and white, knowing how it'll end, and when, and why – this
awareness should comfort me. But instead I have this hollow
feeling in my gut, the way you feel when you drink coffee on an
empty stomach. *She was afraid, so she gave up.* Of all the reasons
for their relationship to end, that has to be the worst.

I scroll back up to an earlier email, my favourite of them all,
and read it again, allowing myself to imagine, just for a moment,
that it was intended for me.

Abigail Hannah Barnes,
You changed my life. A year ago today, when you walked
into it. "Are you here by fate or choice?" you asked me. I
said choice. Now I know better.
I love you!!!!!!!!!!!!!!!! Happy day before your birthday.
Josh

I sit with these words, basking in their simple truth. Then it
dawns on me: my parallel will still be with Josh on her eighteenth
birthday. According to the emails I just read, they won't have
"that conversation" for two more weeks. But if that's true, then
my relationship with Michael couldn't have started the way I
remember it. But clearly it did. I've got a picture of him scream-

singing the lyrics to "Whatta Man" on the dance floor at Alchemy to prove it.

*How is that possible?*

"Easy," Caitlin says after I explain the situation to her. "It's just cause and effect."

"OK, new rule: when we're talking about cosmic entanglement, you're not allowed to use the phrase 'it's just'. It's never '*just*' anything."

"Would you like me to explain this to you or not?"

"Yes. Go."

"If a tree falls in the forest and no one hears it, did it make a sound?"

"I'm serious, Caitlin."

"So am I! You asked why your parallel's relationship with Josh hasn't affected your relationship with Michael. I'm giving you the answer: because no one knew about it. Think about it: the only person at your birthday dinner who knew you in high school was me, and I had no idea that you and Josh were still together. I stopped keeping up with your love life when we stopped talking."

"Ugh. It just feels so gross," I moan. "I kissed Michael that night, and I was still with Josh."

"Abby, you weren't *actually* with Josh. He just remembers it as though you were."

I know this, but I still feel weird about it.

"Abby!" my mom calls from the kitchen. "What time are you leaving to get Michael?"

Yikes. I'm supposed to be at his house in half an hour, and I still haven't showered.

"I have to go," I tell Caitlin. "Call you later?"

"Have fun," Caitlin calls in a sing-song voice. "Fingers crossed your dad does something super embarrassing."

"I'm hanging up on you," I say, and do.

Five minutes before I'm supposed to be at Michael's house, I gun it out of our driveway, one hand on the steering wheel, the other fumbling with the clasp on my grandma's pearls, which I'm wearing for good luck despite the fact that they in no way go with my outfit. After this morning's revelations, lucky pearls seemed appropriate.

At the first stoplight, I enter the address Michael sent into my phone's GPS, expecting at least a fifteen-minute drive. *Estimated driving time four minutes?* I pull over on to the shoulder and look at the map on my screen. Lilac Lane is a short street in what looks like a big subdivision. I scan the names of the streets near it. Daisy Court. Rose Terrace. Gardenia Place. Apparently, the builder had a flower fetish.

One name jumps out at me: Poplar Drive, two streets over. We had a party there junior year, before the road was paved. We left our cars at Tyler's house and walked over. Now the flower names make sense: Poplar Drive is in Garden Grove, a little enclave of newer homes in Tyler's sprawling subdivision. *Michael's parents live in Tyler's neighbourhood?* Whoa. That means if they'd moved here four years ago instead of two, Michael and I would've gone to high school together. Would we have dated? Would my parents have *allowed* me to date him? They let me go to prom with Casey Decker freshman year, but he was only a junior because he skipped first grade, and he only asked me to the dance because the girls in his own grade called him Casey Pecker. I don't think my dad would've been as keen on Casey if he'd looked like Michael.

I wonder what my dad thought of Josh when they met. Not what he told my parallel, but how he really felt. Judging from the tone of their email exchange, Dad was a big fan of Astronomy Boy. Did he like him instantly, or was it a gradual thing? Will my dad like Michael less because he'll compare him to Josh?

Would *I* like Michael less if I could compare him to Josh? Truly compare them, not just how they appear on paper or in memory, but how they really are when you're with them. Michael is smart and charming and confident. Josh is . . . a different version of that. Less . . . knock-you-off-your-feet. More . . . what? The word *right* keeps pounding in my head. *Right, right, right.*

I pull up in front of a modest two-story brick colonial at the end of a cul-de-sac. The numbers 4424 are painted on the kerb. *Wait, is this right?* I thought I turned on Lilac, but this must be Poplar. I've definitely been on this street before. Turning around in the cul-de-sac, I drive back to the beginning of the street to check the sign. It's Lilac, all right. Puzzled, I head back to 4424 and park in the driveway. As I'm walking up the pavement to the front porch, I take in every detail. The grey-blue shutters, the flower bed, the bird feeder in the front lawn. I've definitely seen this house before. My mind is on the brink of placing it when Michael opens the front door.

"Sorry I'm late," I call as I'm getting out of the car. "It was further than I thought it'd be." I'm kidding, but he doesn't know that. His face falls in mock disappointment.

"Bummer. I was hoping we'd live close enough for me to walk over to your house at midnight and throw rocks at your window."

297

He sticks his head back inside the house. "I'm leaving!" he calls to whoever's inside. Without waiting for an answer, he closes the door and comes down the pavement towards me.

"Should I be offended that you're not inviting me in?" I joke. Sort of.

"Definitely not. I want you to meet my mom, but tension is a little high right now. I just told them I wasn't coming home for Christmas again this year."

"Don't you spend Christmas with your dad, anyway?" Michael gives me a funny look. I flounder. "When you said you spent Thanksgiving with your mom, I assumed that meant. . ."

"My dad died four years ago."

"Oh," I manage, wanting desperately to rewind the last ten seconds. "I didn't know."

"I guess I just assumed Marissa would've told you," he says. "Otherwise, I would have." *Like you've told me so much other stuff about yourself?* I fight annoyance. My boyfriend just told me his dad died. I'm supposed to feel sympathetic. I'm not supposed to be annoyed that he's never mentioned it before. But we're supposed to be a couple, and couples are supposed to tell each other everything. Michael tells me almost nothing. Then again, my brain is cosmically connected to a girl living in parallel world, and I haven't said a word about that.

"Hey," he says softly. "I wasn't trying to keep it from you or anything. It's just hard for me to talk about, that's all." I nod, feeling like a bitch for being upset about it. He leans in and kisses me softly on the lips. I expect a quick peck, but it turns into a serious kiss. When I feel his tongue on mine, I pull back.

"Um, isn't your mom inside?"

He laughs. "She went to the grocery store for more eggs. And my stepdad's in his office. In the windowless attic."

"And your neighbours?" I say, looking around the cul-de-sac.

"Don't know 'em," he replies, and pulls me into another kiss, silencing my protest.

A few seconds into it, I hear a car pull into the driveway behind me. I jerk my head back from the kiss. *Not the way I wanted to meet his mom.* "Don't worry," Michael says, looking past me. "It's just my brother." The car door slams, and there are footsteps on the driveway.

"You have a *brother*?"

Michael nods casually. "We're not exactly close."

I smooth my hair and turn around.

My stomach drops.

"Glad you could make it," Michael calls from behind me, his voice dripping with sarcasm.

*Holy shit. Holy. Shit.*

Josh is standing in the driveway, holding a suitcase. Tyler is behind the wheel of his mom's burgundy minivan. Suddenly, I understand why Tyler has been acting weird. It was about Josh.

"You're Michael's brother," I say, stunned. *Josh is Michael's brother.*

Josh just stares at me.

"You know my brother?" Michael asks.

I nod feebly. "We went to high school together," I manage.

Josh's face twists in anger. "That's right!" he says, his voice laden with sarcasm and fury. "We did go to high school together! Then you went to Yale and morphed into a heartless bitch. Here's the part I'm not sure about: at what point did you start screwing my brother? Was it before or after you decided to blow me off?" For a second I think he might spit at me, but he just gets back into the van. Tyler is already halfway down the driveway when Josh slams the door.

"Whoa. What was that about?" Michael looks stunned.

"We used to date," I say weakly, knowing he'll need more detail than that and wondering how I can possibly give it to him.

"You dated my *brother*? Recently?"

"No! We broke up in September. Why didn't you tell me you had a brother?"

"It didn't seem important. Wait, *this* September?"

"It didn't seem *important*?" I stare at him in disbelief. "He's your *brother*."

"We're not close," Michael says evenly. "You had a *boyfriend* when we met?"

*Crap.*

For a second, I consider telling him the truth. The collision, the entanglement, all of it. The words start to form in my mouth. "It's the craziest thing," I start to say. But Michael cuts me off.

"Look, I don't want my brother to come between us," he says. "He's not worth it." Michael steps down off the porch so we're eye level. "Whatever happened between you guys is over, right? One hundred per cent?"

"One hundred per cent," I say firmly.

"Good," he says, and touches my cheek. "Now let's eat."

300

The meal goes surprisingly well considering the massive elephant in the dining room. Two seconds after we sat down, Michael launched into the Josh story, sparing no detail (not even the front porch kiss). My parents smiled politely, but I could tell they were horrified by the notion that their daughter might have broken up with her boyfriend for his older, cuter (and thus, in their mind, less trustworthy) brother.

"I didn't know they were brothers," I offer by way of explanation.

"How is that possible?" my mom asks. "Didn't you know Josh had a brother named Michael at Yale?" The problem, of course, is that I don't *know* if I know that. Fortunately, no one else at this table does, either.

"There are a lot of Michaels at Yale," I reply defensively. "And Michael didn't tell me he had a brother, so I didn't make the connection," I add, glaring at Michael. He brought this up. He can deal with it.

"Josh and I don't exactly get along," Michael tells her calmly, spooning sweet potato soufflé on to his plate. "Before this morning, we hadn't spoken since last Thanksgiving. Wow, these yams look amazing, Mrs Barnes."

"Thank you," she says, then turns back to me. "The name Michael Wagner didn't ring a bell?" she says pointedly.

"His last name isn't Wagner," I snap. "It's Carpenter."

"Oh, so you're *step*brothers," Mom says, as though this makes everything better.

"No, we have the same parents," Michael tells her. "My stepfather adopted Josh when he married my mom two years ago. I respectfully declined the offer." Somehow I doubt there

301

was anything respectful about it. Michael can't even say the word "stepfather" without contempt. *How can two guys have such different opinions of the same man?* Even from my limited memories, I know that Josh adores Martin. Michael, for some undisclosed reason, hates him.

"How'd your mom and Martin meet?" I ask in an effort to both change the subject and gather some clues about the source of Michael's ill will towards the man his mother married.

"He and my dad were best friends," Michael replies.

"Yikes," my dad says under his breath. I shoot him a look.

Mom holds up the platter in her hand and smiles. "Balsamic-glazed parsnips, anyone?"

# 11
# (here)

*You have already told us about yourself in the Common Application, the Short Answer and the Personal Essay. Please tell us something about yourself that you believe we cannot learn elsewhere in your application.*

I stare at my blinking cursor. I should be thrilled that the prompt is so vague. But what if everything about you is already covered "elsewhere in your application"? What if there's nothing left to say?

"See, this is why I'm not Yale material," I mutter. *Why am I even doing this?* Why am I filling out the application if I'm not going to apply?

I start typing. *The Lure of the Ivy, by Abigail Barnes.*

"There are those who have never wanted to go anywhere else," I type, reading my words aloud as I go. "The moment they learned what university was, they set their sights on the Ivy League. Awed by its exclusivity, inspired by its excellence, enticed by its promise of a bigger and brighter future. I have never been one of those people. That is, until the Yale application packet arrived in my mailbox. It was that moment that I felt it: the Lure of the Ivy."

I charge through another four hundred words, then reread what I've written. Definitely *not* what the Yale admissions committee is looking for, but that's fine, since I'm not actually applying. If I wasn't certain before, I am now. My own words convinced me. I'll admit, when I saw that my SAT score was within the median, there was a moment – a millisecond – when I considered it. It's hard not to be enticed by all that history and prestige. But that's not a reason to apply.

*And fear isn't a reason not to.*

I push this thought from my mind. Yes, the fact that the odds are stacked against me has intensified my conviction. Why shouldn't it? Strong sense of self. That's my thing. I know what I'm good at, and I stick to those things. What's wrong with having a realistic grasp of my potential? It's not like I'm resigned to mediocrity. I just know my limits.

*Your limits or the edge of your comfort zone?*

"Enough," I mutter. I'm ready to stop thinking about this. I promised my mom that I wouldn't make a hasty decision, and I haven't. I've thought it through and come to a reasonable and rational conclusion. Yale is not for me. As if to make the point, I drag the "Yale Application" folder from my desktop to the recycle bin where it belongs.

I don't even know why I bothered filling it out. There's a good chance I'll hear from Northwestern today, and if I do, that will be that. Early Action decision letters were sent on 20th November, and a bunch of people on the NU admissions blog have already got their acceptance email. Mine could arrive any minute. Just thinking about it makes me shaky. For the sixtieth time today, I click on my mailbox icon.

No new messages.

I wonder if Caitlin's heard from Yale yet. Even though we haven't spoken since our fight, I'm praying she gets in early. Thanks to Grandpa Oscar, it's the only place she's ever wanted to go. Unceremoniously, I pick up the phone and dial her number. Her voicemail picks up immediately.

"Hi, this is Caitlin. Leave me a message and I'll call you back." *Beep.*

I quickly hang up.

In twenty-eight days, I've called her twenty-eight times. Sometimes it rings a couple of times first. Once the line just went dead. Most of the time it goes straight to voicemail. I'm terrified of an in-person confrontation – I avoid her at school and stopped going to the frozen yoghurt place we both love – but I've called her every single day since our fight. I'm not sure what I'd say to her if she ever picked up, but I keep calling anyway. Afraid of what it'll mean if I stop. In my head, I know there's a good chance our friendship is already beyond repair, but in my gut, I still believe there's a scenario in which we move past this and go back to being Caitlin and Abby. The hardest part is knowing what to do in the meantime.

Time to get moving. The crew team's first-ever pep rally picnic starts at noon, and I'm still all sweaty and windblown from practice this morning. Ever since my foot healed, Coach Schwartz has had me jogging with the team before practice and doing press-ups and crunches with them after, so I end up just as nasty as everyone else. Since I'm pretty close to pre-injury form, I thought about asking Coach P to let me run in the state cross-country meet this weekend, but decided that I couldn't abandon my teammates for the Head of the Hooch. It's the biggest regatta of the autumn season. Coach wants us at the boathouse ten minutes before the picnic starts to hand out our boat assignments. Close to a dozen university recruiters will be there, so everyone is on edge – Josh in particular. This is the first (and only) time this season that scouts from the West Coast will see him row, so if he wants a crew scholarship to a PAC-10 school, Saturday is his make-or-break moment. Not that he has anything to worry about. Our star stroke hasn't had an off day all season.

And, since we started dating, neither have I. The past twenty-six days have been like nothing I've ever experienced. Feast and famine. Fire and ice. My days break down into two categories: moments with Josh and moments without him. When I'm with him, my mind turns off. I don't think. I don't plan. I don't worry. There's no room for thoughts or plans or worries. Every space and crevice is stuffed with happiness, so full it feels like my soul might burst at the seams. Minutes speed by, rushing us to the next and then the next, until our time is up.

That's when I'm with him. When I'm not, time slows down. Seconds crawl by. I watch the clock, counting the hours until I see him again, as I think and plan and worry. About him, about us, about the future. I replay our last kiss and try to plan for the next one. I wonder if he's feeling what I do, simultaneously convinced that he can't be and he must. I worry about what it'll be like to leave him, even though graduation is still six months away.

"You're in love," Mom said when I came home last Saturday night, clutching a giant blue teddy bear. Josh had taken me to the fair, where we'd shared candyfloss and ridden the rickety roller coaster, and he'd won me the biggest stuffed animal on the wall. Afterwards, we went to our swing in Josh's neighbourhood, neither of us caring that the moon was too bright to see any stars. I could still taste his gum on my lips. Big Red. The kind he always chews.

"What?" I said, even thought I'd heard her fine.

"You're in love," she repeated, her smile knowing and kind. "I'm glad."

I blushed and looked away, not ready to acknowledge it, but not arguing with her either.

*I'm in love.*

"Abby!" I hear Mom call from downstairs, startling me back to the present. "Isn't the picnic at noon?"

The party is about to begin when I arrive at the boathouse at quarter till. In the time since practice ended, the Brookside booster club has turned the boathouse grounds into a wonderland of blue and orange streamers and balloons. The Peppery Pig has set up shop under a huge tent in the shape of a Spartan's helmet, giving the crisp autumn air that great charcoal-and-roasted-meat scent. I inhale deeply, relishing it.

My teammates are gathered around the picnic table closest to the river, munching on crisps and dip while Coach hovers nearby, holding his ubiquitous clipboard. Josh, as usual, is the last to arrive. He's never actually *late*, he just doesn't show up until the precise time we're supposed to meet. Class, practice, our dates. Always right on time.

At 11:49, his Jeep pulls into the car park. I smile as he comes down the hill. Untucked polo shirt, Converses replaced by canvas loafers. Hanging out with Tyler is clearly rubbing off on him. He's also stopped parting his hair, and right now it's damp and messy, like he got out of the shower and shook it.

As he gets closer, my mind quiets and everything gets brighter. The blue of the sky, the green of the pine needles, the yellow paint on the boathouse door. My teammates are talking, laughing, buzzing with adrenaline and caffeine, but they've become background noise. The Josh Effect.

"OK, people," Coach calls over the hum of chatter. "We only have a couple minutes before the crowd shows up." The team gets quiet. "We're mixing things up this week," he announces. "In the stern, anyway. Megan, I'm moving you to the men's B." Megan's jaw literally drops. She's been coxing the 8A all season, and the buzz is she has a tentative offer from College of Charleston, contingent on her performance on Saturday. When the COC coach sees that she's been bumped from the A boat, he's going to assume she did something to warrant it. "This isn't meant to be a punishment," Coach is saying to Megan. "I still want you on the women's A. I just want to give Abby a shot at the men."

*Did he just say Abby?*

Since Josh is currently grinning at me like the Cheshire cat, I assume the answer is yes. My hand shoots up.

"You don't have to do that," I blurt out. "Megan deserves to be in the A boat. It should be her, not me." I flash a smile in

Megan's direction, but she doesn't return it. Meanwhile, Josh is staring me down.

"I don't *have* to do anything," Coach snaps. "But last time I checked, *I* was the coach of this team. Which means I make the boat assignments. Not you. Not Megan." I nod glumly. "The rest of the assignments are the same as last week," he continues.

He prattles on, but I stop listening. *I'm coxing the 8A? At the Head of the Hooch?* There's no way that's a good idea. Yes, I've got better at this, but I am not A boat material. I'm not even B boat material. Every Saturday I'm amazed that my shell makes it to the finish line without crashing into the riverbank.

"I'm preparing stat sheets for each of you to give to scouts on Saturday," Coach says in conclusion, replacing the top sheet of his clipboard with a blank piece of paper. "So write down your email address before you go. And I better not see 'crewgirl' or 'mrstroke' or any of that shit. Like I said last week, university scouts are looking for mature rowers, not punk-ass kids. OK, you're dismissed."

"'It should be her, not me'?" Josh asks. "What was that about?"

I shrug. "She's better than I am. And this matters more to her."

"First of all, she's not better than you. More experienced, maybe, but you've got better instincts. Second, impressing recruiters on Saturday could mean a crew scholarship. Or a leg up at a great school."

"The only 'great school' I'm interested in going to is Northwestern," I remind him. "And they don't have a varsity team."

"I know you've got your eyes on Northwestern. But the Ivies are always looking for rowers. Crew could be your way in."

309

"I don't want to go to an Ivy," I snap. "I want to go to a school with a journalism programme."

"Doesn't Columbia have one?"

"Not undergrad. Look, I get it that it's most people's dream to end up at Yale or Harvard or wherever. But that's not what I want."

Josh holds his hands up. "You won't get any argument from me. If it's not what you want, it's not what you want. I thought you weren't applying to those places because you thought you couldn't get in, and I wanted to make sure you knew that rowing could be a way in. *If* that's what you wanted," he adds. "If it isn't, it isn't."

"It isn't," I say firmly.

"OK. So what about USC? A journalism programme *and* a great rowing team."

"Do you ever give up?" *Did he just suggest I apply to USC?* As amazing as things are between us, we haven't gone down that road. There's been no discussion of applying to the same schools, because we both know that would force one of us to forgo our top choice. I look at him, waiting for this conversation to become *that* conversation, but Josh just kisses me on the nose. "Hey, there's Tyler."

When I turn to greet him, Tyler doesn't return my smile. He looks uncharacteristically glum.

"Is Caitlin coming?" I ask, even though I already know the answer. Caitlin hasn't come to a single party or school-related event since our fight. She spends every evening and most weekends at the Tech astrophysics lab. At least, that's what she's told Ty every time he's tried to make plans with her. He and

Caitlin are still friends, but it's different now that she knows how he feels about her. Complicated where it used to be so effortless. No wonder Caitlin's been living at the lab, a place where order is imposed on chaos and not the other way around. It's her escape from the havoc. A haven from Tyler's searching eyes and my incessant calls.

"Haven't talked to her," he says, looking past me to Josh. "Let's get some food while it's hot."

"So I have something to ask you," Josh says as he's walking me to my car, under the close watch of the two park rangers patrolling the car park. They showed up about an hour ago, when the sun disappeared behind the pine trees that line the riverbank. The picnic lasted way longer than anyone thought it would. It'd still be going if the park rangers hadn't kicked us out. Josh and I are the very last to leave. We hung around under the guise of cleaning up, but really we wanted to watch the sunset through the pines. Just before the sun sank behind the horizon, he kissed me. Pressed up against him, I could feel his heart through his chest, beating as wildly as my own.

"Uh-oh. Should I be nervous?"

"Only if you say yes." He smiles at my quizzical look. "Come over tomorrow," he says. "For Thanksgiving. My mom is cooking enough food for a small army, mainly because she's anxious about my brother being in town, and cooking keeps her busy."

"Your brother's in town?" Josh has mentioned his brother only a handful of times and never by name. I didn't quite envision him as the home-for-the-holidays type.

"He will be," Josh replies. "He flies in tonight and leaves Friday morning."

"Quick trip," I say, and then wonder if I should have.

"Yeah. He never stays more than a day. Which is good for all of us, believe me. Things are pretty tense when he's around."

"Sounds fun," I joke.

"Not in the least," Josh replies, still smiling, but his voice is less joking than mine. "Which is where you come in. I'm hoping you'll deflect some of the tension," he admits. "So you'll come? We usually eat around two."

"I'd love to," I tell him, suddenly thrilled that my grandparents decided last minute to spend this Thanksgiving in the Caymans. When my grandma cooks, the meal starts promptly at one, and she expects us to spend hours at the dining room table, relishing every course. With my mom at the helm, there's no way we'll eat before sundown. I'll easily be back from Josh's in time.

"Great," he says. "So I'll see you tomorrow, then."

"See you tomorrow," I reply, and touch my lips to his. He steps forward, resting his hands lightly on my hips as his lips move against mine. We've kissed twenty-three times, but I still get light-headed when it happens. The two on the roller coaster last weekend (numbers nineteen and twenty) nearly made me pass out.

"Hey, you two! The party's over!" An exasperated park ranger is idling in his truck, waiting to shut the gate to the car park.

"Sorry!" we call in unison, swallowing smiles. Josh kisses me one more time, earning us a honk from our chaperone.

"If she was your girlfriend, would *you* want to leave?" Josh shouts to the park ranger as he jogs to his car. He turns back and blows me yet another kiss.

Then, suddenly, it's as if everything slows down. Even the wind that right now is rustling Josh's hair. Details I didn't notice a second ago now jump out at me. The old gnarled tree at the head of the path down to the river. The Sprite can someone left in the car park that got crushed by a car tyre. The small brown bird perched on the edge of the entrance sign. And, at the centre of all of it, Josh. His hand at his mouth, palm open, his kiss having just taken flight. A grin just beginning to take shape. The dark grey USC T-shirt with a bleach spot on the collar.

The moment feels like déjà vu, but more precise. Déjà vu isn't detailed. This moment is all about the details. Even Josh's tiny mole stands out.

Then, as quickly as it slowed down, everything speeds up again, and Josh's back is to me as he jogs to his Jeep.

I'm surprised to see my grandparents' maroon Buick LeSabre parked in our driveway when I pull in. They're supposed to be boarding a Seniors at Sea cruise ship right now.

There's much commotion in the kitchen when I open the back door. My grandma is holding a syringe full of dark brown liquid over a massive raw turkey. There are brown grocery bags on every available countertop.

"Grandma, I think he's dead already," I say as I step inside.

"She gets her sarcasm from you," my grandmother says, looking pointedly at my father.

"Better that than my hairline," Dad replies, and kisses me on the forehead.

"Still waiting," my grandpa says, the same thing he says at the beginning of every visit. I walk over and plant a kiss on his cheek. "That's better," he says, folding me into a hug. "How's my girl?"

"I'm good, Grandpa," I tell him, burrowing my nose into his leathery skin. Tobacco and Lagerfeld cologne. He always smells the same. I smile against his neck. "What are you guys doing here?" I ask, resting my cheek on his shoulder. "I thought you were supposed to be in the Caymans."

"We were," my grandmother replies, squinting at the turkey.

"Thwarted by a hurricane," Grandpa says. "So here we are."

"Surprise!" my mom says cheerily, between large gulps of wine. Grandma shoots her a look, then stabs the bird with all the force her tiny frame can muster.

"So does this mean we're eating at one o'clock tomorrow?" I ask.

"Of course," my grandmother says as she pumps our turkey with brine. "We always eat at one." My mom and I look at each other and mouth Grandma's words with her as she says them in her thick Tennessee drawl: "It's tradition."

314

"Their flight from Nashville to Miami was cancelled because of the hurricane," I tell Josh, "so they drove down here instead." I called him as soon as I could escape the kitchen.

"That's good news, right? You were bummed you weren't going to see them."

"Yeah, but it means I can't come over tomorrow. We sit down at one o'clock and, no joke, we don't finish till five. It's the longest meal of the year. At the end of it, both my voice and my ears are tired."

"You're lucky," he says. "We speed through ours in awkward silence."

"What time does your brother get in?"

"His plane lands at nine," Josh replies. "My mom's at the airport picking him up."

"Are you excited that he's coming?" I ask. I don't mean to pry, but I can't help it. I know so little about Josh's relationship with his brother, and why his presence puts everyone on edge.

"Excited? No. But it means a lot to my mom that he comes every year, so I'm glad that he does. But he treats Martin like crap."

"Why?" Josh idolizes his stepfather. What would make his brother feel so differently? When Josh doesn't answer right away, I quickly backpedal. "I'm sorry, I'm being nosy."

"Don't be silly," he says. "You're my girlfriend. You're allowed to be nosy." He hesitates before continuing. "It's complicated," he says eventually, "but the gist is, Michael thinks my mom and Martin were having an affair before my dad died. My mom says they didn't, and I believe her. Michael claims to have forgiven my mom, but he still hates Martin. He refused to come to their wedding."

315

"Wow." I was expecting a story about a missed curfew or a wrecked car, not something this heavy. "Poor Martin."

"Yeah. It's even worse because he loved my dad so much. They were best friends," he explains. "University roommates. Martin never would've done something like that to Dad. But he can't even defend himself, because he doesn't know what Michael thinks."

"Michael's never confronted him about it?"

"My mom won't let him," Josh replies. "When Michael came to my mom with his theory about the affair, my mom told him that if he ever said anything to Martin, she'd stop paying his Yale tuition. She also made him promise to come home for Thanksgiving every year." He pauses, then says, "Wow, it sounds a lot worse when you say it out loud."

"Where'd the theory come from?" I ask. "If your mom and Martin weren't having an affair, why did Michael think they were?"

"According to my mom, he misunderstood something he overheard. She's always been really vague about it." His line beeps with another call. "Oh, hey, that's her calling on the other line. Call you back?"

"Of course," I say, and we hang up.

"Whatcha doin' in there, sitting in the dark?" It's my grandpa in the doorway, an unlit cigar between his lips.

"Looking at the stars," I tell him, and point at my ceiling. He looks from me to the stars and back again.

"You know there are real stars outside," he says. "A whole universe filled with 'em."

"I've heard that, yeah." I smile in the dark.

"C'mon," he tells me, beckoning with his arm. "Take a walk with an old man."

My grandfather's idea of a "walk" is going to the end of the driveway and back – eleven times – while he smokes a cigar. As we're on our third pass, he pats the arm that's linked with his and says, "I think it's time I told you what happened the night you were born."

"The night I was born?"

He puffs his cigar and nods. "Your dad called around eight o'clock that night to tell me your mother was in labour. We had strict instructions not to get into the car to drive down here until you'd officially arrived, so there was nothing to do but wait. It was a big deal for us, first grandchild and all. And since your parents had waited ten years to have you, we figured you might be all we'd get."

A wave of sadness washes over me. While my mom's the youngest of six, my dad and I are both only children. From what my mom's told me, my grandma struggled with infertility back before there were treatments for it. She lost six babies before having my dad. And my mom, she only ever wanted one. How lonely it must be, to be in your eighties and to be able to count your family members on one hand.

"So, we waited," my grandfather continues, pausing for a few more puffs. "Your grandmother was a mess of nervous energy, banging around in the kitchen, making all this noise, so I went outside. There wasn't a moon that night, so the stars were especially bright – much brighter than they are tonight." *A perfect moon,* I think, elated to tell Josh. Grandpa stops walking and tilts his head back. "And I stood there," he says, "just like this, watching the sky and praying that the Lord would bring you here safely. And then . . . *zzzoom!*" His hand zips through the night air for effect. "A star shot across the sky."

I smile, imagining it. Grandpa turns to look at me. "And that would've been something – a shooting star always is. But then there was another one. And one after that." He looks back up at the sky. "They just kept coming," he says. "Nine altogether."

"You're making that up."

"I most certainly am not," he replies, crossing his heart with his free hand. "And after the ninth one, they stopped. A few minutes later, I heard the phone ring inside, and a few minutes after that, Rose came out to tell me you'd been born. At nine-oh-nine on September the ninth."

Goosebumps spring up on my arm. *That's a lot of nines.*

"I've spent the last seventeen years trying to figure out what it meant," he says then. "'Just a coincidence', most people would say. And maybe it was. But I'll tell you what, it sure didn't feel like one."

"What'd my dad say?" I ask.

"I never told him," my grandfather replies. "Or anyone else."

"Why not?"

"Because I wanted to be the one to tell you about it," he says, giving my arm a squeeze. "When you were old enough to really hear it. As much as I love my son, he can't keep a secret for shit." I stifle a giggle. No argument here. "I always planned to tell you on your eighteenth birthday – 9/9/2009 seemed fitting somehow – but I reckon you'll be off at university by then. Figured I'd better tell you now."

"So if it wasn't a coincidence," I say when we start walking again, "then what was it?"

"A sign, maybe. That your life would be special." He chews thoughtfully on his cigar. "That's what I always thought, anyway."

"Special how?"

"That depends," he tells me, his face suddenly serious.

"On what?"

"What you decide to do with it."

# 12
# (there)

"You owe me one," Tyler says as soon as he opens his front door.

"Here," I reply, handing him a plastic container of yesterday's leftovers. I look past him into the house. "Where is he?"

"Basement." He pulls open the blue cover and peers inside, surveying the contents. "I don't see yams."

"They're at the bottom. Below the parsnips. How does he seem?"

Tyler plucks a green bean out of the container and pops it into his mouth. "Pissed as hell," he replies, chomping on the bean. "So good luck with that."

Tyler steps back to let me inside. His mom, a concert pianist with a penchant for bright colours and expensive kitsch, has painted each wall of the foyer a different shade of magenta. Randomly placed shelves display various treasures she's acquired over the years, only some of which are wall-appropriate. A hand-painted mask with a beaklike nose stares down at me menacingly.

"So that's why you were freezing him out?" Tyler asks. "You were screwing his brother?"

"I'm not *screwing* him," I say pointedly. "And I didn't know they were brothers."

"Why didn't you just break up with him like a normal person?" Tyler asks.

"It's complicated."

"Whose fault is that?"

"I thought you were staying out of it?" I shrug out of my sweater and hang it on the banister. There are sweat stains on my T-shirt. *Why am I so nervous?* This seemed like a good idea when I orchestrated it during this morning's six-mile sprint through my neighbourhood. Having Tyler invite Josh over, pretending to just show up. It seemed like a brilliant plan. Now I'm thinking the endorphins may have led me astray, considering the guy I'm about to ambush promptly hung up on me when I called him last night.

At least things with Michael are OK, if our sunrise drive to the airport was any indication. He was supposed to be in Boston with his high school friends until late Sunday night, but he told me he's taking an earlier train so we can go to dinner when I get back to New Haven.

"Should I stay up here?" Tyler asks, mouth full. He's using his index finger to shovel broccoli casserole into his mouth.

"No. We want him to think I just dropped by, remember? If you stay up here, it'll look planned."

"Whatever. Either way, I've committed a major man-code

violation. Luring him over here with PS3 so that his heartless ex-girlfriend can ambush him?" Tyler shakes his head. "I'm ashamed of myself." He drags his finger back through the broccoli. "Then again, I'll do pretty much anything for your mom's leftovers."

"What if he won't talk to me?" I ask.

"I'd be more worried about what you're gonna say if he will," Tyler replies. "You gave the guy the deep freeze, then showed up on his front porch with his brother's tongue down your throat."

"It was unintentional," I insist.

"If you say so," he says. "How's Caitlin?"

"She's good," I tell him. "You should call her."

"Yeah, maybe," he says. But I know he won't. It's hard to know how to feel about it, especially since neither of them seems unhappy about how things ended up. Tyler has a new girlfriend at Michigan that he's crazy about, and Caitlin can't stop talking about the guy she met last week at STARRY, Yale's astronomy club, who's probably just a Ben replacement but a welcome one. Who knows, maybe Caitlin's right. Maybe it's better this way, maybe Caitlin and Tyler weren't meant to be after all. I'm not sure I buy it – Tyler's girlfriend calls her girl parts "the V-train" and Caitlin's Astronomy Boy wears multiple shirts with popped collars (all pastel and all polo and all at the same time) – but I beat myself up less if I pretend to.

"Ilana's in town," Tyler says then. "Visiting her parents for Thanksgiving. I ran into her yesterday at a petrol station."

"How's she doing?"

"Pretty well, I think," he replies. "Better." My spirits lift just a little. "She told me to thank you for the journal you sent," he says. "She said she's been writing in it every day."

322

With all the drama of Halloween and its aftermath, I'd forgotten I'd sent it. I found it at a bookstore off campus, misshelved in the religion section, wedged between Kempis and Kierkegaard. It was pink, Ilana's favourite colour, and had the word REMEMBER imprinted on the cover. I sent it with a purple pen and a note telling her that no matter what her doctors were saying, she shouldn't be discouraged. There are always anomalies.

"Think she'd mind if I stopped by to see her while she's here?" I ask him.

"I think she'd love it," Tyler replies. "But seriously? You and Ilana?"

"We have more in common than you'd think," I say, and smile.

I follow Tyler down the basement stairs. Josh is muttering angrily at the TV screen, immersed in a game of Street Fighter. He doesn't see me at first, giving me thirty unadulterated seconds to assess. Bags under his eyes. Bed-head hair. The makings of a scruffy straw-coloured beard.

He looks like hell. But even unshowered and unshaven and unrested, he's cute. Cuter now, like this, than he ever was in my head. I feel my pulse quicken just looking at him. *Get a grip, Abby.*

Tyler looks at me, waiting for me to say something. "Hey, Josh," I offer. Josh's head jerks up at the sound.

"What are you doing here?"

"Uh, I—"

"She brought me Thanksgiving leftovers," Tyler interjects, holding up the half-eaten container.

"I did! Leftovers." I bob my head for emphasis.

Josh tosses the controller on the sofa and stands up. "I should

323

probably take off," he tells us, not looking at me. "I told Martin I'd help him with something."

This is most definitely a lie.

"Can we talk?" These words fly out, followed by a rambling flurry of unnecessary explanation. "I know you hung up on me last night, which I guess means you don't want to talk to me, but I really want you to. You don't have to, of course. It's not like you owe me anything. But I hate the way we left things yesterday, and I thought that maybe if we could just talk. . ." I trail off, imploring eyes locked on his flat gaze.

"You want to *talk*." He says this like it's a joke, his words laced with irony.

"Yes. Please?"

He eyes me, unblinking. I blush under the weight of his stare. "OK," he says finally. His shoulders rise and fall in a dismissive shrug. "Let's talk."

"Should I go upstairs?" Tyler asks, a devilled egg in each cheek.

I look at Josh. "Are you up for a walk?" He doesn't respond but reaches for the maroon fleece slung over the arm of the sofa. There's an oar and the words USC CREW stitched in golden thread on the lapel.

"You kids have fun," Tyler says, plopping down on the sofa. "I may be in a food coma when you get back. Don't wake me."

Josh follows me upstairs and out of the front door. No particular route in mind, I just set off down the street, which is still wet from last night's rain.

Josh falls into step beside me. When I look over at him, he's staring straight ahead, his expression blank. Totally unreadable. *Is he always like this?* I wish I knew him well enough to know. All

I have are a couple of months' worth of year-old memories that aren't even mine.

We're halfway down the street before I realize I left my sweater inside. I wasn't cold until I realized it, but now I'm freezing. Josh sees me shivering and unzips his fleece.

"Here," he says, handing it to me. It's the first word spoken since we left the basement. I shake my head in protest.

"Keep it," I insist. "I don't want you to be cold." He ignores me, draping the fleece around my shoulders. "But I'm the bad guy here," I point out. "The bad guy doesn't deserve to be warm."

"This is true." There's the slightest hint of humour in his voice. I run with it. It's risky, but it's all I've got.

"I mean, come on," I joke, "the girl who shows up at your house on Thanksgiving to pick up your *brother* certainly doesn't deserve to wear your jacket."

His face hardens. *OK, so we're not quite to the we-can-laugh-about-this stage yet.*

"So he's the reason you just disappeared?" he asks. "Why didn't you just tell me the truth?"

"I'm so sorry. So, so sorry." He doesn't respond. "I don't expect you to forgive me, but it'd be really great if you would."

Josh just looks at me. "That's it? That's your apology?"

I nod weakly, nearly buckling under the weight of how much more he deserves. This kind, well-meaning guy has become collateral damage. His heart was broken, and he has no idea why. He's telling himself that his ex-girlfriend simply fell for someone else, but that can't be a satisfying explanation because that's not the person he understood his ex-girlfriend to be. "I didn't mean for this to happen," I say softly. Even as I'm saying it, I know how lame it sounds.

"Which part?" he asks evenly. "The part where you acted like I didn't exist? Or the part where I found out why?"

"I didn't know," I whisper, stung by his tone.

Josh stops walking. "You 'didn't know' what, Abby? That Michael and I were related?" His voice is angry now. "Maybe not. But you sure as hell knew how you were treating me. Never mind that I was ready to *transfer* to be nearer to you. And you couldn't even be bothered to pick up the freaking phone?"

I shake my head slowly, my eyes never leaving his. "No." My voice is barely audible. "I didn't know that, either."

Confusion flashes across Josh's face. "OK, now I'm lost."

*I shouldn't have said anything. I should've just let him hate me.* Now he's expecting an explanation, and I can't give him one. He'll think I'm crazy if I try.

I look away. A man in a stiff flannel shirt and work trousers is listening to a football game on his front porch, smoking a cigarette. *Somebody's grandfather.* I suddenly miss mine. I haven't seen him since last Christmas, three days after I found out I'd booked the movie. He was so proud. "Gonna be a star," he told me, not an ounce of doubt in his voice. I laughed when he said it, but he hadn't meant it as a joke.

"Abby." Josh's voice cuts through the silence.

"You wouldn't believe me if I told you," I reply, my voice small. I watch as the old man puts out his cigarette and lights another one.

"Try me."

*Tell him.*

I turn my head, meeting Josh's gaze. Something in his eyes makes me think he might get it. But what if he doesn't? What if he thinks I'm crazy, or worse, making it up?

"Just tell me the truth," he says softly. "That's all I want."

I take a breath and exhale slowly. The truth.

"Something happened on my eighteenth birthday," I begin, because it feels like the right place to start. "Something I still don't completely understand. It has to do with the earthquake last year."

"Your unfortunate twist of fate," Josh says. His eyes dance a little, remembering the words he thinks I spoke. "The day we met."

"Yes. Only. . ." I take another breath. "It wasn't me you remember meeting that day."

"It wasn't you," Josh repeats. He looks at me for a moment, then shakes his head, getting angry again. "What, you're going to tell me you weren't yourself that day? That the girl I fell in love with isn't who you really are? That's bullcrap, Abby." His voices rises but stays steady. "Don't tell me I don't know you. I know you, and you know me."

"That's not what I'm saying," I reply, feeling my own voice shake. "I'm saying that the girl you remember meeting literally wasn't me."

Josh stops walking. "What?"

I force myself to keep talking. "Do you remember Dr Mann from astronomy?"

"Do I *remember* him? Of course I remember him, Abby."

"OK, well, he has this theory . . . about parallel worlds."

"Cosmic entanglement," Josh says. "I know."

I stare at him. "You know about the theory."

"Sure. The basics, anyway. I read Dr Mann's book when I signed up for his class. I mean, I'm not sure I believe it, but—"

"Believe it." Without thinking, I grab his hand. "It happened. On my birthday."

"*What* happened?"

"Our world collided with a parallel world. Became entangled with one. Everyone's memories were erased, and our parallel selves started rewriting our pasts, but no one knows it. No one but me, anyway." I hear myself, how utterly insane this all sounds, and I wonder if I've made a mistake. I back up a little, not wanting to leave anything out. "The parallel world is a year behind ours," I explain. "Well, a year and a day, actually. The earthquake – well, that's just it, it wasn't an earthquake, it was a collision. And it didn't happen *here* on 8 September, 2008, it happened there. In the parallel world. We just remember it as though it happened here. It's called—"

"Shared reality." Josh is staring at me in wonder, but not disbelief. Hope bubbles up inside me. He doesn't think I'm crazy.

"Right! But the thing is, it didn't work like it was supposed to for me. I kept all my real memories, and I didn't get a full set of new ones. My memories from the parallel world stop where my parallel's stop, so I have a year-long gap where everything from her version is just a blank. That's why I didn't know you and I were together. Why I—"

"Stop."

I don't hear him at first. "What?"

"I said stop." He looks down at his hand, which I'm still

328

holding. I start to let go, but he grabs it back. "Just so I'm clear, your explanation for your behaviour for the past month is that there was a freaking cosmic collision? That altered the way we interact in time and space? And that you're the only one who knows it happened? Abby. . ."

"I know. I know how crazy it sounds. But think about it, Josh." I grip his hand, wanting so desperately to make him understand, to give him the peace he deserves. "Think about Abby," I say softly. "The Abby you know. The Abby you love, and who loves you back. The Abby who stopped answering your calls out of the blue. The Abby who didn't respond to a single email or text. Would she *ever* have done that to you?" My heart aches at the thought of what it must've been like for him, all that inexplicable silence. No explanation. No goodbye.

Subtly, almost imperceptibly, he shakes his head.

"She would never have done it, Josh. If I had known what was going on, *I* would never have done it. But it happened, and neither of us had any control over it, and you're the innocent victim, and I'm sorry. I'm so sorry." My voice breaks and I gasp for breath, my hand clutching his so tightly my fingers have started to cramp.

He looks down at the hand I'm holding. "You're saying that everything I remember about our relationship is fiction?"

"Not fiction," I reply. "Just not . . . what happened to us." We both know there's no distinction, not really.

He lets go of my hand. "No." He shakes his head firmly. *"No."*
The hope inside me recedes, like a wave at low tide.

"It sounds impossible," I say. "It should be impossible. But it's the truth, Josh. I promise you, it is."

He's quiet, his body angled away from me, and for a moment, I think he might walk away.

"Please," I whisper. "Don't go."

"You don't remember any of it?" he asks then, his voice incredulous and sad. "Our relationship, I mean. Nothing at all?"

"I remember some of it," I say. "Our first date. The Georgia Fair. Everything that happened before twenty-seventh of November of last year. That's where my parallel's memories stop."

He's still not looking at me, but I can see his tears spill over. He doesn't even attempt to wipe them away. "What I feel . . . these aren't someone else's feelings, Abby. They can't be. The way I love you. . ." His voice breaks. "Don't tell me that's not real."

My insides squeeze and contract. "I don't know what to say," I say softly. "Other than I'm sorry. I'm so, so sorry." The tears that have clogged my throat and shaken my voice since this conversation began are flowing freely now. I choke back a sob.

"I am too," he says sadly. He hesitates for a moment, then pulls me into a hug. "I believe you," he whispers. I exhale and lean into him, letting the weight of my upper body fall against his chest. His neck, soapy and sweet, is warm on my forehead. The scent is both new and powerfully familiar, triggering the dozen or so memories I have of being this close to him. Sitting next to him on that swing in his neighbourhood, the night before our first date. Holding hands at the planetarium two days later. His arm around me on the Ferris wheel. And my most recent one: leaning against a tree on the bank of the Chattahoochee, my head resting on his shoulder, watching the sunset after the Brookside crew picnic. I inhale deeply, allowing myself to imagine what those moments would have been like to live, since the memories of them, while specific and precise, are void of emotion and thus strikingly incomplete. My arms tighten around his neck. I don't want to let go.

"Cosmic entanglement," Josh says after a minute, his voice muffled against my hair. "Definitely not where I expected this conversation to go." I smile, resting my ear against his chest. "Who else knows about it?" he asks.

"Only Caitlin," I reply, distracted by the faint thump of his heartbeat, wondering what it would feel like beneath my palm. "Dr Mann suspects, but we haven't told him for sure."

Josh pulls back and looks at me. "You haven't told Michael?" I shake my head. "Why not?"

"I wasn't sure he'd believe me if I did."

"Do you. . ." His eyes drop to the pavement. "Love him?"

"I don't know," I admit. Josh turns and starts walking again. His brown eyes are heavy with hurt.

"It shouldn't have happened like this," I say lamely. "If I'd known about you . . . about us . . . if I'd had any idea that we were—" The words "in love" are stuck in my throat. *We were in love.* I shake my head, unable to finish. Josh takes my hand and squeezes it.

"So I should blame Thanksgiving, then," he says then.

I look at him. "What?"

"Last year," he explains. "If you'd come over like you were supposed to, you and Michael would've met. Maybe things would've been different if you had."

My rib cage contracts. There's no "maybe" about it. If Michael

331

had known who I was when we met at Yale, he would've expected me to remember him, and I would've played along, the way I did with everyone else that day. At the very least, he would've asked me about Josh. There's no way we'd be dating right now if we'd met under those circumstances.

*Thank God she didn't go.*

I think back, trying to remember what my parallel did instead, but can't. My breath catches in my throat as I realize.

"Thanksgiving hasn't happened yet," I whisper.

It doesn't register at first. Josh just looks at me. Then realization flashes in his eyes and he gets it. "It's still possible," he says. "She could still come by. For dessert, maybe." His eyes are shining with hope and possibility. But there's something else there, too.

*Love.*

Even now, after all that's happened. It's written so plainly on his face. It doesn't matter to him that his memories aren't real. His feelings haven't changed.

*He loves me.*

"Fate could intervene," he says then. His lips, chapped from the cold, curl in a sanguine smile. "We could end up together after all."

*No!* All the fears and anxieties I've been ignoring come rushing to the surface. If my parallel wants to be with Josh, she should be. If she decides to give their relationship another shot next autumn when he tells her he's willing to transfer, then great. I wish them the best. But here, in this world, I should get to decide who I end up with. And I choose Michael. He's the one I'm supposed to be with. What I'm feeling in this moment doesn't matter. In my head I know what's true.

Then again, it's not my head that's the problem.

Unable to meet Josh's gaze, I look past him to the wooden gazebo up ahead. My eyes wander down the hill to the swing at the lake's edge, swaying in the afternoon breeze. Our swing. I blink, pushing the image of us on it from my mind. It's not *our* swing. It's *theirs*.

Memories are tricky little bastards.

"Come on," Josh says, stepping on to the dirt.

"So how do you remember it?" I ask as we settle into the swing. "Last Thanksgiving, I mean. The last memory I have is from the night before."

Josh's expression darkens. "Michael acted like Michael." He glances over at me. "However he is with you, he's different with us. Ever since our dad died." Josh looks out at the water. "Last Thanksgiving was a new low. He said some really awful things to Martin at the table, and my mom just let him." *What kind of things?* I want to ask, but can't. "That was it for me," he says. "I didn't want anything to do with him after that." Josh looks over at me, his eyes sad. "In the driveway yesterday, with you . . . that was the first time I'd seen him in a year."

"Some reunion," is all I can muster.

We're quiet for a long time, letting the wind, even colder coming off the water, rock us back and forth. I lean my head back against the cool wood, examining the muted grey of the sky. "I was in LA when the collision happened," I say after a while. "Shooting a movie, actually." I look over at Josh. "In the real version, I didn't take that astronomy class with you. I took drama and ended up in LA." I look back up at the sky. "It seems so crazy to me now, my life out there. So far away."

"I wonder if we would've met," Josh says thoughtfully, pushing off the ground hard with his feet. "If you hadn't been in my class last year. Maybe we would've run into each other at some coffee shop in Hollywood."

I smile. "Maybe so."

We're swinging in earnest now, the old rusty chain clanking on its hook above our heads. "Aren't you freezing?" I ask him, zipping his fleece up to my neck.

"Nope," he says, pumping his legs to get us going higher.

"I don't think this is the kind of swing you're supposed to do that with," I say, eyes on the clanging hook.

"I'm pretty sure you're right," he replies, pumping harder, his cheeks pink from the cold.

I giggle, pulling my knees up to my chest. A few seconds later, he does the same. We're moving so fast that the swing jerks at each end, nearly knocking me off each time. I reach for the armrest.

"Wimp!" Josh shouts. "Where's the Abby I know?"

We look at each other, and wonder.

Michael calls as I'm pulling into the garage.

"Hey," I say, answering it. "How's Boston?" From all the commotion in the background, I can tell he's at a bar.

"Awesome!" he bellows. I wince and pull the phone away from my ear, noticing that my battery is almost dead. "We're pre-partying at Sullivan's Tap!"

"Tell Sullivan I said hi."

"No, no!" he yells. "Sullivan isn't a *person*. Sullivan's Tap is the name of a *bar* near the Garden."

"Yeah, I figured that. It was a joke."

"Oh! Right." Michael laughs. "So how are things down there?"

"Things are fine. I just miss you." It's only been seven hours since I dropped him off at the airport, but it feels like seven days. Hanging out with Josh was fun, but being with him has left me unsettled. All my parallel has to do is stop by his house tomorrow and my relationship with Michael will be over.

"I miss you, too." Michael says. "I wish you were here."

"Me, too," I say, my throat suddenly tight.

"Carpenter!" I hear a male voice shout. "Car bombs. Pronto!"

"Call you tomorrow?" Michael asks.

"Sure," I say, making the effort to sound upbeat. But he's already gone.

My mom is sitting at the kitchen table, working a crossword puzzle, when I come in.

"Hi, honey," she says. "How'd it go?"

"As well as it could have, I guess. Is there pie?"

"In the fridge," she tells me, putting her pencil down. "So you got him to talk to you?"

"Yeah. We went for a walk." I spot the pie behind a gallon of milk and pull both out of the refrigerator. My mom stares me down as I cut myself a slice.

"Mom. What?"

"Did you *really* not know that Michael was his brother?"

I contemplate continuing the truth trend, but know that will add a level of complexity to my life that I don't need right now. "I really didn't," I tell her. "Since Michael never mentioned

335

a brother, it honestly didn't cross my mind that he might have one."

"And you never thought to look up Josh's brother when you got to school? Josh didn't suggest it?"

"Josh asked me not to," I tell her, with a hunch that this might be true.

"Not an especially good relationship, is it?" she muses, handing me a knife. I cut a hefty slice, then double it. It's been a rough twenty-four hours. The familiar peppery pumpkin spice is instantly calming. I shove another forkful into my mouth. *This is why they call them comfort foods.*

"So what'd you think of Michael?" I ask with my mouth full, not sure I want to know the answer. Both of my parents were pretty quiet after he left last night.

"He seemed very confident," she replies. "And he's obviously very smart." *Confident?* That's like saying a girl has a good personality when asked how she looks.

"So you hated him."

"We didn't hate him! Don't be silly."

"But you like Josh better," I say.

"We know Josh," she replies. "We don't really know Michael yet. But we're looking forward to getting to know him." She smiles.

*Let's hope you get the chance.*

I'm about to bury my anxiety under another piece of pie when the doorbell rings.

"Sorry to just show up," Josh says when I open the door. "I tried calling, but it went straight to voicemail." He's wearing the fleece I had on an hour ago, the collar flipped up around his neck. It smelled like him when I put it on . . . did it smell like me when I took it off? "Am I interrupting dinner?" he asks.

"Nope. I was just in the process of spoiling it." I lift up the plate I'm still holding in my hand. "Want some?"

"Nah, I should get home. My mom's waiting with leftovers. I just wanted to give you this." He pulls his hand from his pocket, and Caitlin's gold bracelet slips to the ground beneath his feet.

"Oh! Where'd you find it?"

"It was stuck to the sleeve of my fleece," he tells me as he kneels to pick it up. I watch as he drapes the delicate gold chain across his left palm, then extends his hand up towards me.

Suddenly, swiftly, I am bowled over by memory. An image – this image – of Josh, kneeling in front of me, his left hand open and raised. Except, in my mind, the ground he's kneeling on is a beach, and there isn't a bracelet in his outstretched hand but a ring. And Josh, wearing khakis and a short-sleeved maroon polo shirt, looks different somehow, older. *Why can't I place when that was?*

Because it isn't a memory.

I grab the door frame to steady myself, my legs no longer sturdy beneath me. Why do I have a mental picture of Josh, down on one knee, holding a diamond ring? Where did that image come from? I wonder, but at the same time I know.

It came from the future. *But whose?*

"Abby? What's wrong?"

*Oh, nothing. I just pictured you proposing to me in elaborate detail, down to the precise shade of you shirt.*

I feign calm and smile, taking the bracelet from his outstretched hand. "Josh to the rescue," I tell him. "Caitlin would've killed me if I'd lost it."

337

"No problem," he says, getting to his feet. He reaches into his back pocket and pulls out a folded postcard. "I also wanted to give you this." He unfolds the postcard and hands it to me. On the front is Dali's *Persistence of Memory*. The painting that brought my parents together. The only painting that survived when the surrealist wing at MoMa caught fire after the collision. A painting whose name perfectly describes what I'm living with now. I run my thumb over the slick surface of the glossy image, marvelling at the coincidence and connectedness.

"Where did you get this?" I ask.

"You gave it to me," he replies, not bothering with the us/them distinction. Something in his face tells me it's a conscious choice. "We went to your mom's Dali exhibit the night before you left for school," he says. "We were on a tour, listening to the docent describe the surrealist view of the subconscious. 'Dreams are more real than real,' the woman said. Right after she said it, you leaned over and whispered, '*We* are more real than real.'"

"I did?" I whisper, even though it wasn't me who said it. We both know that.

"That postcard was in my locker the next morning," Josh says. "You must've got it in the gift store after the tour." He reaches forward and flips it over in my hands. There, on the back, are my handwritten words. *We are more real than real.*

I just stare at the smudged ink, my throat too tight for an audible response. *More real than real.* Something inside me reaches out and grabs hold of the idea. Are there things that transcend our perception of them? Things that are true no matter what? If so, what does that mean for me and this boy I barely know but can't stop thinking about, despite the fact that I'm supposed to be in love with his brother?

"I should probably get going," I hear Josh say. "Early flight tomorrow."

"You're going back to LA already?"

"We play UCLA tomorrow," he replies. "Big game."

"Well, it was good to see you," I say awkwardly, holding out the postcard. My hand trembles slightly. *Why don't I want him to leave?*

"Keep it," he replies. "To remember." He smiles sadly. Without thinking, I throw my arms around his neck. At first, his body feels tense against mine, like he's bracing against the hug. But then, the tension gives way and he hugs me back. Only for a few seconds, though. Then he pulls away. "Bye, Abby," he says, turning to go. "Take care of yourself."

"Do you think things happen for a reason?" I ask suddenly. Josh turns back around.

"Absolutely."

"Do you believe in soulmates?"

"Ask me tomorrow," he says. Then he turns and walks away.

At quarter past one, I'm still awake, waiting for the refuge of sleep. The moon is bright outside my window, casting its light inside my room.

I sigh, rolling over for what must be the ninetieth time since I got in bed, and repeat what I've been telling myself over and over again ever since Josh left. *She's not going to meet him. There's nothing to worry about. She's already told Josh she can't make it. The day will come and go, and Michael will leave early Friday morning to fly up to Boston like he always does. Nothing will change.* I tell myself these things and pretend to believe them, but I am afraid. I don't want to lose Michael. Not now.

Lying on my side, my face inches from the Post-it note I stuck to my nightstand reminding me to "remember Thanksgiving" as soon as I wake up tomorrow, I say a silent prayer that my parallel's holiday will happen exactly the way it's supposed to. I imagine her at the table with my parents and grandparents, eating my grandma's turkey. I imagine her in the kitchen with my mom, washing dishes at the sink. I imagine her on the sofa with my grandfather, watching the black-and-white version of *It's a Wonderful Life*, a movie I've seen so many times I can recite the entire thing by heart. I close my eyes, playing back my favourite scene.

George Bailey's words echo in my mind as I finally drift off to sleep: *What do you want? You want the moon? Just say the word and I'll throw a lasso around it and pull it down. Hey. That's a pretty good idea. I'll give you the moon, Mary.* Except it's not Jimmy Stewart's face I'm seeing behind my eyelids but Josh's. And the name that echoes is my own.

# 13
# (here)

*I'm on a pavement, walking along the side of a stone building that runs the length of the street. The pavement is crowded with people dressed in jackets and scarves, arms full of books and notebooks, hands wrapped around giant cups of coffee, bustling here and there. The air is cold on my nose. "Abby!" I hear someone call. I turn to my right and am facing a black wrought-iron gate beneath a tall stone archway. On the other side of the gate, a guy – dark hair, chiselled cheeks, perfect teeth – smiles at me. Suddenly, there's a beep and the gate opens. The guy comes towards me. "Hi," he says as he gets nearer. "I brought you something." I look down. There's a box in his hands. "It's pumpkin pie."*

I wake up with a start.

The air in my bedroom is heavy with the spicy sweetness of my mom's Pepper Pumpkin Pie, her one contribution to the meal my grandma insists on cooking every year – in our kitchen.

"Thanksgiving isn't a time for recipes," goes Grandma's annual refrain, aimed directly at my mom, who doesn't like to make anything twice. "Thanksgiving is about tradition." Apparently, adherence to tradition requires a modern gourmet kitchen. Grandma refuses to have Thanksgiving any place but ours.

Still in my pyjamas, I pad down the back stairs.

"There she is!" my grandpa announces when I enter the room, opening his arms wide for a hug.

"Happy Thanksgiving, Grandpa," I murmur into his neck. "I'm glad you told me about the stars." I went to bed thinking about all those nines, wondering what to make of them. He squeezes me tighter, and I hold on, not wanting to let go yet. When I finally do, I walk over to where my grandmother is standing, her manicured hands covered in cornbread crumbs.

"Your mother forgot the sage," she tells me, leaning over to let me kiss her cheek. I do, glancing over at my mom in the process. Mom just shakes her head. *Don't ask.*

"Want me to run and get some?" I ask cheerily, setting my phone down on the counter and heading for the coffee pot. "Whole Foods is open till two. Fresh, not dried, right?"

"That would be lovely, dear," Grandma says. "And could you get some scotch? Your mother forgot that, too."

"No, Rose, she cannot buy you scotch," my mom answers before I have a chance to. "She's seventeen. And since when do you drink scotch? There's a bottle of Jack Daniels in the cabinet."

"Scotch has fewer carbs," my grandmother retorts. "But bourbon will do."

"OK, so fresh sage." I dump vanilla creamer into my coffee,

then dig around the Tupperware drawer for the lid to my travel mug. "Anything else?"

"Who's Josh?" I hear my grandfather ask. "And why will he 'miss you today'?" Grandpa has my phone in his hands, the screen lit up with a new text.

"Josh is my boyfriend," I reply. "And he'll miss me because I told him I'd be hanging out with a nosy old man all day." Grandpa swats me on the butt with my phone, then hands it to me.

"Do we get to meet this boyfriend?" my grandmother asks.

"Eventually," I tell her. "Before I marry him, for sure." I blow her a kiss, then dart up the back stairs with my coffee before the inquisition can continue.

"Is it really that serious?" I hear my grandmother ask.

I return to my room just long enough to put on jeans and throw my hair into a ponytail. As I'm passing my desk on my way back out, I hit the space bar, illuminating my screen. With my grandparents' unexpected arrival yesterday, I forgot to check my email when I got home from the picnic last night. My acceptance email could be in my inbox right now. Heart pounding, I click on my mailbox icon, and a pop-up box appears:

Server error. Your message was not sent.

*What message?*
I click on my outbox, and an email opens.
*No.*
I stare at my screen, dumbfounded. It's an email to the Yale admissions office with a document attached. There's only one person other than me who uses my laptop.

*She didn't.*

With shaking hands, I click on the attachment. It's the file I dragged to the recycle bin yesterday morning. The Yale application I never intended to send.

*Oh, yes. She did.*

Fury rips through me. So searingly hot that it burns everything else out. I yank the power cord out of my laptop and storm down the back stairs into the kitchen.

Mom doesn't look up from the mixing bowl she's washing. "Would you mind also getting so—"

"How could you?" I demand, cutting her off. She looks up in surprise. Her face falls when she sees my computer.

"Abby, I just—"

"You just what, Mom? You just needed to know whether I could get in? Whether your precious daughter was good enough for an Ivy?" My voice is shaking and my eye sockets are radiating heat. The edges of things are starting to blur.

"No! It wasn't about that. I—"

I don't let her finish. "You went through my files? Who does that?" I slam my computer down on the counter, not caring whether it breaks. My grandparents gape at me, stunned into silence. I don't behave like this. I'm not careless with expensive electronics. I don't scream at my mother.

I am screaming at her now.

"I didn't go through anything," she says quietly. "I needed to send an email yesterday, and I'd left my computer at the museum. Your recycle bin was open on your screen."

"My recycle bin. *BIN*. What were you planning to do if I'd got in?"

"What's going on in here?" My dad enters the kitchen, hair still wet from the shower. "What's all the shouting about?"

"Did you know about this?" I demand, pointing at my laptop. "Did you know that Mom fished my Yale application out of the *recycle bin* and sent it in without telling me?" From the look on my dad's face, it's pretty obvious that he didn't.

"She filled the entire thing out," my mom tells him, immediately defensive. "When I saw it in the recycle bin, I thought maybe she'd got cold feet at the last minute, and I didn't want her to miss out on a life-changing opportunity out of fear that she wouldn't get in. She's worked so hard, I just thought—"

"But that wasn't your decision to make!" I shout.

"Abigail, don't talk to your mother that way," my dad says sternly.

"No, Robert, she's right. Abby, I—"

I don't wait for her apology. Before she can finish, I spin on my heels and fling open the back door. "You should eat without me," I announce just before the door slams shut.

My car steers itself towards Caitlin's, even though I haven't made a conscious decision to go there. But when I pull up in front of her house, I know exactly why I've come, and it's not to vent about my mom. It's to apologize. And for the first time since we said those horrible things to each other, I'm not worried about what I'll say to her.

I've rung the doorbell twice when it occurs to me that the

345

Moss's family Volvo is gone, and Caitlin's Jetta is parked in the garage. Yesterday's newspaper is still on the porch.

*Charleston.* Duh. That's where Caitlin's grandmother lives and where her family spends every major holiday.

Disappointed but not defeated, I sit down on the porch step and dial her number. This time, I leave a voicemail.

"Hey, Caitlin. It's me. Abby. I'm at your house, sitting on the porch, wishing you were here so I could say this in person." I take a breath, certain of what I want to say, but not sure the order in which to say it. "I'm so sorry, Cate. I'm sorry for what I said to you in the cafeteria, and for bringing up Craig – that was totally bitchy and awful and I'm sorry – but I'm really, *really* sorry for telling Tyler you liked him. For assuming I knew what was best for you. For thinking it was up to me. I can't even imagine how angry you must be. Well, actually I can, because—" I start to tell her about the Yale application, but stop myself. This isn't about what my mom did. This is about what *I* did. "Please let me make it up to you," I rush on. "I'll do whatever it takes." I pause, wondering whether this message is still coherent, as it's morphed into words spewing out from a mesh of tears and sniffles. I'm debating whether to beg her to call me back or just apologize again when I hear the second beep.

The line goes dead.

Suddenly, the depth of the chasm between us is unbearable. I don't want to be in a fight with her any more. She's my best friend. She's part of who I am.

I'm not Abby without Caitlin.

*Please, God, give me my best friend back.*

I'm redialling her number when she calls me back.

"I'm so sorry," I say instead of hello. "Please don't hang up on me."

"I called you," she points out.

"Oh. Right," I say lamely. I can't tell her from her voice if she's listened to my message or not. "I'm sorry," I say again. "Not that you called me," I add quickly. "For what I did."

"I'm sorry, too," she says, and then her voice breaks.

"You don't have anything to be sorry about," I tell her, tears streaming down my face now. "I'm the one who lied to Tyler, and who said those awful things."

"I said awful things, too," she says. "And, in a way, I lied, too. I didn't tell you why I was really mad. It wasn't just the Tyler thing."

"What do you mean?"

"My Yale application was due the next day, and—"

"Oh my God. Your essays." I completely forgot. An excuse almost as bad as the offence itself. *What kind of friend forgets something like that?* I knew how important it was to her that I read them. Her dyslexia has made her super self-conscious about her writing, and these essays meant everything to her. "I'm such an asshole," I say. "No wonder you were mad at me that day."

"Well, that and my sucky SAT score."

"Your *what*?"

"Yeah. It was a pretty shitty week." Her voice is thick with disappointment. "Almost as shitty as this one's been."

"Did you. . ." I trail off. I can't imagine that it's true.

"I didn't get in," she says. "Found out yesterday, right before we left. Wait-listed."

"Oh, Cate. . ." My heart literally aches in my chest. "But you still have a chance of getting in, right?"

"Yeah. Won't know till February, though. So I'm applying to some other places. I figure Grandpa Oscar would be just as proud to have a granddaughter at Wash U or Duke." She makes an effort to sound upbeat. "What about you? Did you hear from Northwestern?"

"Not yet," I tell her.

"You'll get in," she assures me, because that's what best friends do.

"My mom sent in my Yale application without telling me," I say. "Or tried to, anyway. I found it stuck in my outbox this morning. Like fifteen minutes ago, actually. Unsent, thank God."

"She filled the entire thing out without telling you?"

"No, I filled it out. She found it in the recycle bin on my computer."

"Why'd you fill it out if you weren't going to apply?"

"I was confirming that I didn't want to go there," I explain.

"By filling out the application? How very Abby." The familiarity of her voice, its distinct mixture of wit and frankness, delivered with Caitlin's impeccable timing, fills me with an incommunicable joy.

"I missed you," I say. "So much."

"I missed you, too."

Neither of us says anything for a few minutes. We just sit there, relishing the rightness of the world.

OK, so maybe the world isn't all the way right. By the time I get back in my car, I've declined four calls from my mom and ignored three texts. Just because I might be able to identify with my mom's I-know-better mentality doesn't mean I'm in the mood to talk to her right now. And frankly, I don't have the emotional energy to deal with Grandma Rose, or the stamina to endure her four-hour meal. With Caitlin out of town, the only place I can imagine going is Josh's.

I'm halfway to the Wagners' before it dawns on me that I haven't showered or brushed my teeth. Fortunately, there's a pharmacy with a bathroom between Caitlin's house and Josh's. I buy deodorant, a toothbrush kit and a travel-sized bottle of Awesome Apple body splash, which I proceed to spritz on every bare inch of my skin.

*Excellent. I now smell like a green Jolly Rancher.*

It's not until I've parked in Josh's driveway that I realize I haven't told him that I'm coming. I contemplate pulling back out but decide there's a pretty good chance someone has seen me pull in. Not the impression I want make on the family members I haven't met yet. As I'm debating my options, my phone rings.

"You're outside my house," Josh says as soon as I pick up.

"This is true."

"Does that mean you're eating with us?"

"If I'm still invited."

"Of course you are. What happened to the marathon meal?" he asks.

"Long story," I tell him. "So is it OK that I'm here?"

"More than OK," he says. I hear him unlocking and opening

the front door. "Are you coming inside now? Or do we need to bring the turkey to the driveway?" Josh steps out on the front porch in bare feet, wearing wrinkled khakis and a grey sweater and looking exceptionally cute.

"I'm coming in," I reply. Phone still glued to my ear, I get out of the car and walk towards him. "Please excuse my appearance," I say. "I left in a hurry."

His forehead wrinkles in concern. "Everything OK?"

"Yes. No." I sigh and hang up the phone. "I dunno. My mom found my completed Yale application in the recycle bin – where I put it and wanted it to stay – and secretly sent it in. Or tried to. I found it my outbox this morning."

"Wow. Did you confront her about it?"

"Yeah." I don't have the energy to rehash all the details, so I don't. Josh doesn't ask for them.

"You need a hug," he declares, pulling me into one. Just as I start to relax against him, I feel his nose against my neck.

I jump back. "Don't smell me! I haven't showered. And I went a little overboard with the Jolly Rancher spray."

"That's it!" he exclaims. "That's what you smell like. A green one." He smiles and leans forward to sniff me again. "Do they make the other flavours, too?"

"No. I don't know." I move out of his sniff zone. "Can you please not smell me?"

He laughs. "It's kinda hard not to."

"Great," I mutter. "Some first impression I'm going to make."

"The only person you haven't met is my brother, and you definitely shouldn't worry what he thinks." At the mention of his brother, Josh's expression darkens.

"Ouch, bro." I hear the voice before I see its owner. "That hurts." I look past Josh into the unlit foyer, where his brother stands in shadows.

"So this must be the girlfriend," he says, stepping into view.

Tall, dark hair, piercing green eyes. Grey Yale Lacrosse T-shirt. My breath catches in my throat. *The guy from my dream last night.*

"Abby, this is my brother," Josh grumbles. I've never heard him grumble before. It doesn't really suit him.

"Hi!" I chirp, attempting to mitigate the grumbling by going as far to the opposite extreme as possible. "I'm Abby!" The chirpy voice also keeps me from fixating on the fact that I had a dream about Josh's brother last night, a dream in which Josh's brother gave me a pumpkin pie. *How is that possible?* I've never seen him before today.

"Sorry for my brother's rudeness," he replies, extending his hand. "I'm Michael."

An intense sense of déjà vu stalls my next thought. I just stand there, staring at him – trying to place him in a moment – any *real* moment. But I can't.

"You gonna leave me hangin'?" he teases, nodding towards his outstretched hand.

"Oh! Sorry!" I put my hand in his. The moment we touch, recognition ripples through me. I want to ask him whether we've met before, but I know there's no way we could have.

"Are you all planning to spend the day on the front porch?" comes their mom's voice from inside.

"How are you with a fire extinguisher?" Josh asks me. "I told my dad I'd help him fry the turkey."

Michael steps back to let us inside. "Yeah, you'd better go help your *dad*," he says pointedly. Without a word, Josh walks past Michael into the house. Michael keeps his eyes on me.

I meet his gaze. The sense of recognition, of unplaced memory, is overpowering. Those green eyes. The shape of his eyebrows. The tiny scar on his cheek. I blink rapidly, trying to snap out of it.

"Do you have something in your eye?" Michael asks, a smile tugging at the corners of his mouth.

I quickly look away. "No, I . . . I should find Josh." Eyes glued to the ground, I brush past him and step inside the house.

Two hours and one almost-fire later, the five of us sit down to eat. After the scene I witnessed on the porch, I assumed Josh and Michael would be at each other's throats all afternoon, but they appear to be making an effort to stay civil for my benefit. This, apparently, requires that neither of them speaks. The only sounds at the table are the clinks of silver hitting porcelain china.

"So, Michael," Martin says, breaking the silence, "what classes are you taking this semester? Anything in the physics department?" *It's almost December and they don't know what classes he's taking?*

Michael responds with a patronizing smile. "Unfortunately not, Marty."

Martin doesn't react to the diminutive. But he doesn't say anything else, either.

"So what universities are you applying to?" Michael asks. I assume he's asking Josh until I realize that everyone at the table is looking at me.

"Oh, um. . ." My mind is suddenly blank. "Journalism schools," I say after a few awkward seconds. "Northwestern, Indiana. A few other places."

"Why not Yale?" Michael asks, popping a piece of fried turkey skin into his mouth.

I shoot Josh an annoyed look. "I didn't tell him," Josh says quickly. "He goes there, that's why he's asking."

Michael looks at Josh, then back at me. "Didn't tell me what?"

"Nothing," I reply. "I thought about applying there, but decided not to." Suddenly, my mother-daughter drama seems so childish.

"Why?"

"I want to go somewhere with a journalism programme."

"A girl who knows what she wants," Michael says, his eyes never leaving mine. "Nice work, bro." Beside me, Josh bristles. I want to look away – I should look away – but I can't. Michael's gaze is magnetic. Out of the corner of my eye, I see a look pass between Josh's mom and stepdad.

"Mrs Wagner, these biscuits are delicious," I say, changing the subject.

"Oh, good!" she replies, sounding pleased. "It was my attempt at Southern cuisine." She picks up the one on her plate, examining it. "I was expecting them to be fluffier."

"I think they're perfect," I tell her.

"Yeah, Mom. Nice work." Michael leans over and pecks her on the cheek. She lights up.

Michael immediately turns back to me.

"So why do you want to be a journalist?"

The question catches me off guard. Nobody ever asks *why*. "What do you mean?"

"I'm just wondering what prompted the decision. You seem pretty certain about it."

"Oh, I uh. . ." I look down at my plate, embarrassed that I don't have an answer. *Because my friend's mom was a journalist, and I liked the way she dressed.* Is that really my reason? "I like to write," I say lamely.

"She's being modest," Josh chimes in. "She's a phenomenal writer. And she's editor in chief of our school paper."

"Well, if you want to be a journalist, you should definitely apply to NYU," Michael tells me, barely acknowledging Josh. "My best friend from high school goes there, and he interned at the *Huffington Post* last summer."

"Really? Wow."

"I could give you his email if you want."

"Yeah, that'd be great," I tell him. "NYU is on my list, but since the deadline isn't until January, I'm waiting to hear from Northwestern before I send in any more applications."

"How is Ben liking New York?" Mrs Wagner asks Michael.

"He loves it," Michael replies. "He met a girl last summer that he professes to be in love with."

"Ben in love!" his mom exclaims, smiling at the thought. "Have you met her?"

"Not yet," Michael replies. "She's in high school, in Seattle. Ben was hoping she'd end up in New York next year, but according to him she has her heart set on Yale."

"'*Here she comes again!*'" Our heads swivel to Martin, who is now singing in a pretty decent falsetto. "*Duh nuh nuh nuh na na nah.*" Martin taps the tablecloth with his finger as he sings, "'*She's my best friend's girl!*'" Anger flashes across Michael's face, but Martin doesn't notice. "Watch out, Ben!" Martin jokes, an oblivious smile on his face. He's not thinking about his alleged affair with his best friend's wife, because he doesn't know that he should be. He chomps happily on a biscuit, waiting for the rest of us to laugh at his joke.

I glance at Mrs Wagner. Her eyes are glued on Michael, as if willing him not to say whatever it is he's about to say.

"Michael." Josh's voice is firm, the way a parent might speak to an insolent child. Michael's head snaps towards Josh, but his eyes catch mine instead. Our gazes lock for half an instant. Less than a second. And then, inexplicably, he smiles. Not an icy smile, but a warm one, directed entirely at me. "I think you should reconsider Yale," he says then, as if we're the only two people at the table, and for a moment I forget that we aren't. "I mean, c'mon," he continues, "Northwestern may have a great journalism school, but how many of its graduates have won the Pulitzer for reporting?"

"Nine," I say, and smile. "To your four." Michael laughs. I look around the table and realize that Josh and his parents are staring at us. Flustered, I pick up my fork and promptly drop it. And now I'm sweating profusely as everyone watches me fumble to pick it up off the floor.

"I'll get you another one," Josh says, and stands up. I can feel Michael watching me from across the table, wearing a ridiculously attractive I'm-amused-by-you smile. Resolving not to make eye contact with him for the rest of the meal, I stare at my plate. My peas are shrivelled and dry.

"So how'd you and my brother meet?" I hear Michael ask.

Josh responds before I have a chance to. "In astronomy," he says as a fork appears in front of my face. I take it and stab a single green pea.

"So I guess that makes you star-crossed lovers, huh?"

The house is dark when I pull into the driveway five minutes before curfew. I'm mildly offended that no one is waiting up for me. I left twelve hours ago and haven't answered their calls. I could be dead on the side of the road.

I park behind my grandparents' Buick and use my key to go in through the front door, not wanting to wake anybody up with the sound of the garage door opening. My mom is sitting at the top of the front stairs, a coffee mug between her hands, waiting for me. She looks tired.

"How was it?" she asks when I come through the door.

"It was . . . interesting," I say, closing the door gently behind me. "How'd you know I was there?"

"Josh called," she replies. "Don't be upset with him. He didn't want me to worry."

"I'm glad that he called you."

"Don't be upset with *me*," she says then, her voice even softer now. "I was only trying to help."

"I know."

"I just want you to be happy," she tells me.

"I know that, too." Shrugging out of my coat, I climb the stairs and sit down next to her. "I'm sorry I yelled."

She puts her arm around me. "I'm sorry I didn't have a camera to record your grandmother's face when you did." We both giggle, and the tension between us evaporates. I lean my head against her shoulder. "I thought the woman was going to have a heart attack in our kitchen," she says.

"How'd the meal go?"

"About like it always does. Oh, although apparently your grandparents are on the South Beach diet. Neither of them would touch my pie."

"Ooh, does that mean there's some left?"

"Almost all of it. Want some?"

"Yes, please. After the day I had, I could use a slice of normal."

"What happened?"

"Imagine the most awkward social encounter you've ever experienced. Then add cornbread and turkey and multiply it by five."

"That bad?"

"Worse. Over store-bought cherry cobbler, Josh's brother accused their stepdad of sleeping with their mom while their dad was still alive."

"In front of you?"

"I think it might've been *because* of me, actually. If I hadn't been there, I think Michael would've left before dessert. But it doesn't end there. Turns out their *dad* was the one having the affair, and their mom has been keeping it a secret. I guess the woman their dad was sleeping with lost an earring in a hotel room, and the concierge left a message about it on his home number. Michael heard it and assumed the earring was his mom's, and that she'd been with Martin."

"Well, at least the truth is out now, right? So maybe they can get past it?"

"I hope so."

I follow her down the stairs and into the kitchen, where we both have a double slice of pie and a tall glass of milk. As we eat, I tell her about my dream. The pie, the gate, Michael's piercing green eyes.

"It's weird, right?"

"That you dreamed about him? Nah. You and Josh had just been talking about him."

"But I didn't know what he looked like," I point out. "No mental image. And there aren't any framed photos of him at the Wagners' house, either. I looked this afternoon. Besides," I say, licking pie off my fork, "in my dream he wasn't Josh's brother. He was . . . I dunno. My boyfriend or something. And he was giving me pie. *This* pie, in fact. Which, by the way, is awesome as always."

"Hey, at least he has good taste," Mom says, polishing off her piece.

I smile, picturing Michael's face in my head. "Smart, good-looking, and great taste in pie," I muse. "I could do worse."

"We're talking about your dream guy, not your boyfriend's brother, right?" She's teasing, but I feel myself flush.

"Right."

"And your boyfriend's brother? What's your take on him?"

"I dunno," I admit. "He's hard to read. But there was something about him. . ." I trail off, imagining my palm on his chiselled cheek, then catch myself. *He's my boyfriend's brother.* "He goes to Yale, actually," I say, clearing my throat and the image from my mind. "He was encouraging me to apply."

"Did you yell at him, too?"

"Very funny." I open my mouth to make a snarky comment but yawn instead. "Uh-oh," I tell her, "I feel a pie-induced coma coming on."

"Works every time," she replies, stifling her own yawn. She reaches for my empty plate.

I kiss her goodnight and head up to my room. There, on my desk, is my laptop, my outbox still open on my screen. My vision blurs for a sec, and I picture myself standing next to Michael in front of a massive wrought-iron gate, a newspaper tucked under my arm. It's the same pavement we were standing on in my dream last night. *Where is that?* The location feels familiar, but I can't place it as anywhere I've ever been. As if prompted, I open my bottom file drawer and pull out the stack of university brochures I've been meaning to organize but haven't yet. The Yale one is at the bottom, a few errant coffee grounds stuck to the back of it from its brief stint in the kitchen rubbish bin the day I got it. The image on the cover is an imposing stone building, what looks like a Gothic cathedral but probably isn't. The library, maybe?

On impulse, I flip the brochure over. There it is. Phelps Gate, according to the caption beneath the photo. In the photo, there is a student passing through the oversized archway – the same archway Michael walked through in my dream. Michael, a guy I'd never met before today. Michael, my boyfriend's brother, a guy who just happens to go Yale, a place I've never visited and, before this moment, couldn't have connected to a single piece

359

of architecture. Yet somehow, I dreamed about him, standing behind this iconic gate.

My instinct is to doubt myself. Maybe the gate wasn't this gate. Maybe the guy I saw wasn't Michael. Because, really, how could it have been?

*But it was.*

I stare at the image, imagining myself walking through that gate and stepping into the campus beyond it. A thought pops into my head, strange and powerful: *This is your destiny.*

"I don't believe in destiny," I murmur, but this is a lie. I just never considered that mine could be anything other than what I planned.

I riffle through the university brochures until I find the most worn of the bunch, its purple corners bent and soft from use. "This is my destiny," I repeat to its immutable cover, tracing the capital *N* with my finger. But my voice sounds flat and unconvincing.

I look back at the Yale brochure and make a decision. If they send a scout to the Head of the Hooch, I'll talk to him. And if he tells me I should apply, I will.

I drag the email to my drafts box, just in case.

# 14
# (here)

SATURDAY, 28 NOVEMBER, 2009
(GAME TIME)

My eyes fly open and dart to the clock: 6.01 a.m. The yellow Post-it is right where I left it last night, stuck to the side of the nightstand, illuminated by the clock's eerie blue glow.

REMEMBER THANKSGIVING!!!

Not that I need the reminder. It doesn't take much effort to recall this particular memory. It stands out among the others, lodged at the forefront of my mind.

The fight with my mom. Showing up at Josh's house unannounced. Meeting Michael for the first time, not as some unattached and available freshman girl, but as his younger brother's girlfriend. In other words, already attached. Completely and utterly unavailable.

I fall back against my pillow, letting the new reality wash over me. *I'm not with Michael any more.* As of right now, it's as if our two-and-a-half-month relationship never happened.

I wait for that familiar knot in my gut, the sick dread. But it doesn't come. Instead, there are gentle butterflies. The excited kind.

I rest my hand on my stomach, trying to make sense of what I'm feeling. How can I be OK with this?

*Because it means you're with Josh.*

"No," I whisper in the dark. "I am not in love with my boyfriend's brother." Hearing myself say it, I almost laugh out loud. *Who's the boyfriend and who's the brother?* "This whole thing is seriously effed up," I say to my ceiling.

I close my eyes, picturing Michael's face. He makes me laugh. He makes my palms sweat. He's a ridiculously good kisser. All are very important qualities in a boyfriend.

And then there is Josh. A face that is hazier yet somehow more familiar. I don't know him very well at all, and yet, there is something so indescribably *right* about him. About us. When I was with him yesterday, I felt strangely complete, as if I'd found something I'd been looking for. *But why?*

"Is he my soulmate?" I say these words out loud without meaning to. My voice sounds strange in the darkness. "Josh is my soulmate," I add, trying it on for size. I feel a flood of happiness as I picture what could be our future together. Watching USC football when I'm with him in LA. Eating deep-dish pepperoni at Yorkside when he's with me in New Haven.

Yale.

My mind, which until this moment had been calmly evaluating my new set of circumstances, suddenly begins to race. I've been wondering how I could've ended up at Yale without Caitlin around to convince me to apply. Now I know: my mom sent in the application. But my parallel undid it when she found that email.

*I don't go to Yale any more.*

I leap out of bed for my phone, but the battery is dead. My laptop is plugged in next to it on my desk. I bang on my space bar to wake it up, only to discover that it's not on standby but turned off. "Dammit!" I shout, pressing the power button repeatedly. "Turn on, you piece of shit!"

"Abby? What's going on? Why are you up so early? And why are you cursing at your computer?"

My mom is in the doorway, squinting at me in the dark.

"Oh. I, uh. . ."

She reaches inside my room and flips on the light. We both blink from the shock to our retinas. "Is everything OK?" she asks. "I could hear you all the way downstairs."

As my eyes adjust to the light, I see a flash of blue above her head. There, above my door, right where it should be, is my Yale pennant. Caitlin's bracelet is on my dresser.

"Everything's fine." I flash an apologetic smile. "I just need the cordless phone."

"Then come downstairs and get it," she says. "And stop shouting. Your dad is trying to sleep."

"I know, I'm sorry." Tail between my legs, I follow her down to the kitchen to retrieve the phone.

"Who are you calling this early?" she asks as she pours me a cup of coffee.

"Caitlin," I reply, already dialling her number. "Thanks for the coffee," I call as I head back upstairs.

"Are you serious right now?" Caitlin says when she picks up the phone. "It's six fifteen. On a Saturday."

"I need a reality check."

"Your name is Abby Barnes. You're a freshman at Yale. You live with Maris—"

I cut her off. "I know all that," I say impatiently. "Am I dating anyone?"

"Michael," she replies sleepily.

"Michael," I repeat. "Michael is my boyfriend."

"You didn't know that?" asks Caitlin, wide-awake now. "Your relationship with him is new?" For the first time ever, I feel a modicum of her excitement.

*My life is a puzzle. These pieces fit together.*

*There's nothing to be scared of.*

"Not new," I tell her. "I just didn't expect it to still be true."

"Why not?" Caitlin asks. "What happened?"

"In the real version, Michael and I met on my eighteenth birthday, the day after the collision. He was just some guy to me – Ben's high school best friend. But he's not 'just some guy' to my parallel – not any more. She knows he's Josh's brother. They met yesterday, on their Thanksgiving."

"Well, yeah," Caitlin replies. "That's why you're together."

My breath catches in my throat. "What are you talking about?"

"You said you knew from the first day you met Michael that you were supposed to be with him. It's the reason you broke up with Josh. And why you applied to Yale."

*She chose Michael.*

"When was the break-up? Right after Thanksgiving?"

"No, not till April. The day you got back from Bulldog Days."

"Bulldog Days?" I am practically screeching at her. "What the hell is Bulldog Days?"

"Yale's admitted students weekend. You and Michael h—"

"SHE HOOKED UP WITH HIM? While she was with *Josh*?"

"*Hung out*," Caitlin says calmly. "As far as I know, there was no hooking up involved. Not then, anyway. You kept it platonic till September. Your idea, not his. You started dating on your birthday."

You told Josh two days ago, on Thanksgiving. From what you told me yesterday, he didn't take it very well. I don't think you've spoken to him since."

"And Michael?"

"He left yesterday for Boston. He's taking you to some fancy dinner in New Haven tomorrow night."

It's exactly what I wanted. Two days ago, it's what I had.

A lot can change in two days. A lot can change in two minutes.

Order to chaos, then back again.

"We made up," I say. "You and me. Last Thanksgiving."

"Of course we did," Caitlin replies. "What, you thought we'd stay mad at each other for ever?"

I smile. That's the funny thing about life. We're rarely aware of the bullets we dodge. The just-misses. The almost-never-happeneds. We spend so much time worrying about how the future is going to play out, and not nearly enough time admiring the precious perfection of the present.

I close my eyes and see Josh's face. Standing in the middle of the street yesterday, unshaven and unshowered and unwilling to doubt what he knew to be true. *These aren't someone else's feelings, Abby. . . The way I love you . . . don't tell me that's not real.* It didn't matter to him that the past wasn't as he remembered it. All that mattered was how he felt right then, standing there with me. Here, in the present. I inhale, letting myself return to that moment. Letting myself feel what I felt then but couldn't understand. Letting myself step into the future I glimpsed on my porch last night, a future I can't see clearly but trust nonetheless. *Right, right, right.* He is right. He always was.

And Michael is right, too. Just not for me.

I had it backwards. Michael is my parallel's soulmate. And Josh is mine.

Just like that, all of Caitlin's arguments about genetic equivalence fall away. So what if my parallel and I look the same under a microscope? The soul can't be captured in DNA. Which is exactly what Dr Mann meant that day in his lab. *You are a uniquely created being with a transcendent soul.* A soul whose yearnings can't be predicted or effectively explained, whose composition can't be quantified, whose true nature remains a mystery, as mysterious as it ever was. My parallel and I have different soulmates because we're different souls.

"I have to break up with Michael," I say then.

"What?" Caitlin sounds genuinely shocked. "Why?"

"I'm with the wrong brother," I tell her, and promptly hang up.

Forgetting what time it is, I dial Michael's number. He answers on the fifth ring, his voice muffled and groggy. "Abby?"

"We have to break up." It just pops out, the moment I hear his voice. *So much for doing it delicately.*

366

Silence.

"Michael?"

"If this is a joke, it would've been funnier at noon."

"It's not a joke," I say quietly.

I hear footsteps on his end and then the sound of a door closing.

"Can I ask why?" His voice is low and echoes slightly, like he's in a bathroom. I picture him in a T-shirt and boxers, his hair all mussed up from sleep, sitting on the edge of someone's bathtub. I inhale, imagining the smell of him, so different from Josh despite their shared DNA. Briefly, strangely, I wonder if a soul has a scent.

He's waiting for an explanation. I consider giving him a nonanswer, something about valuing our friendship or needing time to myself. But he deserves more than that. He deserves the truth.

"I think I'm in love with Josh," I say softly.

"You think you're in love with Josh," he repeats, his voice hollow. I nod, then realize he can't see me nodding. "And here I thought you were in love with me."

"It's. . ." I begin, then stop. *Destiny?* It sounds ridiculous, even to me. "It doesn't make sense," I say instead. "I know that."

"How could you do this?" His voice is angry now. And hurt.

"I didn't mean to," I say, my throat tight.

"But you did," he replies. "You *did* mean to. It's not like this is an accident, Abby. You're doing this. You're deciding. You're the one throwing our relationship away."

There are a few seconds of silence before the line goes dead. For exactly ten more, I panic. *What if I'm picking the wrong guy?*

I barely know Josh. Yesterday was the first live conversation we've ever had. Everything else I know about him is from memory. He seemed certain, but can I really know for sure that he and I are meant to be together? The answer, of course, is no. We can never know for sure. The best we can do is take what we do know, and what we've learned, and what we believe to be true about ourselves, and then make a choice.

My parallel made her choice. She chose Michael.

I choose Josh.

Momentarily paralysed, I stare at my phone. There's no going back from this. If things don't work out with Josh, I will have lost them both.

I'm praying as I dial Josh's number. *Please answer, please answer, please answer.* After two rings, an operator voice kicks in. "The number you have attempted to contact is not receiving calls from your number."

My heart sinks. He doesn't remember our conversation yesterday. My parallel erased it.

All at once, a sense of urgency takes hold. I've glimpsed my destiny. Not all of it, but a crucial part. If this moment is the only moment I can be sure of, then I have to make it count.

Fingertips tingling, I type "last minute airfare" into Google and hit enter. Five minutes later I'm entering my debit card number for a flight from ATL to LAX that departs in three hours and six minutes and brings the amount in my checking account below three digits.

I throw a change of clothes and a toothbrush into my bag and take a quick shower. As I'm speed-washing my hair, I debate how to sell this impromptu trip to my parents. They like Josh, obviously. But do they like him enough to let me fly across the country on three hours' notice to see him?

"So he doesn't know you're coming," Mom says when I tell them my plan. "You're just going to show up at his dorm room?"

"Not his dorm room," I reply. "His seat. At the UCLA game. I know where he's sitting." Wanting to preserve the element of surprise, I told Tyler that I was hoping to catch a glimpse of Josh on TV and thus wanted to know where he was sitting. Tyler didn't buy it, but he got me the seat number, anyway.

"That's my girl," Dad says approvingly. "Grabbing the bull by the horns." My mom shoots him a look. "What? I think it's romantic."

"Our eighteen-year-old daughter wants to fly across the country to tell a boy she likes him." Mom looks back at me. "Can't you just call him? Or send an email?"

"I told you, he won't take my calls. He's upset about what happened with Michael."

"Do you blame him?" she asks. "You broke up with him for his brother and then kept it a secret."

"I made a mistake," I say simply. I can't explain or make an excuse for the choice, because it wasn't me who made it. But I can't resent it, either, because without it, I wouldn't have what I have right now: clarity. If Josh is my soulmate, then I found him not in spite of Parallel Abby's influence, but *because* of it. She is no longer my adversary, but part of who I am now. "Need some money?" Dad asks, scanning the kitchen for his wallet. "Let me give you some money."

"We're letting her go?" my mom asks him.

"I don't think she was asking for permission, Anna."

"I'll be fine, Mom," I tell her. "Really."

"What about school? Don't you have class on Monday?"

"I'll be back for that. I'm coming back tomorrow morning. My flight back to New Haven isn't until six."

"Anna, this is Abby, remember? Our responsible, levelheaded daughter." My dad hands me five twenties and his Amex.

"So responsible and levelheaded that she deserves a mini shopping spree while she's out there?" I ask with a grin as I pocket the money.

"Ha. Don't press your luck."

"Have you told Michael?" my mom asks.

I nod. "I called him about an hour ago. He was pretty upset," I tell her, remembering the sound of his voice. A wave of panic washes over me. *Did I make a mistake?*

"I never liked that guy," Dad remarks. "He had an attitude."

"You met him one time!"

"I have good instincts," he replies, buttering a piece of burnt toast. For a moment, I feel sorry for the parallel me. She's in for a challenge trying to sell Mom and Dad on Michael.

"Well, I should probably get going," I tell them. "My flight leaves in two hours." I pick up my duffel bag, suddenly nervous. "Wish me luck."

"Break a leg, champ," Dad says, and puts his hand on my shoulder. It's exactly what he said to me the night the autumn play opened last year, standing backstage before the show. Same words, same gesture, same mix of confidence and fatherly concern. I remember being so nervous in the weeks leading up to the show, convinced I would forget my lines and embarrass

370

myself in front of an auditorium full of people. All my energy and anxiety were focused on getting through those five performances so I could get on with my life. I never saw it coming.

I wasn't paying attention.

"Earth to Abby." My mom waves her hand in front of my face. I blink and her face comes into focus. And somehow, so does my entire life.

"I am now," I say simply.

She shakes her head, not comprehending. "You are now what?"

"Paying attention."

By the time my plane touches down in LA, I'm freaking out. Yes, this is what I want, but WHAT AM I DOING? He blocked my calls. What if he refuses to talk to me? Or worse, what if I embarrass him in front of his university friends? I debate waiting until the game is over, but decide that's too risky: odds are Josh will go out with people after. As long as he's at the game, I know where to find him.

The freeways are predictably crowded, and as we approach the USC exit, traffic slows to a stop. Around us, fans display their affiliation with window decals and streamers. My driver is listening to game coverage on the radio. "Would you mind turning it up?" I ask him. He nods and cranks the volume just as UCLA kicks off to USC. Josh should be in his seat by now.

My stomach turns over. I barely know this guy, and I'm about to profess my love to him in a stadium full of people. It's crazy, but I've never been more certain of anything in my life.

Fifty-eight dollars later, the taxi drops me off at the coliseum. The noise from inside is deafening. As I'm approaching the entrance, I glance up at the sky, which, despite the fact that it's the middle of the afternoon on a spectacularly clear day, is streaked with scarlet and amber. I haven't missed the smog, but I have missed its effect on the LA sky. These colours are particularly arresting, which is odd, because usually when it's smoggy, it's also hazy. But today I can see all the way to the foothills. *When was the last time the sky looked like this?* My mind dances on the edge of a memory, unable to make the connection.

"Ticket?" comes a voice, snapping me back to reality. I've reached the turnstile, where a girl in a maroon-and-gold hoodie is collecting tickets.

I look at her blankly. Completely forgot about the ticket factor. "I, uh, don't have one yet," I tell her. "Where can I buy one?"

She laughs. "You're kidding, right? The game has been sold out for months. There are scalpers around, but I doubt any of them are selling for less than two fifty."

"Two hundred and fifty dollars? For university football?"

The girl looks past me to the bear of a man behind me, dressed from head to toe in powder blue.

"Ticket?"

The man brushes past me, nearly knocking me over.

"I can sell you a ticket."

I turn to see a junior high kid in an oversized USC sweatshirt on a bike that looks like it belongs to a five-year-old. The kid looks around the car park like a cop might be waiting to bust him. I sprint to the kerb.

"How much?" I ask in a low voice. "I can't pay a lot."

"Fifty bucks," he replies, pulling a single ticket out of his front pocket and holding it up for me to see. "It's real," he adds, coming to a stop a few feet from me. "It's a good seat, too. UCLA side."

The other side of the stadium from where Josh is sitting, but at this point I can't be choosy. "I'll take it," I tell the kid, digging through my bag for my wallet.

"You don't look like the football type," he tells me as he waits for his cash. "Who you cheering for?"

"I'm not. Hey, I only have twenties and two ones. Will you take forty-two?"

"Sixty."

"But you said it was only fifty!"

"And *you* said you don't got fifty. What do I look like, an ATM?" Glaring at him, I hold out my three twenties. He pockets the money, hands me the ticket, and pedals off.

Once inside, I easily find Section 4. Making my way down the cement stairs, I crane my neck for a glimpse of Josh's dusty blond head. When I finally reach his row, my heart is pounding and the backs of my knees are clammy with sweat. *Here it goes.* I step down one more step so I can see the entire row and scan it, person by person, waiting for the moment that my eyes hit his familiar face.

But he's not there. There are two empty seats in the middle of the row, but no Josh. I recheck the text from Tyler to make sure I'm in the right place. Section 11, Row 89. So where is he?

I quickly dial Tyler's number.

"He's not here!" I moan when Tyler picks up.

"Who's not where?"

"Josh isn't where you said he'd be. Section 11, Row 89."

Just then, USC scores a touchdown, and the coliseum erupts with noise.

"You're in *LA*?"

"I came to tell Josh how I feel about him. I wanted it to be a surprise."

"Aren't you dating his brother?"

"We broke up."

Tyler says something in reply, but USC has just kicked the extra point, and I can't hear anything over the deafening roar. It's a good sixty seconds before he's audible again.

"He's there," Tyler tells me. "He just texted me back. He's with some girl he knows from junior high."

"With her, like, *dating* her?"

"If he were dating her, I'd hope he wouldn't refer to her as 'this girl I know from junior high'. No, he just ran into her on the way in. Her seats were better than his and she had a couple extra tickets. Section Six. Third row."

"Thanks," I say, already halfway up the stairs. "I'm on my way."

"It's a pretty ballsy move, Barnes, flying all the way across the country like that," Tyler muses. "What if he tells you to go to hell?"

"Thank you, Tyler, for the vote of confidence. Goodbye."

By the time I get to the entrance of Section 6, I'm a frazzled, windblown mess. *Lovely.* A quick stop in the ladies' room helps, but also confirms that I look like a wild-eyed crazy person.

Probably because I *am* a wild-eyed crazy person. With sweaty armpits. I stare at myself in the soap-splattered mirror, wondering what happened to the cool and confident girl who flew across the country this morning. "What's the worst that can happen?" I ask my reflection. I don't wait for my reply.

This time, Josh is easy to spot. He's the only guy in red in a sea of blue and yellow. He's sitting three seats in from the aisle, next to a girl with long brown hair and tiny shoulders. As I'm staring at the backs of their heads, trying to get up the nerve to go down there, the guy in the aisle seat leans forward to say something to Josh. At first I only see his arm, resting on the back of the girl's seat. Unabashedly spraytanned. *Gotta love LA.*

And then the girl shifts and the guy's face comes into view.

It's *Bret*. Sitting next to Kirby. Kirby from Boston. The girl Josh knows from junior high.

My eyes zip down the rest of the row. There's Seth at the other end, and Bret's stunt double and the make-up artist the stunt double was always flirting with, and then some university-age guy I don't recognize, who I'm guessing from the black USC T-shirt is a friend of Josh's. Just then, out of nowhere and for what seems like no reason at all, Josh turns his head and looks directly at me. He stands and stares at me uncomprehendingly for a split second, then shakes his head as if to clear it. "What are you doing here?" he calls, inching past the others towards the aisle.

"I wanted to talk to you," I yell.

Josh meets me halfway down the stairs. "Calling would've been cheaper," he says.

"You wouldn't take my call," I point out.

"Three thousand miles. You must have something pretty important to say."

I hesitate, knowing this is my moment but scared of screwing it up. Josh just stands there, waiting, as the crowd begins to chant around us. For a second I think they're chanting for me. But no. They just want a touchdown.

"I think we're soulmates," I blurt out, which isn't at all what I was planning to say. I meant to start with an apology for what happened with Michael, gradually working up to the big, "I made a mistake, please take me back" moment. *So much for easing into it.*

"Since when?"

"Since the first time you took me to our swing," I say, even though that means something different for him than it does for me. "I just forgot for a while."

"What about Michael?"

"I told him this morning. He didn't take it so well." My eyes fill with tears, remembering. I didn't mean to hurt either of them, and now I've hurt both of them. "Josh, I'm so sorry."

Josh is quiet for what feels like an eternity. Then, just loud enough to make out: "I guess he probably deserves to find his own soulmate."

My heart flutters in my chest.

"Are we . . . OK?" I whisper.

He doesn't answer me. Instead, he sweeps me up into his arms and kisses me, and all my doubts fall away. His hands are in my hair and mine are on his face, and it fits, we fit, like we've been rehearsing this moment all our lives. When the marching band starts to play, I imagine the song is for us.

"Just in time to see some Trojan domination," Josh says when I finally pull back, his voice louder and lighter now. He reaches to lift my bag off my shoulder. Bag in one hand, he takes my hand with the other, and I follow him down the steps towards the field.

"So you know Kirby from junior high?"

His eyebrows shoot up in surprise. "How do you know Kirby?"

*Whoops.* "I don't," I say quickly. "I just heard you say her name."

"I didn't think I'd said it."

"So she's from Worcester?" I ask, before he can replay our conversation and realize that he didn't.

He nods. "Two grades below me in school. I was friends with her older brother, Keith. She and her mom moved out here when Kirb turned sixteen."

"And now she's hanging out with celebrities, huh? Isn't that Bret Woodward?" There's not an ounce of envy in my voice. I don't feel any.

"Crazy, right? That's her there, next to Bret, and that's Seth, Dante and Brianna," Josh tells me, pointing each of them out. They all smile and wave, not an iota of recognition in their eyes. *My LA friends.* I can picture all of them at the birthday dinner Bret planned for me the night before everything changed. "The guy on the other end is my buddy Derrick."

"You guys should sit!" Kirby chirps. "Here, take my seat. Seth, scoot down."

Josh lifts my rucksack up and over his head. Watching his tanned biceps contract, my stomach flutters. Suddenly, all I can think about is kissing him. Running my hands through his hair, feeling his chest against mine. As I follow him to our seats, my eyes drop to the waistband of his jeans. Boxers with little red reindeer peek out beneath his T-shirt, which is lifted slightly from his arms being raised overhead. His back is a shade lighter than his arms are, but his muscles are no less pronounced. *Is his butt naturally that perfect or did he work for that?* I'm so distracted by the thought that I don't see Bret's foot until I trip over it.

He catches me before I fall. "Careful there," he says, steadying me.

"Hey, lemme get a picture," Kirby says, waving her mobile phone and splashing beer on Seth's leg. "Squish together."

"She's a menace with that camera phone," Bret whispers to me. As his breath hits my cheek, a lightning bolt of realization rips through me.

*I would have been here.*

Even if our world hadn't collided with a parallel world, I would have been sitting right here, in this very seat, with these people. I wouldn't have come to LA for Josh, of course. I would've already been here for the movie, and I'd probably be at this game as Bret's date. But I'd be sitting here either way. And thanks to Kirby from Boston, so would Josh.

*We would have met regardless.* Even without that astronomy class. Even without my parallel's help. She got me to him sooner, but I would've found him on my own.

And then, a reality so clear it illuminates everything else.

*I would've loved him either way.*

Dr Mann's words echo in my head: *Your path will change. Your destiny doesn't.* Suddenly, it all makes sense. The path doesn't dictate the destination. There are detours to destiny, and

378

sometimes that detour is a short cut. But it's more than that. Sitting here, in this seat, Bret on one side, Josh on the other – wedged between my past and my future – is exactly where I'm supposed to be. It doesn't matter how I got here or where I'm going when I leave. The point is that I'm here. In this place, at this moment, with these people. The dots coming together so exquisitely, crystallizing into something greater than the sum of its parts. All of the past made whole in the present. The picture of my life more beautiful than I ever could've imagined.

More beautiful than I ever could've planned.

*Le mathématicien. Quelle artiste.*

"Look up," Josh says, taking my hand in his. "Puts the night sky to shame, huh?" Above us, the sky is a swirl of breathtaking reds and oranges, like the inside of a candle flame.

"Wow," I breathe. "It's—"

Before I can finish my sentence, the coliseum begins to shake and tremble. Around us, people scream and scurry for cover. "EARTHQUAKE!" someone shouts.

I look over at Josh, and the world goes dark, then quiet. The shaking intensifies, then stops.

Out of the silence, I hear the sounds of a crowd cheering. A whistle blowing. People talking and laughing.

"Earth to Abby."

At the sound of Bret's voice, my eyes fly open. He's smiling like nothing happened. "What was that?" I ask.

"You tell me," he replies with a laugh. "You were sitting there with your eyes closed."

I look past him to the crowd. Everyone is smiling and happy. No signs of an earthquake.

*Could I have imagined it?* I reach for Josh's hand, clutching it with both of mine. "I just had the weirdest experience," I begin, turning in my seat to face him. He's looking at me in surprise.

"Uh-oh," comes Bret's voice. "Should I be jealous of the new guy?" I look from Josh to Bret, and it is at that moment that I realize that Bret is wearing a different shirt than he was five minutes ago. And I'm. . .

*Holy shit.*

Here with Bret. Not Josh.

"Hey, I don't mind," Josh says then, giving my fingers a squeeze. "It's not every day I get to hold hands with a movie star." He laughs and lets go.

*No. Please, no.*

I don't know how I know, and I can't explain how it could've happened, I just know that it has. As quickly as I lost my real life three months ago, I've somehow got it back. The people sitting in this row are my cast mates. I live here, in Los Angeles, where these people think I've been shooting a movie since May.

I don't go to Yale.

I've never met Michael.

I've never dated Josh.

I close my eyes. This isn't happening. *Please God, don't let this be happening. Not when I just found my soulmate. Not when I just made things right.*

Bret is quick to pick up my hand, pressing it between his palms.

"You OK?" he asks. "You look kind of shaken."

Shaken. It's a particularly fitting word, considering.

I open my eyes and look at him, and for a moment, yes, I am

shaken. Unnerved by the notion of beginning again, alone in the knowledge of the ways things were. Of the way things should be.

But then, I look at Josh. And I remember.

*More real than real.*

I'm not alone. Josh is right here beside me. He doesn't know what I know, but what I know is enough.

# *Acknowledgements*

Thank you first and most to the Creator of the universe, the author and perfecter of every great idea, and to his Son, for the gift I can never repay. I am blessed beyond measure.

Thank you also:

To Kristyn Keene at ICM, for finding me and reading my story and believing in it, even when there was work to be done. Besides being one of the loveliest human beings I have ever encountered, I honestly believe that you are the best agent in this universe or any other, and I feel incredibly lucky to have you by my side.

Thank you also to my wonderful UK editor, Helen Thomas, for saying yes and for believing that UK readers might love my story as much as she did, and to everyone else at Scholastic UK, but specifically and especially to Jamie Gregory for my kick-butt cover, to Hannah Cooper and Penelope Beech for getting people to pay attention to this unknown American author, and to Kim Pedder, production controller extraordinaire.

To Garry Hart and Jill Arthur, for seeing the promise in my complicated concept back when it was a TV pilot, and to the television networks that passed on making *Parallel* into a TV show, which is the reason it became a book.

To my LA family – Sarah, Ryan, Suzanne, Brian, Mia, Francois, Katherine, Jay, Cat, Alan, Kelli and Matt – you've inspired me and challenged me and taught me the meaning of grace, and to my women's discipleship group who prayed for a sense of urgency when I couldn't get my ass in gear to write.

To Tyler, for reading every single draft of this book, even the crappy ones, and for fixing my ellipses and mocking my improper use of quotation marks and pointing out every annoying "and yet" and for always using correct syntax in our g-chats. But thank you most of all for being real and true and you. This book and my life are better because of the part you've played in shaping them.

To Rachel, for practically writing the query letter I never actually sent because your blog roll had already done all the work for me (and, on that note, for giving new meaning to the phrase small world). The only thing that would make me love you more is if you moved to LA so we could hang out all the time and do yoga and drink green smoothies and procrastinate about the books we're supposed to be writing.

To my early readers and dear friends Bobbi Shiflett, Lindsey Mann, and Amy Carter, for your encouragement and feedback.

To SK, for being the prototype of Caitlin, which made her so easy to write.

Last, but certainly not least, to my family.

To Mom and Dad, for so many things – your love, your faith, your wisdom – but most of all, your unceasing presence in my life. You've always been there, not just for me, but with me, reminding me that no matter what, you're on my team. So much of who I am is because of who you both are. Plus, I like you better than I like most other people, so there's that. And to Stacy, my best friend and my biggest supporter, the one person who never questioned my decision to quit my job to write (not even when I asked to borrow $300 to pay my electric bill), and to Gregg, for reading my blog when no one else was, and to Hannah, for helping me come up with character names when I was stuck.

To Donny, my husband and partner in all of this, thank you for taking this leap with me and for believing that it would bear fruit. The journey we are on together is the greatest adventure of my life, and I wouldn't change a moment of it. I love you.

And, finally, to sweet Eliot Bea, my Lil Mil. Were it not for your unexpected conception, this book would not exist. You were my writing partner from page one. Thank you for teaching me to embrace the detour and for filling my life (and our house) with laughter and infectious joy.